TONY GALLOWAY

SOUL STONES

DEMON POWERS
BOOK TWO

SOUL STONES

DEMON POWERS BOOK TWO

TONY GALLOWAY

CHATTOOGA PRESS

Copyright © 2023 by Tony Galloway

All rights reserved.

Cover images by Miblart

This is a work of fiction. Names, characters, places, and incidents are either products of the author's imagination or used fictitiously. Any resemblance to actual persons, living or dead, events, or locales is coincidental.

No portion of this book may be reproduced in any form without written permission from the publisher or author, except as permitted by U.S. copyright law.

Print ISBN: 979-8-9868746-3-0

Contents

Dedication	IX
The Road So Far...	XI
1. Breaking and Entering	1
2. Rapid Reflections	11
3. Death Takes a Bath	20
4. Blind Date	24
5. Your Life in Technicolor	34
6. Deathly Distractions	42
7. A New Project	49
8. Smart Board	57
9. Currency of Reprieve	64
10. Cold Stormy Night	66
11. Camping Story	74
12. Changing Tactics	79
13. Hiring Help	83
14. Human Hive	87
15. Visiting the Prisoner	92
16. Rest Stop	97
17. Eli Remembers	105

18. Invitations Sent	111
19. Wild Ride	118
20. Barn Gathering	125
21. Pursued	131
22. Abandoned	137
23. So It Ends	142
24. Whirly Bird	148
25. Praise or Perish	156
26. Strays	160
27. Reunion	163
28. Going to Church	169
29. Darkness Comes	175
30. Training and Planning	181
31. Among the Raff	189
32. Underground Again	195
33. Father Logan's Gambit	200
34. Unlikely Companion	207
35. Double Stubborn	213
36. The Life That Never Was	219
37. Voices of Reason	228
38. Dictionaries and Bibles	234
39. Gates and Dominos	239
40. Unlikely Reunion	247
41. Putting Puzzles Together	253
42. Trust Fall	261

43. Security Meeting	268
44. Patience	275
45. A New Alliance	281
46. Check	287
47. Checkmate	293
48. Reunited	300
49. Convergence	303
50. Left to Melt	308
51. Need an Army	317
52. Spring the Trap	322
53. Questions and Answers	327
54. Some Say Fire, Some Say Ice	332
55. Gate of Ascension	338
56. Near Disasters	343
57. Mass Exodus	347
58. Tower Top	352
59. An Unusual Summoning	357
60. Brave New World	362
Word From The Author	367
Acknowledgements	368
About the Author	370

For Cara,
our four teenagers,
and the many adventures still to come.

The Road So Far...

If it has been awhile since you read the prior installment, *Solomon's Ring*, let me refresh your memory on who's who and where we left off. If you are coming to *Soul Stones* fresh from the last book, or you have an impeccable memory, then by all means skip on to the first chapter. I hope you enjoy.

There are several key factions, families, and notable individuals at play in this world, with different abilities, beliefs, and practices, though all trace their lineage and their power to King Solomon, his artifacts, and the demons with which he consorted.

Most notable among these is the Stewarth family, claiming direct descendancy from the wise king and possessing a ring that grants the wearer absolute control over demons. They have ruled a worldwide shadow empire for nearly three millennia. Alexander Stewarth is the reigning Heir at the beginning of the book, but he succumbs to a mysterious illness, leaving his son Eric as the rightful Heir. Unfortunately, Kurt Levin steals the ring hours before Alexander's death, forcing Eric to ally himself with the Demonriders and attack Kurt's manor in an attempt to reclaim his birthright.

The Protectors are appointees of the Stewarths and enforce law and order with near impunity. These are positions of power and prestige coveted by both Nathan Goodrum and Father Logan. Kurt Levin, Michael Benson, and Brianne Moore are notable examples. Kurt, charged with guarding Alexander Stewarth on his deathbed, "borrows" Solomon's ring to fulfill a twenty-year-old bargain with Azrael, God of Death. Despite the fact Kurt's dead son had been reincarnated some years earlier, he must deliver a thousand demon servants to Azrael before she will reunite him with his child. Though the ring allows him to pay the balance in a single night, Azrael steals the ring before Kurt can return it to the Stewarths, and places it beyond the reach of humanity. Kurt becomes a fugitive as a result and is last seen making a final stand against Eric Stewarth's army and his fellow Protectors in the entryway of his manor. He is presumed dead after a rocket destroys the entryway.

The Demonriders, led by Nathan Goodrum, have turned possession on its head, taking control of the demons they allow inside themselves, to become faster, stronger, and more telekinetically competent at the cost of surrendering some piece of humanity to the endless struggle that ensues. They have little to fear from anyone other than the bearer of Solomon's ring who can strip them of their unnatural power. They are generally despised and looked down on by the other members of the conclave. Summoning demons is a capital offense, but riding them is not technically illegal. This dislike has led the Demonriders to become clannish and socially isolated, largely separating themselves from the others. They live by a strict code and any Demonrider that loses control of his demon is cast out of the order. By the end of *Solomon's Ring*, as a reward for assisting Eric Stewarth's siege, Nathan is appointed as the new Protector, and willingly relinquishes his demon to put the other factions at ease with his new position.

The Prophets are a religious organization that has teetered on the brink of obscurity for centuries. Recently, their numbers exploded worldwide under the charismatic leadership of Father Dravin Logan. Unknown to anyone else, Dravin is using a mysterious cocktail he calls Devotion, to build a large network of psychically interconnected followers, a hive mind of thousands whose wills have been subjugated to his own. Things go awry when Dravin attempts to give Devotion to his prisoner, Brooklyn's boyfriend, David Sterling. With the aid of Azrael, David wrests control of the Prophets away from Dravin Logan, causing him to flee the sanctuary. Though blinded, David can see lines of energy, auras, and other mystical connections and manifestations. At the end of *Solomon's Ring*, David is reclaiming all of Dravin's cells of followers and serving as Azrael's prophet, preparing his people for the apocalypse Azrael predicts is coming. Stripped of his followers, Dravin Logan seeks out a meeting with the newly appointed Protector, Nathan Goodrum. They share a drink and Dravin doses Nathan with Devotion, taking control of his mind and beginning to rebuild his lost influence.

I should also mention the Crafts, a matriarchal family of nomads, sometimes called the Wandering Witches. The most notable members are Erina Craft, the matriarch, and her daughter Bryssa. They operate a traveling circus and are something of a mystery even to the other families and factions. Much is rumored about their unique abilities to control the elements, but most agree these are likely just fantastic stories. No one has ever seen the rumored powers in action. At a conclave meeting early in *Solomon's Ring*, Erina Craft seeks the help of the Protectors in excising a particularly powerful demon from her daughter's fiancé. Kurt Levin assists the family with the unwelcome help of Eric Stewarth. They encounter Prosidris, father of the Wardens, and master of the seas. He's come to Earth to investigate the disappearance of hundreds of lesser demons. Unexpectedly, Eric produces the Ring of Solomon and begins to communicate with Prosidris directly about the missing demons. Kurt tackles Eric under the pretext of protecting him, causing the boy to lose his grip on Prosidris before they can compare notes and conclude that Kurt himself is responsible for the missing demons. Though the Craft family plays only a minor role in the first book, they become increasingly important in the books that follow.

Throughout this story, mundane earthly happenings intertwine with events taking place on a larger cosmic stage. Though most of our protagonists remain oblivious, the puppet master behind the curtain is Azrael. With her continued existence threatened by the ballooning human population and the corresponding number of deaths she must attend, she's hatched a plan to vastly reduce our numbers. Indeed many of the larger happenings are caused by Azrael or by her absence. From Brooklyn's initial possession by Belial, to David's rise to power as leader of the Prophets, Azrael's actions and oversights wreak havoc. She's the reason Brooklyn has two souls, and why Kurt summoned enough demons to weaken the Pull, and now she's unleashed an ancient plague of corn beetles intending to destroy the world's economy, bringing about death from famine and war. While her origins are unclear, and there are hints she wasn't always bound by death, her motive is a simple and understandable desire for self-preservation.

Speaking of the Pull, you might remember it as the force or barrier that keeps the spiritual realm and the earthly realm mostly separate. While not much is known about its origins, it is believed that it was created at some point in the distant past and that prior to the creation, spirits were an integral and natural part of life on Earth. Maintaining separation is the key to maintaining the barrier, which is why summoning is a capital crime and both the Protectors and Wardens work collaboratively to send rogue demons back to Hell. Kurt Levin's extensive summoning to complete his deal with Azrael significantly weakens the Pull in *Solomon's Ring*. Without the ring that is the novel's namesake, there is no easy way to repair the damage. It is also noteworthy that the Pull only seems to affect those who have taken sustenance from humanity. Azrael never experiences the Pull until she strengthens herself using human blood.

And what of our protagonist, you ask? Brooklyn Evers began as a rural Appalachian farm girl and community college student, still living at home in her early twenties with her parents and young nephew, Devin. Her sister, Erin, had gone missing without a trace some three years prior, leaving Devin parentless. Brooklyn works part-time at an insurance company where she begins a relationship with her co-worker David Sterling. Through events beyond her knowing, Brooklyn becomes possessed by the demon Belial and as a result of several brutal interrogations he conducts while controlling her, she becomes a wanted serial murderer. Belial's quest culminates in coercing Brooklyn to attempt assassination of Alexander Stewarth in order to save her own family.

Sentenced to die, Brooklyn is granted reprieve after Azrael pressures Kurt Levin to intercede on her behalf, but Alexander Stewarth ties Kurt's fate to Brooklyn's. If she steps out of line again, Kurt's head is on the chopping block. David, who has been searching for Brooklyn, is reunited with her, but Kurt makes it clear they must both remain safely at his manor due to the risk he is taking to help Brooklyn.

After a botched escape attempt leads to a run-in with both the Demonriders and the Prophets, Brooklyn is injured and David is presumed dead. An angry Kurt hands Brooklyn's training over to his lieutenant and researcher, Riley Martin. Driven by grief over David's presumed death during the conflict, shame at how easily she was defeated, and a desire to exact revenge, Brooklyn vastly improves her abilities. She and Riley grow closer over the next few months and start to become romantically involved. Riley arms Brooklyn with a weapons of his own creation called soul stones. Colored orbs of a metal alloy, soul stones are keyed to their user and cannot be blocked or interfered with by other telekinetic adepts, making them especially deadly.

Later, Riley discovers that Kurt has gone to Brooklyn's childhood home fearing her family may be in danger. Riley and Brooklyn follow and arrive at the Everses' farm to find Brooklyn's mother dying of a gunshot wound. Kurt and Devin are held hostage by Prosidris who is possessing Brooklyn's father. Brooklyn is captured and forced to summon Belial. Belial is commanded by his father to make Brooklyn kill Devin in order to break her spirit. A savage struggle ensues. To save Devin's life, Brooklyn uses her soul stones to kill her own father. Belial prevents Prosidris from taking Devin as a new host and both demons fall back into Hell. Brooklyn collapses from overexertion.

Brooklyn wakes in the medical wing of Kurt's manor, but her reprieve is short-lived as Eric Stewarth, the Protectors, and the Demonriders lay siege to Kurt's manor demanding the return of Solomon's ring. Brooklyn has a run-in with Nathan Goodrum who is bleeding a young girl in order to summon his demon. He insinuates David may still be alive and tempts Brooklyn to join the Demonriders. When she rejects his offer he tries to kill her. With some help from Belial, she gets the upper hand and cuts Nathan's Achilleas tendon with a piece of glass. An enraged Nathan loses control of his demon.

Things end with Brooklyn Evers escaping the siege and taking refuge at the farm of Mrs. Mays. While hiding out, recuperating from battle injuries, and coming to terms with the murder of her parents, she develops an uneasy truce with the demon Belial via their unusual psychic connection. Belial, a prisoner in Hell's library, is coerced into translating the Eternal Collection for Prosidris in exchange for his life. Pitying Belial's plight, and feeling partially responsible for it, Brooklyn summons Belial back to Earth with the agreement he will not try to take control of her again. He arrives with his father's shark-tooth dagger buried in his back and clutching two dragon eggs. After Brooklyn removes the dagger, he buries the eggs near the ocean. They set off to find Devin and Erin, which is where *Soul Stones* begins.

SOUL STONES

1

BREAKING AND ENTERING

Brooklyn crouched on a low branch, ignoring the cramp in her calves. In the last year, she'd lost almost everyone she'd ever loved. Something old and evil had murdered the Evers family, save for herself and her nephew.

The second-story window lit up across the way, causing her to shiver and crane her neck as Devin appeared through the gossamer curtains with an unfamiliar man.

Brooklyn dug her nails into her palms until the ache matched the pain in her calves. *Devin.*

The man walked him around the room. Brooklyn knew the nightly ritual by heart. Check under the bed, in the closet, close the curtains, hugs and kisses, lights out, and wait for the screaming to start.

Waiting sucked. The still night seemed to constrict around her minute after minute until, as always, his screams shattered it.

Shrill and cutting as a razor. If only she could go to him, tell him everything was okay, make him feel safe, but as a fugitive, all she could do was hide in a tree and watch. Light flared in the window, two adult silhouettes this time, a man and a woman. Brooklyn tilted her head but couldn't make out the soothing voices.

Who are they? Foster parents?

Does it matter? Belial stirred restlessly in the back of her mind. Belial was a demon, and both the reason she and Devin were alive and the reason her parents were dead. Gratitude and resentment were uncomfortable companions where thoughts about him were concerned.

He's my family.

You aren't doing him any good hiding in a tree outside his window.

She shrugged.

The light went off, and the screams started again. The woman came back into the bedroom, leaving the light off this time. Brooklyn bit her lip until she tasted blood.

You don't need to hear this every night. It's not good for you.

Maybe it's good for you. She hopped off the limb and clenched her teeth against the impact, grinning when the pain made Belial squirm.

There might be one other Evers still out there. Brooklyn's sister, Erin, had vanished almost four years ago. "I'm going to bring her back to you," she promised Devin as she jogged away into the empty night.

Brooklyn wheeled her stolen SUV into the parking space behind the sheriff's office furthest from the security cameras. She pulled her dark hair into a ponytail and tugged a ski mask over her face before stepping out into the early morning chill. It was strangely cold for late summer.

The station had two floors. The first was well lit, but the second—where the offices were bound to be—was dark.

Her heart hammered as she approached the rear of the building, drawing slightly on Belial's power. It rolled up her spine in an aching wave. The night grew subtly brighter and the damp coolness more bearable.

Brooklyn knelt, took a deep breath, and leapt, pushing against the ground with her mind to boost her ascent. It was imprecise, but she snagged the brick windowsill and, with another haphazard push, pulled herself up.

Balanced precariously on the narrow ledge, Brooklyn eyed the latch through the glass and concentrated until it clicked open. The office was plushly decorated. Definitely not the right one. Investigator Richmond was all business; his office wouldn't look like this.

On trembling legs she crossed the dim room and listened at the doorway until she could slow her breathing, then slipped into the hallway, casting furtive glances in both directions. There was better lighting here.

Silently and slowly, she circled the floor, looking for the right office. Some doors had brass nameplates. None said Investigator Richmond. What if his office was downstairs? *Christ.* Time was getting short. This was supposed to be a quick in and out. She began to sweat. Should she go room by room checking the unmarked doors?

Thinking back, Brooklyn remembered the first time she had seen his face. It had been on television during an interview about a multiple homicide. *Her* multiple homicide. The memory conjured the familiar dread and a flickering image of stacked bodies that she quickly pushed away.

Richmond's face had been seared into her mind. She'd watched in stunned disbelief as he'd labeled her a serial killer, describing her as dangerous, ruthless, and remorseless.

Immediately, she'd wanted him to know that wasn't who she was. She'd had the irrational, unthinkable impulse in that moment to call the number on the screen and explain herself to this man . . . but some things defied understanding or forgiveness.

Riley had tried to comfort her while they hid from the police in a closed clothing store. The night she learned she was a wanted woman, and that she'd never be able to go back to her old life again.

Riley. If not for him, she'd probably be on trial for murder right now. If not for him she might have lost it when David died. Now Riley was probably dead too. Apparently, loving her was a dangerous endeavor.

Regardless, she had adapted well enough to fugitive life over the last few months. It was Belial's fault she was in this predicament. If he had left her alone, Devin wouldn't be screaming in the night. Her mom and dad wouldn't . . .

No. No time for those thoughts. Brooklyn closed her eyes and tried to focus on breathing for a moment. This wasn't the place. This wasn't the time.

There were four offices without nameplates. Circling back to the first unlabeled door, Brooklyn bypassed the lock, her hand shaking as she twisted the knob. A heady scent of roses and vanilla hit her as soon as she stepped inside. She saw a scented candle on the desk, and a woman's scarf draped across the chair. Not a man's office.

Seven minutes until shift change. *Shit.*

The next office was a mess of papers, no pictures or personal effects. She cracked her neck and started rifling through the hoard. Only about half the folders were labeled. If this was the investigator, then she didn't have much to worry about. He'd be lucky to find the case file, let alone actually find her. She needed that file, but it wasn't here. This couldn't be Richmond's office, could it?

Three minutes. She could waste them all in here, or move on to the other unlabeled rooms.

The third office had a standard metal desk with a utilitarian, no-frills lamp. There was an honest-to-God magnifying glass on the desk. A magnifying glass. The leather chair was well-worn. Pictures pinned to a corkboard showed a bearded middle-aged man on a boat, his arm around a blonde woman, two school-aged kids, a girl and a boy, in life jackets in front of them. Was this him?

Brooklyn tried to imagine him cleanly shaven in a shirt and tie like she'd seen on the television. Maybe.

All doubt evaporated when she saw her last name on the first folder in the tidy stack on the desk. She rifled through it, then pushed it aside. The next folder had a name she didn't recognize: Richard Clymer. She flipped it open. There were pictures clipped to the inside. Pictures of bloody bodies stacked like cordwood. Autopsy photos, too. The world dropped out from beneath her. Brooklyn couldn't breathe. His face floated through her mind. She remembered his screams and the way he had begged. She didn't want to know his name. Any of their names.

Brooklyn . . . , Belial whispered with concern in his voice.

"Shut up," she growled out loud.

She slammed the folder closed and snatched the stack with both hands. Clutching it to her chest, she spun to flee, but a large figure filled the doorway. Investigator Richmond, with his gun aimed at her heart.

David wished he could see Israel with his own eyes, but he should be grateful—he supposed—that Azrael had saved him from a fate worse than blindness. He saw it through the eyes of his traveling companions, but it wasn't the same. The images were incongruous with his other senses. More like watching a video than seeing a new place.

"This way, Father Sterling." Avery, one of his aides, touched him on the shoulder to help him orient.

"Don't call me that," David reminded him.

"This way, *sir*." Avery didn't hide the disapproval in his tone.

Reluctantly, he let himself be led away.

Inside the temple was cool, in stark contrast to the midday heat. The minds around him hummed incessantly with information.

The loudest of these was very near and distinguished by its autonomy of thought.

When David had first supplanted Father Logan at the head of this network of minds, he'd expected all of his prophets would be as docile and dependent as the first group.

He'd quickly been disabused of that notion. The prophets he encountered as he traveled the world reclaiming the lost followers were all independently led. Each followed a local leader who reigned with a great degree of free will despite a subjugated connection to David. Similarly, the beliefs varied among different sects and drew heavily from the local faiths. Many prophets were assimilated into other established faiths.

"*Shalom*, may I help you?" asked an elderly man.

David turned and faced the man. "I'm here to see Yosef Kohein."

The man did not reply immediately. The silence stretched for several uncomfortable moments before he said, "Rabbi Kohein is not—"

"Don't lie to me," David cut in. He pressed against the older man's thoughts, following the threads that connected him to Yosef's web of followers. "He's here; I can feel him."

"Yes, I'm here." His accent was thick and regal. Yosef approached from near the Ark. As he did, the first man retreated. "I thought it a great miracle when the yoke of Dravin Logan was cast off, but here you are, a new master to enslave us again."

"Something kinder, I hope. I apologize for the necessity. I'm David Sterling, pleased to meet you."

"Names are not important. A master is a master. I will not bow to you or any other. Outsider."

David spread his hands magnanimously. "You've freed your flock then? Given up the role of master yourself?"

"I would if I knew a way." Yosef crossed his arms. "The whispers never stop. The best I can do is ignore them, let them live their lives without my direction or interference."

"When you are hungry?"

Yosef looked ashamed. "I do not make them prepare meals for me. I do not want them to."

"When you have . . . other desires?"

"*Yetzer hara* tempts us all, Master Sterling. I send the women away and pray."

David smiled sadly. "No one is always strong, and when you give in and feel like a monster, there's some small part of you that likes it, no?"

"No, I don't like it. I would give them free will back in an instant if I could," he hissed.

"I believe you. That's why I'm here. I broke Dravin Logan's control in America and now I'm working to free the other conclaves." A smile tugged at his lips. "There is a way. Do you have someplace where we can speak privately?"

Yosef's face filled with hope. "My office is near where you entered."

David followed Yosef from the main synagogue to his office. David signaled to Avery that he and the others should wait outside. The smell here was different. Scrolls, dusty old books, carpet underfoot. The scents told him this was a working office. David glimpsed the interior through Avery's eyes just as the door swung shut between them. It was enough for him to find a chair. Now the darkness was absolute. Blindness was maddening. Deep breaths and a friendly smile masked the terror. Barely. The urge to look through Yosef's eyes was intense. "So you'll truly give up control?"

"Gladly." The rabbi's voice came from the left. "You killed Father Logan, then?"

David twitched his head in that direction. Damned carpet made it impossible to hear the man's footsteps. "No, I haven't killed anyone. I just . . . disconnected him from the others." David leaned back, resting an ankle on his knee. "I need to understand the history here if I'm going to help you. Can you tell me how you came under his control in the beginning?"

A chair creaked as Yosef settled into it across the desk from David. "It started with letters. He presented himself as a religious scholar and author; he referenced my books, posed intriguing questions. We corresponded for almost two years."

"I'm guessing he traveled here and met with you face to face?"

"Eventually, yes."

"So, how did it happen? He made you drink something?"

"No. I know too well what you are asking, but it was not the dark drink for me. I do not remember exactly how it happened. We were talking, debating deep theology, the nature of free will and sin. Slowly, his points seemed right and my own felt contrived. The doubts deeply grieved me. Uncertainty crept in until a lifetime of faith, once the pillars of my life, suddenly seemed foolish and trivial."

Thick sorrow laced Yosef's words, his voice catching so often David could almost see the man weeping as he continued the tale. "The debate was unbearable. Out of weakness, I conceded the point. Whatever it was, I don't even remember. At once, I felt reassurance and peace inside. We spent many days together, talking, even laughing. He twisted my beliefs only slightly, only enough to control me, and to make me feel that the others he gave me to control needed my oversight somehow. He called me a prophet. When I began to hear the thoughts of others, it was a kind of brotherhood. We were all a part of something much bigger than our individual desires. It felt divine."

"You liked it, then? Being under his control?"

"I liked it then, when I did not see it for what it was. When I did not understand what I was taking from those who believed in and followed me. Free will is what makes us human. I . . . wasn't human for a very long time."

"He gave you something to eat or drink, probably without you knowing it. I don't fully understand it yet, a drug maybe, but it breaks something inside of you. Some part of you that protects your will and autonomy. Some people he breaks entirely, and some, like you, are weakened and conditioned to manage the others." David sighed. "Let me ask you something. Did you sense it when Father Logan was removed?"

"Yes," Yosef answered from David's right. Damnable carpeting. "It was like waking from a nap. Disoriented, blinded by afternoon sunlight. I cried as a baby cries. My thoughts raced. It was the most joyous moment of my life. Then the voices started."

"They were always there." David tilted his head. He could hear Yosef breathing, just barely. "He conditioned you not to notice unless he wanted you to."

"How will you fix what is broken inside of me? Inside the others?" Yosef was right beside him now.

"I'm sorry. I lied about that part." David unleashed the power he'd been holding in check since his arrival. The world sprang to life around him, electricity oscillating in cool blue waves along the wiring in the walls. Yosef himself glowed faintly in mixed waves of green uncertainty and sullen red outrage. His feelings spread throughout the building and further, racing along invisible filaments to all of those subjugated by him.

"You're a monster just like him." Yosef struck him across the face with a large book. David tumbled out of his chair onto the floor.

David quelled the urge to lash out at the rabbi. This required a delicate touch. Push too hard and his mind would break and make him as useless as the others. He felt the frustration and terror in the other man, as if the feelings were his own. He soothed them away, robbing Yosef of his passions.

After a few moments, he helped David to his feet and offered him a tissue to wipe his bloodied nose.

Touching the rabbi's mind again, David took inventory. Several highly placed prophets in the government, both in the prime minister's office and the *Knesset*, the legislature of Israel. There were half as many lower-level officials in various military, religious, and local government positions. There were hundreds of unremarkable followers as well.

David released the connection. "I thank you for meeting with me, Rabbi Kohein." He stuck his hand out, and the rabbi shook it.

"Not at all, Father Sterling. The pleasure was mine." He smiled genuinely, all traces of doubt and uncertainty gone from his demeanor.

Maybe it really was better this way. Maybe free will was the root of all misery. And maybe, if David kept thinking it, he'd find a way to believe it.

2

RAPID REFLECTIONS

Brooklyn froze at the sight of the gun. The barrel seemed like the yawning mouth of a cave. She clutched the files to her chest as if the investigator might try to snatch them away.

The window behind her was the only other exit. If she moved, he'd shoot. Would her summoned shield deflect bullets when she still struggled in practice with tennis balls? Fear rooted her to the floor and panic set her heart skipping like a stone across water. She couldn't be caught, not now. Devin was counting on her and so was Erin, even if neither of them knew it yet. There was always her soul stones. Though they looked like colored marbles, they were killing tools, fast and accurate. At the thought, they twitched in her pocket as if eager to come to her aid, but she didn't want to kill this man.

"Keep your hands where I can see them," Investigator Richmond bellowed as he reached for the radio on his belt, never breaking eye contact.

Kill him, Belial urged. *He's calling backup.*

No, I won't hurt him. Brooklyn lashed out with her will and slapped the radio out of the officer's hand. It skittered out into the hallway.

"Goddamnit." He cast a quick glance at the radio without ever really taking his attention away from her. He narrowed his eyes. "Get on your knees. Do it slow. Keep your hands where I can see them."

"Don't shoot. I don't have a gun, and I didn't do the things you think—"

"Get on the floor now!" The intensity of his scream was as shocking as a slap.

"Okay, okay." She rocked forward onto her knees and looked up into the gun's barrel. It was the bullseye, and if she missed . . .

"Cross your ankles and—"

With a whisper of will, two of her three soul stones leapt free of her jeans pocket. The pink one blurred as she shot it into the opening of the gun barrel, plugging it. Another lanced out behind her. Glass exploded, drawing Richmond's attention, and Brooklyn surged to her feet. Before he could react, she shoved her power against his bulletproof vest, knocking him off balance and thrusting herself backward.

He recovered quickly, and fired. The explosion was deafening. The pistol barrel split at the end. There was a puff of silvery pink dust.

As she fell backward through the broken window, pain lanced across the backs of her legs. Brooklyn clung to the files as she fell and pushed her power down to slow the fall, but the ground rushed toward her. She slammed into the dirt, driving the breath from her.

Nothing felt too broken . . . Air finally filled her lungs like molten lava and her ribs screamed in protest as she forced herself up. Her mind fogged with pain, black spots swam across her vision, and her body was responding too slowly. Brooklyn struggled to get out of the shrubbery and stumbled when she put weight on her right leg.

Cold raced up her spine and numbed the pain. Brooklyn hobbled around the corner of the building, with Richmond shouting from the window. She called her soul stones back, but only one of the two responded. Brooklyn couldn't feel the other one anymore. *Damn it.* Riley had made them for her and now one was gone. *Should have been smarter, faster, more careful.* She clutched the folders to her bosom and wondered if what was inside would be worth the sacrifice.

More shouts filled the air. Apparently, backup had arrived. She hugged the building and clung to the shadows. Relief washed over her when she finally reached the Jeep Cherokee. Brooklyn's body protested as she hauled herself into the driver's seat, desperate to get away before being spotted. Barely breathing, she pulled onto the road without headlights. Dangerous, but not as dangerous as being seen.

Killing him would have been quieter and a lot less painful.

Brooklyn shivered. *He's got kids. Besides, killing got me in this predicament to begin with. How bad am I hurt?*

Two cracked ribs, sprained ankle, wrenched knee, a few cuts, loads of bruises.

Great.

Hey, you asked!

Brooklyn glanced in the rearview mirror for the hundredth time, fully expecting blue lights, but there was only the dark road vanishing in her wake. The adrenaline faded, leaving her with the shakes.

This is double stupid. You shouldn't be here of all places.

Ignoring him, she turned into a small subdivision and parked the SUV on the street outside the investigator's house.

Are you trying to get caught?

He'll get it back to the owner.

And what? He'll think, 'Oh she's not so bad. She probably didn't kill all those people since she returned this car. Let's just let her go'?

Shut up. She dragged herself out of the driver's seat, got into the Chevy Cavalier she'd left there a few hours prior, and pulled away feeling much safer having swapped cars.

Brooklyn switched on a police scanner and listened as they coordinated the search. Tires whispered on the pavement and she wanted nothing so much as to rest and lick her wounds. Staying clear of the main roads, she made herself drive slowly so as not to draw any attention, winding in no particular hurry through the hills toward the lake communities.

Pulling the car into the driveway of a little brown-and-white cottage on the water, she sat with her forehead resting on the steering wheel for a long moment. She'd been using the place as a hideout for several weeks. It was a summer home for a couple in their fifties, judging from the pictures inside. Fortunately, they had yet to stop by this summer.

Letting herself inside, Brooklyn drew on Belial again to numb the pain. Dropping the files on the dining room table, she stumbled to the bathroom. Her pants were shredded and soaked with blood. The gashes on her thighs were long, but shallow. The injured ankle was swollen and already bruising. Her ribs ached with every breath.

Brooklyn cleaned the cuts and scrapes with alcohol, relishing the way the pain made Belial squirm. She tended her wounds as best she could with Band-Aids and toilet paper, then limped to the kitchen, filled a couple of Ziplocs with ice, and grabbed the files on the way to the living room. Brooklyn sank into a recliner and put the cold packs on her knee and ankle.

You need to put the car in the garage before someone notices it. This house is supposed to be empty.

Brooklyn ignored Belial. Who knew a demon could be such a nag? She flipped the first folder open. There was a list of names. Victim names. The last two names drew a shocked gasp. Pain roared through her cracked ribs. Her parents' names. The police thought she'd killed her own parents? How could they think that?

There were several pages of handwritten notes, interviews with people who had known her, former employers, friends, and even David's mother. The next section contained interviews with the families of the people she—Belial rather—had killed.

Are you looking at this? You did this.

He didn't answer. Apparently, she wasn't the only one who could choose to ignore. Further in the stack she found autopsy reports stapled to images of corpses, some badly decomposed, black with frozen tissue. Causes of death varied from stabbing and asphyxiation to blood loss and hypothermia. There were hundreds of pictures. There was mixed information on David. It appeared they couldn't decide if he was an accomplice or a potential victim. There were grainy security photos of her and Riley together; she recognized her outfit from their one and only date. She read a lengthy summary of therapy sessions with Devin. His account of events, while quite accurate, had been written off as a traumatic fabrication.

She sighed and closed her eyes. Her mind expanded out along the wall and into the kitchen. Brooklyn popped the fridge open and felt around for a soda. Line of sight made this sort of exercise much easier, but her ribs ached and she needed the practice. By her own estimation, she was still much weaker and less skillful than even the least of Kurt's Adepts. *Kurt oh Kurt.* Her chest clenched. Was he still alive out there somewhere? The news reports had centered primarily on the burning of the town, with no mention of the events at Kurt's manor. They had coined it an incident of domestic terrorism.

I think if anyone could have survived the battle, it was him. He fought my father and lived. He was dueling with another Protector the last time I saw him, just before I came to you. When she didn't respond, he went on, *I know you cared for him.*

"And I know you hated him."

He betrayed his office. The Protectors and Wardens have worked to keep the worlds in balance for centuries, and then he turned on us. I hated him, but I don't now. Silence stretched for a long moment and then he said, *I don't hate you.*

"I don't hate you either, not really."

You should. It's my fault you're a fugitive. It's my fault your parents are dead—

"It's also your fault Devin is alive, and that I'm alive, for that matter. I try to remember that when I want to kill you."

Brooklyn popped the top on her soda and flipped the next folder open. This one contained more information about her parents. Photos of her home burned to the ground. When she came to the autopsy photos of her parents, she slammed the folder shut and tossed it away. The image of their burned bodies would haunt her for the rest of her life.

The last folder was older. Years older, edges worn and bent. It smelled musty. The other folders had been neatly marked with typed labels; this one was handwritten in black marker. This was it. This was what she'd sacrificed one of her three soul stones to get. What if there was nothing inside to help her?

Belial stirred restlessly behind her eyes. She lifted the cover back. There, on the very first page, was Erin. Her high school yearbook photo smiled up at Brooklyn, stapled to the missing persons report. It was the same photo that had graced posters and television for months after her disappearance. Erin's eyes were as dark as Brooklyn's were light. Her walnut hair framed her pale face in loose, looping curls, accentuating a mischievous smile.

I think this is a bad idea for which we do not have the time to spare.

"Devin needs his mother."

He has a new one, and a father too this time. He's in a better home than you or your sister can give him.

"You don't get it."

I get that this is not about Devin, it's about you. Search for Riley, David, or even Protector Levin instead. You will not find her.

"She's the only family I have left. For all I know, the others are all dead anyway."

Brooklyn thumbed through the case file. There was less to go on than she'd hoped. Erin had gone to a concert in Asheville with some friends. The group of girls had met at a friend's house and rode together in one car. Early the next morning, they'd come back to sleep at Kindra Miller's house. A little before noon the next day, Erin left to drive home. Her car was found later that night on a side road with the keys in the ignition. An abduction in broad daylight.

The investigator's notes mentioned suspected drug use. There was cocaine found in the car. Her dad had always blamed her disappearance on drugs and hanging out with the wrong people, but Brooklyn never believed it. Erin was a mom, a wonderful mom. There's no way she was out doing drugs while Devin was waiting at home.

It's not something people advertise to their families.

"It doesn't add up. We were close. As close as sisters can be. I would have known."

Cocaine in the car.

"Somebody else's. It means somebody else was in the car. If she were an addict, she would have taken it with her."

If it was somebody else's, why would that person not have taken it as well? Your logic is flawed.

Brooklyn flipped through the rest of the file. There were recorded interviews with Erin's friends, the girls that attended the concert. They were on microcassettes. She'd have to find something to play them on. That meant going to an electronics store, which she wouldn't be able to do for a few days.

You've been up all night, and you are hurt. You need to get some sleep.

For once, she didn't argue with him.

Erin's face flickered through Brooklyn's dreams. Childhood forest forts melted into all-out fights with punching and hair pulling. Conversations flitted by faster than Brooklyn could follow. It was like watching several videos at once on fast forward.

Erin was aging before her eyes, growing from a grinning first-grader into the gorgeous woman in the investigator's photographs.

Next a blur of whispered conversations, many of them at the shallow cave the sisters had used as a hangout and drinking spot in their early teen years. There they gossiped about boys and school. The blitz of images suddenly froze and melted away, leaving Brooklyn disoriented as her focus resolved on a single moment.

Erin was crying and trying to hide it. Rubbing her eyes with the heels of her hands had made things worse. They were sitting on the floor in Erin's boyfriend's apartment amid a semicircle of half-packed boxes.

Brooklyn pulled her sister close and hugged her. "It's okay. You're too good for him, anyway."

"He's not coming back, Brooke." Erin wailed.

"You're going to be okay, I promise. You'll move back home for a while."

"I can't do that. Dad—"

"He'll get over it."

"I can't do it."

"We're your family. It's what families are for."

Erin didn't answer, but she sat up straight and wiped her eyes, with a little more success this time.

"Where is he going?" Brooklyn turned to face her sister more directly.

"Chicago, for school. Said he had an uncle there to stay with." She took a deep, shuddering breath and let it out.

"You've had breakups before . . . I've never seen you this upset."

She shrugged and hugged herself, looking very small. "Yeah, well, I've never been pregnant before."

Brooklyn opened her mouth to reply, but the dream jumped ahead.

She was in the living room at her parents' house. It was raining outside. Devin was about a year old and he was screaming. Brooklyn held him, trying to soothe him. Erin had the phone pressed to one ear and her finger in the other.

"You need to do something for him. He's sick," Brooklyn's dad yelled from down the hallway.

"We know he's sick." Brooklyn touched Devin's forehead, feeling the fever.

"Why are you holding him? Let his mom take care of him. It's her job."

"She's on the phone."

"Tell her to get off!"

Brooklyn went upstairs to her bedroom with Devin and shut the door. The yelling downstairs soon escalated. She could hear her mom becoming involved and Erin's voice rising shrill and angry. Brooklyn held Devin and rocked him back and forth until his sobs dwindled to whimpers and finally to sleep.

The front door slammed and from her bedroom window Brooklyn saw Erin's car careen out of the driveway, spraying gravel.

The images started to spin again, and Brooklyn realized what was happening. She froze the images. *What are you doing?*

I'm learning about your sister. Searching for clues.

I don't want you pilfering through my memories.

There might be something that can help us find—

No. Brooklyn waited until she felt Belial withdraw to the back of her mind where he belonged. Then she closed her eyes again but, try as she might, sleep evaded her.

3

Death Takes a Bath

Riley stared dejectedly out the window at the unchanging landscape. There wasn't much else to do. It was better than the plain gray walls surrounding him and the empty food tray discarded by the slot in his door. The setting sun cast long shadows across the field. He pressed his face against the cold glass and imagined he was anywhere else. Imagined he was with Brooklyn.

The air outside was chilly, as if summer had never quite gotten a foothold in the mountains. Several strange, colorful insects lit on the window. He had never noticed them before his captivity, which, by his nearest estimate, had started six months ago.

In the beginning, before the cornfields in the distance had foundered, planes had frequently passed overhead dusting the fields with pesticides. Apparently, that hadn't worked. Now, each evening as the sun set, the strange bugs gathered on the western wall of the manor, chasing the fading warmth. Perhaps a cold winter would do for them what pesticides had not.

Riley was losing his mind, and he knew it. Under his pillow was a screw that he had carefully worked loose from the bed frame over several days and then painstakingly sharpened to a razor's edge during the subsequent weeks. This was not a weapon with which he intended to harm others; he had seen no others for the duration of his confinement. He couldn't imagine doing anything more than hugging another human being at this point. No, it wasn't a weapon at all. It was a tool that let him cling to what sanity he had left. A promise he made to himself every morning and every night when he held it loosely in his hand under the pillow. It was the possibility of a final escape. He'd pressed it against the tender flesh of his wrist more than once, but memories of Brooklyn's smile and their brief time together were enough motivation to live another day.

Endless questions whirled through his mind, driving him mad. Tormenting his dreams. The world went on while he rotted away, forgotten. What had become of his friends? Kurt was likely dead, but Riley refused to give up hope until he knew for certain. Had Belial gotten Brooklyn to safety? Not knowing was stealing his sanity. Riley was tired of his own voice, the familiarity of his own thoughts, and—most disconcerting of all—the dying dialogue with his internal companion. The latter made him feel most uncomfortable. As the months ticked by, he had interacted less and less with that other part of himself. Their partnership, built on a mutual love of arcane research, had atrophied. There was nothing to study here apart from the four walls and the landscape beyond the window.

Insects landed against the window with little tapping sounds, not unlike raindrops. Riley tapped the window, and they ignored him. He tapped harder. Still nothing. He banged his head and his fists, but they continued to crawl, oblivious or uninterested in his presence.

There was a metallic snap behind him. He whirled to find the food tray had been removed. This was another reason he was going insane. In six months, he had never seen the tray arrive or get taken away. Never heard footsteps. He pounded on the door, calling out, his voice strange and thick from disuse. No one answered.

Several times he'd spent entire days staring at the door. On those days, they simply hadn't fed him.

Riley turned back to the window and looked down. Four stories. It was inviting. He'd gladly trade a couple of broken legs for some human interaction. The window, unfortunately, would not break. He'd lost count of how many times he'd tried.

He reached inside the lock on the door with his mind. It was filled with tiny clockwork. Hundreds of moveable parts. Riley had never encountered a puzzle like it before. Normal locks he could often bypass without a key. Safes, with enough time, could be cracked. But this? He didn't even know where to begin. At first, he'd tried mapping it out mentally, depending on his companion to maintain the integrity of his visualization. The next day, what they had pieced together no longer matched up, as if the lock had changed itself overnight.

For the first few weeks, he had feared execution, but now he thought it might be a pleasant change of pace. Darkness stole away the outside world and made a mirror of his window, and he was so tired of seeing only himself. Riley collapsed onto the bed. "Goodnight," he whispered.

There was no reply.

Azrael, God of Death, sighed as she reclined into a hot bath. It was the first uninterrupted bath she'd taken in at least four thousand years. Generally, she found herself flickering in and out of whatever task she was trying to accomplish, several times each second. If someone died, she was there to untether the soul and see them off. Now she had help. They were slow and unskilled helpers, but there were a lot of them.

She flicked at the bubbles with her fingers. The Buddhists were really on to something with this "being present in the moment" thing. For a while, things had gotten out of control. As the human population grew, so had the number of deaths occurring each moment, taxing her to the point she had literally broken apart. Fortunately, she'd found a solution. Now she had time to bring her plans to fruition, time for leisure even. The population was still growing, but not for long.

Corn crops around the world were failing. Humans had become too reliant on it, and now it would be their undoing. Fuel prices were at record highs. The prices of food, soft drinks, and plastics were increasing steadily. There wasn't enough feed for livestock and as a result the prices of poultry, pork, and beef had already doubled. Everything, it seemed, had corn in it.

She'd dropped a pebble in the pond and now she had but to wait while the ripples spread.

4

BLIND DATE

Belial could smell ruin in the air. While Brooklyn prattled on about the ever-rising price of gasoline, he teased out the various scents blowing through the open car window.

This plague of corn crop–decimating beetles gave off a heady aroma. Ripe, decadent, and unnatural. Something old had spewed them forth into the modern world. Something old and foul.

Illinois countryside sprawled around them in a carpet of brown rot. Each cornfield with half-grown stalks broken and splayed at odd angles seemed its own ground zero.

They were heading northwest, following an obscure, years-old lead that was bound to be a waste of time. He hadn't argued the point, though. Brooklyn was prone to doing what she wanted regardless of his opinions, and anything that took them further away from the manhunt, or woman-hunt in this case, wasn't a bad thing.

Belial was itching to return to Driftwood Beach. How long would it take for dragon eggs to incubate? With winter coming in a few months, might they need to be moved further south? If only he could have gotten them to a more Mediterranean climate.

There was really only one way he was going to get back to that beach. He had to help Brooklyn find out the truth about her sister. That, or point the clues back toward southeastern Georgia, but she was too smart to fall for that.

I'll make you a deal.

She didn't answer.

I think you're going to want to hear me out on this one.

"If I'd known you'd be this annoying, I'd have let you stay in Hell with your father."

We were talking long before you invited me in.

"What's the deal?"

I help you solve this thing, and you get me back south to check on the eggs before winter.

Brooklyn didn't answer. That was okay. At least she had not rejected him out of hand. So he waited as the fields rolled by. She would acquiesce in time.

Several minutes later, she finally responded. "Help how? Aren't you already helping?"

That was good. She was at least nibbling at the offer. *Data analysis. I can put information together faster and more objectively than you. I can work while you sleep. Last night was just a taste of what I could do if you'd allow me some freedom.*

"What is it you think you accomplished last night? Besides invading my privacy?"

I learned quite a lot about your sister, her temperament, background, and motivations. I don't know what use it will be just yet, but at the very least, I can offer a different perspective.

He waited while she changed roads, casting a quick glance behind her. This was another human limitation, no true capacity for multitasking.

"Alright, but our original deal doesn't change. I'm in charge at all times. If I think you are trying to manipulate me even a little, you're gone."

Sure.

"And you can only look at memories that include Erin. I catch you in any other part of my mind, you're toast."

These threats are really beneath you, child. Where's the trust?

"Don't call me child." She slapped the steering wheel for emphasis. "What have you done to earn my trust? Besides getting me a shot at a debut on *America's Most Wanted?*"

I saved your life and made an enemy of my father. I've followed your rules and taken a lot of verbal abuse. Now I'm offering you my help. Take it, or drive around the Midwest by yourself. I'll find another host.

Brooklyn growled in frustration. "Fine."

Fine. Now pull over at that grill up ahead. I want a tenderloin sandwich.

"*You* want a sandwich?"

He didn't answer, but when she pulled off the road, he couldn't suppress his satisfaction.

Brooklyn had to admit, it was a pretty good sandwich. The inside dining room was full, so she had ordered at a walk-up window and now ate at the picnic tables. It was midday, and the weather was warm. Could she let her guard down and trust Belial? She didn't know. He had wrecked her life, but his motivations had not really been about her. He'd been trying to uphold ancient laws of separation between the physical and spiritual worlds. It just so happened that doing so had resulted in the loss of her boyfriend and her family, and had made her a wanted criminal. It was true he'd been perfectly compliant since she had aided him in escaping his father though.

Brooklyn wondered how Riley had kept Belial in this world without allowing him inside. She knew there was a way, but then, Riley did lots of things normal people couldn't do. And there was a strange connection between her and Belial. She could draw on his power anytime, no matter where he was. A fact that had even confounded Riley.

She sighed, missing Riley. He'd been there for her after she lost David. He'd been the friend she needed, and then more than a friend, and now he was lost or dead too.

A crow landed on the edge of the table and cocked its head at her. She tore a bit from her bun and tossed it. The bird watched it bounce, and then its beak lanced forward and devoured it. She guessed the corn collapse was hurting everyone. There were several of the strange beetles around, but it seemed the crows were not interested in eating those. Brooklyn picked one up as it crawled onto her sandwich wrapper. It was shaped like a ladybug and gave off a faint, unpleasant odor. She felt Belial stirring with interest, so more by reflex than thought, she flicked it away.

She turned her thoughts inward. *So now you've had your sandwich. What help do you have for me?*

I need you to take a nap, so I can learn everything there is to know about Erin. I do not think following a five-year-old lead of a possible sighting is going to pan out. They didn't find her there then; we won't find her there now, and it likely wasn't her at all.

Brooklyn closed her eyes and felt the breeze on her face. *You think she is dead? Don't you?*

I think it's likely.

It wasn't what she wanted to hear, but she sensed and appreciated the honesty. So the next step to finding her sister was to take a nap. Of course it was. *I'll find a secluded place to park the car and you can get to work. How long will you need?*

I can finish in two hours.

She stood up and tossed her trash in the can. Inside her, something burned painfully, something she hadn't really let herself feel in a while. Something called hope.

David sank into his bed. It was good to be home. He had visited more of the world in the last few months than he'd ever dreamed possible and now had direct contact in most first-world nations, in government, finance, and private industry.

At each of Father Logan's lost churches, there had been a new leader. Someone who had regained autonomy. David still heard their cries of anger and frustration when it was quiet. They hated him for taking it away. They were right to hate him. He hated himself for it.

Azrael wasn't here. He'd half expected she would be, shining bright as a star in his unsight. He felt lonely and, as always when he felt alone, his thoughts drifted to Brooklyn. Was she still alive? Did she know he was alive? How had things gotten so crazy?

He imagined the life they would have had together. A normal life with jobs and kids, a dog. Maybe his band would have gone places. They might have wound up in Nashville in some other life. A life without demons and Protectors.

His stomach growled as he eased himself off the bed and started a warm shower. He didn't hurry, though food would be coming soon. They'd wait until he was ready and deliver it at the right moment. He'd have steak, a baked potato, and salad tonight.

The knock came just as he finished dressing. They entered right after. Two men set up a folding table and two chairs. They placed the meals and retreated.

The steak smelled perfect. David wasn't sure if his sense of smell was more acute because of his blindness, or if he was just that hungry, but he imagined he could smell the individual seasonings.

Barely seconds later, a lighter, more hesitant knock sounded. "Come in."

Information about his visitor, Nicole, flooded his mind, unbidden. With concentration, he pushed the knowledge aside. She entered and took the empty seat, gracefully smoothing her skirt as she sat. Her companion, Emily, moved to sit on the edge of the bed, just behind David's left shoulder. She would be his eyes.

Through her, he could see his dinner companion. Her passing resemblance to Brooklyn had been heightened and emphasized by the careful application of makeup. The way she moved, the quirk of her smile, all subconscious adjustments she'd made based on what she sensed he wanted. Each gesture was an ache of familiar longing laced with guilt.

He smiled warmly. "I hope you like steak."

"It's my favorite." She tucked a strand of hair behind her ear, another Brooklyn gesture. Nicole was a vegetarian. The information seeped through the block in his consciousness. He could feel her inner revulsion being quashed by her desire to serve him.

"Leave the steak for Emily. It's alright." He picked up his knife and fork and cut into his own steak. It was tricky watching himself through Emily's eyes, but months of practice had improved his coordination. The first bite was heavenly.

"How was your day?" He focused on fully blocking their psychic connection in hopes of an intelligent conversation. He'd never tried this before, but his experiences reclaiming lost cells over the past few months had given him the idea that it might be possible.

She didn't answer immediately. Instead, she speared a cucumber and munched on it thoughtfully. "This morning we had chapel, devotions, and prayer to Azrael. After that I helped in the daycare. I met Eli for lunch in the cafeteria. Eli's my boyfriend. We were making plans to see a movie this evening and then . . . I can't remember what happened after that. I was just here knocking on your door." Her brow furrowed with concern. It was a prim expression, not at all reminiscent of Brooklyn. "You don't want to know about this, do you?"

Even without a direct connection, she adored him. He could see it in her concern, which was not for her own predicament, but born from a worry that he would not like it. "It's fine. So would you say it was a good day?"

She wiped her mouth carefully with a napkin. "It was good," she answered without really looking up from her plate. The playful smile from earlier seemed to have vanished inside this reserved persona.

Feelings about Eli warred with a sense of devotion and duty inside of her. David felt shame when she regarded Emily, her best friend. It was as if she were looking into his eyes directly. He could feel frustration and anger pulsing just beyond the block he'd created between them. The block crumbled and her face became suddenly serene. Enthusiasm and peace filled her eyes, and Brooklyn's doppelgänger was smiling at him again.

David cleared his throat. "So, overall, a good day?"

"Yes," she answered at once. "It was an amazing day."

"That's good. I appreciate you having dinner with me. It was a tough day for me."

"My pleasure." She smiled coyly through the steam that rose from her potato as she cut into the skin.

"Nicole, are your parents a part of the church?"

"Yes they are, and please, call me Brooklyn." She bit her lip and frowned, sensing his turmoil.

He sat his fork and knife on his plate. "I don't think that's a good idea."

Her expression switched from reproachful to defiant. The expression was one Brooklyn had given him often, just as a big argument was brewing. "My name is Brooklyn. Don't call me Nicole again."

David picked up his fork and sat it down again. His hands were trembling. "I don't want you to be Brooklyn. I just want you to be yourself."

She stood, her chair tumbling over backward. "Who's Nicole? Are you cheating on me?"

"You are Nicole." He reached for her hand, but she pulled away. "You're just confused. Please sit back down and I'll show you."

"Who. Is. Nicole!"

He blocked the connection and watched Brooklyn's rage melt away. She gasped, clutching her chest. "I'm Nicole?"

"Yes. Everything is okay. Just breathe. Just breathe."

"You were trying to make me *be* her." She swayed on her feet, putting a hand on the table to steady herself.

"I wasn't."

"You were. And it isn't . . . it isn't the first time. I remember. I remember what you did. What I . . . what you made me do."

He put his hand over hers on the table. "You're just confused. There's nothing to remember."

She looked down at his hand as if it were a large, disgusting spider. Her fingers curled around the steak knife and she slashed his arm. Screaming, she slammed into him, driving him to the floor.

All he could see from Emily's vantage point was Nicole's back as she straddled him and raised the knife with both hands. He flung his arms up blindly. Fear coursed through him. Mortal terror. He felt people all over the complex responding to his distress. They were too far away to save him. How had he been this stupid? Emily was moving. Her hands were around Nicole's hands as they struggled on top of him. The block. He was still holding it. He let it go.

The effect was instantaneous. David saw it through Emily's eyes, and felt Nicole change, all the resistance melting away as she became Brooklyn again. Then he felt it through each of them as Emily, bent on protecting him, drove the knife into her best friend's heart, and he lost Brooklyn all over again.

They came to meet his needs. David needed to be far away from the body and the smell of blood. Needed it gone. He wanted desperately not to see through the eyes of the prophets that had burst into the room in response to his summons, but he didn't dare block the connections.

He felt like he was supposed to say something, to offer some explanation. But they didn't ask for one and he didn't have the words.

David was a pitiful sight, bloodied and pale, with blind eyes that stared blankly. He saw himself as they saw him. When he noticed the throbbing pain in his arm, it wasn't long until gentle hands began to clean and prep the wound for stitching.

David had expected his goddess to appear and pluck him like a child from the mess he'd made. Instead of her glowing visage, he'd seen a monstrosity. Where he'd expected the compassion and precision of an angel, there had been something crude and soulless. Nicole had deserved better than a demon to usher her soul from this world.

Emily's eyes flicked between the corpse on the floor and the man cleaning David's wounded arm. The man was Eli.

He worked with quick, methodical motions. His expression was grim and determined.

David touched Eli's mind. It was alive with impotent rage. The woman he loved lay dead on the floor, and every fiber of his being was compelled to serve her murderer.

When the stitching was finished, David took a shuddering breath. Around him, men and women worked in gruesome silence.

This was his fault. He was so weak. He had allowed his desires to ruin the lives of others. Without his direct guidance, this whole situation would continue to spin out of control.

At his direction, Emily came to sit beside him on the bed. Carefully, he pressured her to forget what had happened this evening. She would throw her bloody clothing away, shower, and go to bed.

One by one, he dismissed the others similarly. When only two remained, he had them gather all the bloody clothing and burn it. The body was another problem. He didn't know what to do with it. He couldn't trust these men to plan, only to follow directions.

Should they burn it or bury it? They couldn't dump her to be discovered because his DNA was all over her.

How stupid he was. The answer was obvious. This was a church, and there was a graveyard out back. He sent them to dig the grave beyond the tree line at the furthest corner of the cemetery. That left him to wait alone with her. In death, she really did not resemble Brooklyn much at all. He was oddly grateful to be blind in this situation. Not seeing the body now somehow made things easier. She did not look like Brooklyn . . . and yet, the thought did not comfort him.

Was he one of the bad guys now? Like Father Logan, his predecessor, or Nathan Goodrum, leader of the Demonriders? At least they had a purpose. What was his purpose? Stealing free will and instigating murder? David wanted to flee the room, but he made himself stay with her. That at least he could do. He wouldn't sleep here tonight—or ever again—but he could sit with the girl that had been so alive and full of plans and dreams just a couple of hours ago.

David fumbled his way into the closet and rummaged around with shaking hands until he found his guitar, and sat on the bed and played a quiet melody, his hands becoming steady. David played until they returned for the body and returned afterward for debriefing. He played until the alarm clock sounded the next morning. When the last notes trembled in the air, almost visible, and faded, she was gone forever, and nobody would remember why. How he wished he didn't know, either.

5

YOUR LIFE IN TECHNICOLOR

Images swirled around Brooklyn in a visual cacophony. More intense than the previous time when Belial had worked with a light hand to camouflage his intrusion as a series of dreams. Memories ripped by with nauseating speed, trailing the associated emotions behind them so fleetingly that she couldn't identify them by name.

What's this? Belial asked, bringing one image to the front. It was a Saturday morning and Brooklyn had accidentally walked in on Erin in the bathroom. She was taking a pill, the prescription bottle open on the counter beside her. What made it notable was the look of startled guilt. The bottle was generic because she didn't know what the medication treated.

It was some kind of antidepressant.

So, she was depressed?

I guess so. After Devin was born with no father. It wasn't how she'd wanted things to be.

Belial unfroze the memory and Erin yelled, shoving Brooklyn into the hallway and slamming the door.

Okay, tell me about this one. The images swirled again, and Brooklyn packed for a weekend ski trip with her two best friends. Erin sat on the bed talking to her while she did.

"Is Justin going to be there?" Erin asked, referring to Brooklyn's boyfriend.

"Nope, just Megan and Jennifer. It's a girls' weekend."

"Sounds like a lot of fun."

"You sure you don't want to come? I told you I'll pay."

She smiled faintly. "I have 'responsibilities.'"

Brooklyn placed the neatly folded stacks of clothing into her suitcase. "You have a baby. It doesn't mean you have to stop living your life. Mom would watch him for a couple of days."

"Just drop it, Brookie. Thanks, but no thanks."

The image evaporated. *She wasn't happy*, Belial mused.

Lots of people aren't happy. That doesn't mean anything.

You believe the pills were hers? That they were antidepressants?

Well, that would make sense if she wasn't happy, wouldn't it? Postpartum depression is common.

You two were close. Why would she hide something like that from you?

Brooklyn paused for a moment. *I don't know*, she admitted at last, a kernel of uncomfortable doubt taking root.

Look at this. A new image blossomed in her mind's eye. Christmas Eve, Devin's first. He was dressed in a Grinch onesie, with a matching hat. Erin held him in her arms, looking down at him.

"Oh, he's so cute! Let me hold that grandbaby."

Erin looked up, startled out of whatever private thoughts she'd been having. "You want to go to Grammy?" She lifted him up and her mom took him. Erin's eyes lingered on him for a moment, and then she rose amid the familial chatter, mumbled something about the bathroom, and slipped down the hallway.

Wait. Brooklyn reasserted control, pausing the memory. *Why is this significant?*

I'm not sure yet. This caught my attention.

The images rippled forward at least half an hour. Devin was in Brooklyn's mother's arms when the kitchen door opened quietly and Erin entered the room.

See? She never came back down the hallway, which means she left through a window and came back in through the back door sometime later.

Just because I don't remember her coming back from the bathroom doesn't mean she didn't. These are memories, not video footage. The doubt blossomed larger inside her chest anyway.

The images spun again. *Maybe so.* A new image resolved, and Brooklyn recognized it immediately. This was the very last time she had seen her sister. Erin was gorgeous in a dark emerald dress and cowgirl boots. Her hair curled carefully, and her nails painted. She was bursting with anticipation.

Brooklyn trailed behind her, Devin on her hip. Erin was busy moving everything from a large purse into a smaller one that would be easier to carry. She had everything dumped out on the bed.

"So, who all is going?" Brooklyn asked.

Erin continued to sort through her belongings. "Jenna Beck and a couple of girls I hung out with at college. You don't know them."

"Any guys going?"

Erin chucked the rest of her belongings back into the old purse and tossed it aside. "Hmm?"

"Is it just a girls' thing?"

"Supposed to be."

Brooklyn put Devin down on the bed where he sat looking back and forth between them. "Be careful, have fun, but call me if you need a ride, okay?"

Erin hugged her. "Don't worry, Brookie, I'll be fine. Don't wait up." She gave Devin a kiss on the forehead, grabbed her purse, checked herself in the mirror with a nervous sigh, and was gone.

"Let's get some supper, little man," Brooklyn said, sweeping Devin up into her arms.

She came back to herself suddenly. The sun was much lower in the sky than it had been when she'd parked the car in a copse of trees just off a small side road.

"Why did you show me that?" Her mouth felt dry, and her voice was husky. She fumbled in the backseat, looking for a bottle of water.

It was different. The contrast struck me as significant.
"No pill bottles this time. Nothing pointing toward drug use."
She was nervous.
"Just excited. She was going to a concert."
He didn't say more. Brooklyn found the water and used it to wash down a couple of aspirin. Her head throbbed as she started the car and got back on the road.

Dravin Logan considered himself a patient man. Growing up on a farm, he'd learned the value of planting seeds, working hard as a steward to ensure their survival, and eventually reaping the reward of harvest. But, from an early age, his ambition had burned hot, urging him on to other places and bigger challenges. Growing up, he had often chafed under the menial responsibilities a family farm heaped onto him, especially the expectation that he would someday take it over. Toward the end, he had considered his family a source of frustration more than anything.

He felt similarly impatient now. After years of amassing a worldwide network of followers, he had been reduced to control over a single man. An unambitious man at that. Nathan Goodrum had been willful, but lacked direction and vision. Dravin could help with that.

Still, he was restricted to controlling only Nathan. An unfortunate side effect of stripping Nathan's free will was that it left him unable to control a demon or other spirit. As Nathan was the leader of the Demonriders, this presented certain . . . logistical problems.

Leaving him independent enough to not raise suspicion, but still firmly under control, had been a careful balance to strike. Fortunately, Dravin had been doing this sort of thing for years.

He took a stroll through the manor house, with Goodrum at his side, to assess the reconstruction. The place was the customary seat of the Eastern District Protector, the man or woman responsible for maintaining law and order east of the Mississippi, and beholden only to the Heir himself. A position Goodrum had long coveted and finally obtained several months ago.

Removing the previous Protector had been a messy affair. The main entryway had been heavily damaged by a rocketeer, causing much of the marble floor to collapse into the lower level. Repair work was coming along swiftly, however.

The men they passed nodded with stiff deference to Goodrum, but eyed Dravin with carefully veiled distrust. Instinctively, Nathan moved to reprimand the men. Dravin allayed the impulse before Nathan could act. No sense in letting the others see their leader act out of character.

Dravin suppressed a shudder as they turned the corner away from the Demonriders' cold, calculating glares. Demonriders practiced intentional and persistent possession. Pitting their wills against the wills of demons in a never-ending struggle for dominance. If successful, they could take the demon's power. Make themselves faster, stronger, and more telekinetically adept. At the same time, they courted disaster. A slip in concentration, a moment of weakness, even an unchecked emotion could allow the demon to seize control and wreak havoc. If that happened, and if they survived the repercussions, they were stripped of their demon and cast out of the order as failures. Dravin couldn't fathom why anyone would choose to live life like that, even if it granted them power.

These musings rattled through his head until they reached the dining room. Today, it had been reconfigured to serve another purpose. A semicircle of mahogany tables was arranged around a dais and lectern. There were seats enough for thirty people, though Dravin didn't expect that many to attend.

The serving staff that had been retained were busy preparing an evening meal for the expected guests. Goodrum busied himself with checking on the arrangements. Dravin secured an unobtrusive seat on the front right-hand side of the room. The more important guests would fill in the central tables.

"I'm surprised to see you here, Father Logan."

Dravin jumped and immediately chided himself. *Never show fear, especially in a room full of Demonriders.* He turned to find the speaker wasn't a Demonrider at all. "Lord Heir, I hadn't expected your attendance either."

Eric Stewarth smiled. "I've learned it is important to provide oversight. If half of what I've heard about your recent luck is true, I wouldn't have been surprised to hear you'd called it quits."

Dravin flashed his own dismissive smile. "Just a minor setback. Grossly exaggerated. Theological differences. Most faiths experience splits from time to time. Growing pains, if you will."

"I'd love to hear more about it sometime."

"Of course. We could discuss it over a drink, perhaps?"

Eric raised his eyebrows and spun a chair around, sitting in it backward and resting his elbows on the back. Something his father never would have done. "You and Nathan seem to have become quite close. I thought you despised these blasphemous Demonriders?"

"I despise men who lack ambition and passion."

Eric's face clouded over. "What about Kurt Levin? Do you think he was a man of ambition?"

"I think he was passionate, but not particularly ambitious. Who could say what his motives were? To serve so loyally for decades and then do something like that . . . it's unthinkable."

"What was it you said earlier, a minor setback? The ring will find its way home. Until it does, there are plenty of other tools in my family's toolbox."

"No doubt. Your father was the latest in a long line of legendary men. I had tremendous respect for him. If there is anything I can do to support you, you need only ask."

Eric nodded. "Thank you for your loyalty. It means a lot."

"Of course." Dravin leaned back in his chair, considering the young man and the room beyond, which had filled up noticeably during their exchange. He recognized several people, including the Wandering Witches, Erina Craft and her daughter Bryssa. Regal as always, with raven hair and green eyes, something about them screamed Eastern European descent. They were rumored to have a secret skill with the four elements, but nobody had ever seen proof of it outside of fire-breathing circus performances.

"I should mingle," Eric commented lightly, his eye on Bryssa. As he stood, touching the ribbon that held back his long, dark hair, four guards materialized from among the serving staff and shadowed him.

Interesting.

Nathan had taken a seat at the table just right of the center, flanked by his Protector compatriots, Brianne Moore, leader of the Protectors, and Michael Benson, the Canadian Protector. A row of blank-faced Demonriders stood directly behind them. Dravin thought he saw Brianne wrinkle her nose in distaste.

Del Stewarth, Eric's mother, occupied the central table. Dravin knew little about her, but she had apparently developed a strong rapport with Goodrum, leveraging his help in deposing Kurt Levin in exchange for the Protector title he'd always coveted.

Across the way was a Scotsman, Tristan Barrett. Dravin had only met him in passing at prior meetings. He was talking animatedly with a large woman in overalls. Mrs. Amelia Mays. Dravin's stomach lurched. What in all of creation was *she* doing here?

He made to look away, but wasn't quick enough. She caught his gaze, scowling with disapproval. Fortunately, before she could cross the room to speak with him, Eric banged the gavel, calling the meeting to order. Begrudgingly, she sat, staring holes through him. It was going to be a long meeting.

6

Deathly Distractions

"You could have ruined everything!" Azrael raged.

David watched her impassively. She was one thing he could always see despite his blindness, as bright as the sun, wings drawn back in an aggressive posture. "What is 'everything,' exactly?"

"Our plans! All our hard work. Everything we've built."

Her aura seemed to be tinged with hints of green. He'd never seen that before. "You mean your plans, my hard work, and everything we've stolen?"

She crossed the room to perch beside him on the bed. A warm arm around his shoulders. "I don't understand what's happening to you. I need to understand."

"What's the point of this? Any of it? Why are we controlling these people?" David's anger chafed under Azrael's comforting arm, but a smaller, more desperate part of him craved the contact.

"They aren't really people anymore. They're broken. They were broken when we found them, but at least you can give them purpose."

"Like I gave her purpose?" He gestured to the floor where Nicole's body had been.

"Yes. Absolutely, yes. If you'd allowed her to serve your purposes, she'd still be alive. Happy even!"

David pushed her away. "This power is turning me into a monster."

She folded her wings and turned to face him. "This power is doing exactly what you tell it to do. If what you see it doing is monstrous, don't blame the power, learn to control it, or better yet, learn to control yourself."

David rose and walked to the window, gazing sightlessly out at the trees where Nicole was buried. "She deserved something better than that ugly demon that came for her. It should have been you."

Azrael put a hand on his shoulder. "I don't care about her. I care about you."

"What if I had died? What if she'd stabbed me? That demon servant of yours would have been my last look at this world and my first at the next, and you'd never have even known it happened."

"But she didn't, and now you know to be more careful as we go forward."

David turned and met her eyes. "I'm not going forward. I'm done."

"Why—"

He held up his hand for silence. "You know why."

She sighed softly. "Brooklyn again?"

"Just find her and bring her to me."

"You ask for the one thing I cannot give you."

"Why?"

"I'm bound not to interfere with her life further. If I could do this for you, I would."

"I don't understand what that means. How have you interfered with her in the past? Why are you bound now?"

"You don't need to understand. I can bring you a hundred girls that look just like her, but Brooklyn Evers is off-limits to me. That's all you need to know."

"She's a goddamn fugitive for something she didn't do! We have to help her. I can't just sit here and leave her to the inevitable."

Azrael pulled him over to the bed and pushed him down. "There's a war coming, and thousands of people depend on you to lead them. If you continue to wallow in self-pity and personal pursuits instead of making the preparations I've outlined, then they will die of starvation or disease before the fighting even starts."

"I won't let that happen. You know that." David bowed his head, looking away from her scorching aura.

She moved onto the bed, lithe as a cat. "I do know that. I picked you for that very reason." She spread her wings around them both in a protective cocoon.

The voices of his many subjects were suddenly silenced. The relief was instantaneous. He wasn't alone, however, and as she kissed him, desire rioted against his better judgment, and he knew he'd lost again. David wouldn't allow his people to die, and Azrael knew it. He couldn't say no to her. But he wasn't a puppet, or a broken thing, and he wouldn't give up on Brooklyn either. Not ever.

Nathan Goodrum cleared his throat and looked up at those gathered for the conclave. "I have personally made lifestyle changes to better serve in the role of Protector, but it is not reasonable for me to ask the same of the other Demonriders, and I won't."

A low murmur went around the room.

"There is nothing illegal about our practices. This debate has raged for generations. I've defended my place on this council time and time again because of bias and bigotry. It's time we stop squabbling among ourselves and unify around our shared values." Goodrum cast his eyes around the room entreatingly.

Dravin refrained from interfering as a fierce three-way debate broke out between Goodrum, Mrs. Mays, and Eric Stewarth. Mrs. Mays had begun by establishing her right to attend, a right inherited from her deceased husband and son. Once that had passed, she wasted no time in launching an all-out assault on Nathan Goodrum's appointment as Protector and the proximity of his Demonriders to her farm.

Eric cleared his throat. "I have decided. Nathan Goodrum is the Protector of this district. This is not a democracy. I make the appointments."

"He can't protect anybody. He wallows with the very things he's supposed to keep us safe from. Your father tolerated them because he could control them. He had Solomon's own ring. What have you got? What's stopping the lot of them from slitting your throat just as soon as your guard is down? No sir, he's no Protector of mine. Next time a gang of 'em comes traipsing across my property in the middle of the night chasing folks, they'll get a face full of buckshot." She punctuated the last part with a solid fist on the table, then pointed right at Dravin. "That goes for you too."

Goodrum rose to reply, but Dravin stopped him with a thought. The truth was she had plenty of reason to hate them both, and it was better to let Eric defend his decision than for Goodrum to defend himself. Eric looked at Goodrum expectantly. Nathan shook his head with a smile. "Sorry, sir. I have nothing further to say. As always, the decision is yours and I serve at your pleasure." He gave a deferential nod and sat back down.

Eric nodded. "The matter is closed. I'll hear no more about it. We will move on with new business."

Mrs. Mays harrumphed, but took her seat.

Eric nodded to Tristan Barrett. "News from Scotland, Mr. Barrett?"

"Aye, all is quiet in the homeland. For what it's worth, I throw my lot with Mrs. Mays."

Eric's ears reddened slightly, but he gave no other sign the comment irked him. "Any petitions from the ladies Craft?"

Erina stood slowly. "Please accept our condolences on the loss of your father. He was a good man, and I knew him for many years. Also, I want to offer my support to Protector Goodrum. I supported his predecessor for many years, and he was not a man who feared spirits, and really, that is all a demon is. My family's power is nearly as old as yours and we believe the Wisdom of Solomon passes to his heirs. For this reason, we will follow and support you and provide honest counsel always." She curtsied gracefully and sat.

"Let's hear from the Protectors. At our last meeting, which has been far too long ago, there were concerns about disappearances, several lesser Adepts and one of your own members as well?"

The three Protectors stood, Brianne Moore in the middle with Nathan Goodrum on her right and Michael Benson, a skinny dark-haired man with glasses, to her left. Brianne spoke for the group. "Some were identified as victims in the Brooklyn Evers investigation. Law enforcement has not released specific information to the public, but I have contacts in the FBI who confirmed the identity of several victims and they all matched up with our missing Adepts."

"Any word on your missing Protector?"

"No, sir. He's been missing for more than a year, and covering his territory has been a strain for me. A new Protector needs to be appointed to Mexico as soon as possible. In fact, due to all the activity in that region, I would recommend appointing two and splitting it geographically."

"Protector Goodrum. Last year you reported three deserters from the Demonriders and suspicions of a splinter organization. Can you provide this council with an update?" Eric's eyes shifted down to notes on the lectern. "According to the minutes, their names were Hayleigh Vinson, Marco Goff, and Conner Day."

Dravin was impressed with the businesslike way Eric kept the meeting moving. Gone was the tentative air the boy had displayed for most of his life. He had seized his new position with fervor. Dravin felt hesitation through his connection to Goodrum.

"Yes, sir, Marco Goff was among Brooklyn Evers's victims. I believe the other two may have been as well, but as yet, their bodies have not been identified. They may still be out there somewhere."

"We will come back to Miss Evers in a moment. What of the splinter group?"

"We've heard nothing further about them. The disappearances ceased around the same time. I presume they were wiped out."

"Alright, Brianne, identify potential candidates for me to consider for the Southern Protector position."

"I will, sir." She nodded and took her seat. A moment later, Michael and Nathan did the same.

Eric bowed his head, looking at the podium for a long time. Others in the room shifted uncomfortably as the moments crept by. At last, he looked up. "Brooklyn Evers. She's brought a lot of unwanted attention to our community. If justice had been served, she would have been executed when my father still lived. The traitor, Kurt Levin, vouched for her, and in one of his rare lapses in wisdom, my father commuted her sentence."

Dravin noticed that several people around the room were nodding vigorously in agreement. Mrs. Mays, Brianne, Michael, and Erina, however, were not.

"There is a reason we do not allow Adepts to roam unaffiliated. They put us all at risk. With Kurt Levin deceased, would any of you volunteer to accept her into your organization or family? If she were willing?"

Dravin looked around. The question hung heavy in the air. Several people shifted uncomfortably under his scrutiny. He considered the possibilities. If someone accepted her, they would bring her in alive and give her the opportunity to join. Eric seemed confident no one would want the liability. It was a clever political move, making them all complicit in her execution. Any of them could save her and none of them would. Dravin could offer her asylum himself. It would be simple enough to slip a few drops of Devotion into her food or drink and earn himself another powerful tool. Alternatively, he could have Nathan make the offer. He could cite feeling responsible, as she had been the ward of his predecessor.

Before Dravin could speak, Eric did. "I thought so. In that case, I will offer her asylum." A collective gasp went up around the room. Ignoring it, he continued. "By the Wisdom of Solomon, I decree Brooklyn Evers a fugitive. She is to be captured on sight and brought unharmed before this council for my Judgment and offer." He turned slowly to the Protectors. "Let's make sure we get her before the police do."

7

A New Project

After showering, Riley wiped the fog from the mirror so he could brush his teeth. One benefit of his lengthy incarceration was the opportunity to practice excellent oral hygiene, or maybe it was just something he could control. If he had enough floss, he could have flossed fifty times per day. He was just getting to his molars when he heard a throat being cleared impatiently. This was it. He'd finally gone crazy and started hallucinating. Riley quickly wrapped a towel around his waist and yanked the bathroom door open.

Eric Stewarth sat on the bed. "I am in a hurry, but I'll wait while you put pants on."

"You're really there?" Riley demanded in disbelief. "Why have you been holding me here all this time? Where are the others? Is Kurt alive?"

"I have questions too. After you put your pants on, maybe we can help each other out." Eric smiled.

Riley groaned but grabbed a few items from the closet and went to the bathroom, casting glances over his shoulder to reassure himself Eric hadn't vanished into thin air and left him all alone again.

When he came back, he half expected to find the room empty as always, but his guest still waited. What's more, he waited with cold beer and even offered one to Riley, who gladly accepted. He'd watched Eric grow up, tutored by Kurt, but sitting here now, it was hard to reconcile the man Eric had become with the boy he had been not so long ago.

Riley twisted the top off his beer and took a long pull. "He's dead, isn't he?"

Eric looked at him hard for a moment. "I think so, but we haven't found a body."

He nodded. "He loved you like his own son, you know."

"I know that, but it doesn't change anything. He took away all my options and left me one hell of a mess to clean up. I'm not even sure it can be cleaned up."

"Where are the other Adepts?"

"Nope, it's my turn to ask a question now. Where did Kurt hide *my* ring?"

"He didn't. It was stolen from him before he could return it to your father." Riley locked eyes with Eric. "That's the truth, I swear."

"Stolen by who?"

"Isn't it my turn? Where are the Adepts?"

Eric sighed. "They were all executed for treason months ago."

Riley chugged the rest of the beer and dropped the empty bottle on the floor. "You're a monster." He said it with no particular conviction or malice.

Eric pushed another one into his hand. "That's your question?"

"No, tell me why I'm being held here if you executed all the rest."

"Kurt was my last connection to the ring. You are the only remaining connection to him. I need to know what you know. If what you say is true, who stole the ring from him?"

"I don't know."

Eric slapped him across the face; stars exploded across his vision. "Ah, see now, the game doesn't work when you lie. Try again."

Riley tongued the inside of his cheek, glaring holes through Eric. There was, he supposed, no actual harm in sharing the identity of the thief. For better or worse, Kurt had concluded his dealings with her by now. "He told me the ring was taken by the angel of death, Azrael." Riley readied himself to intercept another blow, but one never came.

Eric slouched back onto the bed thoughtfully. "It makes sense. I just didn't think there were any left untainted. Do you know why this angel stole it?"

"I don't," Riley answered truthfully. "How long do you intend to hold me here?"

"As long as it takes."

"As long as it takes for what?"

Eric ignored him, pulling something small from his breast pocket. "What's this?" he asked, tossing the object onto the bed between them.

Riley picked up the small metal sphere, rolling it between his fingers. "Looks like a marble or a ball bearing." He shrugged and tossed it back.

"Lying again. I thought we were past that."

Riley took another long drink and considered for a moment. "Put something on the table, *Lord* Heir."

"I'm not here to negotiate. You are a prisoner. I could keep you here or have you executed. You will cooperate."

"You could, but it's not polite to *say* it. That's where you fall short of your father, Eric. He was not a man to cut himself and blame the knife."

Eric bristled, but said nothing, gesturing for him to continue.

"Your family has stayed in power for generations not because of that ring or any special abilities, but because of cleverness and wisdom. People followed you for stability, for decisiveness, and because you were good leaders. If you can't learn a little about politics, Goodrum or one of the other snakes will have your throat cut before the year is out, regardless of what you do with me."

"I guess this is the part where you tell me you can 'advise' me?"

"Only if you give me some sign you'd be a leader worth advising."

"The last man you advised is dead. That's not much of a track record." Eric crossed his arms.

"He was stubborn and didn't listen. Every time you open your mouth, you remind me of him."

"Alright, I'll put something on the table just as soon as you admit you know what this marble is and why I can't affect it with my mind."

Riley stared at the orb fondly. With just a whisper of will, it rose off the bed and hovered in the air between them. "That enough of an admission for you? Where did you find it?"

"We found it during an investigation into an unregistered mystic group in the vein of the Demonriders. We found it near dead bodies."

Though the healed hole in his stomach itched with the memory of that night, Riley held his face impassive. With the stone, he could kill Eric, smash the window, and be gone before the guards fumbled through the infernal lock on the door.

Eric clapped his hands, smiling wanly. "That's amazing, truly. When I try to take it from you, my grip slides right off of it."

"You were about to offer me something?" Riley murmured.

"Here is my offer: you relocate to my family estate in Nashville, I'll set you up a lab to work for me on a special engineering project in exchange for some freedom. If you complete the project successfully, you walk away, fully pardoned, a hero, and a very wealthy man."

"And if I refuse?"

"You can get back to flossing your teeth and I'll check in with you again in three months to see if you've changed your mind, assuming the Pull hasn't failed entirely by that time." Eric shrugged. "Killing you does me no good, and you won't be bullied, so appealing to your better nature is all I have left."

"So, what's the project?"

Eric pulled a sheaf of papers from a briefcase by his feet and unfolded a diagram on the bed. "I want you to re-create Solomon's ring."

Brooklyn threw the tape player across the room in disgust. "These interviews are worthless." It had taken her most of two days to locate a store selling the obsolete microcassette recorders. "They didn't even have the right name for the guy she left with. I can't believe her friends were this dumb. I can't believe she was this dumb."

Maybe it's by design. Belial stirred languidly in the back of her mind.

"They chose stupidity?"

Maybe Erin purposefully kept them in the dark about this guy. Gave them a false name.

"She didn't know him either. They met him at the concert."

Maybe.

Brooklyn paced around the room. It was a cheap hotel with rust rings around the bathroom drains and threadbare blankets. The TV didn't work and there was a musty smell. Fortunately, the front desk was happy with cash and no questions. Unfortunately, they were running low on cash again. "You know everything I know about Erin at this point. What's your theory?"

I'm going to come out for this. It will give you a chance to practice tethering, anyway.

She shivered as an icy sensation raced up her spine and then Belial was standing in front of her, stooping to avoid bumping his head on the ceiling. He stretched four large wings covered in lidless eyes that drank in the light as surely as the azure scales around them reflected it. Folding them carefully, he shrank until he could stand comfortably. Brooklyn sensed the Pull, the strange force that kept the physical and spiritual worlds separated, tugging at him through the invisible filaments that connected them.

"It's much easier than the last time I tried," Brooklyn marveled.

"The Pull is growing weaker and weaker. At this rate, it will fail in a few months. Every demon that crosses strains it further."

"Fail? As in demons coming through whenever they want like what happened last year?" She shuddered at the memory of the chitinous insect that had clawed its way free of Kurt's throat and tried to seduce her with promises and visions.

His voice softened. "No, that was like a momentary power outage in an isolated area. I'm talking about a permanent blackout."

She thought on that for a moment. "There's nothing we can do about it, is there?"

"Nothing I know of. At least, not without Solomon's ring."

Brooklyn imagined the monstrosities that haunted Devin's dreams strolling into the real world to torment the boy. The monsters were real and she couldn't protect him. If she didn't find his mother soon, there would be no choice but to give up and risk going back for him herself. "Let's get back to Erin. You had a theory, I believe?"

"I think the answer is a simple one, and you aren't going to like it. I want you to promise to hear it through before you dismiss it."

She rolled her eyes. "Fine. Please proceed."

"Your first memories of Erin are when she is approximately eight years old, so I'm unable to assess what the dynamics of her life were like before you were born or during your infancy. However, there are many little indicators of discontent. Her relationship with your father grows more and more discordant and at the same time, you begin to supplant her as the favorite child."

"I wasn't the favorite child!" Brooklyn raised her hands in disbelief.

Belial held up a claw-tipped hand for her to be silent. Only when she nodded her acquiescence did he continue. "I'm unsure if there were drug problems, but depression is clear, especially after the unplanned pregnancy derailed college and her relationship with Devin's father. She clearly felt trapped, and my observation of your memories leads me to believe she was having trouble bonding with her child. All her family relationships were weakening. Even her relationship with you is romanticized in your memory, even though the actual memories show a different dynamic entirely.

Biting her tongue, Brooklyn gestured impatiently for Belial to get on with his analysis.

"I propose she knew the man from the concert and had already arranged to bump into him there. I'm not sure who he was, but I'm positive she knew him. Did you ever meet Devin's father or see a photo of him?"

Brooklyn racked her brain. "No, I don't think I did. You think that's who kidnapped her?"

He shook his head. "I think she wanted to leave for a long time, and she finally just snapped and did it."

She considered that for a moment. "People don't just walk away from their families, from everyone they know and love. From a child. She wouldn't have."

Belial rustled his wings uncomfortably. "Did you bring the map in?"

Brooklyn dug through her backpack and spread the map out on the bed between them.

He studied it intently for a moment. "Here is your hometown and here is where she was allegedly spotted years ago. The dead lead we're chasing."

"Yeah, I don't get your point."

"Here is Chicago. Didn't you say that's where Devin's father had gone when he left her?"

She studied the map. The three points were as close to a straight line as they could be considering the layout of the interstates. "Her car was found here, though." Brooklyn pointed to a place southwest of home, almost in Georgia.

Belial shrugged. A gesture all four of his wings mimed along with his shoulders. "Maybe the intent was to mislead. The good news is that if I'm right, she's probably alive and just not wanting to be found. The alternative is a lot grimmer."

"Either way, we'll find out soon enough. Let's go get some cash so we will be ready to roll out first thing in the morning." Brooklyn didn't wait for a response. She gave a tug on the threads of energy connecting them and wrenched Belial back inside her mind. How could Erin abandon her mom and dad? Devin? How could she have abandoned *her*? It didn't feel right, but there was a nagging voice in the back of her mind that wouldn't be silenced, and it didn't belong to Belial. Brooklyn knew all about abandoning people, didn't she?

8

SMART BOARD

David finished a bowl of soup and retired to his new office on the other side of the worship center. He'd mostly been living here since the unfortunate night with Nicole. The office had been Father Logan's previously and was filled with fascinating books he couldn't read. Although, he knew if the itch to read them grew too strong, someone would doubtlessly find their way here to read to him. He hated being dependent on other people for such basic things, and yet he knew he should be grateful he had such vast resources and so many other eyes to borrow.

He locked the door against well-intentioned intrusions and settled into the overstuffed leather chair behind the desk. He closed his eyes, an unnecessary but comforting reflex, and reached out through his network of followers.

Information flooded his brain in a wave of indistinguishable sensation. He could simultaneously attend a United Nations meeting, a Chinese business function, and a French theater production if he wished, but he shunted most of the information aside, searching out specific followers. The ones he'd dispatched to locate Brooklyn just after Azrael's departure.

His goddess could have located Brooklyn and brought her to him in the blink of an eye, but she denied him this one thing. The only thing he'd ever really asked of her. The unfairness of it gnawed at him. What prior oaths had she made regarding his girlfriend? And to whom?

He'd used his contacts in government to get all the most recent intel available on her, of which there was precious little. She had broken into a Tennessee sheriff's department and taken the investigator's files right out of his office and promptly vanished.

The world thought she was a killer, but David knew better. She was a victim of an unwilling demonic possession and nothing more. He'd been aggrieved to learn her parents had perished in what authorities deemed a homicide-arson. Brooklyn was the primary suspect in that crime as well.

If he could find her and get her safely to the chapel, he was sure he could keep her safe, help her disappear. He longed to hold her, to hear her voice, to smell her. He'd never look at her again, at least not through his own eyes. God, let her be okay.

He contacted each of his followers in quick succession, reviewing their efforts to locate her, giving new directives; they reaffirmed their unwavering desire to locate her and keep her safe.

David checked in with the FBI. He had teams reviewing random reams of video footage from traffic cameras along major interstates and large cities. He had to find her before some local authority wound up in a shoot-out with her.

Somehow, she was staying well off the grid. David doubted she had a cell phone or a credit card, and couldn't imagine she had a car unless it was stolen. He had another small team gathering information about any stolen cars in Tennessee, working out in concentric circles from the town where she'd abandoned her last one. So far nothing, which was puzzling.

David sighed. It was a waiting game. His first impulse was to allocate all of his resources to searching for her, but Azrael had made a good point. If he didn't prepare for what was coming, his followers across the globe would die.

He turned his attention to those he'd charged with making preparations. Large shelters were being constructed on every continent and stocked with purified water, canned goods, sanitary products, bedding, medications, and a host of other things. The costs were exorbitant, but Azrael assured him currency would soon have little value anyway.

A quick check-in with his accountants reminded him they were in little danger of bankruptcy.

As for Azrael, she'd vanished as quickly and inexplicably as she'd arrived. He opened the desk drawer and felt around inside until he found what he was looking for. A soft raven's feather, the only thing she'd left behind after their night of passion and reconciliation. He held it between thumb and forefinger while he waited. It wasn't long before a girl of maybe fourteen arrived and offered the leather thong and glue he'd wanted. He kept her there so he could see as his deft fingers twined the cord around the quill end and applied the glue.

After a few moments, when the glue had hardened, he slipped the necklace over his head. Touching it gave him reassurance. If things got out of control, he had a way to reach her.

He closed the drawer and reached out through the network. He liked to observe his followers, experience their thoughts and feelings, live as they did for a time. There was a soothing simplicity to their needs and the ways they met them, something pure and childlike in how they worked together in the absence of his influence. Something about it gave him hope that the world could be better, if not for him, then at least for other, more deserving people.

Riley was overwhelmed. After months of almost no mental stimulation, he had a challenge worthy of his skill. The mental dialogue with his internal partner, which had atrophied during his incarceration, suddenly flourished again.

"Do you have everything that you need?" Eric asked, looking around the room at the strange collection of instruments Riley had requested.

Riley glanced around, assessing. It was like his old lab, but much better funded. Instead of folding tables, he had stainless steel workspaces, and in place of his old mini fridge, a climate-controlled cabinet full of alchemical supplies. Good old blackboard and chalk had been replaced with a state-of-the-art smart board. Not everything was super modern, however. There were all manner of supernatural books from antiquity. "Oh yes, I think so. Almost everything has arrived. I think I'm ready to dive in."

"Excellent, I've loaded a copy of the diagram along with descriptions and notes into the smart board. Use the intercom if you need anything." Eric gave him an encouraging pat on the back and left, the electronic lock clicking into place behind him.

Riley pulled the diagram up on the board. The notations were all in an unfamiliar language. That would be the first barrier. He jotted down a few notes and dove into the books. It took him several hours, with the help of the demon in his brain, to decode the first few lines that read:

With this seal take dominion over the winds.

With this seal take dominion over the birds of the air, beasts of the field, and fish of the sea.

With this seal take dominion over the Jinn and all unclean spirits.

With this seal bind and be bound.

What the heck did that even mean? He turned to one book and brushed the dust from the cover. *Solomon: Man, Myth, or Maniac?*

He thumbed through it. There were several colorful illustrations of Solomon, some sitting upon his throne, and some with demons and spirits bowing down before him, his glowing hand raised high. In yet another, he appeared to be levitating massive boulders for the construction of a temple, with white concentric circles projecting from his forehead. There were several in which he rode on a flying carpet, his beard whipping in the wind. Riley skimmed the pages, speed reading the information and retaining it with assistance from his other half. It was mostly fables, legends, and the author's observations about Solomon's actions within them. It barely mentioned the ring at all, which was described only as a gift from the Archangel Michael in response to a prayer.

He turned back to the diagram, using the smart board to zoom in on specific sections. The diagram was interwoven with text and notes in several languages, a few ancient, others far more modern. He'd expected to find a pentagram or the six-pointed star of David, Solomon's father, but that wasn't the case at all.

The central pattern was a swirl, like a spinning sun casting off rays of light at odd angles. At its center were etched four strange, flowing symbols from a language Riley had never seen. The intricacy and detail of each symbol seemed beyond human comprehension. The second and fourth symbols appeared to be the same or at least very similar.

You know, even if we succeed, he will never let us leave this place alive with the knowledge to create another ring, his companion muttered gravely.

It was a chilling thought, but one that had already occurred to him. *We will have to plan for contingencies.* Riley reached out, hit the buzzer beside the door, and notified the person who answered that Eric Stewarth was needed immediately.

A few seconds later, Eric's voice boomed from the tiny box. "What do you need?"

"I have several questions. I'd like you to come down and look at this with me."

The line went dead, but shortly Eric was striding through the double doors. "What have you figured out?"

"I've translated part of the inscription above the diagram and identified most of the languages used for the notations for later translation. What I need now is some firsthand knowledge. Can you tell me what the ring looked like?"

"It was yellow gold, ornate to the point of gaudiness, with a dense black stone that seemed to devour light. When in use, it appears as a bright white light to a demon's eyes."

Riley jotted notes into a spiral pad. "Do you have any idea what kind of stone it was?"

"Something celestial. My father thought it was moldavite, though that's usually green."

"Do you know if the color is important to the function of the ring?" Riley's mind was alive with possibilities.

Eric shrugged. "I'm not sure."

"Describe to me what it felt like to use the ring. Did it drain your energy? Did it require a lot of willpower?"

"Hmmm. It didn't really feel like a lot of effort. It was more like placing the last piece in a puzzle, or suddenly understanding a riddle. Things just click into place. Does that help?"

Riley furrowed his brow. "Maybe. It tells me that the ring is more than just a focus for your own abilities. It draws power from some other source."

Eric's eyes lit up. "Oh yeah. I remember Dad saying something about it using a demon's power against it."

Why didn't you share that up front? Idiot, Riley didn't say. Instead he forced a smile. When Eric smiled back, there was something of the cheerful boy he remembered. "Eric, look at what I've translated so far. Is any of this familiar to you? Is there any other helpful information you might have forgotten to tell me?"

"Not really. I know the part about jinn and unclean spirits refers to demons. The rest doesn't really fit. I know my dad believed King Solomon never intended the ring to be passed on after his death, so maybe there are things about it we never discovered."

"So, this diagram was not a blueprint from the construction of the original ring?"

"I don't think so. I think the heirs that came after pieced it together."

Riley sighed. "I was afraid of that."

Eric leaned against the workbench and crossed his arms. "This needs to move along. What do you need from me to get things moving?"

"I'm putting together a list of materials we will need to even attempt this. Some of it is going to be expensive and some just difficult to find or procure. Once I get the list together, I need every scrap of written or photographic information you have about the ring, about Solomon, about controlling demons. I need to expand my knowledge extensively to even attempt this."

Eric stood up straight. "Okay, I'll make it happen. Anything else?"

Riley's face tugged into a mischievous grin. "Yes actually. I'm going to need some of your spinal fluid."

9

Currency of Reprieve

Azrael watched the sun set over the Pacific. On the beach below, parents were packing up their sun umbrellas and fishing reluctant children out of the foamy waves.

When twilight fell, only a few teenagers remained, flitting between islands of firelight like moths. The night was theirs, seductive, full of mirth and possibility. One couple left the warmth of the fire for the privacy of darkness, their ritual as cyclical as the tides lapping against the sand.

They were, all of them, beautiful creatures. Each bright and fleeting and so virile, defying the clockwork of the godless universe meant to contain them. Beyond the furtive couple, in a world apart, sharks went about their cold business.

In each person, she could sense a dusting of the creator, an energy that sang out to her from their very blood, even at this distance. The Pull was a constant reminder of why she must not succumb again. Though its tug seemed to lessen a bit each day, she could still feel its hooks deep in her essence.

The giddy couple returned to the flock, cheeks flushed. The boy held the girl close and whispered something as they turned toward the firelight, hand in hand.

It was a shame they had to die.

Azrael spun a vial of dark red liquid between her bone-white fingers and wondered why the machinery of the world seemed engineered to crush her and why the currency of reprieve had to be paid in loneliness and blood.

10

Cold Stormy Night

Brooklyn felt her jaw drop open and made a conscious effort to close her mouth. Belial materialized beside her, barely relying on her tether to remain fixed in the physical world. The image on the television bobbed and bounced as if the cameraman was struggling to keep his footing. Around him, dead fish littered the beach, thick enough to make walking difficult. The reporter's face twisted in revulsion, though she fought to keep it placid. Her hand drifted subconsciously to her nose and back down again several times as if she wanted to pinch it closed. The camera panned to show what the reporter described as environmental protection agency scientists, all wearing hazmat suits, examining the bloated fish. The waves were tinged red, and crimson threads were visible in a close-up shot of one of the fish.

Images flashed to a news anchor interviewing a university marine biologist who explained a lengthy theory about ocean floor fault lines releasing ancient parasites. Brooklyn clicked the television through several more news channels in quick succession. On every one it was more of the same.

"It's like the corn beetles, isn't it?"

Belial studied her for a moment before nodding his agreement. "It's my fault. My father would have never let this happen to the seas, but he's gone because of me, and if he ever gets back topside he's going to be pissed."

"Bah. It's not your fault. If you hadn't sent him back to Hell, I'd be dead and so would Devin. Besides, what's the worst thing he could do?"

"Last time he got really angry, a place called Atlantis went missing."

"A problem for another day. Someone is behind this. We need to figure out who." Brooklyn pulled on a red hoodie and grabbed her keys from the bedside table. "And we're broke again, so let's go knock over a few gas stations. We need cash."

The routines were familiar to her now. If the station was empty or nearly so, and the attendant was male, she flirted. It was a subtle distraction. A suggestive posture and a big smile were often all it took for the cash drawer to open unnoticed and the hundreds to slide onto the floor, around the counter, and up into her hands. A few promises for the end of his shift and a fake number scribbled on his palm made for a clean exit. She always felt guilty for leading them on.

When the attendant was a woman, or the station was crowded, or on rare occasions when she couldn't woo a man, she resorted to other distractions. One of her favorites was to plug the fountain drink drain with ice and then telekinetically depress all the dispenser levers at once. A waterfall of soda was usually a sufficient distraction for an entire store full of people.

At other times she had toppled displays, shattered glass, flooded bathrooms. Really, anything that created a distraction could work. Brooklyn tried not to think about the consequences her thefts might carry for those she duped. She hoped nobody had lost a job over it. It was a necessary evil. At least, that's what she told herself. The alternative was getting captured and convicted of mass murder. Still, thieving was shameful.

On a good night, she could pull anywhere from fifteen hundred to three thousand dollars. It seemed like a lot, but it went fast to food, ever-increasing gas prices, and hotel rooms. Tonight, she hoped to break five grand. She needed a few days to focus on the search for Erin. Belial's theory left her at once comforted and uneasy. She had always held the belief that Erin was alive, somewhere, but she'd never entertained the idea that she might be alive and staying hidden of her own accord. It seemed unlikely a kidnapper would keep her alive for years, though there were some accounts of just that sort of thing.

Brooklyn couldn't decide what would be worse, finding her sister alive and shattered by the abuse of some pervert, dead, or alive after willfully abandoning her child and family for some selfish reason. Each was its own flavor of agony.

Belial was with her, watching her thoughts rise like mist and burn away. Normally she would have pushed him to the back, and walled away her reflections, but maybe it wasn't necessary. He had been perfectly compliant, no matter how much she gave him cause not to be. The only time he'd broken her rules had been to help her with the search for Erin, which she couldn't really fault him for.

It began to rain, a misting at first that didn't warrant the wipers, but soon it fell in sheets that battered the car and drowned out the radio. Ahead, she saw the first gas station on her route. She pulled beneath the canopy and parked beside a pump. The sudden silence was startling, and the wipers moved with such speed as to gently rock the small car.

Brooklyn ran in, ducking from the pump canopy to the eaves of the station as quickly as possible. Even so, she was all but dripping and her sneakers squeaked on the tile floor with each step. She shivered; it might be wise to invest in an umbrella. Maybe some men were into the drowned rat look, but it seemed unlikely.

Water ran from her hair in icy trickles down her back. The woman at the counter looked to be in her midfifties, though she'd aged well. She watched Brooklyn approach with lips pursed against a smile. An expression that at once made Brooklyn feel like a necessary nuisance and welcomed.

Brooklyn smiled back and inquired where she might find the umbrellas while simultaneously drawing on Belial's power to form a clot of ice in the soda fountain drain across the way. She squeak-stepped her way back to the indicated area and chose a full-sized black model before dropping it on the counter and pulling out a twenty to pay. As the cash drawer opened, Brooklyn started the soda. The cashier paused, looking at the fountain, first in wide-eyed confusion and then disbelief. Brooklyn slid the large bills from the register without looking away from the fountain. "What in the world is happening?" Brooklyn asked in her most innocent voice as the soda spilled over onto the countertop and cascaded to the floor.

The woman didn't answer, slamming the register closed and dropping Brooklyn's twenty beside the umbrella. She rushed over to the growing mess in dismay, then vanished through another door, presumably to cut the power. Brooklyn tugged the bills from the floor into her waiting hand. She ripped the barcode tag free from the umbrella and left the twenty on the counter with it.

Back in the car, Belial manifested in the passenger seat. "You are getting much better at managing multiple threads," he complimented.

"I still need more practice. I'm not close to Kurt's level."

"It takes time, but you will be beyond his level long before you are his age if you keep progressing."

The rain continued to fall in torrents through the next four jobs. So far, she'd taken thirty-three hundred dollars, and it was four in the morning. The five-grand goal seemed overly optimistic now and her bones ached with weariness.

Belial likewise had grown lethargic, his normally chatty demeanor lapsing into a sullen silence.

The next all-night station was at least twenty minutes further on, probably more with the foul weather. She drove in silence, taking her cue from Belial.

There was a small jolt and one tire began making a steady thumping noise. "What is it?"

"Flat tire," she murmured, easing the car onto the shoulder. The rain was an endless roar, and the wipers swatted it away as dutifully as a cow's tail would flies, and with about as little success. She leaned forward, looking up at the sky through the windshield as if the answer to her problems might be divined there.

It was a lonely stretch of road. Nothing but pastures and trees visible in the sliver of night the headlights cut away. She checked her throwaway phone and couldn't get a call to connect. *Well shit. And who could I call anyway?*

"Do you know how to change a tire?" Without waiting for an answer, Belial ghosted outside to examine the damage. The rain passing through his visage, lit from within, became a cascade of colored sparks. There was something majestic about him, as if she could see past azure scales to some piece of him that wasn't fallen, something that could be trusted, something divine. But he wasn't divine. He was a demon, and she'd do well to remember that.

The thought was cut short by a shouted warning from Belial. "Ambush!"

He settled into the back of her mind just as she opened the car door. The rain soaked her almost at once, running like liquid ice down her back. A lanky man emerged from the embankment above the car, closing on her at a brisk jog. A car with no headlights pulled in behind her Cavalier.

Are they the police?

Not a police car, Belial murmured. *At least, not a marked one.*

Should she dart into the woods across the road and try to vanish into the trees? Her heart sped up and she began drawing together a rudimentary shield.

As the jogging man reached her car, the driver's door of the other vehicle opened and a short stout man stepped out.

Her breath hitched in her throat when the shorter man spoke in the even, measured way of a Demonrider.

"Miss Evers. You need to come with us."

"We're here to help," the lanky one offered as he stepped in front of her car. The headlights struck him and she saw blood on his shirt. A lot of blood.

Without thinking, her fingers drifted up to the scar from the last Demonrider who had offered her unwanted help. "Think I'll pass."

"The Heir has named you a fugitive. Protector Goodrum wants you brought in alive for Judgment. That's what we are here to do."

Protector Goodrum? That can't be right?

Pay attention! They're flanking you, Belial growled.

He was right. While the lanky man held her attention, the short one had sidled several steps to her right side. The pouring rain and deep darkness almost concealed him entirely.

Cold energy slid up her spine, freezing the rivulets of rainwater in its wake. The darkness receded a little bit and her soul stones rolled down her sleeves and came to rest in her palms.

"You're going to have to come with us and get this sorted out," the tall man implored. As he spoke, the shorter man lunged for her legs with unnatural speed.

Even with Belial's power, he almost got her. She leapt aside.

A fallen tree branch flew out of the woods and struck her legs just above the ankles, dumping her onto her back. Pain lanced through her still sore ribs. The tall man was already stepping over his floundering companion, and two wicked-looking throwing stars floated near his shoulders. "We have to bring you in alive," he said, "but alive doesn't mean uninjured."

The stars lanced down at her as fast as arrows. She pulled the shield back together and the wedge of it pushed them wide of her.

Unperturbed, her attacker advanced on her with measured steps while continuing to batter his razored weapons into her shield again and again.

Use the stones.

She didn't want to kill. There wasn't any other option, though. The green and blue blurred toward her attacker.

He was unearthly quick, batting one aside with the flat of his throwing star and ducking the other. The shuriken was wrenched from his grip on impact and careened into the woods.

The soul stones swooped back around and the tall Demonrider turned to face them, pulling up a shield that made hers seem like paper-mache and continuing to hammer at her with his remaining weapon. She was outclassed and he knew it, else he wouldn't have dared turn his back on her. It didn't matter. Both the green and the blue punched through his shield and a spray of blood mixed with the falling rain. The last throwing star clattered onto the asphalt. The man followed. Falling first to his knees, a look of shock etched on his features, and then flat out on the road. A blue spirit, scraggly as a hyena, floated out of his fallen form and vanished.

The remaining Demonrider was back on his feet, looking at his dead partner in dismay. As Brooklyn struggled back to her feet their eyes met. The man reached beneath his jacket and drew a large, black gun.

Could she shield against bullets?

Give me control, Belial begged.

No.

The soul stones came whistling out of the rainy darkness just as the Demonrider leveled the barrel at her. There was a soft double oomph as they impacted. The gun roared, its muzzle flashing like lightning. Brooklyn flinched and closed her eyes, waiting for the pain. After a long moment she realized he'd missed.

The Demonrider was on the ground on his side, struggling to raise the gun in her direction for another shot. She crossed the space between them quickly. Her ears rang as she stomped on his wrist and bent to pry the weapon from his fingers.

The man laughed and coughed.

"What's so funny?"

"Be ashamed if Protector Goodrum knew one little girl got the best of me," he wheezed out.

"Yeah, well. I got the best of him once, too. I don't guess he can hold it against you."

He shuddered, and his eyes took on an alien glint. He shuddered again. The demon rose out of him, smooth-scaled like a snake; it regarded her for a long moment, as rain pounded through its translucence, and vanished.

"I'm sorry," the man murmured, but Brooklyn wasn't sure he saw her anymore. His eyes had taken on a glassy, distant look. "They'll go for the boy now."

"What boy?"

The man didn't answer.

"What boy?" she shouted over the rain, prodding the downed man with her boot.

He's dead. Belial appeared beside her in the rain.

"They know about Devin."

Sounds that way.

The horror of Devin in the hands of these monsters ran through her like a jolt of electricity. She tucked the pistol into her waistband. "Come on. I'll teach you how to change a tire."

11

Camping Story

Thirty minutes and two hundred dollars later, Brooklyn had a brand-new tire and a new toy. She tugged the razor-edged throwing star from her back pocket and dropped it into the cup holder. The technician who changed her tire had found it inside the old one. It was identical to the two her attacker had used.

"We should go back and search the area for clues," Belial suggested. "They anticipated which way we'd come and laid a trap. How could they have known?"

"There's no time. They know about Devin. We need to get back to North Carolina and make sure he's safe."

"Do you think they really know where to find Devin? They didn't say his name."

She gripped the steering wheel until her fingers ached. "We've got to assume they do. I'm going to stop in the first halfway decent-sized town we come across on the way back and hire a private investigator to continue the search for Erin."

"That's a waste of money and time."

"I can't just give up on her."

"Are you sure? Because to me it looks like you are just using this to keep busy and avoid all of your problems. You're a fugitive. You should be laying low somewhere. Hiding out."

"No, I'm . . . ," she began and trailed off. Was she sure? Maybe this whole search was wasted time. Something she was using to keep her mind off her own situation. Would it have been time better spent searching for Riley or Kurt or even following up on Nathan Goodrum's cruel insinuations that David still lived? Goodrum. Everything that man said was poison. She could still hear him screaming at her: *Belial is the only thing special about you. Without him, you are nothing!* Had he been right about that?

Belial grunted. "You're what?"

"What? Oh. I was saying, I'm sure Erin's out there somewhere."

"How do you know?"

"I just know." The midmorning sun on the horizon had her squinting and wishing for sunglasses. "When we were kids, Erin and me, we snuck out one night. Thought it would be fun to go camping. Dad had told us no when we asked, so we waited until the house was quiet. We took our sleeping bags and slipped out a window.

"It was so quiet you could hear your own heartbeat. We knew this place by the river, an old campsite with a ring of stones for a fire. I think we probably picked it for the noise of the water. We couldn't get a fire going, though. We tried for a long time. The wood was all damp and our box of matches used up. We huddled down in our sleeping bags; it was freezing so close to the water. We talked through chattering teeth until we finally fell asleep."

Belial watched her impassively. She didn't look at him. She looked out the window. "You already saw the memory"—she brushed her hair back—"you know what happened next."

"Tell it anyway. Just because I saw doesn't mean I understood."

"I woke up colder still. The world was shrouded in a shadow haze. There was a man there with us. I guess the roar of the water had kept me from hearing his footsteps. He had Erin out of her sleeping bag, his hand over her mouth. I don't know why he was out there in the early morning. He kept asking her what a girl like her was doing in the woods alone. It was like he couldn't see me, and she couldn't either. I saw her eyes, wild and searching. She looked right at me, and her eyes just slid off.

"She was terrified. Years later, she always said she knew I was there. Even after he wrestled her down, she said she couldn't see me, but she could feel me there with her. She said she saw the rock float up from the fire pit like magic. I couldn't have done it that way back then. I was holding it with both hands, arms trembling. She couldn't see me. That black fog muted everything, like looking through a window screen. It took every ounce of strength I had to swing that rock into his face."

Brooklyn gripped the wheel until her knuckles turned white.

"The shadows were flickering by then. He saw me in snatches. Enough to track where I was. I was trying to help Erin when he came with the knife. I can still remember the way it gleamed in the moonlight. The way he looked with blood in his teeth. I tried to turn, but I wasn't fast enough. I'd already done the math, and I was dead."

She shivered at the memory.

"He got me right between the shoulder blades so hard I went down in the dirt on my belly. It wasn't a sharp pain, it was blunt. It knocked the wind out of me. I rolled over and there he was, looking shocked with eyes so big it almost made me laugh. He still had his hand around the knife handle, except it was hilt-deep in his own belly.

"We left the sleeping bags; we left everything and ran all the way home."

Brooklyn shook her head to clear the cobwebs of the memory.

"When we find Erin and ask her, she'll tell you I appeared out of the darkness like a ghost and saved her. She'll tell you she knew I was there all along, that she felt my presence.

"That's how I know she's out there somewhere. I can feel it."

Belial was quiet for a long time while the road whispered under their tires. Finally, he spoke. "I didn't pick up on the details of that memory. I just saw you pick up a rock and brain a creep that was trying to hurt your sister. I missed the supernatural element entirely."

"It doesn't matter. It was just an instinctual response to stress. Before I knew what I could do or how to do it."

"I'm not so sure." Belial stretched his wings, letting them ghost through the sides and roof of the car.

"Stop that, somebody will see." Brooklyn waved the back of her hand irritably.

Belial curled his wings tightly. "You said it was a dark fog and that it seemed to flicker?"

"Erin said I flashed in and out like a strobe light. Why?"

"I need to review your memories again, slower this time."

"We don't have time for that."

Belial harrumphed his disapproval. "There's a bigger game here, and we need to understand who the players are and what's really going on before we wind up dead."

"When the next one of these comes at us," she said, gesturing to the shuriken, "I need to be ready, not taking a nap while you paw through my brain."

"You'll have to sleep soon. I'll do it then."

David felt the first throwing star leave his man's hand. For him, it was a strange sensation to feel the mental tug as the star was nudged in flight, its course corrected by feel and instinct. An ability he'd never been able to master himself. It was a skill he envied. A critical one as the weapon vanished into the torrents of rain and sliced through fingers of fog too quickly for the eye to track. Only the sensation of mental grip remained.

The star stopped abruptly. The sound of the impact was inaudible over the storm. He felt it though, a jolt and then the star becoming lost in the larger matter of the car. It was a miss. Another throwing star was in flight before David even realized the first had failed to find a tire. This one sank home with a satisfying sensation and the throw was rewarded almost instantly with the flash of brake lights.

He refrained from urging the man off the embankment. Brooklyn wouldn't respond well to a random man approaching her broken-down car on foot in the middle of a rainstorm on a deserted stretch of road in the dark. Instead, the man turned back toward the car he'd hidden in a copse of trees, and walked into someone. The stranger was tall and thin. Rain cascaded off the wide-brimmed hat he wore. Before either David or the prophet he controlled could react, there came a flash of silver and a hot agony in his throat.

David scratched at the phantom pain beneath his own shirt collar as his man choked on blood and stumbled into the attacker. The stranger lowered him to the ground with something like gentleness and took the remaining throwing stars from his numb fingers.

"Thanks for your help catching her," the stranger whispered mockingly.

He recognized the robotic cadence of a Demonrider's speech. He watched in horror as the man stepped over his dying prophet and disappeared down the embankment toward Brooklyn's car.

Get up! he commanded.

His man tried and failed. A heartbeat later, their connection fizzled out of existence.

12

CHANGING TACTICS

"What do you mean they are missing?" Father Logan asked incredulously.

"Missing," Goodrum replied with maddening calm. "Gone."

Dravin ran his fingers through his hair. "All of them?"

"None of the searchers have checked in or responded in the last two days." Goodrum shrugged. "Maybe they found her. Maybe she killed them."

"No." Dravin shook his head for emphasis. "No way one person kills eight Adepts, let alone Demonrider Adepts."

"I only know they have not checked in since . . ." Goodrum shuffled through a messy stack of papers. "Since about fifteen miles south of Champaign, Illinois."

Dravin stood and paced the room, feeling Goodrum's eyes follow his back-and-forth march of agitation. He wanted an explanation, but getting an independent opinion out of Goodrum was unlikely. "We could send a smaller team to look for the missing Adepts, but what are we sending them into that the last eight couldn't handle?" he mused aloud. "Where is Eric? Still here?"

"Yes. Said he was going to stay awhile. He's expecting I'll produce the girl in short order, I think." Goodrum ran his fingers over his shaved scalp. An idiosyncratic habit he'd developed since drinking the Devotion. As if he needed to mirror the emptiness inside his head by rubbing his hand across it as a constant reminder.

"We could ask him for resources, men to search. It is his project, after all."

Father Logan began to raise a hand to forestall further idiotic suggestions, but let it hang. He wasn't certain what he planned to do with Brooklyn if—no, when—they captured her, but handing her over to the Stewarth boy for God only knows what purpose was not high on the list of probabilities.

Nathan had wanted to force her to become a Demonrider once. There had never been a grade-three demon broken to a human's will. She could have been the first, and with the ring gone it would have tipped the balance of power to Nathan's people in a big way.

Dravin wasn't interested in making a Demonrider of her though. He saw her more as a lever to move others. After her Judgment, when Kurt had tied his fate to the girl's, Dravin and Nathan had wanted to use her against Kurt, to oust him from his position as Protector. They had formed an uneasy alliance and attempted to do just that. It hadn't worked out well.

Now, with Kurt out of the way, she'd be an excellent tool to force David Sterling down off his pedestal. The Blind Prophet would surely forsake his stolen followers if it meant keeping his lover from becoming Dravin's thrall. If not, she could still be a powerful ally, or perhaps he'd let Nathan turn her into a half-demon abomination after all.

Still, maybe there was a way to let the Heir do the heavy lifting and leave him empty-handed and none the wiser for it. "Ask him for a hundred men, not Adepts, regulars. Break them into ten teams of ten and put one of yours with each group. Make sure when they find her, they know what to do."

Goodrum nodded, not needing specifics as Father Logan's will was impressed upon him with all the clarity of his own thoughts.

CHANGING TACTICS

Riley dropped the phone with a sigh. He'd been trying to reach Eric for the better part of a week with the same pat answer from the house guards every time. Something about his "highness" being unavailable and could they provide any assistance in his research.

Research was progressing nicely, though he'd taken some time off during the Heir's absence to replace his lost ICMs, or soul stones, as Brooklyn would call them. They were an insurance policy of sorts against what the voice in his head had termed "their eventual disposal." The silver orb Eric had brought when he first approached Riley had been taken back by the Heir and was no doubt being reverse engineered at another location even now.

Riley called up the diagrams on the big screen and let his eyes follow the now familiar curves of the script, the angles of the black stone. If he'd had the original item to study, he was sure he'd have cracked its secrets by now.

He checked the shape of the script against the writing in one of the oldest books on demon summoning he'd ever encountered. It had no title, just a worn brown binding that seemed newer than the fragile pages it held. Even here, he found no match. The ring script was something older, maybe something older than humanity. Staring at the swirling symbols for too long left Riley feeling queasy and dizzy. If he unfocused his eyes, the symbols seemed to writhe and squirm.

What is this? Riley asked his partner. *You researched in the library down under. Didn't you ever see anything similar?*

No, but I had a thought.

And that would be?

If you were going to record a method for the creation of soul stones, would you just write it down with complete diagrams for someone to come along and follow, or would you leave something out or add something in? A missing piece, or a key to unlocking things. Think security or encryption from thousands of years ago.

Riley sighed, rubbing his temples. *You think the symbols are smoke and mirrors?*

I think something is. Was the ring made or given by an angel? Does moldavite have some special properties we don't understand? Do these symbols have any meaning or power?

Riley glanced at the workbench where his moldavite samples were arranged on a felt cloth. They were all green and blue. Some so deeply green they verged on black, but none truly were. He didn't think the color mattered. Stones and gems and crystals harnessing supernatural energies was all new-age bullshit.

He closed the diagram, leaving the smart board a gleaming square of empty light. "Everything has an explanation," he mused. "There's no such thing as magic, just the things we don't understand yet. This ring is just technology. Old technology. Alien technology, or celestial technology, or just genius technology we can't seem to grasp."

What's the point? Why are you talking out loud? I'm sure you are recorded in here.

"I don't care. The problem is the solution. We are trying to re-create somebody else's solution instead of tackling the problem head-on. We're like cavemen trying to build a glider from airplane blueprints. What are we trying to do?"

Build Solomon's ring?

Our goal is to build a device to control demons. We should study demons, not these diagrams! Riley cleared his workspace with a sweep of his arm and reached for the books on summoning.

13

Hiring Help

Brooklyn looked up at the sign above the door, wooden, hanging from a cast-iron spindle. Faded and chipped paint declared, "Innovative Investigations Inc," or as she'd dubbed it when she found it in the phone directory, Triple I. The place was just another glass door in a row of identical strip-mall stores.

She tugged open the flap of her new messenger bag and touched the money tucked inside. She smoothed the front of her skirt and fingered her now shoulder-length blonde hair. Brooklyn was, hopefully, unrecognizable. New clothes, new hair, makeup.

A bell tinkled above her when she pushed the door open. The lobby was tiny, with three mismatched chairs that may have been salvaged from a dumpster, and a wobbly coffee table. Not what she expected. She was about to leave when a tall man with a hawkish face and a peacock's plumage of unruly black hair appeared from a side door.

"Hello, miss. Come in, come in. Alvin Whittaker at your service. Can I take your jacket?" He was shaking her hand with one hand and reaching for her jacket with the other before she properly had time to retreat.

"I'm not sure . . ."

"Well, let's talk it through. No charge for consultations, after all. I should put that in my advertisements. Like one of those television attorneys. Would you like some coffee, Miss . . . er?"

"Elroy. Jacqueline Elroy. No coffee, thank you."

"Pleasure, Miss Elroy. Please follow me."

He led her down a narrow hallway to a space barely large enough for the desk and pair of wooden chairs that occupied it.

Feeling wrong-footed by his incessant talk, Brooklyn decided to take the initiative. She seated herself without invitation and launched right into the questions she'd put together, mainly from internet searches. "So, tell me about your experience investigating missing persons."

"Ah . . . well." He hurried around the desk to his chair. "I haven't much of that, really." The admission seemed to deflate him somehow. "Mostly I do freelance jobs for divorce attorneys, surveillance, child custody cases, affairs, that kind of thing."

"What are your success rates like?" she pressed.

"Uh . . . success rates are average, I guess. I'm not sure."

"Do you have any references, former clients, perhaps, that could speak to your skills?"

"I could think of a couple of people, sure."

She began to ask the next of her rehearsed inquiries, but he held up his hands to forestall her.

"Listen, Miss Elroy, I'm a good investigator and that's the truth. If I take your case, I'll do everything I can to find the person you're looking for. I can't promise success, but I do promise I'll work hard and earn my pay." He smiled, half-blushing. "Business isn't exactly booming right now, you might have noticed, so why don't you just tell me who you're looking for and why, and maybe I can help?"

Brooklyn did. Posing as one of Erin's four friends from the concert, she described how the mystery had been eating at her these past few years while the police did nothing. And so, when her great aunt had died and left her a modest amount of money, she'd decided she couldn't rest easy until this was put to bed once and for all.

They went over what she knew of the man from the concert. The fake name he had given, Richard Willow, and the somewhat conflicting reports of the man's appearance gleaned from Erin's friends' police interviews. She proposed he might have been a college student in Chicago and may have gone by the name of Scott instead of Richard. She provided pictures of Erin and lapsed into silence, waiting for Mr. Whittaker to speak.

"That's a very cold case, Miss Elroy. A lot of maybes in it."

Been telling her that for some time, Belial chimed in.

Brooklyn gave him a mental shove before addressing her host. "Will you take the case, Mr. Whittaker?"

He steepled his fingers and leaned back in his chair, sighing loudly. "This young man seems to be the best bet. If we can pin down where he went to university, we can probably get some info there. He's probably on an alumni call list or email group someplace." He leaned forward. "Sure would help if we had a legitimate name, or a picture, something more concrete to go by. You said you saw him? Maybe you could spot him in a yearbook or graduation photograph, something like that?"

She shrugged. "It's doubtful. I saw him once at a concert eight or nine years ago. It was dark, loud. We had been drinking. I don't know."

Mr. Whittaker leaned back in his chair. "I'll help you, but you gotta give me more to go on. See if you can't come up with an old photo, confirm a surname, something."

"I will," she assured him quickly. "I'll keep trying."

"Well then. My usual hourly is fifty dollars, but I'm not exactly overwhelmed with clients right now, so—"

Brooklyn pulled the money from her bag and put it on the desk. "Fifty seems reasonable. There's four thousand dollars for eighty hours, plus some extra for expenses. I'm going to check back with you in a couple of weeks, but I'll leave a phone number. Most likely you'll need to leave me a message. I expect by the time I get back you'll have some photos for me to look at, and I'll have money for your expenses and hopefully something more solid for you to follow up on. Is there any paperwork I need to fill out or anything like that?"

Mr. Whittaker smiled and stuck out his hand. "I shake on my business deals."

After shaking, she dug into her messenger bag and produced a folder. "This is a copy of the original missing person investigation. There's an envelope inside with a couple of microcassettes, recordings of the interviews with Erin's other friends. I want you to listen to them, then I want you to find these ladies and interview them again. There must be something more to go on."

"Miss Elroy, I'm happy to do that, but in my experience, in a case like this, the police are usually pretty thorough."

She shrugged. No sense disagreeing. Playing detective had turned out to be a lot harder than she'd imagined.

"I don't suppose you have current contact information? For these other ladies?"

She shook her head.

"I'm sure they'll be on social media. If not, I have other tools."

"I really appreciate your help, Mr. Whittaker."

Mr. Whittaker eyed her speculatively. "If she can be found with the info we have, I'll find her."

14

Human Hive

Visions writhed in David's skull. Put there, he had little doubt, by Azrael to hasten his preparations. The world was an overripe melon waiting for the worms, and every night he saw it devoured in a new way. The message was clear: the end is coming.

He watched the chaos starting sometimes on television, and sometimes from the viewpoint of one of his flock, but always through someone else's eyes.

Small skirmishes were breaking out across the African continent and the Middle East. Partially a result of curtailed foreign aid programs from wealthier European countries.

Too many interests, David thought. Dogs fighting over scraps. No sense of the greater good. Not like his flock, working cooperatively, quietly preparing for the uncertainty ahead.

David felt secure at the center of his great web. The only piece of the puzzle he couldn't pin down was Brooklyn. After the Demonriders had killed his man and gone after her, he'd feared the worst. He'd paced all night, sick and unable to help her. Then the bodies of three men had been found. One was his man and one of the others was the stranger who had killed him. The third was doubtlessly another Demonrider. Brooklyn, along with her car, had vanished and the trail had gone cold again.

David's prophets weren't the only ones looking, either. There were more Demonriders on her trail. He'd killed some of them in an ambush just this morning, but there were surely others. It didn't matter. They were less than human as far as he was concerned. He'd kill them all if it meant her safety.

In a state as narrow east to west and as long north to south as Illinois, there wasn't much use in knowing somebody was traveling generally north. That was, if her destination even lay in the state. She might be running haphazardly, staying on the move, but he didn't think so. It didn't feel right. The Brooklyn he had known was a systematic thinker, spontaneous, but not reckless, not prone to flights of fancy. She was going someplace specific.

His other person of interest, Father Logan, had turned up in the most interesting of places, at Kurt Levin's manor, now Protector Goodrum's manor. "Protector Goodrum" was an oxymoron if David had ever heard one. And a regular moron too, he thought with grim amusement. It made a certain sense. They'd been together when they ambushed him and Brooklyn in the cornfield, though all information pointed to them being well-known rivals, that hadn't seemed to be the case that night.

With a thought, more funds were wired to the men searching for Brooklyn. His request becoming an irresistible compulsion for his accountants. At the same time, men in the field became aware of the incoming funds and how he wished for them to proceed.

He found he was getting better at this. Better at parsing what he needed from the constant noise of thousands of overactive brains. He was learning the shape of many of them. The flavor of their thoughts. Free will, he'd decided, was not necessary for personality and individuality.

The Prophets were expanding. He had an entire team working on recruitment. This was the way humanity would survive what was coming. Not through competition, but through cooperation. It wasn't so much the human race that would emerge victorious on the other side as it was the human hive.

Dravin Logan was painfully aware of the explosive growth of the Prophets under the leadership of his usurper. Claiming Goodrum, and by extension his Demonriders, had seemed like a quick way to rebuild some influence. He'd expected David Sterling to flounder about directionless—like a boat—dead in the water and easily recaptured. He just didn't understand it. There was nothing exceptional about the boy. He should have quickly undone himself with the mindless pursuit of his own desires. Instead, he'd moved with unerring precision in claiming the entire worldwide following and then expanding it. He had to be stopped. The only question was how.

An open assault was out of the question, too noisy and unlikely to succeed. This would have to be done quietly. That meant it had to be done internally.

The first frost of the autumn lay like silver gossamer as Dravin picked his way into the forest behind the manor house. Sunrise was a pink promise on the bellies of the eastern clouds. The little light offered faded away quickly as he ducked beneath pine boughs. He snapped on an LED flashlight with a red filter. The morning chill quickly gave way before his exertions as he climbed and in less than fifteen minutes, he was sweating.

The gloam surrendered at last to a clearing with a circle of large stones. A place visited often in the past by the former Protector Levin and his ill-fated Adepts. Dravin had never understood why Kurt dragged his coterie up this god-forsaken mountain for training that could have been accomplished more effectively, and more comfortably, in one of the many training rooms or the gym housed within the manor.

He sat on the boulder catching his breath and watching the sun summit the horizon.

When his heart no longer beat in his throat, Dravin stood and shouldered his small satchel. He set off around the top and down a ridge on the far side. The sunlight grew wispy and weak as he descended into the mountain's shadow along a crooked trail he'd trimmed into the heart of a laurel thicket. Even so, branches snagged his clothing or pack at almost every turn.

When he came to the place he'd sought, he was breathless once more. Breathless and irritated. He didn't have time for this with David Sterling growing the Prophets out of control and his own influence reduced to Goodrum's rabble.

He stood in a tiny clearing, barely large enough for two or three people. At the center, a gnarled laurel jutted from the steepness of the mountain at a ninety-degree angle, unlike the surrounding foliage reaching for the sky.

Dravin knelt at the base of the strange shrub and released a slide lock, tugging until the bush and the surrounding ground swung up with ease on oiled hinges. Below the trapdoor, concrete stairs descended into damp darkness.

The stairs wound down through rough-hewn passages and vast caverns, snaking through a world of dancing shadows. Dravin fancied he could feel the weight of the mountain poised above him, like a breath drawn and held before the guillotine drops.

Further in, the path became less irregular. This section was newer. The footing even and the passages wider. The irregularity of the natural cavern melded with man-made renovations until at last he stepped from damp stone onto corrugated metal stairs. He estimated he was somewhere beneath the rear yard, between the manor and the mountain.

He believed there had once been an entrance from the basement of the Protector's manor, but an unfortunate explosion had filled the likely section of basement with marble and rubble. Unfortunately, excavating it had not been a priority for young Stewarth, and both Dravin and Goodrum lacked the funds for such an extensive cleanup.

Dravin turned into a small side passage and followed it to the end. He emerged into a round room with four doors spaced equally along the perimeter.

He slowed now, letting his weight settle quietly with each step forward. Dravin steeled himself against the smell as he drew nearer to one door. The smell of death? Maybe just shit.

He felt along the wall beside the door until his fingers found the switch. With a click and a buzz, warm light filled the cell beyond and illuminated the small viewing glass set into the steel door. Inside, curled in the corner with emaciated arms raised against the sudden brightness, was what remained of Kurt Levin.

15

VISITING THE PRISONER

Kurt had been with Mary and Tyler at a hockey game at Bridgestone Arena. The concessions here were awesome. Tyler was tearing into a Nashville hot chicken sandwich. Kurt's stomach growled as he eyed his own plate of chicken and waffles. He reached for the food and his fingers passed through it, trailing an afterimage of colors before snapping back to normal.

Kurt looked around. The place was packed, but nobody seemed to notice his predicament. He tried again, slowly. It happened just the same. A delicious meal he couldn't eat. His stomach growled more insistently. Mary smiled at him in that tolerant way women smile at mischievous children. "Better eat." Her voice was soothing and encouraging.

"I can't." The words buzzed in his throat like they might strangle him. He coughed. There was something in his throat, dry and brittle, each convulsion of his esophagus an agony of sharp edges and broken glass.

His stomach growled loud enough to draw the attention of those seated around him. First a few and then more and more faces turned toward him, eyes going wide with horror. Except Tyler. He kept eating and watching the game. Mary's tolerant smile melted into a lopsided grimace of disgust.

He dropped the plate, food forgotten. "Help me," he tried to say, but the only sound he made was an insectile chittering.

"Dad!" Tyler whined, gesturing to the ice. The players were staring at him, masks raised, puck forgotten. The stadium lamps swiveled from all directions, crucifying him on beams of light. He raised his arms against the glare and coughed again. A large roach spilled from his lips and onto his forgotten plate, black carapace tinged pink by blood.

The smell of it overpowered him, twisting his stomach like a knife. Kurt looked for Mary, reached for her blindly with one arm while pressing the other over his aching eyes. He yelled her name, but nothing escaped his lips but more chittering. Kurt heard the footsteps of the people nearest him as they shoved their way to freedom, gagging and retching. He would die here, he realized, as fresh blades tore at the tatters of his esophagus. Not another one . . .

Someone tugged at his arm, and the light clawed gleefully at his watering eyes.

He came awake gasping like a man nearly drowned. It came back slowly. The gnawing ache in his stomach his constant companion. Followed by the stink of his waste and the ruin he had become. The light, though, was a sweet pain, one he'd thought to never feel again. How long had he been dreaming?

He heard the door scraping across the floor. "Who's there?" he rasped. His throat felt like he'd chewed up a box of Christmas ornaments and swallowed them. The voice that answered was the one he'd expected, Dravin.

"You don't look well."

Kurt's eyes were mostly working now. He saw Dravin standing in the doorway, a large bag hanging from a strap across his shoulder and chest. "What's in the bag?"

"You already know." He stepped back out of the doorway. "Come to a fresh cell so we can talk."

Kurt struggled to his knees, placing one foot flat and using the knee and both hands to lever himself upright. His legs trembled violently and threatened to dump him back in the muck. Dravin gave him a wide berth as he stumbled through the doorway and across the chamber to the next cell.

Following him inside, Father Logan rummaged in the sack and produced a bottle of water and tossed it to Kurt. Kurt held it up to the light, inspecting the seal on the lid. Satisfied, he popped the cap and drank deeply. The water stung his dry throat in the most delicious way.

"I hardly need to poison you. If I wanted you dead, I could just leave and not come back."

Kurt ignored this. "You bring food?"

Dravin patted his pack. "All yours, after we talk."

Kurt's stomach growled in protest. He looked down at his arms, the way the skin hung loose. He was dying, starving to death. "Afraid if you feed me, I might muster enough strength to kill you?"

"Yes," he answered without guile.

Kurt grunted. "What do you want?"

"I need to find Brooklyn Evers before Eric or Nathan get her."

Kurt laughed. He saw the look of indignation on Dravin's face and laughed louder. The echoes of it reverberating through the cavern beyond the door. "Why would I help *you*?"

"Because Goodrum has Eric Stewarth's ear. The boy lives in the Protector's manor with all those Demonriders. You remember the kind-hearted boy you stewarded and trained? He's gone." Dravin hesitated, eyes haunted by some painful memory.

"Out with it," Kurt prodded, dread supplanting the hunger in his belly.

"The way he slaughtered your people. It haunts me." He wrung his hands in distress. "The young lady with the bad teeth . . . wounded in the fighting. What was her name?"

"Tessa."

"Yes, the poor girl couldn't walk because of her leg injuries. They dragged her from the infirmary, out on the front lawn, and staked her facedown. He made the others watch. I . . . it's too gruesome."

Useless. Pompous. Sniveling. Kurt regarded him coldly. "Finish the story, *Father.*"

"The Demonriders carved her up, separated her ribs from her spine, and pried them out on either side like bloody wings. At first she screamed, but then she couldn't anymore."

"And you *watched?*" Kurt spit. "Coward." The rage boiled inside him, impotent.

"I watched them all die. One by one. So did the Protectors. The Heir made it clear dissenters would get their turn. He may not have the ring, but Eric intends to maintain control. Call me a coward if that makes you feel good. I'm a survivor. I mean to keep my ribs inside." Dravin shrugged. "You created this situation. I'm just adapting to it. Young Stewarth is after Brooklyn; he's put a price on her head. He'll have her, too, if I don't find her first. At this point, I'm her only hope."

Kurt trembled. Was it rage, horror, or physical weakness that shook him? He folded his hands in his lap to keep them still. He didn't know where Brooklyn might be, but was encouraged to know she had escaped after the assault on his manor. The details of that day were still hazy. Explosions could do that to a person, he supposed. He opened his mouth to tell Father Logan he couldn't guess where she might have gone, but then he closed it again.

Something Alexander Stewarth said once rattled through his groggy brain. *It's Dravin Logan you should worry about. Goodrum despises you openly, but Logan is twice as clever and hates you for reasons you don't even know.*

Kurt felt the tickle of an orb inching down his shirt sleeve, responding to his unconscious desire to put a hole in Dravin Logan once and for all. He didn't, though. Instead, he spoke, his tongue thick with some emotion he couldn't name. "Alexander told me once that you were one of the good ones. I didn't believe it at the time, but now I do. I'll help you find Brooklyn if you promise you intend to keep her safe."

Father Logan smiled magnanimously. "Of course, you have my word on it."

"And—"

"And?" Logan furrowed his brow.

"And, if you bring me one thing from my office. It's nothing really, just a little bauble that belonged to my Mary. Bring it to me, to comfort me as I lay here dying, and I'll tell you anything you want to know."

16

Rest Stop

The door to the laboratory slammed open. Startled, Riley dropped the moldavite he'd been examining and turned, lifting the magnifying loupes from his eyes. Eric stalked toward him, face red, fists balled menacingly at his side. "What do you think you are doing?" he demanded, jabbing a finger into Riley's sternum.

"Research," Riley stammered in confusion, "for the project you asked me to complete."

"I asked you to summon demons? In my house!"

"Oh, that . . ."

"Yeah, that."

"I hit a dead end with the materials you provided. I decided to proceed in a different way by studying the problem instead of attempting to study an incomplete record of someone else's solution. And I'm making progress."

Eric glowered.

"It's perfectly safe," Riley continued, filling the uncomfortable silence. "I had no idea the diversity of demons. Consider this one, for example." He hurried out from behind the workstation and approached what looked like a medium-sized lizard-dog with bat wings. "Mostly nonsentient, affinity for fire, but watch this." He studied a row of colored boxes on a nearby shelf, selecting a red one about the size of a cigar box.

"I'm watching," Eric said, some of the ire draining from his voice.

"Right, so let me just power this up and . . ." The dog-lizard stopped pacing in its cage and turned to regard them with amber eyes. "Up on your back legs." The creature complied. "Roll over." It did. "Play dead." It fell to its back, one rear leg twitching theatrically.

Eric's anger had evaporated. "How does it work?"

"It's like a subatomic entanglement. There's a tiny bit of a demon in each controller, and a tiny bit of me. Those pieces are still connected to their source on a quantum level. When I power this thing up, the two bits inside become entwined with one another, creating a connection between me and Rivera."

"You named the demons?" Eric smiled in disbelief.

Riley shrugged. "There's not a lot of company here."

"Each demon has a separate controller?"

"That's the primary problem right now. I'm not sure how to create a more universal effect. It's not feasible to manually summon every demon and create a controller for it."

"Could you make one controller for four or five demons?" Eric ran his fingers through his hair.

"Probably, it would be complicated. It wouldn't be able to run on batteries and would require a lot of willpower to operate. Why do you ask?"

"Because it buys time. If I can give the impression I've reclaimed the ring, proof even, then I won't have to worry about usurpers. At least for a while."

"I haven't even tried this on a significant demon, nothing sentient for sure. I'm not positive—"

"Get to work on it right now. Make it your top priority. You'll have whatever resources you need." Eric grabbed Riley and pulled him into a hug. "You're a lifesaver. Literally. I'll bring you information on the demons I want to control."

Riley opened his mouth to respond, but Eric was already out the door. The whole bipolar exchange had spanned less than three minutes.

He's unstable.

Says the voice in my head?

When we can replace the ring, he will kill us to safeguard the knowledge.

A pang of fear touched Riley, but he pushed it aside. *When we can replace the ring, he won't be able to. For now, we play the part of the timid scientist. Trust me, I have a plan.*

As the sunset pointed long shadows at the dark mountains in the distance, the whisper of tires on pavement tempted Brooklyn to close her eyes. She hadn't slept the last two nights running, but it was just a few more hours until she could make certain Devin was okay. Afterward, there would be time to sleep and figure out how to make sure he stayed that way.

Belial supplied a thin trickle of cold energy that helped her push through the fatigue, but she knew from experience, even that had its limits.

You need to rest. Just an hour.

"I can't afford the time."

You can't afford to arrive too exhausted to fight either. You think that Demonrider turned helpful on his deathbed? Belial shot back.

"No. I mean maybe. He seemed remorseful."

Belial laughed. *Or he was baiting you into a trap.*

"Dying with dedication?"

Well he was dying either way. If it had been you on the ground bleeding out, would you have changed your loyalties and whispered something useful to the Demonriders with your last breath?

He had a point. Maybe it was a trap. But, to lay a trap, they would have to know about her nephew and know where he was. If they had that information, he wasn't safe and that was reason enough to go back whatever the risk.

The sky darkened as night fell. The headlights of oncoming cars pained her tired eyes. Twice she caught herself nodding off and drifting onto the shoulder rumble strips. When a gas station appeared ahead, she turned in.

"Five minutes," she murmured. "Snack, bathroom break, and an energy drink. After that, back on the road."

It was a small station. Four gas pumps, one diesel pump, and a self-serve air compressor. She parked on the side and stumbled out of the car to stretch. Her back protested as she straightened her spine.

Inside the station smelled of pizza and Brooklyn's stomach gurgled. When had she last eaten? A quick search for the restroom turned up a sign that proclaimed: Restrooms around back. *Typical.*

She gathered an armful of energy drinks in brightly colored aluminum cans from the cooler. At the register she added a plastic bottle that promised energy for hours and a slice of pizza.

It was almost full dark as she deposited her haul in the car and went in search of the restroom. It was cleaner and less sketchy than expected.

She stooped over the sink to splash some cold water on her face, and froze. The woman in the mirror was deathly pale with dark circles under her eyes. The bleached hair added to the ghostly undead look. Would Devin even recognize her? Or would he think some new monster had come to claim him?

The bathroom door opened, and a tall woman with dark hair stepped inside. She was pushing thirty and looked as wrung-out and tired as Brooklyn felt. Judging by the scrubs, she was probably a nurse.

The newcomer joined her at the sinks and set a purse on the countertop. "Long day?"

Brooklyn nodded. "A few in a row."

The woman smiled. "I know that feeling."

Splashing more water on her face, Brooklyn considered if Belial might be right about the need for some rest. Maybe it would be smarter to find a secluded place to park and crash for an hour than to arrive delirious with exhaustion.

"Name's Cindy," the woman said, flashing a tired smile.

"Jacqueline," Brooklyn lied.

"Cute name," the other woman offered, touching up her makeup in the mirror, and never looking Brooklyn's way. "From around here?"

"No. I'm actually from Kentucky originally."

Cindy spread out a paper towel on the countertop and pulled a small leather pouch from her purse. With practiced ease she opened it and pulled out a vial, a hypodermic needle, and an alcohol swab. When the other woman glanced at her, Brooklyn quickly looked away. What was she doing?

"It's not heroin," Cindy said with a laugh. "I'm diabetic."

A blush heated Brooklyn's cheeks. "I didn't think that. I mean I didn't . . ."

"It's fine." She swiped the alcohol wipe across the vial and drew up the clear liquid and flicked it twice. "Makes some people uncomfortable. I get it."

"Doesn't bother me, but I do need to get going. Have a good one."

"You too, Jacqueline."

Brooklyn pulled the bathroom door but it didn't budge. She grabbed it with both hands and rattled it.

"What's wrong?" Cindy asked. "Is it locked?"

"Seems to be," Brooklyn muttered as she grabbed the pull handle with both hands again. This was just the kind of luck she'd been having lately. Wasn't it about time for things to go right for once? Before she could yank the door again, a sharp pain lanced through her shoulder. *Shit.* She looked down, already dreading what she knew she'd find.

There was the needle, stabbed right through the sleeve of her shirt and hanging loose from her arm. She took it gingerly between thumb and forefinger and winced as she plucked it out. It clattered on the tile floor. She looked up and took a step toward Cindy.

"Whoa now," the other woman yelped, taking a step back and raising both hands in surrender.

"Why did you do that? What was in it?" Brooklyn shouted.

"Just a sedative."

"Why?" she screamed, slamming her hand against the stuck door for emphasis.

Cindy tugged nervously at the pendant she wore and winced in pain, and then a thin tendril of smoke rose from between her thumb and the necklace. Her face stilled, the tiredness faded, and her eyes glinted with new perception. "I heard you were halfway clever. It's obvious, isn't it?" she asked in the cool and clipped cadence of a Demonrider.

Brooklyn launched everything in the bathroom that wasn't nailed down at Cindy, including the purse on the counter and the hypodermic on the floor.

The other woman didn't shield, instead, faster than thought, she plucked the items free of Brooklyn's mental grasp and let them fall to the floor between them.

Shit.

She's a lot better than you, Belial agreed.

That's super helpful. Any other great tips?

Kill her with your soul stones?

Brooklyn yanked on the door again. It didn't budge.

"Let's talk about this," Cindy said in a low voice you'd use on a child or a skittish dog. "The options are all gone. Even if you managed to kill me, that door isn't opening for at least fifteen more minutes, by which time you'll be falling down drunk or completely unconscious. But, let's suppose you kill me and get the door open. Four of my friends are on the other side of it waiting. You'll be captured. But, go a step further. Say you kill me, get the door open, and fight your way free. You're still on a timer." Cindy tapped her shoulder for emphasis. "You'll collapse out there, someone will call 911, and you'll wake up in a hospital, handcuffed to the bed with a couple of US Marshals for company."

"Why can't you people just leave me the fuck alone?"

"Protector Goodrum—"

"Goodrum is scum."

"—has charged us with bringing you in alive to face Judgment before the Heir, Eric Stewarth."

Brooklyn launched the items on the floor at Cindy again. Just like before, they were wrested from her control leaving a phantom ache between her eyes.

Kill her. Use the stones.

"And then what?" Brooklyn said out loud.

Cindy's eyes narrowed. "You'll face Judgment and whatever happens, happens. You can't roam unaffiliated, killing, breaking into police stations, robbing convenience stores, and drawing attention to the community. It's against our law. We're not the bad guys here. You are."

Laughter bubbled like acid in her throat. "A lecture on law and ethics from a Demonrider?"

Cindy smirked. "Says a wanted serial killer? It's really better this way. Now that we have you there's no reason to involve the boy."

"If you touch him, I'll kill every last one of you," she snarled.

"Oh! Tough threats. I'm not sure you can back them up though."

Brooklyn rattled the door again to no avail. She leaned against it heavily, and reached for her soul stones. They responded sluggishly. Killing her captor with them would still be doable, but there was no next step, no viable escape. The sedative was working now; she could feel it. Better to keep her tricks hidden and hope she got a chance to use them later than to risk losing her only weapons. She hid them away in her clothing.

A jolt made her eyelids flutter open. When had she closed them? How had she gotten onto the floor? She tried to stand up and fell again. The bathroom door opened and two men wheeled a medical gurney inside. After that, everything was a blur.

17

Eli Remembers

David watched the massacres on television. He had prophets watching different stations so he could absorb the information concurrently. His network of followers extended through much of Europe, Africa, and Latin America, but grew thin to nonexistent in the Middle East, Asia, and Russia. It was as Azrael predicted: food shortages and soaring food prices were gasoline on a fire, especially in countries where there were already glowing embers of unrest. Several uprisings in Russia were being resolved with automatic gunfire. North Korea's ongoing invasion of South Korea, shaky snippets of armed soldiers herding civilians. Governments were overthrown in Egypt, Venezuela, and Thailand, with ongoing coups d'état in Taiwan and Turkey.

On other programs, there were debates raging about the United States' and other United Nations members' responsibility for the current conflicts. One station's political commentator was advising strategic military involvement to stabilize the unrest in key areas. His guest argued back that relief funds would be a better approach to achieving stability.

On and on the debates raged as the world seemed to tilt off the tracks like a mine cart in a tight turn. What was it Azrael had said at her last visit? "This is just the beginning of the end. Wait and see." How much longer before they tipped off the rails and pitched into the abyss?

The conversation about the Red Contagion had all but been abandoned in the wake of the burgeoning global conflict. The contagion had first appeared on a popular beach in Southern California and was believed to be a reemerging prehistoric fungal spore that affected both fish and humans. Azrael had foreseen the catastrophe and thanks to her David had made certain his prophets were out of harm's way before the outbreak.

The death toll was still mounting as the CDC and WHO tried to quarantine anyone who may have had contact with infected persons. They also advised against eating seafood, swimming in the ocean, and traveling. Unfortunately, their public service messages were competing with other global tragedies for screen time.

He turned his attention elsewhere. The search for Brooklyn had gone colder than cold. Three more small groups of Demonriders spotted near the last confirmed sighting location. Whether they were searching for Brooklyn or their missing comrades, he didn't know.

David stood, using the eyes of those around him to make his way quietly from the chapel as the sermon droned on. He felt, rather than saw, the hard stare from behind, reached out, and found Eli drowning in rage and grief. His mind filled with a single image, Nicole dead on David's bedroom floor, and David covered in blood, cradling his cut arm, small and pale in the lamplight. David turned on Eli, directing his focus at the man, pushing the image from both of their thoughts. He encouraged Eli to forget this obsession, coaxed him until, reluctantly, he turned his terrible gaze from David's blind eyes and back to the sermon about Azrael and her righteous prophet.

Outside the chapel, David leaned his head against the cool stone wall. Eli remembered things he'd been made to forget. That was dangerous. David reached beneath his shirt and stroked the feather Azrael had left him, but today it brought him little comfort. He hadn't thought something like this was possible. What else might Eli be remembering? And how quickly could that spread across a web of interconnected minds? David was at the center of the web, and he wanted to stay there. What that meant for Eli, he hadn't quite decided yet.

Kurt Levin fought against the darkness. In a way, he'd been doing that all of his life. But now it was a more literal fight. He couldn't guess how many weeks or months he'd spent in this pitiless void.

The madness had come on slowly as the hunger and thirst mounted and his resolve weakened. The symbol hung before him whenever he closed his eyes, familiar arcs and hollows, soft promises of respite bespoke by the pregnant swell and swooping curves, nothing here of lines or angles. *Infesta.* The word had rolled free of his lips in a dry rasping whisper, some weeks ago in the dark. That's when the dreams had started.

Kurt stood in the dark, pacing blindly. He couldn't afford to fall asleep before Father Logan's next visit. He needed to be ready. The satchel hung on the door, the meager food Dravin had left, rationed and organized inside near the canteen. His captor liked to give him less than half of what he needed to survive. The floor was clean for now, but it wouldn't stay that way. Don't eat where you shit, his grandpa used to say. "Wish I had that choice."

The dreams called to him in Mary's voice, her touch and memories made real. They started soft and seductive, so full of sweet promise it made him weep, but they always turned to nightmares. Nightmares he couldn't escape. It was as if that last demon he'd summoned, the one that had gotten the best of him, was saying, "You could have had this, but since you threw me out, fuck you."

He paced across to the satchel Dravin had left after their last conversation and took it down from the doorjamb. He checked the food inside, all prepackaged as best he could tell in the dark, so that Logan had no chance of poisoning him. His stomach growled with menace. Kurt was so hungry, but if he ate the food now, it would be gone later, and he would need it more later than he needed it now. Kurt hung the bag back up.

He was starving to death, could feel the frailty bone deep. How much longer would it be before his hair fell out, maybe his teeth? *Scurvy dog*, he thought.

The orb rolled up his spine, creeping along his skin like a fat beetle. This was his ace in the hole. This was the way he'd deal with Father Logan, but he had to be careful. It wouldn't do to kill the man with the door locked.

Then what? Where would he go? He didn't know the answer, but he knew one thing now. He knew who would die after Logan. It would be the new Protector and all his little Demonriders with him.

Footsteps!

Kurt crowded close to the door, ears straining for the sound. Nothing for a long moment and then there it was again. It was too soon for Dravin to be back. There were still four packages of food in the satchel. Which meant probably seven or eight more days. Dravin liked to give him plenty of time to starve and weaken before each visit, coward that he was.

"Help me!" he tried to shout, but only a hoarse whisper came out. He fumbled for the stainless steel canteen and turned it up, choking in his haste. Kurt called out again, getting his voice to a respectable volume this time. He listened, stifling the cough in his throat.

The footsteps came closer, not in a hurry about it either. "Who's there?" he called out.

A light grew on the other side of the peephole and then a face seemed to melt through the surface of the door, casting a pale light. It was Tyler. "Hey, Dad, let's catch a game?" He motioned for Kurt to follow.

"I can't, son . . . the door."

Tyler looked puzzled. "There's no door. Come on. Quit playing."

Kurt put his hand against the door to demonstrate, but his hand passed right through.

With a tremendous effort, he opened his eyes. He'd fallen asleep standing up. He slapped himself across the face hard. Then again, harder. "Stay awake. Got to be alert when the bastard returns."

The thought of Tessa tied down and broken apart like Logan had described haunted him. He thought of all the cowards and traitors watching and not acting. First Logan, then Goodrum and every Demonrider. Then Eric Stewarth, heir without a ring. "I should'a took that ring from your daddy a long time ago and put an end to all this foolishness." *I was weak, but I won't be next time*, he thought. *I won't be next time.* The anger warmed his belly.

The Pull's insistent tugging had never had much of a grip on Azrael. For most of her pious life, she hadn't broken the rules. As far as she knew, she might very well have been the last to take sustenance from the blood of humanity.

Of course, she'd regretted it in the days and weeks following her act of weakness as the fingers of the Pull scrambled to gain purchase on her, a constant reminder of her failure. Over the past months, it had gone from insistent to barely noticeable, and now to nonexistent. It was ironic. She, the good one, and the most damned, had cheated the fate of all her brothers and sisters. The Pull faltering just as she fell from grace seemed a divine serendipity, a cosmic nod for her to continue.

And continue she had, nudging dominos as old as the world itself, watching them topple. She was the god of death, and eventually all things must die, even worlds.

She waited for the man before her to die. His breathing became irregular, one side of his chest seeming to inflate more than the other. His eyes were open, but he was beyond seeing. The hospice morphine was to blame for that. This wasn't how men died a thousand years ago, even a hundred, ushered out of the world on chemical comfort, oh no. Dying was an honest business in those days. It was *supposed* to hurt.

She wished she could see the light leave his eyes, but she couldn't. He'd closed them. She saw the soul leave, though, in a flicker of brilliance every bit as bright as the mother she remembered. Her grotesque servant cut the trailing tendril free and in a flash the soul was gone, onto someplace else. She tried to reach after it with her hands, and with her mind, but as always, this way was shut to her.

Azrael could cage it, prevent it from leaving, force it back into the dying corpse even, though that usually didn't accomplish much. But she could not follow. She wondered, not for the first time, what might happen if she ate one, free of its human blood. Would the Pull wrap clawed fingers around her throat and drag her to Hell, or would she be nourished and made whole like in the old stories of the All-Mother?

Azrael sighed. It wasn't worth the risk, not now. She needed to focus on the plan, on nudging the dominos at just the right moment.

18

Invitations Sent

Belial hung on a tether, small as a ladybug crouched in Brooklyn's hair as she lay unconscious on a gurney.

He could hear tires humming on asphalt as the ambulance jostled back and forth. The only windows were in the double doors at the compartment's rear. It was dark outside, and there wasn't much else to see.

His host lay sprawled on a stretcher with straps across her shins and waist, wrist cuffs, and some sort of shoulder harness. A bag of clear fluid hung on a pole dripping a steady supply into Brooklyn's arm.

The two men who rode in silence near the front of the compartment could have been paramedics but for their stiff postures, the looks of almost constipated concentration they bore, and the flat, robotic way they spoke on the few occasions they found cause to exchange words.

Demonriders.

Belial found their practice of capturing and subjugating lesser demons to bolster their own power repulsive, but it wasn't strictly prohibited in the original covenant between King Solomon and Prosidris that had created the first Wardens and Protectors.

Belial couldn't beat them alone, and while Brooklyn slept he was vulnerable. Based on the setup around him, they obviously wanted to keep her unconscious until they got to wherever it was they were heading. Probably back to Nathan Goodrum. The thought stoked a murderous rage in his heart. That bastard had tried his damndest to kill Brooklyn twice. The first time had left her scarred, but the second time she'd gotten the better of him.

He needed to wake her up, and had been shouting inside her skull for an hour with no response. He eyed the two men. They weren't looking his way, so Belial scuttled down Brooklyn's head, using her hair like a tangle of ropes to drop near her right elbow. He wrapped his clawed hands around the needle where it was taped to her skin and channeled frost until slowly the liquid inside turned to ice, then punctured the tubing with his claws, allowing the medicine to leak into the blankets. It was the best he could do. Belial let the tether draw him back inside to wait.

Humming to himself, Dravin packed his satchel with a few extra snacks, prepackaged stuff to put Kurt at ease. He'd been neglectful of his pet, but he didn't want Kurt dead. Not yet. Not with Brooklyn in custody and on her way here. Tomorrow was going to be a big day for him. Finally, the leverage he needed to reclaim what had been stolen from him and so much more.

He made sure the canteen was full of water. On a whim, he grabbed a bottle of whiskey from Kurt's private stash. This *was* a special occasion, after all. Lastly, he pried the third stone on the left side of the fireplace and pulled out the trinket Kurt had asked for. He looked it over critically until satisfied it was as harmless as Kurt claimed, then tucked that too into his bag.

Dravin paused at the door, remembering how warm Goodrum's secretary, Lauren, had felt when he had climbed out of her bed this morning. It would have been good to spend this frosty evening staying cozy, not traipsing around in the mountains. He needed to do this, though. And he needed to get back quickly to complete arrangements for Brooklyn's arrival. He didn't think he would get to sleep anytime soon.

Eric Stewarth howled like a wounded animal. He pounded his fists on the ancient purple-heart desk of his ancestors. With an effort, he mastered his rage. He waited for his pulse to slow and his breathing to quiet. Heat burned his ears and tears stung his eyes. In the hallway, he recognized his mother's light steps; then she knocked.

Part of him wanted to call her in, wanted to hear her soothing words and discuss the source of his anger. He needed advice, but when he opened his mouth, those weren't the words that came out. He sent her away. A part of him marveled that she left, acquiescing to his newfound authority. Eric thrilled in it for a moment, but the mirth was quickly edged out by despair.

With a trembling hand, he reached for the crumpled letter on the floor and unwadded it. He smoothed the sheet against the desktop, pressing out the creases with his palm. It read:

Hey Twit,

I have a certain piece of jewelry you might be interested in. I think we can work out a mutually beneficial trade. Meet me at my old house—what's left of it anyway—at sundown tomorrow. Bring Riley and no one else. Break that rule and I'll find another buyer and we'll see how long the little boy gets to keep playing king.

Warm Regards,
Brooklyn Evers

David felt the slap as if someone had struck him. The sensation blotted out the buzzing from the rest of his followers' thoughts. He focused until he was looking through a different pair of eyes. It was one of the men sent in search of Brooklyn, tied to a chair, arms twisted uncomfortably behind him.

"We want to talk to your boss," the voice repeated in the strange, flat tone of a Demonrider as the stranger drew back to hit again. He was a small man, but thickly built and balding.

"You have my attention," David said through his servant's swelling lips. A trickle of blood tickled his chin.

The man smiled and hit him again anyway. "Father Logan wants his prophets back."

David twisted his puppet's lips into a smile, although it hurt and caused the man's bottom lips to split and bleed anew. "No."

The Demonrider's backhand cracked across his face, fingernails raking through his right eye on the follow-through. The pain was so intense David almost cut the connection, but the thug had dropped something onto the table in front of him. David blinked until he could get a clear view through the uninjured eye.

It was a picture. A picture of Brooklyn in a hospital bed with today's issue of the *Chicago Tribune* spread across her chest.

The man took him by the hair and pulled his eyes away from the photo. He got down low, nose to nose. His breath smelled of cloves. "One chance to trade for her. Tomorrow at sundown, at the burned-out shell of her old house. No tricks, don't be late or—"

He felt a gun barrel under his chin; then everything went white.

Kurt didn't know if he was hallucinating or not. The sound of footsteps approaching and the bobbing of a flashlight beam seemed real enough, but so had all the other things he'd seen. It wasn't until the overhead lights stabbed like knives into his eyes that he knew Father Logan had returned.

He pulled the orb further up his sleeve, lifting his other hand against the savage light.

"You don't look well," Dravin noted as the lock clunked and the door swung out. "I brought you a few extras today in light of your willingness to cooperate." He pulled the bourbon from the satchel with a flourish, then looked around as if remembering there were no chairs here. Dravin shrugged and seated himself against the doorjamb. He produced two tumblers, let Kurt inspect the seal on the bottle, then opened it and poured them both a drink.

Almost dropping it, Kurt took a glass with weak fingers. He downed it in one shot, relishing the burn and the warmth spreading in his belly. It had been a long time.

Father Logan raised his glass to Kurt and then took a small sip. "I brought you a lot of food today. I see the bag from my last visit doesn't look quite empty. Eat up, there's more coming. We need to put some weight back on you."

Kurt regarded him through half-lidded eyes. He was hungry, but there was a hook somewhere. He'd learned that. There was always a hook. Dravin was unaccountably happy. Something had changed since their last conversation. Kurt wondered what that was. Anything that made him this happy was certain to be bad news.

"I know what you're thinking," Father Logan said. "Poison! Right? That's what you always think. No worries, everything in here is still in its original packaging." He smiled.

Kurt pushed his tumbler back across the stone floor for a refill. "What are you so happy about?"

"Redemption! Rising from the ashes!" he shouted in a jubilant mockery of a southern preacher. He smiled again and poured the bourbon. "Take that slow, Kurt. You don't weigh what you did."

Probably good advice, Kurt thought as he gulped the whiskey down.

"You wouldn't believe what a bottle of good Kentucky bourbon costs nowadays. What with the corn crisis and all. Apparently, the whole friggin' world runs on corn. Who knew, right?"

Kurt was feeling the alcohol now, and the warning Alexander Stewarth had given him about Dravin—what seemed a lifetime ago—echoed in his head. He pushed the cup back again; this one he would sip. "So, tell me why you hate me."

Father Logan's mouth quirked in a sneer. "Why should I?"

Accepting his third cup to Logan's second, Kurt shrugged. "Are you afraid to?" He took a sip.

Rage twitched Logan's features, but he stilled it so quickly Kurt barely caught it. The alcohol was getting to him then. "Atti Berry."

"Never heard of her," Kurt replied, watching Dravin intently.

"*Mister* Atticus Menard Berry," he replied, "paranormal researcher."

The name was familiar; it came to him slowly. "Two-bit, piece-of-shit demon summoner? He was one of my first cases as a Protector."

"You killed him."

"He didn't want to be arrested, and he tried to kill me first, as I recall. Friend of yours?"

"Brother." Logan downed his drink in a final gulp.

"For what it's worth, wish it hadn't gone that way."

He shrugged. "Doesn't matter. This time tomorrow, the world is going to be a different place. I don't need your help to find Brooklyn anymore. We have her. You could kill me if you wanted. I know you are able, but you won't. If I die now, she'll be delivered to Eric Stewarth, and that's something I wouldn't even wish on you."

Dravin stood and dusted his jeans. He turned the satchel upside down, dropping the canteen with a thunk amid a mound of potato chips and peanut butter cracker packages. "Eat up, get healthy. I'll have penance and work for you soon. The next time you see me, I'll be king of the world."

Kurt watched him as he turned his back. The orb rolled into his palm. Just one shot. He closed his hand around the orb. Hard.

Dravin locked the door. "I'll leave the light on for you."

Kurt waited until the footsteps faded and were gone; then he scrambled across the stone floor, knocking the bourbon aside. He dug through the food until he found what he sought at the bottom of the pile. A single black raven's feather.

19

WILD RIDE

Brooklyn drifted in a fog of vague unease. In the back of her mind, Belial hissed at her to make no sounds, not to move, to keep her eyes closed. She couldn't make sense of it and sank back into the darkness. Every part of her felt so heavy, so fatigued. It felt good to surrender to sleep.

The cold woke her again. It ran in a sharp line along her spine, a ridge of frost between her and the bed. Brooklyn tried to move and found she couldn't. She was tied down. Panic swam through her sluggish brain, but Belial whispered to her, telling her what was going on. It was a terrible predicament. Strapped down, drugged, guarded by Demonriders, being transported to an unknown location.

Brooklyn quested outward with her mind, searching for her soul stones, and found them still in her jeans pocket. When she tried to pull one free, it responded sluggishly. She couldn't muster the concentration to fight right now. Too tired. She was just . . .

The next time she woke, the vehicle was not moving.

It's now or never. Open your eyes, Belial whispered.

Sunlight streamed through the back glass and danced across her stomach. Brooklyn smelled gasoline. The Demonriders were taking a pit stop, apparently. Belial was busy refreezing the IV tubing. She reached for the soul stone again and this time it leapt from her pocket and into her right hand. Brooklyn turned her focus on the wrist straps. If she could get one hand free, she could escape this bed.

Unfortunately, this task was harder than it should have been. Her focus was still fuzzy and the soul stones were far more forgiving than other things. It was finicky work, applying pressure to the portion of the strap she needed to move and excluding the strap loop. After a few tries, the clasp gave way and her right hand was free. She fumbled with numb fingers at the strap across her shoulders. Then she heard a mechanical clunk as the fuel pump shut off. *Crap.* Time was running out.

Belial! she screamed mentally. *I need to roll.*

Brooklyn prayed he understood what she needed him to do. As the rear doors opened, she tossed her soul stone against the front wall of the ambulance and pushed with every ounce of psychic strength she could muster. The result was gratifying. The gurney shot through the double doors, knocking both men on their asses. Though the impact with the ground took her breath and almost made her vomit.

It was a large gas station next to a busy interstate. With no further effort, momentum carried her away from the kidnappers at a brisk pace. Brooklyn tugged her soul stone back to her hand in a blur of green light before she was too far away, then fumbled with the straps at her shoulder and left wrist.

The two men were after her on foot and gaining as she approached the incline down to the interstate. Brooklyn dropped her stone to one side and pushed to avoid rolling into the ditch and flipping. The ambulance started up and swung around in a hasty turn. As she crossed the first lanes of traffic, horns blared and cars swerved, one so close she was sure she left a few strands of hair in the bumper. With an effort, her left hand sprang free, and with both hands she finished the shoulder straps.

Brooklyn sat up in the bed as it turned by force of gravity and began to flow with traffic down the steep incline of the road. She realized she would wind up in the dip at the bottom where it turned uphill again, something her captors seemed to have figured out already as the ambulance, siren blaring, raced past her and pulled into the grassy median at the bottom. The gurney rocked dangerously in the wake of a passing big rig; Brooklyn threw out energy, pushing against the opposite side to stabilize.

Icy terror gripped her. She'd be lucky to make it to the bottom without splattering herself all over the asphalt.

The bed shimmied side to side, each sway a little further than the last.

Steady it or we are going to flip, Belial shouted in her mind.

She pulled the blue stone free of her pocket and pushed it against the pavement on her left, then did the same with the green stone on her right. Brooklyn winced as twin trails of sparks leapt up on either side, but the gurney stabilized.

The blacktop raced by with glittering malice. The sun shone off the glass of the cars she passed, most slowing as they approached the ambulance and its flashing lights. A little boy in the backseat of a Subaru waved at her as she went by. Brooklyn waved back. His solemn face reminded her of Devin. She felt afraid, but oddly calm. A side effect of being drugged?

The wheels beneath her whined, stressed beyond their purpose, as they jolted over tar snakes. Brooklyn summoned the stones and held them tight against the flesh of her arms though they were painfully hot to touch, and leaned forward, worrying at the strap across her shins. The Demonriders behind her were almost out of sight. The two ahead were waiting expectantly by the roadside as she approached. Blood from where the needle had ripped out made her fingers slick as she worked her right foot free. Brooklyn was going to arrive with one ankle still strapped to the bed and get shoved right back into the ambulance. She couldn't let that happen.

Brooklyn looked around frantically. Traffic behind her had stopped. A few cars were going around in the right lane. She sent her blue soul stone soaring in an arc down into the back of a passing pickup truck and held on. It caught against the inside of the tailgate and the tether jerked taut, nearly toppling the gurney. Brooklyn clung to the gurney for dear life as it fishtailed wildly across both lanes of traffic and left a long gleaming scrape down the side of a black sedan.

She shot past her would-be captors as they scrambled back inside the ambulance. When the truck started up the other side, the strain of hanging on settled on her like lead and quickly morphed into sharp agony. Brooklyn couldn't spare a moment's concentration to free her left foot. Her head throbbed just behind her eyes with a malicious pain.

Since she couldn't even afford to look over her shoulder, Belial let her know the Demonriders were weaving through the accumulated traffic, dipping across the grassy median when no other way was open. They were coming fast. Brooklyn drew on his strength. Ice rolled up her spine and made the pain behind her eyes distant, burning away some of the drug-induced fatigue and fuzziness. It wasn't much, but it was bearable.

Fumbling with one hand at the ankle strap, Brooklyn worried it with numb fingers as the ambulance pulled alongside her and the passenger window went down.

The man that looked out at her was ugly, with squashed features as if he'd been hit in the face with a frying pan. He lifted a hand in her direction and the gurney slowed, drifting sideways toward the grass. She lost her grip on the blue soul stone and the gurney quickly lost speed, moving in slow motion toward the shoulder. There was nothing she could do. The wheels caught in the dirt and the sky and grass blurred as she tumbled down the embankment.

Floundering in a daze of pain, she struggled to take a full breath. Her wrist and shoulder were numb, maybe broken. This was bad. Brooklyn moved her legs experimentally then sat up with a groan, shaking her head to clear it. Sparkles and black spots danced across her vision. *Great.*

Doors slammed at the top of the bank; then came the sound of running feet. This was worse. Panic kicked her already thrumming heart to a stuttering gallop that pounded in her ears.

Touching the black barbed wire scar that twined between her breasts, she remembered Nathan Goodrum's weight on top of her as he tried to drive a poisoned blade through her chest. She'd escaped him that day, because of David's sacrifice, but David couldn't save her now. She'd have to do that herself. Brooklyn stumbled to her feet and hobbled toward the tree line, Goodrum's cold, passionless threat ringing in her mind. *Soon you will beg for the poisoned knife again.* It would be better to die here than to become his prisoner. Shuddering, she limped a little faster.

Pine needles gouged at fresh scrapes as she pushed through the trees.

One foot in front of the other. But for every step she managed, Brooklyn heard several pounding footfalls behind her.

Give me control, Belial shouted. *You can't outrun them.*

Unable to breathe a reply, she just shook her head. One step, one more, and one more. She risked a glance back; her pursuers had reached the bottom of the embankment.

Please, just until this is over. His voice took on a pleading tone she'd never heard before. *I can fight them.*

Memories of slaughter, of thawing bodies stacked like firewood, flitted through her mind. The helplessness of being locked away as a passenger in her own skull. She brushed them away. "I know you can," she wheezed, clutching her ribs with her good hand. "So can I."

Three more belabored steps carried her into a small clearing where she turned to face the pursuers. Brooklyn thought they might demand her surrender, or reason with her to come back willingly, but they never slowed. The ugly man who had shoved her off the road raced into the clearing and dove for her. She stumbled to the side, falling on her already tender shoulder. Arctic power coiled within her like a wound spring, or a snake ready to strike. Merciless cold. It killed slow and soft like a smothering snow, or as sudden and harsh as a fall from an icy cliff, but it always killed.

Icicles as large as swords erupted from the earth to meet her attacker. One he battered aside with a meaty fist and unnatural strength, but another took him under the ribs, his own momentum driving it deep. His eyes were wide, uncomprehending, and the blood on his lips hung, bright as berries, until it dropped and steamed on the ice, turning to rust.

Brooklyn rolled back to her feet, the thrill of winter numbing her pain. And then the second man arrived. He was wary now, eyes darting between his companion and her. *Good. He should be wary.* "Just go. Leave me alone," she called, hiding the shortness of her breath with short sentences.

"He was my brother," the man choked, emotion breaking through the robotic speech Brooklyn associated with Demonriders.

She almost pitied him, but couldn't quite make the leap. Not after they had taken David from her. Everything bad that had happened to her could be traced back to Nathan Goodrum or one of his Demonriders. She just couldn't feel *that* for one of *them*.

"I didn't ask for this." It was the closest she could come to an apology. She might have said more, but there were two more Demonriders somewhere up on the road coming this way.

Her last soul stone left her numb fingers in a green blur barely discernible against the darker green of the pines all around. She looked away as he crumpled, turning her attention back to the first man who wasn't quite dead. With a grimace, she punched a hole through his skull with her soul stone and ended him, too. As she turned away, something gruesome flickered at the edge of seeing and was gone.

Images of a knife dripping blood and bodies stacked like cordwood surfaced again, but she pushed those thoughts away. There wasn't time for guilt or self-pity now. She forced herself to look back at what she'd done—been forced to do.

With fascination she watched as two small spirits writhed free of the broken men. Small and squat, mottled like hyenas, they regarded her in silence. She waited for them to be sucked away by the Pull, but it never happened. First one, then the other, turned and loped away into the shadows between the trees.

20

Barn Gathering

Riley squinted. The world seemed to be on fire as the sun touched the horizon and cast its final rays through the burnished autumn leaves. There was old magic in Appalachia, Kurt had always said. Old spirits that lingered in the stones and welled in the trickles of underground springs seeking the surface. Kurt always had been a little superstitious though.

Beside him, Eric fidgeted with the bulky controller in his pocket.

"What are we doing here?"

Eric didn't respond for so long Riley thought that he wasn't going to.

Kill him now and let's be free. We have work to do.

It was certainly a prime opportunity, alone with young Mr. Stewarth, far from his family and house guards. Secluded with no witnesses. He could drop the boy and walk away. An orb hung just inside his sleeve.

But no . . . better to wait and see what had Eric in such a twist.

"Just follow my lead and everything will be as it should be, for both of us," Eric snapped irritably.

"That's not mysterious," Riley grumbled, leaning back against the bumper of Eric's SUV.

The chilly air took on a biting edge as the night crept in around them. Riley stepped into the lee of the Everses' barn to shelter from the wind. Eric seemed oblivious to the cold, his eyes scanning the tree line, the paved road, the dirt driveway, and all the open fields that sloped away from the barn. The two demons linked to the controller sat at attention, mostly invisible against the shadowed ground.

Riley straightened, tilting his head to listen. "Somebody's coming."

David placed a hand on the dash to steady himself as they left the pavement and began bumping their way down the long driveway to the Everses' home. The message had been clear: come alone. But he wasn't sure they understood how hard it would be to drive all this way blind. He tried to keep his attention focused outward, looking and listening. He had eyes hidden all around the meeting spot, but the failing light offered him only the silhouette of two men, shrouded in shadow, and it was hard to tell if either was the man he had communicated with. Granted, he'd been looking up through swollen eyes, with the panicked thoughts of his scout roaring in his mind. Might one of the two be Dravin Logan? The thought of another confrontation with Dravin thrilled and terrified him in equal measures. If anyone held the secret to restoring his vision, it was the man who had taken it away.

He took a calming breath, steadied his connection to the men in position to help him, and blocked out the rest of his followers so he could focus. Brooklyn was here. This was his one chance. At a thought, the driver slowed some distance from the barn where the two men waited.

Taking a breath and stepping out into the brisk night, David reached a hand beneath his jacket and stroked the soft raven's feather suspended there on a leather thong. A part of him wished to use it, to summon his dark goddess to keep him safe. But she would not help him, he knew, not where Brooklyn was concerned. So, with a nervous sigh and a heart full of hope he couldn't afford, he turned and headed straight for the barn, the two men, and the strangely luminescent sentinels he should not have been able to see with his own eyes.

Kurt fought the madness of exhaustion and nightmares until he found the calmness he needed to send the summons. With the feather clutched between his fingers, he issued the call. Nothing happened. No whoosh of air, no sultry voice, no icy touch. Just the quiet of a crypt broken only by the rattle of his breath.

The madness threatened to overwhelm him again. It wasn't real; none of it had ever been real. The orb rolled free of his hand and rose to float in the darkness beyond his seeing. This was all he had left now: a way out. He'd rolled the dice one last time and lost. Kurt wondered how much it would hurt. Probably be best to aim for an eye. Of course, this was a coward's way out, but if he could see Mary and Tyler again, see them without the twisted dreams, wouldn't that be worth it?

"Well, go on then," a bemused voice murmured.

Kurt searched the cell, settling on a darker patch of darkness within the shadow's pitch. "You came!" He scrambled to his knees, fighting dizziness, putting a hand down to climb the rest of the way to his feet.

"You wanted an audience, so go on, paint the wall and I'll cut the line and we'll be done with this place." She cast an uneasy glance upward. What could make a god uneasy?

"Help me? Get me out." Kurt's voice sounded weak and wheedling to his own ears. He stood then, making his spine straight despite the way his legs trembled beneath him. "We had a deal, you and I, and your end hasn't been upheld."

Azrael stepped closer, stretching her wings and folding them like twin capes down the length of her back. She was as otherworldly beautiful as he remembered, but didn't flicker anymore; she was wholly present. Somehow, impossibly, that made her more imposing. Kurt stood his ground. He wouldn't be cowed again. Even in this pit, standing in his own excrement, he would not duck his head or avert his eyes.

"Hasn't it?"

"Our deal was that you'd deliver my son to me safely. Even if I believe that my boy's soul is in Brooklyn, you didn't deliver her into my presence, and she's no son."

"Our deal is done. Unless you want me to deliver her here to you?" She looked around theatrically. "Looks safe here."

"No—"

"I wasn't finished," she hissed, reaching out to touch his face. Her hand was warm, almost fever hot, not the coldness he'd associated with her in the past. "As I said, our deal is done, but I'm not unwilling to make another."

Kurt swallowed; his parched throat ached. "What do you want?"

"To continue. To rule in a new world. The same thing everyone wants, freedom and control."

"How can I give you that?" He took a step back, leaning against the wall.

"What will you do if I set you free? Reclaim your role as a Protector? Seek vengeance? Succumb to insanity?" The last words dripped from her mouth like honeyed poison, full of implication.

He opened his mouth to reply.

"Don't deny it," she purred, pacing around his left side like a jungle cat. "You pulled something too big and now you're damaged." She tapped her porcelain forehead for emphasis. "Scrambled eggs."

Kurt cleared his throat and his stomach dropped as he asked the question he feared the answer to. "So, what's your point? What do you want in exchange for a ride out of here and a safe place to heal? And a safe reunion with Brooklyn, not her left unconscious on a couch in the middle of a siege, either. Real safety."

"For all of that plus a little help with . . . you know." She tapped the side of her perfect little head. "All I ask is your life, or what remains of it, spent in my service. Don't answer too quickly. I'm offering death. Death to the proud Protector, death to your indulgence and destruction." She kicked the empty liquor bottle away. "You'll be a new man. You will be my sword. You'll fight for me without question, without complaint. You'll die for me if I ask it of you. You will lead my armies and guard my prophet. That's the deal. I'll accept nothing less than your life, your service, and your uncompromising loyalty."

"Are you sure you don't want me to throw my soul in to sweeten the deal for you a little?" He pushed off the wall. "I'd hate for you to feel cheated. After all, a lifetime of servitude is the going rate for an air ticket and a few nights at a hotel."

"I would very much like your soul, but you should save that for our next exchange, seeing as how it is all you have left. My offer stands. Ring me up when you are ready." Azrael plucked a glossy black feather from her plumage and dropped it at his feet. Then she was gone.

Kurt picked up the feather and rubbed it between his fingers. He'd spent the last twenty years paying off his last bargain, and he still didn't have what he'd sold his position and values to get. It was too much. She demanded everything, but what was the alternative? Die of starvation, knowing Dravin had captured Brooklyn and he could have helped her? The years remaining to him were already forfeit one way or the other. It wasn't much of a choice. It wasn't fair, but then again, Azrael never was.

Father Logan felt unaccountably nervous. He didn't know why. He'd planned, prepped, and prepared for this. Even for the loss of the girl, though he hadn't given up hope of recovering her just yet. When the sun was well and truly set, Dravin knelt in the ashy remains of the Everses' home and prayed to a forgotten god. After a moment, peace and reassurance flooded through him and with it a bone-deep certainty that there was still a purpose, still a plan.

The moonlight illuminated the figures near the barn, but their features were indistinct. From beyond the barn, a third man approached the others on foot, feeling his way carefully. *Almost like a blind man*, Dravin thought. This was the one to take alive.

Get eyes on his car, Dravin thought at Goodrum. *There's at least a driver, maybe more. See, but don't be seen.* As Goodrum moved to obey, Dravin patted his jacket pocket, reassuring himself the small glass vial was still there. His brother's research and life's work distilled into a few dark drops. The last few if things didn't go well tonight, but things would go well. He wouldn't allow failure.

Dravin sat up straighter. David Sterling had stopped his approach and was tilting his head as if listening to something. Back at the barn, the other two men were like statues, eyes trained on David. His sudden pause seemed to have made them uneasy as well. Father Logan reached out to Goodrum again. *Have the girl ready and in position, wait for my go-ahead.*

21

Pursued

Baying hounds in the distance sent a shiver up Brooklyn's spine. They had her scent. She labored on, cutting across open fields and taking every opportunity to plunge into thick woods and up the steepest sides she could find. If it was hard going for her, it would be hard for the dogs, too, she reasoned. What she really needed was a river or at least a creek. Something she could use to trip up the dogs. Or a car. A car would be nice. The cuts and bruises that would have surely been her undoing otherwise were kept in check by Belial, and the steady stream of icy power that seemed to flow out from her spine to all extremities.

Brooklyn didn't like leaning on him. She had been careful to maintain a clear separation these last few months, to make sure he knew she was the one in charge and that he could be ousted at any moment. But now, like so many things, it seemed she didn't have a choice. She hadn't had a choice when he'd chosen her in the beginning, destroying her life and enmeshing her in this new world. And worse still, she couldn't seem to extricate herself from this spider's web of Heirs, Protectors, Prophets, and Demonriders. They just wouldn't leave her alone. *That's okay*, she thought. *Once I get out of this mess, I'll deal with them.*

Brooklyn paused at the top of a particularly steep incline to listen. For long moments there was nothing but the ragged rasp of her own breath. She held it for a moment, and then she heard it.

The dogs were closer now. Judging from the eager notes of their baying, they knew it, too.

She looked back down the way she'd come, the last few yards of treacherous stone. She scrambled back down far enough to reach it with her outstretched hand and drew on Belial. Frost spread across the stones in an icy rush. It wasn't much, but maybe it would be enough to send the dogs or their handlers tumbling back down the ridge.

Satisfied, she rose and turned to the northwest and began picking her way down the other side. Brooklyn wished more than anything she could just fly away from this mess, shoot into the clouds, and vanish. She couldn't, though. She had to find a solution here, on the ground. It wasn't long before one presented itself.

The cliff before them dropped away for thirty or more feet, the ground below littered with boulders and smaller stones.

Belial, how far can we jump?

She felt his uncertainty before his careful reply. *Farther than we can safely land.*

Brooklyn drew on Belial then, hard enough the cold made her teeth ache, and the energy burned painfully behind her eyes. The shadows below receded, revealing the treacherous landing.

Drawing harder until every muscle thrummed and burned with cold energy, Brooklyn gave a yell and ran with a certainty that surprised even herself, leaping from the edge and pushing with all her might, out into the open air.

The wind whipped her hair about her face and for a few glorious seconds she was free from everything. Free of doubt, free of regret, free of her pursuers. But then gravity reasserted itself and she was falling, fast. The stony ground rose up to meet her almost before she could recover her senses. She took her own willpower, augmented by Belial, and pushed it down. Blinding pain exploded in her skull, and warm blood tickled her upper lip. The earth rushed up and she tensed, cringing. Her feet slammed into the ground and her shins and knees screamed in protest as the demon's cold power filled her muscles. The impact jarred her other injuries back to life. Shoulder, wrist, ribs. She felt broken; every joint ached. If she lived until tomorrow, she'd be sore as hell.

Turning unsteadily, she peered back at the cliff top. The distance was dizzying, or maybe that was the darkness creeping in around the edges of her vision. Her stomach growled insistently. Riley had warned her about this; she needed food before overexertion sent her into a coma, or worse, stopped her heart. There was no time to dwell on it. The dogs were close now. She had to keep moving, get out of sight or this whole stunt would be in vain. With a grunt of effort, Brooklyn turned and ran for the fields of softly rolling clover that spread out like a patchwork ahead.

David smiled as he approached the other men, hands up where he hoped they could see he held no weapon. The hive buzzed insistently in the back of his mind, trying to feed him information he didn't want to be distracted with right now.

"Hello, gentlemen." He turned to face the closest man, examining him through the eyes of a prophet with a scoped rifle some two hundred yards away. Was this Dravin Logan? "I thought this was a private meeting." He jerked his head at the other man standing beneath the eaves of the barn.

The view shifted to the other man; he was just a wiry silhouette in the shadows. The two were too far apart for him to see them both at once, which was damn inconvenient.

Turning his own attention back to the first man showed him nothing but the faintest traces of blue energy tethering him to the two glowing demons in the shadows.

The man stepped forward. "Who are you?" His voice rang with confusion. It wasn't the emotionless voice of a Demonrider as he'd been expecting. Further, it was youthful, with the barest hint of an accent he could not place.

Something wasn't right. The obnoxious buzzing in the back of his mind picked up again, forcing him to pause for a moment and silence it. Should he lie? Wasn't he expected and thus known? He couldn't see the harm in the truth, so he told it. "I'm David Sterling. I'm here for Brooklyn."

The young man paced forward. David swiveled his man's rifle scope back on this fellow. "What do you want from her?" the young man asked, voice dripping with suspicion.

"She's my friend. Is she here?"

"Not yet. But when she comes, she's mine, Mr. Sterling."

David felt his anger tightening the finger on the trigger of the rifle pointed at this arrogant bastard's head. With a supreme effort of will, he anchored himself in the moment and willed his man to relax. *RELAX!* He waited for the crack of rifle fire. One heartbeat, then two, then three, until at last he knew it wouldn't come. "Brooklyn's not yours or anybody else's. She'll leave here tonight with whomever she chooses."

"Wrong." David had barely registered the word and the blur of motion in the scope when the man hit him across the face, hard enough to drive him to his knees. A sharp spike of pain ran from his ear down his neck, the taste of blood, hot and metallic. "Do you know who I am?" the man railed indignantly.

David couldn't see, but if he could, he was almost certain this guy was literally foaming at the mouth. He spit blood on the ground, but before he could answer, the other man spoke. A voice unfamiliar, the edges of a true southern genteel dulled by a formal education someplace far away.

"Eric, stop this."

He snapped at the other man. "Have *you* forgotten who is in charge? Are you the Heir, or am I?"

"Heir without a ring," a female voice called gleefully from the darkness. "Little boy playing king."

David scrambled to his knees. *Brooklyn? Could that be her?* "Brooklyn!" he called out, rising. "Brooklyn!" His voice high and laced with desperation.

"Enough of your games. Come here now," Eric bellowed. Each word a sharp spike driven into the night.

"Brookie!" David screamed as he gained his feet, turning wildly in search of her voice. The hive mind buzzed again, an impatient, restless, unwelcome distraction. He couldn't muster the focus to push them back any longer. The information swirled in a whirlwind of images and sounds. "Broo—" He choked on her name. The images danced like ghosts behind his blind eyes, unmistakable. This was what they'd been trying to tell him. She wasn't here; she was on the run from the police.

Beyond the barn, the girl laughed again, and behind him gunfire erupted in the trees. David reached out for his people, for their eyes to see, but he'd already felt it. They were dead, and the only thing he could see now was the twin blurs of blue energy, demons racing to battle.

Riley ran for Brooklyn as the first shots rang out. He could just see her, a familiar shape darting away in the shadows. The fields were open, but the night was thick as ink, with only a few slivers of moonlight slicing through the clouds above. She was making a beeline for a smaller outbuilding, a hay shed if memory served.

He held himself short of running full out. The ground was uneven and treacherous. As she vanished around the structure, Riley was struck by the cloying odor of rotting hay and shit. *Why would anyone want to live on a farm?* "Brooklyn, it's me, Riley," he half shouted, half whispered. Somewhere in the distance, thunder clapped, or was it more gunfire?

He turned the corner, seeing the open side of the shed, the stacks of hay rising to the tin roof. Where had she gone? She'd been just in front of him. He was sure of it. He stopped to listen. Forcing himself to breathe slowly and quietly. The wind rustled the tall, dead grass in the fallow fields. The shed creaked and the metal roof rattled ominously. *Turn around*, the voice inside his head commanded. With the hair on the back of his neck standing at attention, he slowly turned and there she was, pointing a pistol at his head.

"Brooklyn, it's me." He reached out to her but dropped his hands when she clicked the hammer back. She circled him, edging left and left again, almost as if she wanted to be behind him again. Almost as if that made it easier to shoot him somehow. "Brooklyn, please I—" Just then the clouds parted, and moonlight illuminated her face. She wasn't Brooklyn. This was a Demonrider.

"And now you finally understand," she said in that emotionless way they talked. Before he could make sense of it, she pulled the trigger.

22

ABANDONED

Brooklyn had taken her body and her mind beyond their limits. Her heartbeat throbbed in every part of her being, a desperate staccato counting the seconds until she would be caught out in the rolling open fields. The sound of police helicopters filled the air, their spotlights gliding over the trees, crisscrossing the mountains behind her. UFOs come to beam her up. A panicky little laugh bubbled up in her chest at the thought. In just a few minutes, they would make their way here, where there were no trees to shield her from view. The choices were to hide in the trees and wait for the dogs or cross the clover patch and get caught in the open. *There are choices*, she thought, *just no good ones.*

Hunkered low and casting furtive glances back over her shoulder, Brooklyn set out across the field. Belial was stretched, too. She could feel his ability to numb her many injuries and boost her stamina waning. The clover was still green and in the most lush places it reached halfway up her calves. When the copters came, maybe she could lie flat enough to be hidden from the searchlights. It was a feeble hope.

Like that time they had stayed in a cabin when she was a young girl, Brooklyn knew she had to keep moving. On the opposite side of the lake there had been a paddle boat, dragged up on the bank, scant feet from the water's edge.

She had wanted that boat, wanted the freedom to glide across the water. It called to her as they sat in the shallows splashing one another, and later, when the older kids were engrossed in a sandcastle, she slipped away. She'd learned to swim young, and it wasn't so far.

She paused at the floating safety line warning swimmers not to go further. With a little dip of her head, she was under it and stroking into deeper, colder water. At the halfway point her stamina began to fail. The burning in her chest, the ache in her shoulders and thighs. Her strokes slowed, barely keeping her afloat. The boat on the opposite bank seemed further than when she'd started. Behind her, Erin and their cousins still hadn't registered her absence.

Brooklyn didn't know if she should go on or go back. Everything seemed exhaustingly far away. She tried to shout for her sister, but water filled her mouth and nose, choking out her cry.

The burning in her lungs as she went under sent a jolt through her. When she surfaced again, her vision was blurred by water and sunlight. Erin was just a smudge of color with a black spot above her, like some great raptor had descended onto her back. She wiped her eyes and saw clearly now. Erin was coming for her, shouting obscenities all the way. Reluctantly, Brooklyn turned and swam back. So tired when she reached her sister that she dragged them both under.

When they finally made it to the beach, Erin finished scolding her with something strangely like terror in her eyes. Brooklyn had sat in the sand coughing and watching the sun glint on the shiny blue-and-white hull of the paddle boat.

This was the same thing, except the prize was freedom, and the consequence of failure was letting others continue to control her fate and leaving Devin to their mercy, too. She wasn't about to do that, and Erin wasn't here to save her this time either.

See how bad it is, she commanded Belial. Instantly she felt more tired and dozens of alarms went off in her brain as he spiraled up trailing a frail tether, and all her pain came flooding back like a classroom of excited children all vying for her undivided attention.

Each footstep felt leaden and cumbersome. Brooklyn longed to drop into the clover and close her eyes, just for a moment. Even her heartbeat felt more labored, her breathing harsher. The dizziness came in waves now and a cold sticky sweat coated her body.

The copters were approaching the last of the hills, banking in slow circles as they swept daylight across the treetops. What would she do when they finally trapped her? Would she kill to stay free? These weren't Demonriders; these were men with lives and families. These were supposed to be the good guys.

Black spots swam across her vision. Brooklyn reached through the tether to draw a little more strength, and ice seized her that had nothing to do with Belial's power. The tether hung loose, a gossamer kite string twisting in the wind, falling. He was gone. For the first time in months, she was alone.

He'd abandoned her . . .

There wasn't time to dwell on that fact because the search beams were in the clover now, and gunfire erupted in the distance, first in front of her and then behind. She ducked instinctively. Were they shooting at her? The search beam raced across the field, and a group of stunned deer, eyes glowing brightly for a heartbeat and winking out again, turned to run. Brooklyn dove face-first into the clover.

Inhuman screams rang out. David flexed his arms against the zip ties around his wrists until they hurt, and watched the demons mauling someone. In his sight, they glowed like blue neon, but the man beneath them was darkness. Only the spray of his blood had any glow, and that was gone in seconds. Everyone else was dead, and David was alone and blind for it.

"I said don't move." It was the voice of a Demonrider. David remembered the voice of Nathan Goodrum from a cornfield what seemed a lifetime ago. This wasn't Goodrum, but he spoke the same inflectionless way.

Ignoring the man, David turned his head, following the faint blue lines leading from the carnage and into the lee of the barn where Eric was hiding and controlling his demons. *He's smarter than me*, David mused. *I'm bound, blind, and alone. At least he still has a chance.*

They had his only surviving companion, Marshall, trussed up in the backseat of David's car. All he could see was the faint illumination of the radio clock. The car stank of fear and sweat now, and Marshall's heart was galloping in a way that made David feel as if he were having a heart attack.

"Why do you keep looking at that barn?" the guy behind him asked. "You got somebody in there?"

David shook his head. "I'm not looking anywhere, man, I'm blind."

The man grunted and his boots crunched a couple of steps toward the barn. He worked the slide on his rifle, a nervous tick apparently. He'd checked the weapon three times already.

David reached out to his followers. There wasn't any help within two hours' drive. Just Marshall. The hunt for Brooklyn continued and apparently included helicopters now. How had she escaped her captors? It didn't matter. At least she was free. *Run, baby, run*, he thought.

A bright light brought David back to the present. Well, not a light in the traditional sense, but glowing energy, the kind he could see. It approached the two demons quickly and deliberately and fell like a scythe. Both of the creatures blinked out of existence.

"He's in the barn. Bring him alive." The voice came from the source of that light. It was a voice David knew. It gave him chills at first, but those quickly blazed into hatred.

"Father Logan," David shouted hoarsely. There was no answer, so he shouted again. "Logan, you coward, answer me!"

"Well, if it isn't Mr. Sterling," Dravin called out cheerfully. David could hear the smile in his voice. To his left, there was a ruckus in the barn.

Eric let loose a string of curses and David followed the dull blue glow that seemed to emanate from the boy's waist. They brought him closer and shoved him down beside David.

"Logan, you spineless rat, you'll burn for this, I swear it. I am the Heir of Solomon, and you swore an oath to me!"

"You aren't worthy of my oath. We are all descendants of Solomon. What makes you so damned special?"

"Untie me now and we will work this out," Eric implored, exchanging threats for negotiation.

"Gag that one. He talks too much. Then let's find winner number three so we can get this party started."

23

So It Ends

Riley tasted coppery metal and bile. The pain came in crescendos, each trying to outshine the last. It was a pain so enrapturing that he couldn't seem to pull his awareness out of his own skull where the agony centered. All that he was curled around that sensation, all eyes inward.

The pain is a good sign, his companion noted. *It means we are still alive.*

Riley didn't respond. Vaguely, he became aware that he was upright and walking. Well, walking might have been an optimistic assessment of things. He was stumbling along between two other people who were supporting most of his weight, but his feet were definitely moving on their own.

In a moment—or maybe an hour, time had gone all fuzzy on him—they arrived back at the barn. He recognized the smell of hay, aged timbers, and something cloying that was once probably horse shit.

Someone was speaking to him. It was a familiar voice. Riley's tongue felt swollen, thick in his mouth, but he made it work well enough to spit out some blood and utter Father Logan's name like a curse.

"That's not the articulate boy I remember. That's okay though, there's really nothing to say, anyway."

Riley tried to track Father Logan, but his vision blurred, and even the weak light from the moon felt unbearable.

"Tie him like the others, and someone clean him up so he can see," Father Logan called out.

Riley welcomed the distraction of the pain in his arms as they were twisted behind his back and zip-tied, taking his attention, for a moment, from the agony in his head. Then came the sound of tearing cloth and the sloshing of water and sweet coolness against his face. Almost a comfort but for the rough, scrubbing nature of the strokes across his eyes and the bridge of his nose, which he felt fairly confident was broken.

"He's a bloody mess. I thought I told you clean kills or capture unharmed?" said another familiar voice. Riley turned his head and squinted. *Nathan Goodrum.*

"My fault, I'm afraid," the fake Brooklyn murmured. "I shot him point blank. I didn't think he had time to shield." She shrugged. "Once he was down, I thought you might rather have him alive." Riley heard a whisper of leather and a gun cocking. "Was I mistaken?" she asked, pressing the barrel to the back of his neck.

As the seconds ticked by, Riley struggled to breath. Would he hear the shot? Would he feel it? Would the real Brooklyn ever know what happened to him?

"Put your gun away, Cindy," Goodrum commanded.

When he heard the snick of the hammer being lowered, Riley sagged with relief.

"Yes," Father Logan said, stepping into the moonlight and clasping his hands piously. "Let's get started."

Dravin felt alive, wonderfully and truly alive, maybe for the first time since the blind upstart had taken everything from him. *Let's get them ready*, he thought at Goodrum.

Goodrum began barking orders almost instantly. Dravin left him to it, making his way behind the barn to David's car. He opened the rear door and patted down the squirming driver until he found the keys in the man's breast pocket. Dravin felt a brief twinge of guilt. Marshall had been his driver once, long ago. He hated to see him suffering so, but it was an unfortunate necessity. It was David's fault. He'd created this situation after all. "All will be made right," Dravin whispered to the man, though it appeared he found little reassurance in it.

The engine purred to life, all eight cylinders thrumming with power. He pulled carefully around the barn until he was facing the three men on their knees, the six Demonriders flanking them, two per prisoner, and his ever-patient Mr. Goodrum.

Whistling because he just couldn't contain his glee, he turned on the high beams and declared, "Let there be light!" He hopped out of the SUV and opened the back door, pulling Marshall into a sitting position and manhandling him out of the car and pushing him down on his knees facing the other three men. He leaned close to Marshall's ear and breathed a single word in the tiniest of whispers. "David."

David Sterling twitched in response.

"Good, just making sure. I wouldn't want you to miss this next part because of the whole 'not being able to see' thing."

Him first, he thought at Goodrum. When Nathan pulled the gag out of Eric's mouth, he immediately began babbling again.

"You are my sworn protector. I am the sole and legitimate Heir of King Solomon himself. You know this! By God, do your duty! Protect me."

The boy just didn't seem to grasp the gravity of the situation. Even when Nathan pried his teeth apart and forced a funnel into his throat, he continued to blather, or maybe he was crying, or gagging. It was hard to tell.

"Shhh . . . ," Dravin said. "I'm not trying to hurt you, I'm trying to help you." He pulled the glass vial from his pocket, its contents blacker than the night around them. "Believe you me," he whispered, "I wish there was another way." Then he unstopped the vial and upended its contents into the funnel.

David watched the proceedings through Marshall's eyes. A few seconds after the liquid had been poured down Eric's throat, nothing happened, but they pinched his nose shut until the desperation for air caused him to swallow—his throat working reflexively and repeatedly as if the liquid were thick as tar—and a sudden light flared up. Not a light David could see with Marshall's eyes, but a light for his eyes alone. A glowing blue line of power erupted between Eric and Father Logan. And as he looked more closely, he saw another line, fainter, easy to overlook, like an afterimage on the retina, but there just the same. This line connected Father Logan to Nathan Goodrum.

Dravin's face seemed to light up with understanding. At once he turned and marched over to the other man, the one whose nose they'd broken. "You are next on the roster, Riley, but I've just learned some very interesting things from my *liege* Eric about you and your research. If we follow our plans for the night, there might be some pretty significant side effects for you in the areas of creativity and intuition. I think you still have great things to do, so for you, my friend, a stay of execution. We'll chat more later." He patted Riley on the cheek and sauntered over to David. "Now for the main attraction, the stealer of minds, the Blind Prophet, the one and only David Sterling."

David half expected applause, but it never came. He saw a silent pulse along the line between Father Logan and Nathan Goodrum, and Goodrum pulled the funnel from Eric's mouth and wiped it on his jeans. He turned to David with an unpleasant smile.

"Do the Demonriders know?" David asked in Father Logan's direction. "Do they know their leader swallowed the same sludge you are force-feeding us?" David could hear murmuring and shuffling feet.

"Lies!" Goodrum roared, closing the distance between them and wrenching David's head back by the hair. He shoved the end of the funnel against his lips hard enough to bust both and possibly to loosen one of his teeth. The funnel was in his throat gagging him before he could utter another word. Through Marshall's eyes, he could see Father Logan unstopping a new vial. Marshall fell forward in his desperation to answer David's call for help, but he was trussed from head to toe and flopped with the futility of a fish on a boat deck.

Sweat trickled down David's neck, dampening the leather thong of his necklace. His necklace! He could feel the feather under his shirt tickling his chest. *Azrael!* he screamed again and again. *Azrael, I need you!* Marshall rolled, and he caught a half a glimpse of Father Logan upending the vial into the funnel. A second later, David gasped; then everything went black.

Belial ascended higher and higher above Brooklyn. He could feel her teetering on the precipice of unconsciousness. He looked to the west and saw a train track, to the north, fields and farms in the dark, a pinprick of light here and there, not enough to make sense of the patchwork of shadows and darker shadows. To the southeast, there were mountains, lights, barking dogs, and helicopters. The searchers were in the tree line now; from this vantage he could see the futility of their situation. The expanse of open field before them was vastly larger than they'd been able to judge from the ground in the dark. The distance they'd covered—that Brooklyn was continuing to cover—was a fraction of the whole. He estimated they would catch her less than halfway across.

The night seemed alive with energy. He felt it like the caress of a warm breeze across his face. He flared his wings and turned their many eyes toward the source of that heat. His heart dropped. There was movement ahead of them in the trees, a lot of movement, a lot of people. Who were they?

He gently severed the tether, letting the Pull take him—only it didn't really. Instead of the inescapable lurching yank he was accustomed to, he felt a lazy tug, one he could shrug off. He thought then of the Demonriders they'd killed earlier, and the beasts they'd left behind in their passing. Things that should have been swept from this world that had instead wandered out among the trees.

As the Pull edged him out of the physical realm, the scene below changed. Brooklyn became a brightness that blinded. Beyond her, lesser lights dotted the landscape, some brighter than was natural, but none matched her, not even by half. Still, those bright lights meant something unfortunate.

"Demonriders." The word left him with a sigh. For a moment he was back in the sea watching Tais getting swept away by his betrayal as much as by his fath—Prosidris's machinations.

He remembered her mismatched eyes. Eyes that had once only shone with love and trust now held something different. Not surprise, exactly, more like anticipated disappointment. As if she'd expected to be let down all along. This was Tais all over again; he was about to fail someone he cared about just like he always did. Except instead of his father it was the police and Demonriders, and instead of an ocean it was a sea of clover that would be the stage for a young woman's undoing.

Belial started back toward Brooklyn, but then he hesitated. If he reconnected with her, what could he do but give her the strength to run and be caught a few hundred yards further from where she was now? The helicopters illuminated the field now. She would be caught in minutes. Going back down there would not help her. He turned and winged back the way they had come.

24

WHIRLY BIRD

Riley thought the pain in his head couldn't get any worse, but all the cursing and yelling were proving him wrong. Father Logan raged. There was no other word for it. He stumbled as if drunk, holding between his forefinger and thumb a charred feather, dangling it into the car headlight beams as if they might reveal the answers he sought.

The curious part of Riley's mind wanted a closer look at that vial of black liquid. Something about it taunted him, an insinuation just beyond his understanding. Something he'd read maybe, about Solomon's ring. Were the two things connected in some way?

The Demonriders were hard at work, dragging bodies from the trees and storing them in the barn. Riley could hear their uneasy whispers to one another, and saw the furtive glances they shot at Nathan Goodrum, Father Logan, and the now sedate Eric Stewarth. That was a mutiny in the making. The Demonriders wouldn't follow Nathan for long once word got out that Father Logan had compromised him. They walked wide of the area where the Blind Prophet had been. Spooked by his impossible disappearance. The funnel from his mouth lay broken as if he'd partially bitten through the spout.

Goodrum pulled his SUV up beside the other car and got out. One by one, his men came and handed him their assault rifles to be stored in the cargo rack. He spoke to each man in a low voice and ended with a familiar slap on the back. Clearly trying to undo the doubt David had cast on him. Afterward, they milled about beside the barn, standing in a loose huddle discussing something in low voices. When all the weaponry was securely stored and the bodies dragged into the barn, Goodrum unslung his own rifle, working the slide to check the ammunition. Satisfied everything was as it should be, he raised the gun and opened fire on his men.

The bullets tore into them so quickly the shock of betrayal did not even register on most of their faces. Eight men were dead in as many seconds. Riley could see their demons set free, dim, low-level creatures blinking in surprise at the sudden and unexpected freedom. Each waiting instinctively for a tug that never came, until at last, realizing it wasn't coming, they dispersed, fleeing from the scene of the slaughter with yips and howls. Had the woman who shot him been among those killed? He wasn't sure.

Riley's ears rang with a new pitch of agony. On the ground before him, the Blind Prophet's driver wriggled frantically, no doubt anticipating his turn coming.

Goodrum didn't come for him, though. He placed his rifle in the SUV and then began dragging the bodies of his former brothers and sisters into the barn with the others. Eric Stewarth rose, unbeckoned, and helped him. When it was done, Goodrum produced a jerry can from within the barn and began to slosh its contents among the dead and the dried timbers and hay. He ran a trail out of the barn and then tossed the empty can back inside.

He rummaged inside the vehicle for a moment and appeared again with a book of matches. It took him three tries before the trail of fuel ignited, the flames racing its length in half a second, a whumph as the whole structure went up. Riley felt the impact in his chest, then the heat that scorched the back of his neck and set him forward in the dirt, squirming and wiggling away. The heat became bearable as he reached the trussed driver. Riley watched the fire dancing in the other man's eyes.

These were vile men. Riley longed to kill them as much for their crimes against him as for those against their own people. He vied for the soul stone forgotten in his jacket pocket, but that, like focusing his eyes, proved a task beyond him.

We have to escape! A familiar voice in his head with an unfamiliar note of hysteria.

"There is no escape," he mumbled numbly. He could barely see, and his mind felt sluggish and dull. When they came for him, he didn't resist, but he couldn't help much either. They had to carry him by his arms and legs, and had just buckled him into the prophet's car when he threw up, retching into his lap and the floor.

"Piss on it!" Goodrum roared, rage and frustration in his voice unequal to the offense. Moments later, the other man was shoved into the car and the door slammed. The engine purred to life, but Riley couldn't have said where they went. He was unconscious before their tires found the pavement.

An explosion boomed out across the clover field. It was enough to drag Brooklyn bleary-eyed and aching back to reality. Instinctively, she reached for Belial, but he wasn't there. He was more absent than he'd ever been. In the past, even when they weren't connected by a tether, she could still reach out to him, draw on his cool energies for strength.

Ahead of her, the hillside erupted into flames. The smell of smoke and something more acrid drifted to her on the breeze a moment later.

She turned as a new calamity met her ears. It was the search party advancing with their dogs unleashed, their guns leveled, and bellowing a confusion of shouted orders. Brooklyn turned to run, but a sudden weight took her behind the knees; then everything was a blur of snarls and teeth. She covered her face with her arms as the dogs pinned her, dragging her by the leg and shaking her when she struggled. Brooklyn quested for her last soul stone, but it was pinned between her own body and the ground. A moment later, the dogs were pulled back and her wrists were cuffed. Dimly she could hear the officers shouting at her, adrenaline making their voices wavering and high. A loud thumping drew her attention, and she knew without looking that it was the remaining helicopter setting down.

With the blades still spinning, the pilot leapt out. The dogs went wild, tugging against the leashes, startling their handlers. The spinning propellers blew the hair back from her face and Brooklyn locked eyes with the pilot. She saw confusion there, a man suddenly roused from a dream only to find upon waking that he didn't know where he was. The moment stretched on uncomfortably until some instinct kicked in and the man drew his firearm and charged directly at her.

Behind her, the dogs frenzied, and the men screamed. The pilot leapt over her, his handgun popping off a stream of shots as steady as a drumbeat. She rolled onto her back, struggling to sit up, wounds reopening and oozing blood. Awkwardly, she gained her knees. The grass was trampled and bloody. One of the dogs stood over its handler, jaws locked on his throat. The officer's feet kicked convulsively.

Another officer clutched his wrist to his chest, blood flowing freely from his arm as he used his uninjured arm to yank ineffectually on the second dog's leash. This dog was attacking the other one, snarling and tearing at its fur-bristled back. One of the pilot's bullets tore the attacking animal free of the downed man and sent it tumbling away with a yelp.

Why were the dogs turning on their handlers and one another? Brooklyn wondered as she struggled to get to her feet. She didn't want to be lying prone when the dogs turned their attention her way, so she backed away from the massacre on trembling legs, keeping her eyes on the crazed animals.

The surviving dog growled low in its chest and bared bloody fangs. It lunged for the two remaining officers. One of them turned tail and ran; the other dropped to a knee and began firing at the approaching dog. Muscles rippled under the dog's fur as he stretched himself to full length, closing the distance in bounds. The cop's gun clicked empty and the German shepherd gathered itself to leap upon the man. Another shot rang out and the dog fell into a heap, lifeless as a pile of dirty laundry.

"Thank you," the man choked out, struggling to get back on his feet. "You saved my life."

The pilot, who had fired the shot, went rigid and shuddered as if suffering a chill. After a long moment he offered the kneeling man a hand. When the officer was halfway to his feet, the pilot pivoted, driving an elbow into the man's jaw with all his weight. He crumpled back to the ground and didn't rise. "Now I've saved your life."

"What the hell?" Brooklyn murmured to herself, still trying to coax her traitorous legs into doing their job and getting her the hell out of there.

The pistol dropped from the pilot's nerveless fingers, forgotten. He turned toward the mountain where a dozen more lights were approaching in the distance. Brooklyn tensed as he came for her. She turned to run and took four loping steps before her legs turned to jelly and dumped her back into dirt.

He grabbed her then and she kicked him in the shins. She almost took his legs out from under him, but he recovered and hauled her roughly to her feet. She struggled to break free of his grip as the pilot dragged her toward the helicopter. He gave her a rough shake and spun her around. "Stop it. I'm trying to help you."

Could she trust him? She glanced back at the mountainside where dozens of flashlight beams bounced wildly among the trees. She really didn't have a choice it seemed. One questionable ally versus two dozen angry police officers. Before she could consider it further, he opened the cuffs and hoisted her into the helicopter.

"Strap in," he ordered, flipping switches and checking gauges. The blades whirred to speed above them, but she could hear gunshots ringing out over them. The police radio squawked with demands until the pilot reached over and shut it off. Then, with a lurch, they shot up and angled away.

"Where are we going?"

He didn't answer, instead focusing all his attention on the controls and gauges as they rose higher. She studied him and wondered why he'd want to help her. Did she know him? Chiseled face, too square to be attractive or expressive, a severe jaw and a broad nose, clean shaven, hair cropped close to accommodate a receding hairline.

The fields and trees rolled beneath them like a dark sea. Brooklyn didn't know who this man was, or why he'd turned on his own people to help her, or where they were going, but she didn't have the strength to pursue her curiosity.

She leaned her forehead against the cool glass of the canopy and slipped away for what seemed only a minute, but when she woke, the quality of the light seemed different. "Why won't you talk to me?" she asked after what seemed an interminable silence, broken only by the sound of the propellers and the winds that jostled them left and right.

"Concentrating," he answered through gritted teeth as if speaking while flying were a taxing endeavor.

Brooklyn wanted to say more, to ask more, to understand who this strange man was and why he'd ruin his own life to help her escape. He could be a Demonrider, she mused, or one of Father Logan's prophets. Might she have been better off with the police?

She called out for Belial over and over, but there was no reply. No whisper of his icy presence. Tears stung her eyes, but she blinked them away. She didn't want to admit it, but she'd become attached to him, and now he'd abandoned her at the worst possible time. Feeling very stupid for believing a demon could be her friend, she curled around her loneliness and slept again.

Brooklyn woke with a start; the world lurched around her. Another jolt broke her stupor and the sound of the rotors spinning down let her know they'd landed. The first hints of gray dawn spilled across her lap as she fumbled for the harness release. Brooklyn reached for Belial and found nothing. She couldn't stop seeking him, like a tongue returning again and again to probe an empty tooth socket.

Her attention turned to the pilot, busily unbuckling his own safety belt. His face was a picture of exhaustion, dark circles, strain lines, the whole nine yards. She reached out tentatively and touched his shoulder. He grew still, then turned to face her.

"You should get out," he said flatly. "I can't leave the bird here."

"Oh." She didn't know what she'd expected, but it wasn't this. "Thank you," she added at last. He had kind, brown eyes. The moment stretched, and he looked as if he were about to say something, but then shook his head softly. She felt like she should know him. Something about him was achingly familiar, but damned if she could place it.

"Go," he said, flipping switches and reconnecting the harness he'd just unbuckled.

She opened the door and climbed down, keeping her head low as she stumbled away from the windy vortex. He lifted off and turned in a lazy circle before angling north and west, fleeing the rising sun. She watched him until the beat of the blades no longer reached her ears and a while longer until he vanished across the twilit horizon.

Her legs trembled. It was cold, and she wasn't dressed for it. Brooklyn took stock of her injuries, plenty of which still oozed blood. There were countless other pains that bespoke her unhealthy exertions from the night before.

As the dawn broke at long last across the distant mountains, Brooklyn realized where she was. The last time she'd been here, these fields were full of failing corn, but now they lay fallow, cut, and cleared. Beyond the fields were a shed and an old house. "Mrs. Mays." She said the old woman's name reverently like a prayer as she hobbled toward safety.

Mrs. Mays, not the kind of woman to let a helicopter landing in her fields go unnoticed, met Brooklyn in the yard with a shotgun tucked casually under one arm.

"Mrs. Mays," Brooklyn called out, her voice cracking with an emotion she couldn't name.

"Brooke?" The large woman rushed over, pulling her into a bear hug that left her wondering if she might still have some cracked ribs as well. Breaking the embrace, Mrs. Mays ran her eyes along the tree line at the edge of her property. "Come on, it isn't safe for you out here." She stooped under one of Brooklyn's arms and sped her toward the house.

25

Praise or Perish

"Fool! You risked everything, everyone! Do you know how many people depend on you?"

"This is your fault." David bristled. The caution that normally censored his tongue when speaking to all-powerful supernatural entities seemed to have abandoned him. "I do whatever you ask, and in return I ask but one thing, only one, and you won't help me. One. Damn. Thing." He turned away. She was a brightness that hurt his blind eyes, and brighter still when angry. After a steadying breath and a moment he continued. "I'm glad you saved me, I . . . thank you for it, but I won't stop looking for her."

"Logan's coming for you, you know that, right? You stole everything from him."

"We stole everything from him."

"You should never have exposed yourself like that. You have tens of thousands of expendable people you could have sent. An army of people, any of whom can be replaced." She stepped close and touched his cheek gently, her hand fever warm. "You cannot be replaced, David. Do you understand? You are not expendable. If you die, they are cut off from me. If you die, they all die. You are their head, so you need to start using yours."

"Then why won't you help me find Brooklyn? Bring her here where she can be safe with me. Then everything will be fine. Then I'll be safe."

"I cannot." She breathed it softly, a note of exasperation in her voice. "A prior oath prevents me."

"What oath? To who?" His mind raced. How could he find Brooklyn now? Could he help her escape? All he needed to do was—

"Just concern yourself with your oaths to me, David." She touched him between the eyes with her fingernail and the world exploded into light. The universe was a mirror, shattered and spreading across the unfathomable darkness, suddenly recalled to wholeness, all the pieces and the light they held snapping back into place. "I'm growing stronger every day. I'm consolidating power because the dam between worlds is breaking, and when it goes, this world will never be the same. There must be hope in the chaos. You and I must be ready to stand against the tide. Do you understand how important this is, how important you are going to be?"

"I think so." He gasped, his brain on fire, a silver splinter at its center expanding until it felt like his skull would burst open.

"I cannot give you what you want, but take this gift, use it to remember this world and these people, use it to understand what you—we—are fighting for. It won't last, so treasure the hours you have." With a whoosh, she was gone.

On the floor, rapidly losing its mystical glow, another feather. Then, like the breaking of dawn, the shadows lifted from his vision, colors swirled in a teary kaleidoscope, and then the room snapped into focus and he sobbed to see it.

David hurried from his room and down the stairs, out into the chilly morning air. The sun was rising, gray light taking on a tinge of pink that slowly darkened to a virgin's blush, until a shock of yellow broke across the blue ridge mountains.

He pushed the image out, feeding it into the brains of all those in his giant web. Giving sight for the first time instead of taking it from others. He pushed the image to his driver, Marshall. David could feel the man's terror and the pain of being tied up for so long, the darkness, and the smell of vomit. He showed Marshall the sunrise, letting its glory blossom in his mind and eclipse his fears and discomforts. *Praise Azrael*, he thought, and all around him, the praise rang out. He felt the words leave Marshall's lips and heard another man asking from the darkness what he'd said. Marshall said it again, louder, as the mountains took on a royal blue and the sun burned away the night, drawing mists upward to lie like scarves across the ridges.

Did you say Azrael? the voice asked Marshall frantically. *Is that what you said?*

David smiled and felt Marshall's lips curl as if they were his own, then form the words, "She's coming. Praise or perish."

As the sun struggled free of the horizon and began to climb, David reached out to Marshall in his moment of jubilation and cut the threads that bound him to this world.

Dravin Logan had only felt terror, true heart-pounding fear and dread, a handful of times in his life, and this was one of those times. The stakes had never been higher. He'd had the world, the whole damned world, in his hands and now it was slipping away like sand between his fingers. He held the feather in his lap and examined it with his flashlight. Its surface, once glossy black, was charred, and it looked as if it might crumble to dust at the slightest provocation. This was the only thing remaining from the usurper's disappearance, and he'd seen its twin only hours before. Seen it and delivered it, like a fool, to Kurt Levin.

Part of him wanted to rush into those underground caverns and verify Kurt was still safely imprisoned and withering away. The other part knew if he had escaped, going down would waste precious time needed to solidify his influence. Only one thing had gone as planned. He had that little jerk, Eric, on a leash now.

Whatever had happened with Kurt and his feather, it was already past tense. He had to believe that. He would play it safe, stay under heavy guard, and if another month went by without Kurt showing up on his doorstep looking for revenge, he would go down and see the body to put his mind at ease. Another month without supplies would be enough to finish the old bastard.

Having thought himself to this conclusion, he felt the edges of his panic fraying under the pressure of solid reasoning and necessity. There was nothing to worry about because it was already done and decided. No choices for him to make, no further chance of failure.

He reached out across his tiny web to Eric and let him know what he wanted him to do. Then, with an almost frantic energy humming in his veins against the fatigue building into a dull ache behind his eyes, he steeled himself for this last, crucial thing. For the next part of his plan to be successful, he needed supplies, very special supplies. Supplies he could only get in one place. For the first time in close to a year, he was going home.

26

Strays

Belial felt himself fraying with the effort of keeping his host on task. To take full control and lock the man away in his own mind would have been an easier task, but the problem was that he needed the pilot's knowledge and skills to operate the helicopter. It was a constant balancing act to keep enough control to influence the man's behavior, but not so much that his host lost usefulness.

Besides his own fatigue, his host's exhaustion and terror fell on him like unrelenting waves, taxing his concentration and his will. He kept telling himself, a little further, just a little longer. He wasn't sure how far they had come or how much of what was happening his host would remember tomorrow. The safest course of action would be to plow into the side of a mountain and eliminate any memories the pilot had made. It's what his father would do. No loose ends.

It was going to be hard enough to get Brooklyn to trust him again, temperamental as she was. Hopefully she would understand there wasn't time to discuss, only time to act. With the dogs closing in and a band of Demonriders waiting ahead of them in the trees, he had no choice but to act at once. Killing someone unnecessarily wouldn't go far in regaining her trust.

These thoughts were cut short by an insistent buzzing and a glowing dash light that proclaimed *Low Fuel*. He could feel his host's response. This was a serious issue, but it wasn't his issue, so he slipped free of the pilot and let the last vestiges of the Pull buffet him out of the flying machine and onto the spiral path between worlds where all the souls of Earth and spirits of Hell burned like Christmas lights, and where some, like the one he searched for, blazed like dying stars.

The Pull was as weak as it had ever been. A casual suggestion in place of the unrelenting compulsion he was accustomed to. It was weak enough that even in his drained state, he knew he could escape it. It was weak enough that he feared his father could throw it off as well. Prosidris would come for him, and soon. There was power in the Tomes, power Prosidris wanted, power he would use Belial to access since the timeless texts opened like flowers beneath his claw-tipped fingers, yielding up their secret truths with an eagerness that was almost perverse.

The Tomes tempted him even now, calling with the promise of knowledge and understanding. Power to throw off his shackles and be truly free. But Brooklyn was hurt, on the run; she needed him. Even if she didn't admit that to herself. If Prosidris showed up while Belial was with Brooklyn, she would be caught in the crossfire. He couldn't protect her from his father any more than he'd been able to protect Tais all those long centuries ago.

Brooklyn needed him, but she didn't understand the dangers that lay ahead. Somewhere in those Tomes were the answers to all the problems looming on the horizon. So, with a heavy heart, he fell.

Mrs. Mays really couldn't say why all the strays found their way to her house. Not just Brooklyn, but all manner of cast-offs and wander-abouts. Today it was a tabby tomcat that looked like he hadn't eaten a good meal since being weaned from the mama-cat's tit. He was scraggly and lean, with a tail like a corn cob.

At the thought of corn cobs, she looked out on her fields wistfully. Mrs. Mays wasn't sure she'd ever taste corn again, not the slop from a can, but real golden ears, buttered and salted.

"Easy, old boy," she crooned as she approached the glider where he lay stretched.

There was a wildness in his eyes as she approached, a growing tension and distrust. He drew his feet under him and eyed her as if to say, "One more step and I'll run, old woman." Mrs. Mays didn't go any closer. Tom was going to take some persuading.

She backed away and pulled the screen door open. After rummaging in the kitchen pantry, she came up with a can of StarKist tuna, trundled back out, and eased into her rocker, setting the open can down between her chair and Tom's glider.

Tom took immediate notice, sitting up, nose and whiskers twitching. "Well, come on, fella, come fill your belly, won't you?" she cajoled. He came, eyeing her suspiciously the whole way. When he was deep into the tuna, she settled a well-worn hand on his back and stroked him lightly. She knew from experience when the eating was done, the purring would come. Cats and people were a lot alike.

Her other stray hadn't done much but sleep since she'd dropped quite literally out of the sky yesterday. Brooklyn was pretty banged up. She'd been on the run for a long time. Mrs. Mays had followed the news reports and wondered where the fool-girl was going and what she was up to, breaking into sheriffs' offices and riding gurneys down the yellow line.

Tom finished his food and purred as she knew he would, nudging his head upward against her hand. She was scratching his ears and gazing out to where the fields sloped up and joined the mountain. There, amid the trees, a shadow was moving. She sat up straighter, squinting against the noonday sun until her third stray in not as many days staggered out into the light.

27

REUNION

Kurt could already tell that Azrael was going to be a bitch to serve. On the sealing of their deal with a not-unpleasant kiss, she had kept her word in extracting him from his subterranean prison and left him shivering in the woods to sort the rest out for himself. He knew he couldn't go home and there was only one other place to go. So, he'd put his back to his—well, Protector Goodrum's—manor and started off at a measured pace.

The sunrise, when it finally came, was a thing of blinding beauty. His eyes ran like faucets, the sweet pain of morning. The last time he'd made this walk, he'd been brimming with nervous energy and righteous anger. Now he made the walk as an old man, joints aching and footing unsure, picking his way carefully around the mountainside toward the farm of Amelia Mays, and worrying all the while that if he fell, he might not rise again.

Out here in the open, the preceding months took on a surreal quality, like a long, laborious dream, the details receding like shadows before the sunlight, until only a sense of unease remained. A quickening of the pulse in the presence of unnamable terrors.

He stopped once, in a clearing that seemed familiar, and pulled the last of the food from his filthy rags. It was a beef-and-cheese stick. There in the day's warmth, with a gentle breeze stirring, it may have been the most delicious food he'd ever tasted. Afterward, he leaned back against an old hickory tree and tilted his head back to watch the squirrels chattering above him. They moved in sprints, up or down the trunk, or out onto swaying limbs, taking daring leaps from one leafless branch to the next.

Kurt closed his eyes and sank into a blessedly dreamless sleep.

Brooklyn came awake by degrees, first aware of a headache, throbbing and refusing to let her sleep longer, then the stiffness of her muscles, and finally the memory of yesterday. Her body felt like one enormous bruise, and when she tried to sit up, the muscles in her stomach protested with sharp agony. Her arms were bandaged, and she was clean, could still smell the soap in her hair. The nightgown she wore was several sizes too large and hung loose and billowy to her ankles.

How bad is it? she thought at Belial, but he wasn't there. Brooklyn was alone in her head. It didn't matter. She shouldn't have expected anything more than betrayal from a demon anyway. She slid to the edge of the bed and settled her weight onto her legs, making sure they intended to do their job before she took the first tentative step toward the bathroom. A Walmart bag hung from the doorknob with jeans and shirts, a toothbrush and hairbrush, and deodorant. Not the brand she normally used, but what was that saying about beggars?

Taking the stuff with her to the bathroom, she emerged almost an hour later, feeling mostly alive again. There was a shoe box on the desk and a coat with the tags still on it draped across the chair. She hobbled to the window and peeked out. The slant of the sun told her she'd already slept most of the day away.

Brooklyn descended the stairs gingerly and followed the sound of the television into the living room. When she rounded the corner, there was Mrs. Mays and—and Kurt. Not the Kurt she remembered, this was a shell of that man, with slumped shoulders and hollow eyes, but when a grin broadened his face, she saw the man she remembered wasn't wholly gone after all. He stood and opened his arms and she fell into them.

"It's good to see you," he rumbled.

"You too," she said, feeling wrong-footed by this surprise. "We thought you were dead."

"Almost was," Mrs. Mays interjected. "How about you both sit down? You ain't made of glass." She gestured impatiently at the television they were blocking.

Brooklyn settled onto the sofa beside Kurt. She knew the news would be about her before she even glanced at the TV.

"—aerial footage available," the newscaster commented as the view shifted to a camera man in a helicopter. A great cloud of smoke hung over the clover, and other whirlybirds were dumping foam on the blaze. Next, they flashed photos of Brooklyn and a square-faced man with receding hair. It took a moment to place him as the pilot that had ferried her to safety. "If you have any information, call 911 immediately. Both should be considered armed and extremely dangerous."

Mrs. Mays clicked the television off with a grunt of disapproval. "The Heir named her a fugitive at the last conclave, and now he's called another meeting out of turn. It's gotta be related."

Kurt looked at Brooklyn like she'd just said something really interesting, but she had not spoken. It made her feel uncomfortable and self-conscious. He was old enough to be her father. Why was he looking at her so . . . intensely?

"When is this conclave?" Brooklyn asked.

Mrs. Mays grunted. "Hmm. Near about two weeks. They've called everyone in, from all over the world."

"We have to find somewhere to hide you, someplace safe where you can keep your head down," Kurt added.

Brooklyn quirked a smile. "Witness protection, huh?"

"Something like that, yeah."

The conversation about how best to keep her safe continued on, but she lost the thread of it. Was that what she wanted? To live in hiding? The last year was a blur, always on the move, looking over her shoulder. But for Belial, the loneliness of it might have driven her mad, and now he had abandoned her. There was no way to clear her name of the murders; for all intents and purposes she *had* committed them. There would never be a normal life for her again. She had only this new world in which to carve out a place for herself, and now the supernatural leaders wanted to make a fugitive of her as well.

"—then after a while we could get her out of the country." Mrs. Mays finished some point she'd been making.

Kurt nodded. "That could work. Though it won't be easy."

Brooklyn laughed. "I'm done with running and hiding. If Eric Stewarth wants to put me on trial or offer me asylum, he'll get his chance at the conclave. I'm going."

"The hell you are," Kurt rumbled at her like distant thunder and at the same time Mrs. Mays said, "No, you won't."

Brooklyn regarded them both levelly. She had known they would be against it, but she couldn't account for the intense disdain she felt bubbling up in her throat like some caustic chemical. Who were either of them to tell her where she could go? What claim did they think they had on her? The unexpected intensity of her anger thrilled and terrified her in equal measures. So caught up was she in this rapture of indignation, she didn't notice the barest wisps of warming vapor snaking free of her clenched fist.

It made a certain sense. Kurt was the man that had held her, and David, against their wills for weeks. Might David still be alive if Kurt hadn't forced them into a situation where they had to flee in order to be free to see their families again? Hell, David might really be alive if she could trust in the poisonous words Nathan Goodrum had spewed at her last year.

Brooklyn looked at them both. Kurt, with his sunken eyes and hanging jowls; the only thing that hinted at the position and power he'd once held were his too-bright amber eyes. The way they tracked her face, flashing with challenge, with some authority he clearly thought he had over her. Mrs. Mays with a softer, more concerned expression, like the look a parent might cast after a child headed down a bad path and denying it all the while. It was a mixture of helplessness, disappointment, and worry that reminded her of her own mom during those last days when the screen door would slam behind Erin, and in the vacuum of silence that followed she would gaze at the door, or out the window, watching through the gauzy curtains until Erin's car turned on the main road and vanished. Forlorn. That was the word. Her mother had looked forlorn and now Mrs. Mays was looking forlorn, too.

Huffing a deep breath, Brooklyn said, "I'm not running anymore," meaning it to sound firm and resolute, but it came out dripping venom.

"Brooklyn"—Kurt favored her with a tired, patient smile—"even if you go and somehow get into the meeting, what do you expect the outcome will be? How do you think you'll get out again? What will this accomplish?"

"What do I want to accomplish? I want them to leave me the fuck alone. And as for the rest of it, I don't know yet. I've got two weeks to figure it out." She softened her voice, looking between them so she didn't have to meet the fiery intensity of Kurt's gaze, or see the tears brimming and balanced on Mrs. Mays's bottom eyelids. "I need your help with getting in and out again. I'm not willing to be stopped, but I would be grateful for help." These were the right words. She felt them leaving her lips and already knew, with a sly sense of self-satisfaction, how they would be received.

Kurt sank back in his chair, shaking his head wearily. "You remind me so much of my boy."

"She reminds me of mine, too," Mrs. Mays added in a hoarse whisper. She cleared her throat. "We'll help you, but we are also going to do our best to talk you out of this foolishness every hour of every day between now and then." And she added, "You best watch your language in my house."

This seemed to Brooklyn a perfectly reasonable and fair agreement.

Over dinner, they marveled at how the world had changed since they last saw one another. They discussed the Protector's mansion and what the security would be like, and talked about the tunnels under the mountain. Kurt shuddered at the mention of reentering them and advised against it, claiming the tunnels had collapsed behind him from the rocket explosion as he escaped into them during the siege last year. One big dead end, nothing but a tomb now.

Kurt didn't last long and was snoring softly in a recliner before Mrs. Mays had rinsed the last plate. Brooklyn wasn't tired and busied herself cleaning the table and sweeping the floor, relishing the aching of her bruised muscles, and falling back into the languid rhythm of farm life as easily as if she'd never left. It was soothing, mindless work. She hadn't realized it until this quiet moment that something about her was different. She couldn't say what it was or when it had begun, but she knew it to be true just the same. Knew it as surely as she knew her own name. What was it, though? The question worried her like a persistent fly, buzzing, demanding attention, always flitting away before she could clap her hands closed on it.

28

GOING TO CHURCH

Hell had gone—well—to hell since the last time Belial had been here. The soul sun hung heavy as a rotten peach in the center of all things. Across the barren landscape, a seething carpet of creatures vied for position near a dozen or so rippling distortions in the air, like fumes over gasoline. Growls and snarls intermingled with grunts and yelps. Claws and teeth flashing like dueling blades in the sullen light.

The higher caste, those with wings, like himself, flitted above it all looking a lot like the angels they were, he supposed, or once might have been, in this religion or that one. *No, that's not right*, he thought. They looked more like a swarm of dragonflies. The throng grew thickest toward the Colossus, a sprawling complex of structures built from the same dried-out and flaking semi-stone the whole place seemed to be formed from, like some toddler's abandoned play-dough world, poorly executed and forgotten. At the center, a tower rose so high it seemed, by some trick of angle and proportion, to touch the glowering face of the sun.

Unfortunately, the library lay inside the cliffs on the far side of the Colossus. There was no getting there easily. By foot would be a slow and dangerous trek through the hoards, and the heart of the city, and by wing would present the danger of recognition. Word would doubtlessly find his father more quickly than he could make the trek. He froze with indecision, and the crowd raged around him like a river parting around a stone. He felt claustrophobic in the press, but steeled himself resolutely and put one foot before the other, and kept his wings tucked tightly behind him along with thoughts of Brooklyn, Tais, and the dragon girl whose name he'd never known.

Father Logan knelt to pray. He tugged up the collar of the sweat-ripened army jacket he'd bought from a homeless man that morning. Around him were eyes and ears that fed information to David Sterling, just the way they'd fed it to him once upon a time. He needed the eyes to slide over his dirty face without recognition, noses to smell the harmless cologne of body odor, and ears to detect an unfamiliar voice. He needed to be overlooked and invisible.

The service droned on a litany of praises, prayers, sermons, and so forth. He heard no mention of Azrael here. This was his third service in as many days. He didn't want to seem overeager. Recruitment was a seduction, and sometimes one had to be coy.

He hung back as the service ended, taking his time admiring the biblical stories rendered in ornate stained glass. Here the crucifixion, there the resurrection, the last supper, standard fare. It took a long time for the crowd to filter out, but he wanted to be the last man out the door past the aged, balding man bestowing blessings on all these righteous attendees. Not the pastor that delivered the sermon, but some secondary minister or apostle, or perhaps he had once been the leader of this congregation, relegated in his dotage to a more circumspect role.

The man watched Dravin's downtrodden approach. He played up the slowness with a slight limp, and the fellow actually smiled with some saintly patience for Dravin's afflictions that he himself couldn't have mustered. He longed to sprint the last few feet and get this done finally.

But he hadn't suffered three days of boring sermons to jump the gun now. Instead, he plodded up with his uneven gait, and never quite met the other man's eyes as he said, "I . . . I'd like to learn more."

"Bless you," the man crooned, raising a liver-spotted hand to his shoulder and resting it there without the slightest indication he was repulsed by the general filth and body odor of his supplicant. "There are pamphlets outside with all our services and events listed. There's a family night barbeque this Wednesday that—"

"I don't have any family . . . not really." He chanced a look up to gauge the other man's reaction and got nothing but kindly eyes that might have belonged to Santa Clause for all their joy and fervor.

"Oh, that's unfortunate. You live alone then?"

Was that eagerness he heard behind the question? He struggled to suppress a smile. This was almost too easy. "Guess you could say that," he mumbled. "I stay at a week-rate motel when I got the money, the rest of the time . . ." He shrugged and left his homelessness unsaid.

"Well, it's a terrible thing to be down on your luck. We work with several other churches in the area . . . It's a ministry to help people who might otherwise go overlooked. You know, fall through the cracks, so to speak."

"I'm not looking for a handout," Logan interjected. "I don't want you to think that!"

"Of course, of course," the other man placated, "but you are looking for something, aren't you? Something more than you've been able to squeeze out of life so far? To have purpose? To be a part of something bigger than yourself, perhaps?"

"Something bigger." He repeated the words slowly, even felt his eyes go watery with emotion. "Something bigger sounds nice."

Santa Clause magicked a card from his sleeve and pressed it into his hand. "This is an invitation to an off-site meeting, a service for those looking for something more . . . immediate." He closed his hands over Dravin's, wrapping his fingers tight around the card. "Don't lose it. You cannot get into the service without this invitation. I hope we'll see you there."

Dravin looked up and met the man's gaze at last, as if only now able to muster the self-worth to look into those kindly eyes, and said, "I'll be there."

Kurt woke when the sun was still just a gray promise beyond the mountains, a fragile thing that he could almost believe might never struggle free of the horizon. He imagined a world stillborn into eternal twilight. *Was that a twinge of the old madness?*

It didn't bear thinking on, so he got up and stretched aching muscles, then went about the business of dressing and starting his day. As soon as he stepped into the hallway, the scent of coffee let him know he wasn't the first one up this morning.

He stepped lightly as he passed Brooklyn's door, put his hand to the stained wood for a moment, and eyed the brass knob speculatively. *Not your boy anymore*, he chided himself, and pushed on down the hallway.

In the kitchen, he found a plate with apple slices and a solid handful of the horse pill vitamins Amelia had been shoving down his throat since he stumbled into her fields a week ago. He wasn't sure if they were helping or not, but he swallowed them all at once with a gulp of coffee and a grimace.

Outside, the sun had waxed orange and cast narrow shadows across the porch steps. Kurt descended on legs that still weren't as strong and steady as he would have liked. *It's a bitch being old and malnourished.*

What's the matter, old man? You've endured worse.

Yeah, but I endured it with a little liquor to help me along.

He found Mrs. Mays in the barn. He followed a series of staccato thwapping sounds until he saw her at the far end circling a homemade wooden practice dummy. It was a cylinder as tall as a man with wooden appendages spaced around its circumference at various heights and angles. The top section spun; a wooden arm whistled toward her head. With a dancer's grace that belied her size and build, her arm rose and stopped the blow cold. By some unseen mechanism, all the arrested momentum transferred to the lower section, which sliced the air with speed. She deftly blocked by shifting subtly and raising a leg to intercept. The middle section leapt into action immediately, forcing her to duck down, avoiding the appendage, but rising instantly to slap the next one away. As that section spun in reverse, both the bottom and the top engaged opposite directions. The next three blocks came like automatic gunfire then a softer impact as the dummy took her legs, spilling her onto the dusty, packed earth.

Kurt offered a hand; she shook her head and climbed to her feet. "That the one Riley made for you?"

She slapped her hands across her jeans. Small dust plumes erupted from the denim. "So it is." She smiled. "Want a turn?"

Kurt shook his head. "Too old and feeble for that." He scratched at the stubble on his chin. It still felt strange without the matted beard he'd worn in captivity. "You should teach Brooklyn."

She leaned against the wall and raised her chin. "Why you angling to help this girl? She's cost you a lot already. I expected you'd be gone by now, scheming your way back to the top."

"It was never like that—"

"It was always like that, and you know it. So, tell me what's different now. Tell me why you haven't tried to take that girl and bargain your way back into good graces."

Because she's my son, he didn't say. Kurt fumbled for an answer. He'd saved Brooklyn before he even knew she was the vessel Azrael had chosen to hold his son's reincarnated soul. He'd risked himself and his position to do it, but Mrs. Mays had good reasons to see him the way she did. Nothing he said would ever change that. "It's not that simple." He rubbed the back of his head and turned a steel bucket upside down to sit on. "Selling her out wouldn't do me any good. He thinks I stole his birthright, his family's greatest weapon, that I betrayed his father. There's no buying back good grace after that.

"Besides, if the things Dravin told me are true, Eric's beyond forgiving, and I'll see him die for what he did to my people."

"Mhmm," she said. "See, that's the problem. So many young people with power they ain't ready for yet. Sometimes they turn into monsters, and sometimes they die like my boy, and sometimes they get old, like you. But what they never get is ready. So, if you want to help Brooklyn, you talk her out of this foolish idea, and if you can't do that, you help by getting her ready. If you don't, a quick death is the best option she'll get."

Kurt wanted to make a retort, but wilted under the heat of her gaze. So instead, he said, "I'll help her get out of this mess alive. I swear I will." She studied him for a long time, as if sieving sand for sincerity. Finally, she nodded and turned back to her practice.

29

Darkness Comes

Riley glared at the charred feather on the table. Azrael's feather. Father Logan wanted its secrets sussed out. He had questions, and for the moment at least, he believed Riley could provide answers. But how to keep him believing it? Maybe he could draw the task out for months. Maybe. So long as Dravin believed Riley could and would help, there was little fear of less pleasant outcomes.

Father Logan wasn't prone to fits of impatient rage like Eric Stewarth had been, but he associated Riley with Kurt. And he hated Kurt, and by extension, Riley. There wasn't much Riley could do about it, though, so it wasn't really worth worrying over. The greater danger, he believed, lay in completing the task and thus having no promise of immediate usefulness to his captors. The other danger lay in producing too little progress and frustrating them.

You know where the answers are hidden, his companion crooned inside his head.

Indeed, he did if "hidden" meant buried under a metric ton of rubble three stories below him. To give the location of the Tome to Logan would be to betray Kurt, well, his memory anyway. More importantly, it probably meant drinking a funnel full of darkness because he was no longer needed. There were very few ways forward that left his free will intact. He'd best tread carefully.

Why do you suppose David Sterling is still alive? Didn't Kurt say there was no chance he'd survived? And why would Azrael be working with him now? Was it some arrangement of Kurt's? A final deal with the devil he knew before he died?

"I don't know." Riley sighed under his breath. "It really doesn't matter. What we need is a plan to get out of here." He gestured vaguely in the door's direction and the infernal puzzle lock that defeated his every attempt to escape.

For all your brilliance, you really are quite stupid sometimes, his companion commented with a tremulousness that verged on restrained laughter. *Remember how you heated the Tome trying to make the words appear? But that didn't work here in this world, did it?*

"It was the temperature differential that did it. At a certain temperature, my approach would have worked. Plus—"

Remember when you were trying to create the first soul stones?

"They were called ICMs. Inanimate corporeal manifestations," he retorted, though he hadn't thought of them as that since the night Brooklyn renamed them. "What does this have to do with anything?" Riley could hear a whiny quality in his voice that he didn't like. *Why does being called stupid make me so . . .*

Angry? My apologies, now may I continue?

Riley stood and walked to the window, gazing out across the early winter fields. There were mountains beyond them, but the day was drizzly, and a dense fog followed the course of the river and shrouded everything like a bridal veil. *Of course, please continue*, he thought.

Remember the trouble you had? How many times did you almost give it up for being impossible?

It was true. He'd worn himself ragged with his efforts. He'd read accounts of primitive people who had cut their own toes off to use the bones as telekinetic weapons. One night, after a particularly brutal series of failures, he'd settled the cool weight of a cleaver against his pinky toe. Pressing by degrees until a thin line of blood beaded around the blade, the pain made him flinch and fling the knife into the corner. The solution had come to him then, wholly formed, understanding as fragile as an egg, but with as much potential. How to fuse the organic and the inorganic.

I remember, he thought at last.

When you play the game by the rules, you play it brilliantly, and you lose. Your most astonishing successes have always been when you swept aside the rules, what others defined as 'truth,' and upended the whole game. It's why I joined with you in the first place. So please, quit fiddling with that lock, which was clearly designed as an intentional distraction, and quit weighing the likely outcomes of helping Dravin Logan versus thwarting him. That's you playing their game, and rule number one of their game is that you don't get to win. Look around! You have the tools, and materials, and more knowledge than anyone alive, and you have me. You're the fucking Engineer, so build something.

Riley swallowed. When had that lump formed in his throat? His companion was right. He looked around at all the implements from his lab at the Heir's mansion. It was all in disarray, but it was here. Enough of it to do something, to make something. He looked back at the charred feather and thought, maybe even enough to summon something.

David wept in his room, on the floor with his back against the door to bar any of his followers that might sense his distress and feel compelled to come help. His vision had dimmed a few hours after sunrise on the second day. At first a dark spot straight ahead, that spread like an ink stain until only a thin halo of blurry color filled his peripheral, and now only darkness.

He hadn't realized how much he missed seeing in the traditional way. Not the lines of energy his eyes showed him now, but true colors. Even in the euphoria of first seeing he hadn't realized, not until it was gone again and the grief had overtaken him, left him sobbing, inconsolable as a small child. This was worse even... even—dare he think it—than when his grandpa died. And it was all Brooklyn's fault for dragging him into this mess. It was true. It was a terrible thought to think, and it nagged at him like a hangnail, snagging on other thoughts, putting him off balance, but it *was* true.

The sobs continued like the seismic aftershocks of an earthquake. Until after a time they passed, and acceptance settled on him like the cold weight of stone. Or exhaustion. But there was work to be done, and very little time. He understood at long last the scope of Azrael's ambition, and his role within it, but he couldn't figure out how Brooklyn factored into prior promises from the goddess.

He needed to find Brooklyn himself, he needed to do it covertly, and there were things he needed to learn about, to understand. At the speed of thought, he began dispatching his people. One to identify the country's leading experts on the spiritual, another to locate and bring said experts into the network so David could know what they knew. Others to scour the news and contact organizational affiliates who might have an inside perspective on the Evers investigation. Others he sent to the roof so he could watch one more sunset. A dozen other, lesser directives, and when that was done, he came back to himself, his back aching from sitting against the door. David gained his feet gracelessly, bracing against the wall as he muttered, "Old before my time."

Dravin didn't notice the stink anymore, though he noticed the averted gazes of those closest to him, or the casual cupping of a hand over the nose, as if to pinch the bridge. That was okay.

This was his penance. This was what happened when arrogance led to a fall. He kept his own gaze averted mostly, hoping not to be recognized.

This service was different, not dressed up as a new understanding of the region's prevailing variant of Christianity, but openly pagan. Around the room acolytes watched the congregation, observing who left, put off by the heresy, and, he suspected, noting who stayed, who nodded along in agreement. The speaker reached a crescendo, and although Dravin hadn't really been following the specifics of the rhetoric, he bobbed his head enthusiastically. Pens scratched on paper.

Dravin half expected Mr. Sterling himself might make an appearance, but no such luck. The service was winding down, and in the words of the preacher, *'praise Azrael for that.'* There were only about twenty people remaining in the room. A small draw. It would be easier to remain unnoticed in a larger group, but the fact they were rationing recruitment gave him hope his hidden stores of Devotion remained undiscovered.

They invited the few devout who remained to come forward and drink from the vial of life and death. In a somber line, they did, each taking a crystalline vial. A young woman in front of Father Logan hesitated. "What is it?" she asked the minister. Her voice was a mouse's echo that nevertheless carried around the large room.

"It is a gift from Azrael. It is salvation from the wars and ravages that are coming. It is liquid death, the water Styx, purified so that we, like our goddess, may stand alive at the door of death, without fear. But do not make this choice lightly. If you are unsure, wait and pray about it. Maybe that would be better, yes?"

She was pretty in a pale, too thin kind of way, like an alley cat, he thought. When she wrinkled her nose he thought, not a cat after all, a rabbit, definitely a rabbit. Others in the line were getting restless, losing their nerve as this young girl delayed them with her indecision and gave them more time to consider. To the side, those who had already drank stood in a neat line.

"You heard him. You aren't ready," Logan rasped, as he pushed his way past the others in line, plucked the glass vial from her fingers, and gave her a little shove. As she stumbled back a step, Dravin swapped the vial he'd been palming with the one he'd just taken and upended it. Blackberry juice filled his mouth.

Then he changed his demeanor, slowly sitting the empty vial back into the rack on the table and moving purposefully to stand in line with his compatriots, adopting the same pleasant expression and neutral stance. The girl was leaving, escorted by one of the watchful scribes from earlier. She glared at him over her shoulder, but the man had her by the elbow and was pulling her along firmly. Dravin pretended not to notice. If she only knew, he thought, she would thank him. If she only knew what he'd done for her. Then he slipped the precious vial of blackness into his pocket for later.

30

Training and Planning

Brooklyn reached for Belial without thinking and the familiar coldness of their connection crept up her spine for the first time in days, but weaker than it should have been. *Where are you?* she thought urgently. She waited, her breath lodged like an apple, but no answer came.

"What's the matter?" Kurt asked, smoothing the front of one of the flannel shirts Mrs. Mays had pulled out of the attic for him. It had been her husband's, and apparently he'd been a big man. Kurt looked a little like a boy playing dress-up in his daddy's clothes. Brooklyn couldn't help but smile at the thought until it took her mind to Devin.

"You look pale. Want to take a snack break?"

Brooklyn let the connection drop. Now wasn't the time. "No, let's keep practicing."

Kurt nodded emphatically. He drew back and threw overhand like a baseball pitcher. Except what came at her chest was a bowling ball, and faster than even the major leaguers could pitch. She pushed a wedge to one side of the missile and let it glide along the surface of her construct. As it passed her and threatened to careen away, she brought up a curve of energy and felt it banking behind her. She pushed, accelerating it until the U-turn was complete and the ball returned to Kurt along the same trajectory, but faster. In a breath, it was back at her, almost too fast to see. She pushed the wedge to the opposite side this time, and they passed it back and forth in an infinity symbol until, after several minutes, Kurt flung it wide and high, all that kinetic energy sending it far into the cornfields behind Brooklyn where it landed with a meaty thunk in the damp soil.

"I need a break," he said, a little breathlessly.

She could see he didn't have the stamina he once had. Drops of sweat hung from his nose and chin like desperate climbers despite the early morning chill. She felt a little shakiness deep in her thighs, but whether it was adrenaline or hypoglycemia, she couldn't distinguish. A snack then, just to be safe.

"I never thought I'd be able to do something like this, not alone," she said, surprised at the note of breathlessness in her own voice. "Not without . . ." *Belial*, she thought and didn't say, but Kurt knew what she meant. Of course he did. Kurt, the taker-in of failed Demonriders. That's basically what she was now, right?

"Don't go next week. Give me a year to train you and I believe you could have a real shot at what you want to do. It's too soon. We aren't ready to take this on yet."

"I can't—"

"It's just like the bowling ball. You are trying to take this head-on." He stopped on the porch stairs, leaning back against the railing, looking tired and old.

"They have to pay for what they've done to David, to you, to Tessa, to—"

"To you?" She looked for something in his eyes, mockery or understanding, anything to gauge his judgment. She found only weariness and resignation.

When he spoke again, his voice was low and rough. "None of those people are going to come back to life if you kill Goodrum, and Logan, and Eric Stewarth, and none of them would want you dying for them, so don't pretend this is about them. It's about you. It's about your revenge."

She recoiled like a person slapped. "It's not *just* that! It's making sure they can't hurt us anymore, or anyone else either. It's the only way I can have a life and be left alone. I didn't come looking for this. I was drugged and dragged back here. I was trying to check on my nephew, to make sure he was safe. Or have you forgotten? I'm not sitting around in hiding for a year just to learn a few more tricks. This is the chance I have. While they are all in one place, I'm going to take it."

"Brooklyn—"

"Did you know David is still alive? Or was this time last year?"

Kurt looked genuinely surprised. "This is the first I've heard of it. Where is he? Who told you this?"

"Nathan Goodrum told me when we fought during the siege. He told me you knew and kept it from me."

A look of disbelief and then an amazed, roguish smile lit Kurt's face. "You fought Goodrum and came out on top?"

"I walked away, and he didn't." Brooklyn suppressed her own smile at the irony. "Now answer me. Did you know and keep it from me?"

"No. I swear it. If I'd known, I'd have found a way to see him free. Demonriders lie, but I hope that part about him being alive is true."

Brooklyn nodded. She believed Kurt. "Now you understand. If Father Logan has him, if he's alive, well, you are proof of how he treats his prisoners. I can't sit here playing catch with you for the next year while David rots in a cell somewhere."

"You aren't ready. It's a suicide—"

"I'm going to get the bowling ball. You go eat something. We can finish talking later." Brooklyn didn't wait to see if he went or not. She just turned and headed out into the cornfield. He was afraid. She'd probably be afraid too if she'd been locked in a cavern for the last eight months with very little food. But how could he not want revenge? If not for David, then for Riley or Tessa or the twins?

Stormy thoughts carried her like a dark wind to the crater in the soft topsoil and the red clay beneath. She tried to connect with

Belial again, but felt only the barest chill along her spine. Plunging her mind down into the earth, she found the ball she couldn't see, grasped it with her will, and tugged it up and up. She jiggled it this way and that when some irregularity of the hole impeded the ascent. It surfaced finally with a wet sucking sound. Brooklyn stooped to scoop it up, ignoring the mud smears it left across the front of her shirt.

Back at the barn, she dumped the ball in a corner with some other junk. The old barn sighed with the wind, hay dust floating lazily in the loft. Her stomach growled, and she still felt tremors like microshakes in her thighs. Brooklyn didn't go in the house just yet, though. She wasn't ready to face Kurt again and continue the debate. Instead, she walked through the barn, which was nearly as big as the main house.

From the storage area where she returned the bowling ball, she passed into the open main area. Along the far wall there were dozens of plastic fuel tanks, some red and others blue, presumably gas and diesel. Mrs. Mays had been stockpiling, it seemed.

In the final third of the barn, she found the dirt bike she'd left behind. It looked like it might even still run. Brooklyn thought of throwing a leg across the saddle and disappearing into the mountains, heading back to North Carolina to check on Devin. For a wild minute she imagined taking him from that foster home and throwing him on the back. Living on the road.

If she did, how long would it be before another team of Demonriders ambushed her, and how would that fight go with a five-year-old in tow? *Do they really know about Devin? Is he safe?* Belial hadn't believed Devin was in danger, she reminded herself. The dying man hadn't called him by name after all. It had only been a way to bait her into a trap, and it had worked. If she was ever going to find Erin and reunite her with Devin, she needed to get these people off her back first. It would be hard enough to search while dodging the police, let alone a bunch of supernatural demon thugs.

TRAINING AND PLANNING

She sighed and ran a finger over the dusty seat, gave the handlebars a pat, and headed inside to face Kurt. Brooklyn had made up her mind. There would be no running away from what she must do. Even if she did give that old motorcycle a final glance before she closed the barn door behind her.

When the screen door slammed behind Brooklyn, Kurt was at the kitchen counter, carefully applying mayonnaise to bread and studiously avoiding Mrs. Mays's eyes. The old woman was bright-cheeked and staring like a predator. She didn't look away for several long, uncomfortable seconds. Then, all at once, she turned to Brooklyn and smiled, the heat fading from her expression. "Are you hungry, girl?"

"Course she is." Kurt looked up from his plate finally. *Safe to do so*, Brooklyn thought, *because Mrs. Mays won't pursue whatever they were discussing before I walked in. Which probably means they were talking about me.* "Come on, get something." He gestured at the sandwiches and chips on foam plates.

She did not need to be told twice. Her stomach gurgled eagerly and a heavy soreness settled into her shoulders and thighs as she took a seat on a barstool and began to eat with a little more gusto than was strictly civilized. Though she did have the courtesy to swallow before speaking. "I don't know what you two have been arguing about, but I'm sure it's something to do with the best way to stop me. You both figure this is a suicide mission, but I think if you'd help me come up with a plan, a good plan, then we could figure a way in, and more importantly, a way back out."

Mrs. Mays was wiping her hands vigorously on the thighs of her jeans and appeared to be literally biting her tongue. Kurt just looked tired, worn down, as he scratched the stubble on his cheek. Except for his eyes. There was always a lot of life and energy in those honey-colored eyes. "So, what is your plan to get in?"

"She ain't got no plan," Mrs. Mays burst out. "No plan but to get herself killed, or something worse. Look what they did to you, old man! You're more than halfway dead. If you can't stand up to these people, how can she?"

"Hey, hey! Amelia, we're just talking, just talking, nothing else right now. Sit down and talk with us, please? Nothing's decided, it's just talk. Okay? Hypothetical. Let's hear her out and help her out, and if the plan isn't good. If it can't be done. Well, we'll smack her on the head and tie her up out in the barn or something."

Mrs. Mays laughed, and it seemed to surprise even her. "Always the smooth talker; you're every bit the politician the rest of them are."

He smiled, unabashed as always, and with a long-suffering sigh she sat down, folded her arms, and frowned fiercely. Something in that look broadened Kurt's smile until his eyes crinkled. "Good, well then, Miss Evers, I believe you had something to say?"

"I was thinking, the problem really isn't getting in, it is getting away after." As she spoke, Brooklyn found herself sharing Kurt's sentiment about avoiding the stern eyes of Mrs. Mays. "I could walk in the front door if all else fails. They want me, apparently pretty badly, but then how do I make sure I get a chance to tell my side? I've been through this kangaroo court once before. I don't want to walk into the conclave as a prisoner. I want to walk in as a . . ."

"A what?" Mrs. Mays asked.

"Sounds like she wants to be an affiliate," Kurt murmured.

"That'll never happen," Mrs. Mays scoffed. "You are either born into an affiliated family, you join an affiliate group, or you marry in."

"Well all those families got in somewhere along the line."

"I only know I want to walk in with my head held high, and I want to make sure I get my shot at Nathan Goodrum. And that it's a fatal one."

"So, it is about revenge after all." Kurt shook his head. "How does that solve the bigger problem? You'd still be a fugitive with Nathan dead."

Brooklyn sighed. "It's not only that. He's tried his damndest to kill me twice, and those were Demonriders that had me drugged up and strapped down to a gurney. That means he sent them. They know about my nephew. One of them said he was plan B."

"They just said that to lay a trap. They wouldn't know where to look. Bet they don't even know his name. Did they call him by name?"

"No," she admitted.

Mrs. Mays cleared her throat. "The Heir offered her a trial and amnesty. When no one else would. Maybe walking through the front door ain't the worst idea."

"It would be a hell of a gamble," Kurt commented. "If half the things I've heard about Eric's time as Heir are true, she'd be better off with Goodrum."

"Did you get a lot of unbiased news down in your dungeon cell under the mountain?" Mrs. Mays snapped.

Excitement jolted through Brooklyn. "What about the tunnels? Is there some way through?"

Kurt twitched. "I don't think it would be safe—"

"She didn't ask about safety," Mrs. Mays said crossly. "Is there a way through or not?"

"I don't know for sure, but maybe. I know Dravin came the long way around when he brought me food. He complained about it more than once." Kurt rubbed his temples. "When the explosion happened, I just . . . reacted, you know? Just pushed everything away from me as hard as I could, even as I was falling. That I wound up in the tunnel instead of under all that marble was just blind luck."

"I have to go in and see. If I can't find a way through, or come up with a better idea, there's always the front door. But if I can find a secret way in, then I'll also have a secret way out if things go bad."

Kurt shared a look with Mrs. Mays, and Brooklyn recognized it well. She'd seen it on her mother's face many times. The look was resignation. Weary resignation. Inside, she cheered a little. This battle was won, but she was also afraid. Some small part of her, either the cowardly part or the smarter part, had hoped they would stop her.

31

AMONG THE RAFF

The gates of the Colossus were thrown wide and their glossy black half curves reminded Belial of nothing so much as a couple of humpbacked buzzards squaring off to fight. He'd killed eight demons crossing the sea of vermin to get here. He still had the ichor on his hands, though it was drying and flaking under the heat of the always high noon sun.

The worst had been when one gargoyle-looking creature with vestigial wings had singled him out, stepping into his path and blocking all attempts to go around. Like flies to a fresh corpse, the others came to watch.

As they gathered around, his instinct screamed "take flight," but he'd clamped his wings even tighter, willing them to remain unseen, and faced his towering adversary. Like magic, the hoard had cleared some space, their tightly packed bodies creating a claustrophobic ring of win or die.

Tall and ugly wasted no time, giving a tremendous roar and charging, swishing a python-sized muscular tail with daggered barbs on the end. Just then, in another world, Brooklyn had reached for him, a split second of distraction that nearly cost him his life. He pushed her away savagely as he began to move, but too slowly; the brute was on him.

It would have driven him straight down into the dirt if he hadn't slipped aside enough to take the blow at a glancing angle. Even so, it staggered him and when he spun with the blow to grab this monstrosity around the neck to rip its ugly head off, his fingers only grazed leathered skin and found no purchase. Before he could recover his balance, the thing's tail wrapped around his torso twice like a whip, and one of the barbs lodged deep in his shoulder. White-hot pain exploded through his arm and neck.

The gargoyle never slowed, barreled straight ahead, unfurled its tail, and flung Belial like a Frisbee into a wall of bodies that clawed, bit, and bashed him back into the center of the ring. For a second there was respite as the creature turned and stalked him with the playful feline grace that so terrifies mice.

Cold energy filled Belial's shoulder, numbing the pain as it pooled in his hands waiting to be used. The gargoyle feinted a rush and Belial flinched away. The crowd was a roar of hoots and guttural sounds that might have been laughter. The brute seemed to swell with confidence, glorying in the attention, and relishing the power he held over his weak victim. He made another feint, and the hoard cheered again when Belial staggered aside, stumbled, and almost fell. A third followed, and though Belial reacted to it, the crowd didn't respond. There were a few scattered cheers, but a much larger undercurrent of impatient growls.

The gargoyle seemed to sense that his showmanship was losing favor with the crowd. He swished his great tail twice and leapt headlong for the killing blow. Rather than flinching away, Belial shaped the icy power in his hands, rolled forward into his opponent's embrace, and buried two crystalline blades into the monster's chest, twisting savagely and breaking them off inside.

The giant roared angrily, thrashing blindly for a grip, but Belial slipped through his questing claws. The beast whirled about and its tail swept the feet out from under Belial, dumping him onto the gritty, ashy ground. He rolled instinctively and a moment later the dagger-tipped tail crashed down and pulverized the place he'd been. The tail flexed and writhed until the spike ripped free of the earth. The crowd had warmed to the contest again and churned out an endless rumble of catcalls and jeers.

Belial considered flying away. He could make a clean escape, find somewhere safe to hide, and regroup. Instead, he kept his wings folded and leapt hopscotch-style over two more lightning-quick tail swats. The beast whirled to face him and paced forward in a crouch, shielding its wounds from view. A low rumble emanated from its chest, a growl meant for him this time, not the crowd. Playtime was over.

Above them new spectators wheeled in lazy arcs, looking down, and these Belial knew would recognize his ice magic if he did anything flashy. Even so, he gathered his strength again until his claws ached with the pressure of unspent energies.

As the gargoyle grew still, preparing to pounce, Belial took a knee and plunged his hands into the earth. His sudden move of submission had the intended effect. Belial felt the brute's steps vibrate through the earth twice like gongs, and then it launched itself at him like a missile.

Belial leapt straight up and flung handfuls of ash into the beast's eyes as it passed beneath him. Coming down behind his enraged adversary, he was promptly smacked into the dirt by its tail. He rolled and, like before, the barb drove through the loose ashy soil and into the more solid ground below and lodged there.

Taking to his feet, Belial sprinted past the writhing tail, bringing his claws down on the place where the great serpentine muscle met the body. Again and again in a flashing arc that sprayed ichor on the thirsty earth, he chopped away at his enemy's flesh. The energy he'd packed into his claws gave his cuts a razor's cold edge. The creature howled in agony. He'd severed whatever nerve or tendon drove the flexing cylinder of muscle at the root. *Good.*

The gargoyle whirled back on itself snapping at its own ass like a dog after a flea. Belial stepped astride the tail and continued the job of separating it completely, clinging with his thighs and one arm while sawing tissue with the claws of the other. Each frantic jerk and lurch sent a jolt of agony through his injured shoulder. Blood pulsed out of the gouges and gashes he'd inflicted, slickening his mount. Cheers pulsed all around him as he came finally to bone and searched out the space between the vertebrae and sliced through it. The gargoyle lurched drunkenly, all its feline grace gone. Belial could have finished it then and there, but he didn't need to. Instead, he gave the cripple a hard shove right on the bleeding stump and sent it stumbling drunkenly into the crowd. They fell on it like the hyenas they were.

Belial grabbed the tail by the spiked end and dragged it behind him, leaving an ashy gully of blood in his wake. The upper caste of demons above dispersed, moving on from this momentary entertainment to more pressing matters. He approached the edge of the circle, and again, as if by magic, a path through the crowd opened before him. A wide path.

He knew the way ahead would be less hellish than the trek across the desert had been, but the dangers here were of another sort. Here he would be scrutinized. The lower castes, called Raff, were not permitted in the city. He mustn't appear to be one of them any longer, but neither could he afford the recognition of being himself, Prosidris's wayward chap. For his father had a presence in this place, was feared and respected in equal measures. So, bloodstained as he was, Belial scooped the gargoyle's tail up and draped it around his shoulders like a boa. He'd pose as an off-duty militant who'd run afoul of the animalistic Raff during an outing. A third son's job at best, but one that wouldn't turn heads or raise horns.

The obsidian gates shone like black diamonds beneath the soul sun. Just through the gates, the first curious eyes turned his way. Some studied him openly, curious about the barbed tail he carried like a trophy. Others, with indifferent, passionless eyes ran the numbers, estimating his place in the hierarchy, figuring what he might have worth taking, how much trouble he'd be to kill or maim in order to take it, and if the risks would be worthwhile. These were the gutter dogs of the upper caste, just barely better off than the brutes forced to dwell on the ash plains. It was the ability to be curious and to make these calculations that set them apart. This higher level of thinking made them more dangerous, oh yes, but also more useful, for though they lacked the fierceness of the Raff, their cunning meant they could be reasoned with. The Raff understood only fear and aggression. The eyes that examined him now were self-aware.

He strode with his wings tightly folded. Few with wings ever needed to walk through the main gate, and none would want to spend time down here on the Slopes. They would spend their time on some level or other of the Colossus. Seeing a winged demon down here would surely be noteworthy information. Belial didn't acknowledge the curious or appraising glances. He held his head high and let his eyes slide along, focusing on none too long.

The streets here were a haphazard, unplanned, crooked labyrinth and as apt to dead-end as to meander on in the general direction one wished. They shared little in common with the streets of any Earth-side city Belial had seen, which were laid out like grid work. And where the bustling streets there would be filled with people moving purposefully from place to place, and vendors selling hot dogs "2 for $3 all day." The smells of coffee and donuts even. But no—none of that here. Here there was no purpose and nowhere to go. No hot dogs, donuts, or coffee either, because no one here ate or drank. Even currency didn't exist because for the few things of value that could be bought or sold, barter and violence were fine enough money.

As he made his way onto the higher streets, he started to see shelters, little lean-tos barely bigger than umbrellas, but big aplenty to provide occasional respite from the sun above. Here the looks were more furtive, and the assessments more complex. Not only were they estimating his place in the pecking order and of what value he might be, they were also measuring his threat. These who congregated around their little shelters like families had something to lose, however meager it might be.

It was then that Brooklyn reached again. He felt the ice inside begin to flow and clamped down on it. Too many eyes. She'd just have to manage on her own for the time being. He'd done all he could to keep her safe.

Last year, Prosidris had commanded him to dominate Brooklyn and make her kill Devin with her own hands to prove he'd mastered her. When Prosidris gave orders, they were carried out. Always. Belial and Brooklyn had refused to kill the boy and fought him to a draw when he tried to do it himself. The Father of the Wardens was prideful. He wouldn't let defiance like that go unanswered.

Brooklyn was worried about keeping her nephew safe from Demonriders, but she didn't really understand the scope of things. The next best thing to a god, a being whom even the oceans obeyed, had been told "no" by a human girl and a lesser demon. His hubris would never let that stand.

The tower loomed ahead, a massive spike of ashy stone that threatened to break the sun like the yolk of an egg. Prosidris was likely taking his ease near the top on one of the ringed balconies, higher than Belial's wings could carry him, or beyond the Colossus in the Tome Keeper's vaults. That meant he had to climb the stairs inside. As much as he dreaded it, he'd have to face his father here because once he came to Earth, there would be no stopping him.

32

Underground Again

Kurt stared storms at the dark descent into the cavern before them. He liked the morning sun on his neck and the lazy drizzle of autumn leaves letting go, but didn't much relish the thought of another minute spent underground where he'd been imprisoned for so long. The sausages and pancakes from breakfast had turned to lead in his belly.

"It's not the mines of Moria." Brooklyn stood between him and the open trapdoor, bleached hair blowing and blue eyes alive with merriment. She looked nothing like his boy had, and yet . . . the way she looked over her shoulder at him, one eyebrow raised, that mischievous grin . . . was somehow familiar.

He shifted his pack and rummaged for a flashlight. Sure, he could find his way in the dark, but he wasn't going to unless he had to, damn it.

Brooklyn eyed his pack but didn't say anything as he dug through cans of food and bottles of water. He knew what she must be thinking: thirty pounds of supplies they didn't need for an outing that ought to take less than half the day. To her credit she didn't tease him about it. He'd been starved and nearly killed in this very cave. So if beanie weenies was the security he needed to show her the way, then why should she care?

Kurt closed his eyes, basking in the warm daylight for another few seconds. He wondered when his dark mistress might call him into service and hoped it was a long while yet. With a resigned sigh, he opened his eyes, strode past Brooklyn, and vanished into the darkness like a penny down a well.

Brooklyn followed, hesitated for a moment, and then pulled the disguised trapdoor closed behind them. She felt the weight of the mountain poised to crush her, and took a few deep breaths. Kurt would make sure they got out safely. It was better that the door was closed; she didn't want their passage into the earth noted by an unlikely passerby.

The last time she'd been here was with David. Then they'd depended on the weak illumination from his watch and the faint luminescence of the walls. Now she snapped on the smallest of three flashlights, courtesy of Mrs. Mays, who had declined to join them on this fool's errand. It cast a strong LED beam that she played along the passage walls and ceiling and settled on Kurt's boots to avoid blinding him. He aimed his own beam further into the cave.

The chill and the damp made her shiver. An odor of old stone and turned soil hung heavy as a freshly dug grave. "Lead on," she murmured, voice pitched low so as not to invite an echo.

They came swiftly to the chamber she had discovered with David now more than a year ago, though it seemed much, much longer. Kurt never hesitated, turning from one passage to the next with rote familiarity. He set a brisk pace for a man who wasn't quite recovered from near starvation. His anxiety puzzled her; it was out of character. Though, she mused, what did she really know about his character or what he'd been through all those months down in these caverns?

Footsteps, the far-off trickle of water, and her own breathing were the only things she heard. Flashlight beams showed the caves in slices of light, never whole. Even so, she was able to piece together a rough mental map of the cavern. There were several passages that led off from this primary hub. Kurt veered toward the third from the left without hesitation.

"Where do the others go?" she called after him, in that same shouting whisper she'd used earlier.

"Dead ends mostly," Kurt bellowed back; his booming voice echoed around the chamber. "One has storage and cells."

Where you almost died, she thought.

"I'll show you on the way back out."

They walked single file most of the time. Occasionally the passage widened enough they could walk side by side, but invariably it narrowed again. The air here was drier than in the first parts of the cavern and verged on warm.

"Do you think I'm crazy to think I could pull this off?" she asked.

He cocked his head thoughtfully but didn't speak for a long time. She thought to ask again, but before she could—at last—he spoke. "Maybe you are a little crazy. I don't see how somebody could lose the things you've lost and not be." He looked up at the stone ceiling, the tons of earth above them, seemed to wrestle with something, then spoke again. "Crazy's one of those things you can't fix or change. It just is. Sometimes it takes a little crazy to do what's right. A lot of the people I admire had a little crazy in them. Take Rosa Parks, for instance—"

"Wait, you think Rosa Parks was crazy?"

"Hell yes I do. She had nothing and nobody on her side and she set herself against the bus driver and the police in the Deep South."

Brooklyn tucked a strand of hair behind her ear. "She wasn't crazy. She was brave."

"I'll give you brave, because she sure was, but she was crazy brave. Changed the whole damned world that one woman did. You've got a spark of that in you, too."

The passage widened out again, so she moved up to walk beside him. "So, you think I can do it?"

Kurt let out a long, belabored sigh. "I think you think you can do it. But I think you shouldn't try, not now. The odds aren't good and if you lose, the best outcome you can hope for is a quick death. If they took you alive, well, I think that might be a whole lot worse."

"Worse how?"

"I think in time they'd break you. Hell, Dravin Logan came near enough to breaking me, and he's a gentleman compared to Nathan Goodrum. Or Eric Stewarth for that matter, if what I've heard about him is true. Nathan would torture you and try to make you into a Demonrider, but Eric would use you. For leverage, for power, or maybe just to make an example to others. That's what happened to Tessa. Eric had her staked down and . . ."

"They won't take me alive."

"God, girl, you remind me so much of my son. You know that story, some of it anyway. Was a long time ago, but he was just as stubborn and reckless as you. I should have done more to keep him safe. He was his own worst enemy in that regard, thought he was invincible. That's the arrogance of youth."

"What happened to him? I mean, I know he died after your wife . . . I mean, you never really talked about the details."

He stopped and turned to her. She could just see his face in the darkness, enough to see the sorrow there. "I brought it down on them both. I wish I'd never been named Protector. He got in over his head with some summoners that felt I'd wronged their family, and he asked his mother for help instead of me. He was afraid of how I would react, I guess. I was too hard on him when he was a boy. I talked too much, listened too little, and pushed him away when I should have been drawing him close. That's the way it's been, though, with dads and sons since the very beginning."

He cupped her cheek. "There's more to tell, but I'd not tell it today or here. Just know I'm going to look out for you the way I should have looked out for him." He dropped his hand to his side and turned back to the path ahead. "Come on. Let's be done with this."

Brooklyn touched her cheek where she could still feel the phantom of his roughened palm.

They were getting close now. The irregularities of the caves had given way to a mostly uniform path, one that must be man-made. His words echoed around in her head. *That's the way it's been with dads and sons since the beginning.* She thought then of her own dad, dead and buried—she didn't even know where—and how maybe things were just the same for daughters as they were for sons.

33

Father Logan's Gambit

Former Father Dravin Logan placed himself on janitorial. No one told him to do this because nobody ever had to give directions in a place like this. If you were here, you were expected to know your role. And who knew better how to blend in with puppets than a puppeteer?

Janitorial was a good team to be on because it was perfectly reasonable to see them emptying trash upstairs as well as down here. Upstairs was where he needed to be, but also where the risk of bumping into someone who knew his face was the greatest. He didn't head straight up, however. Instead, he followed his initiate bunkmates to the chow hall and ate his breakfast. There was a low buzz of conversation around the room, but no one spoke to him. That was just as well. Every interaction was a risk of discovery. He ate as quickly as he dared and bussed his tray.

He knew just where to find the custodial supplies he needed, and why not? It was common knowledge, and common knowledge was shared knowledge here. It wasn't a bit unusual that the new guy seemed to know just where to go. He filled a big yellow mop bucket with floor cleaner and water, stuck a roll of trash bags in his back pocket, and headed to the elevator. He even whistled the *Andy Griffith* theme for good measure.

The ride up was fast and as solitary as he'd hoped, and the doors opened on a familiar hallway. The door he wanted wasn't far ahead, but he turned first to the public restrooms on this floor and gave them a thorough mopping until his bucket of blue soapy water had turned brown and murky.

Back in the hallway, he shuffled along, careful not to slosh the water onto the burgundy carpeting. The door he wanted opened into his old office, directly across the hall from his quarters, where even now his enemy likely slept.

He listened at the office door for any sound of movement inside. After he was satisfied, Dravin ducked inside with his mop and bucket, closing the door softly behind him. The room looked untouched. It was sparsely decorated and unremarkable. The desk was still arranged as he remembered, with notes and half-written sermons in neat stacks. Behind the desk was his bookcase. He removed his copy of *Divine Demons of the Fall* and stuck his arm into the space between *Blood Gods: A History* and *The Case Against Free Will*. His fingers found the familiar latch and with a little tug, the bookcase slid easily to the left. Behind it, set into the wall, were several shelves. On the shelves were vials containing liquids of various opacities.

Dravin wanted them all, but he didn't think he could carry them all in a single load, so he selected the ones he needed most and then took as many extra as he dared. These he lowered into a new trash bag from which he removed as much air as possible before tying it thrice. He lowered it into the scummy mop water and placed the mop on top to ensure the whole package remained submerged.

He had his hand on the doorknob when he heard the door across the hall open and then close. His heart dropped.

This was it. If David came into the office, he would have to be killed, and quickly, before he could summon help, before he even knew he was in danger. Was the gun still in the desk drawer where he'd left it? He didn't know. He held his breath and waited as the footsteps faded off toward the elevator. His heart hammered in his chest. Dravin counted to one hundred, then put his hand on the knob, but gave it another fifty count before opening it and rolling the mop bucket back toward the elevator.

Dravin felt giddy, the adrenaline still coursing through his veins as he reentered the custodial supply closet. He drained the bucket and put his dripping treasure inside another trash bag and wadded up handfuls of paper napkins to obscure the contents of the clear plastic liner and to keep the vial clinking to a minimum. The bag was heavy, but he didn't mind the weight, not a bit. He hoisted it over his shoulder and headed for the orange exit sign in the back of the lobby. Carrying trash out the front door would be suspicious. He didn't let himself hope he'd gotten away with it until he was two blocks away, sitting in the backseat of a Chevy Tahoe, with the vials between his ankles, and Goodrum behind the wheel.

Riley reviewed the lab report on the charred feather. He'd had it run on a small sample by a trusted friend with access to a full medical lab. As expected, much of the test results were indeterminate, possibly because of the burn damage to the sample, but he didn't think so. When he had ordered the test, he wasn't even sure the sample would contain DNA. What he was reading now, for about the seventh time, was a summary of the findings, and there was DNA. There were enough undamaged cells to determine sex, two X chromosomes, but the eerie thing was the sample came from a feather, yet the DNA sample was conclusively human. He wasn't sure what he'd expected. Avian genes maybe?

There hadn't been time for a full genome sequencing, but he suspected such an extensive test would unearth some very non-human genetic material, and he believed the preliminary testing, which identified species at a ninety-nine percent match for Homo sapiens.

What does it mean? his companion asked.

I think it means Azrael was human once, Riley thought back. He'd been trying to keep these deliberations internal rather than speaking out loud, and didn't know for certain, but suspected he was being watched from time to time.

Maybe she still is. Human, I mean.

Even if she is, from a genetic standpoint, she's also a freaking angel or goddess or something. DNA tests don't cover the celestial or spiritual.

His companion stirred, sifting through a blur of memories, tidbits, and facts with a disorienting speed that left Riley a little woozy. He sat down heavily on the stool behind the workbench.

When the blur finally stopped, he said, *How about a little warning next time? Geez! What are you looking for, anyway?*

If she was once human, then something changed her into what she is now. I was trying to remember if I've ever heard of anything that could do something like that.

Well, have you? Riley asked impatiently.

His companion paused, then replied, *No.*

That's... anticlimactic.

Maybe, but it's not useless. We know she was human or something close to human once, and we know with reasonable certainty that something—we don't know what—changed her into something more than human. Sound familiar?

You think she's like us, an ascendant, but on a much higher level?

There's a lot we haven't figured out yet; it's just a thought. Here's another: maybe she's not a human and spirit ascended together, maybe humans are descended from whatever she is.

Riley sighed. *So basically, we know nothing?*

Bingo, boss!

He threw the report down on the table with disgust and turned his attention back to the smelter suspended above a hissing burner. In it he stirred mostly melted gold with a long-handled spoon. Laid out on a towel to his left were several samples of finished and raw moldavite stones. To his right, a mold for the gold, but not a ring; instead his mold was to make a pair of brass knuckles... er gold knuckles. Riley was a practical man. A nonfunctional ring would take longer to make and be worthless if the experiment failed. At least with these, if he failed, he could still hit people with them. Or use them as a paperweight. Whatever the situation called for would be fine, he supposed.

He had a heavy apron and extra-long heat-resistant gloves. He even had eye protection. Safety first, wasn't that the motto?

On the other side of the room, safely sealed in a copper hoop on the floor, were his summons. They were lesser demons, but not the mindless, animalistic kind. These were sentient, smart, and, by all appearances, pissed off at their predicament.

"Won't be long now," he reassured them. "Soon it'll be do-or-die time." He was talking as much to himself as his summoned captives. He picked up the molten gold and poured it quick and sure until the mold was filled to the brim. That done, he turned to the table with all the moldavite.

He selected four likely looking samples and gathered his handwritten notes with all the information he'd gleaned, transcribed, and translated about Solomon's ring. There was much he still didn't understand, but he thought he understood enough for a trial run. Each demon had a unique sigil, like a supernatural fingerprint that defined them.

Riley had a sigil for each of the four demons that were locked inside his circle. He shuffled the papers until he had the one he wanted, then picked up a graver tool and set about transcribing it to the first of the four stones. It took a long time; usually the sigils were placed on vellum using the summoner's own blood as ink.

That was how he'd gotten the demons here, but now he needed to replicate the effects of Solomon's ring.

The sigils were all squiggles and crazy angles that made him dizzy and threatened to trick him like one of those *Magic Eye* books he used to pore over as a child.

It took him the better part of an hour just to finish and check one stone. He started on the second and worked until his eyes ached from squinting and his fingers cramped. Riley did not want to chance making a mistake, so he set the stone and scribing tool aside and went to the fridge for a Coke.

He brought his drink to the work table and examined the gold in the mold. It looked solid, so he put on his heat glove and submerged the plaster mold in cold water and waited for it to dissolve.

Waiting was never his strong point, so he went back to the moldavite stone with the finished sigil and checked it against the original copy. If there were inconsistencies, he couldn't see them. Riley picked up a dagger from the workbench and pricked the end of his middle finger with the tip. He squeezed the finger until a fat drop of blood welled up from the tiny wound and touched it to the sigil, watching the blood fill the shallow channels he'd gouged.

As soon as the last line of the design filled with scarlet, the demon closest to him uttered a low growl. Riley sensed him through the stone, and knew instinctively that it was a "he," grade five, comparatively weak, tugging against their connection like a kite on a string.

As expected, the stone had no influence over the other three demons and was in fact more similar in function to Kurt's Celtic-knot pendant than to the Ring of Solomon he was trying to re-create. Baby steps, he reminded himself. Now he had a working model, something to study.

The golden knuckles were ready. He pulled them from the water and toweled them dry. There was some finishing to do, lacquer to cover the sigil on the stone, setting the stone into gold, and three more stones to finish carving and setting as well. If it worked, he'd be able to control four demons simultaneously. It wasn't the universal power of the ring, but it was more than any human summoner he'd ever seen could do. Then again, maybe it wasn't a fair comparison. He wasn't really human anymore, was he?

34

Unlikely Companion

Belial slung the spiked tail off his shoulders and dropped it at his feet. It was a crude weapon and a poor disguise for where he was going. The fellow in front of him looked it over with an appraising eye. "How fresh?"

It was a fair question. It wasn't likely to rot and decay here as it would have done on Earth, but it would dry out and fossilize given enough time, robbing it of most of its utility.

"Can't say for sure, but less than a day." He nudged it with his foot. "Still has a lot of flex left in it."

"Hmmm," he said.

Belial took this as an assent. "I'll trade even for that cape you're wearing." He wanted the cape to hide his wings from those inside the tower, where he expected closer scrutiny.

"Bah," the spiky old fellow allowed, "hardly worth that, is it?" He ran a finger pad over the fabric that looked like green leather, doubtlessly skin harvested from Raff of one variety or other and cured under the soul sun. "What do you want with it, anyway?"

"Just looking for a little portable shade. I might need protection when I get to the top."

Old Porcupine, a name Belial had made up for the vexing stranger, guffawed loudly. "Ain't nobody goes to the top. I've been sitting within spitting distance of that big black toothpick longer than you've been alive. Everybody I ever saw tried for the summit never came back. Make your pilgrimage, climb as far as the first gate to pay your respect, and then head back."

"I'm going to the top. Maybe instead of sitting out here another thousand years, you ought to join me?"

Old Porcupine looked down at his meager belongings, a small lean-to of the same green fabric, a collection of stone arrowheads, and some rope woven from sinew. "Well," he said, stooping to retrieve the gargoyle tail, "I'm not going to the top. I value my hide more than that." He gave the tail an experimental flick. "I'll go as far as the first gate if that suits you. And I think I'll take you up on this trade after all." He unclasped the cape and passed it over.

Belial took it with a ghost of a smile on his face and fastened it around his own shoulders. The weight of it felt nice.

Wrapping his meager possessions into a satchel made of the same green leather—apparently, he'd gotten it wholesale—Old Porcupine slung it over one bony shoulder and then draped the tail over the other. "Let's go then!" he barked.

A few hours later, they stood in the Colossus's shadow near the solitary entrance. It wasn't well guarded like he'd expected, but he'd never approached at ground level before, either. The archway was unremarkable. No door, it reminded him of the entrance to a subway station sans signage. It looked like subterranean, poorly lit public access. Except there was no public accessing it, the present company excluded.

Belial went through the door with quick, sure strides, projecting a sense of purpose and trying to pretend he belonged. He heard Porcupine keeping pace behind him, and didn't see guards or any other travelers, but he felt them. There was a bone-deep sense of being watched closely. He ignored it.

Inside, the tower was lit by a spiral of ascending slots in the wall spaced like sconces. They provided ambient light from the sun outside. The light marked the passage of a winding staircase cut from the same black stone as the rest of the tower proper. Apart from the stairway, there was little else to see. Just like that lighthouse he'd climbed with Brooklyn last year, but on a larger scale. She was probably all healed up now and giving Mrs. Mays hell.

The thought of her sent a twinge of remorse through him, but there was no help for it. If he didn't strike preemptively, his father would find his way topside soon. Then he wouldn't need to worry about anything anymore.

"Are we going up or what?" the old fellow growled, his voice somehow like gravel under truck tires.

Belial bit back a couple of smartass retorts that sprang to mind and settled for, "Lead the way, old-timer."

He stepped past Belial, eyes narrowed. Apparently, trusting wasn't in his nature. Belial gave him his best smile and a wink as he passed. The old guy might have mumbled something profane as he passed, but who could say for certain?

The stairs were wide enough to accommodate five men abreast, so after a few minutes of making his wary companion uncomfortable, Belial stepped up beside him and nodded. Old Porcupine nodded back, and they climbed in companionable silence for a while.

"You've been partway up before?" Belial panted.

"Several lifetimes ago," the old fellow confirmed. "Only so far as the first gate. I hear there are nine."

"I've heard a dozen."

"Seems unlikely. Look how far we've climbed and not yet seen the first gate. If they are spaced evenly, that is, there couldn't be more than, say, five? How high do you think we've climbed? I'm thinking maybe a fifth?"

Belial puffed a little with exertion. "Not even a twentieth." He glanced over his shoulder. You really couldn't tell how far you'd climbed. The sharp curve of the stairway hid progress as quickly as it was made. "Think it touches the sun like in the stories?"

The old guy furrowed his spiky brows. "Hmmm. Sure looks like it from the ground, but nah, couldn't be, could it?"

"I plan to find out," Belial replied.

His companion guffawed again, a deep laugh reminiscent of stones in a blender. "Going to sprout wings and fly, are you?"

Belial didn't take the bait. "I'll find a way to the top, however I have to get there."

"Why? What's up there you want so bad?"

"Don't know."

"I don't either, but you sure seem to be on a mission." The old fellow regarded him shrewdly. "This is more than just a pilgrimage for you, ain't it? It's . . . more personal than that. Hmmm. Somebody on a higher level you looking for, maybe?"

It was Belial's turn to laugh. "Just want to spit off the top of the world. How about you? Awfully quick to pack up and make this trip yourself."

Old Porcupine tugged at his makeshift cape. "What else I got to do? Way I see it, this may be the last adventure I get a shot at. Everything . . . everything has gone crazy out there." He gestured vaguely behind them. "The ones with wings don't land anymore. The Raff are tearing each other apart down on the ground to get near those shimmering rifts that keep opening." He gave the gargoyle's tail a shake for emphasis. "Everybody trying to get out, like rats on a sinking ship."

"Not you though. Why is that?"

"Bah." He waved a claw-tipped hand dismissively. "What am I going to do up on Earth? Run a pawn shop? That's not our place, not anymore. And me? I don't miss it much. Life is life wherever you live it. That's what I say!"

"You don't want to be someplace better?"

Old Porcupine laughed. "Hellfire and brimstone, if the Pull falls, this might *be* the someplace better, ever think of that?"

Belial suddenly felt cold. "No, I suppose not." He really hadn't. The thought that this place—a place many referred to as Hell—might be the best thing going this time next year had never occurred to him. How long would it take the Earth to wither into a wasteland after the barrier collapsed? A year, maybe? A decade? Either way, such a thing would be irreversible.

"Thinking about it now, though, ain't you?" His grin split his lips and revealed the pale canines that lined his gums. "It's an ugly picture, like turning a pack of starving lions loose in a preschool, huh?"

Belial didn't want to picture it. That was why he was here, after all. To run preemptive damage control on Prosidris. He was about to pick a fight he couldn't possibly survive with a being who literally had oceans at his command.

"Never see Wardens anymore either," Old Porcupine continued. "Used to be you'd see them all the time flitting about keeping everything separate."

"I guess I hadn't really noticed," Belial admitted. He wished the old fellow would shut the hell up, no pun intended, and walk in silence for a while.

"Noticing things is important. It's one of the few things I've gotten good at over the years. Take the Melody for example. Same groaning hurdy-gurdy of despair and misery for thousands of years and all of the sudden there's this fresh note of discord and the whole thing seems faster, more frantic, like it is racing to a crescendo."

Belial couldn't restrain his irritation any longer. "Do you ever notice anything useful?"

"Well, sure I do, young one."

"Like what?"

"Well, I notice that we have finally reached the first gate." He lifted a spiky arm in a gesture meant to say, *Go on, have a look.*

Across the stairwell, a tall gate seemed to shimmer into existence from the empty air, wrought from the same black stone as the Colossus, and hinged and latched by a black metal Belial had never encountered. Written across the latch-work was a symbol of the Old Tongue. It meant—

"Determination is what it says," the old fellow interjected.

Belial eyed him warily. "Few read the Old Tongue."

Porcupine just smiled slyly and winked.

Belial grabbed the gates and pulled them apart. Or, rather, he tried to, but they wouldn't budge. Anger flooded through him, and he pulled harder. Still nothing.

"Well, maybe this is a sign we should turn back. It wasn't meant to be."

"No," Belial growled. "I'm going to the top. I will not be stopped." He let out a snarl and redoubled his efforts. For several long seconds, he strained until the corded muscles of his arms felt like they would tear free. Then finally, slowly, the gates parted with a sound like cracking bone.

35

DOUBLE STUBBORN

Kurt fought against the anxiety rising in his chest. Being back in these tunnels where he'd nearly died, twice, was not agreeing well with his nerves. The tunnel roof ahead sloped toward the floor, and in its lowest spot, a mound of rubble rose to meet it.

"Think we can dig it out?" Brooklyn played her flashlight over the mess. There were plenty of pieces not much bigger than bowling balls, but there were also plenty the size of a refrigerator.

"We can try shifting some of the smaller ones. Might be safer to do it from a bit back in the tunnel just in case something falls." They moved back several feet and then began grasping at stones with their minds, finding the ones that were loose. It was grueling work, harder than it would have been to do it manually, but it was safer and good practice for the girl.

More than once a cascade of dust and smaller detritus rained down from the ceiling and billowed over them, coating their faces in powdered stone. What was it people used to say? All cats are gray in the dark.

"Let's take a break," he wheezed after half an hour, shambling over to the wall where he'd placed his pack. "Want some water? A snack?"

Brooklyn nodded, huffed a series of short coughs, and came over to sit on the cool stone floor beside him. She took a long pull from the bottle he offered her, then asked, "Why did you bring so much food? There's enough in there to last a month."

He laughed. "Two weeks, maybe, and not that long if we're burning energy trying to dig our way out of a cave-in. Last time I wound up spending more'n half a year down here and hungry most of it. Wouldn't wish that on anyone."

"It just seems like a lot."

"Just shut up and eat something. I'm an old man, and I've got my reasons whether or not you think they make sense."

The work resumed and only grew more grueling as the smaller stones ran out and they had to coordinate together on the larger pieces. The dusty air grew thicker and heavier with heat. Kurt tugged his shirt irritably as it stuck to his sweaty back. The tunnel floor behind them had grown toward the ceiling by nearly a foot, and the once straight shaft was now a maze of turns around pieces of displaced rubble.

"Got to be careful we don't wall ourselves in," he observed. He stretched his back and watched Brooklyn as she plopped down right where she stood. She looked a mess. Her bleached hair had taken on a granite sheen, as had her face and arms. Said hair was plastered to her sweaty neck, and she looked exhausted and dull-eyed.

"How much further do you reckon?" she huffed.

Kurt thought he could see something of Tyler in her. Something in the way she lounged boneless and exhausted called to mind images of Tyler after football practices. He blinked and shook the thought loose. Wishful thinking that was, and not likely to make what came next any easier. He shrugged. "Wish I knew, girl. Wish I knew." He ran his fingers through his short hair thoughtfully. "This is enough for one day. Let's get out of here. We can come back in a day or two. We've got time."

Brooklyn nodded wearily and climbed to her feet.

The trek out was quicker, even with a short detour to show her the circular room full of cells where he'd been kept for so many months.

She stepped into the chamber that housed the cells and cast her eyes around, taking it in. "This is why we're doing this," she said. "For Tessa, for Saul and Raul, and David and Riley. For everyone they've hurt." She turned to look at him. "For you, too. This is the kind of thing we have to stop from happening to anyone, ever again."

She looked like some sort of avenging angel there in the dim light with her jaw thrust out belligerently and fire dancing in her eyes. He'd never felt more proud of anyone in his whole life, or more wretched with himself. As she looked away, he dropped the backpack inside the doorway and slammed the outer gate closed between them.

Brooklyn whirled, confusion giving way to dawning comprehension and then horror as she understood what was happening. "Why?" she demanded. "Why are you doing this?"

"For the only person you didn't include on your list. For you, Brooklyn. Don't you see? Told you I'd do what I had to do to keep you safe. I've failed my children before, but that won't happen again."

"I'm not your goddamn kid, Kurt. We've been over this. Open the gate!"

Kurt sighed and felt his weariness and years settling on his shoulders like a physical weight. "When my boy died, I struck a deal with an angel, a sort of reincarnation arrangement."

Brooklyn blinked. "You told me before. A thousand demons paid over twenty years."

He nodded. "I didn't understand what that meant exactly at the time. I thought I'd get my boy back just the way he was, but . . ." He gestured at her helplessly. "Now, maybe I'm glad things turned out this way."

"What do you mean?" she whispered.

"I realize that you aren't him, but there's a part of him, the best part, in you, and I can't watch that die again." He hung his head and blinked. *Must have gotten some dust in my eyes*, he thought.

"You think that it's me?" Brooklyn laughed with disbelief, as if she thought he was teetering on the cusp of some kind of mental breakdown. Probably from coming back into these tunnels so soon.

Kurt watched her steadily until she finally spoke again.

"Okay, can we just talk about this? It doesn't have to be this way." She rattled the gate in its frame for emphasis. "Please? This isn't right. Open the gate and we can talk this out."

"Maybe it ain't right, but the one thing I've learned from all of this is that being in the right doesn't keep you safe. Power and intellect do that. Right or wrong don't make you strong." He felt a little ashamed to say it, and couldn't pinpoint exactly when he'd begun to feel that way, but the words felt honest and true as they echoed around the small chamber. "In three days when you walk out of here, the scales will be balanced. You'll have nothing to fear from the Heir or the Demonriders. And if I'm still alive, you can kill me for this. I wouldn't blame you if you did."

"Just open the gate and we'll figure this out together."

Kurt winced at the pleading note in her voice. He knew the feeling. Knew it so well he dreamed about it most nights.

"What if Dravin comes back and finds me here? He knows about this place."

"He won't be back. I was lucky to see him once every three weeks, but if he does happen by, put a soul stone through his skull. You'll likely never get a better chance than that to do it and get away with it."

"Please. Don't leave me here. I'm scared."

"I'm not sure I believe that." Kurt took a steadying breath and straightened his spine. As he walked away, she screamed his name. She swore, begged, bargained, and made promises that echoed through the earth. A while later, he opened the hidden door and stepped out into the evening sunshine, but there was no warmth in it for him and no relief in the open air. He trudged back to the farm alone and couldn't quite swallow his regret.

Brooklyn shook the door for the hundredth time. Reincarnated? Was he serious? Her throat felt raw and torn from yelling. She wasn't sure if he could still hear her or not. The last echo of footsteps had died away at least an hour ago.

She paced the perimeter of her prison. It was circular, with individual cells spaced around the edges like spokes off a hub. The entirety appeared to be hand hewn. A dungeon to hold monsters, she supposed.

Reincarnation. Was he kidding with this shit? She had nothing in common with his dead son. The anger and disbelief were fading and left her tired. Or maybe that was all the rock work from earlier. Either way, she rummaged through the bag Kurt had left for her. There was a blanket, but no pillow. There were canned meats and veggies, and one of those metal mess kits you could buy at sporting goods stores. It had a steel plate and matching spork. There was a can opener. There were bottles of water and a couple of cans of Coke. Even toilet paper, but she didn't even want to think about having to use the bathroom down here.

Christ, Kurt! she thought savagely. Brooklyn took the blanket and crouched near the door, as far away from the two cells across the way as she could get, pretty sure she could smell his old, fetid shit and piss over that way.

Would the betrayals never end? Kurt hadn't changed at all. Here he was taking away her free will, trying to force his choices on her. Again! She'd thought she could trust him. She'd almost thought she could trust Belial. Maybe people and demons just weren't really capable of changing after all.

He was just like all the rest. Every damn person in this world had an opinion about what she should or shouldn't be allowed to do, where she should go, and every damned one of them thought their say mattered more than hers. They'd taken everything from her, and they just kept on taking. She'd be damned if she was going to sit here on her hunkers and wait for three days. She'd bust out of here or die trying.

36

THE LIFE THAT NEVER WAS

Porcupine was entirely too cheerful to suit Belial. Despite his resolution to see the first gate and then call it a day, he'd done nothing of the sort. Nothing but continue the climb, prattling on about the Raff, the tower, the gates, every being he'd ever met. And what had he expected traveling with a millennia-old shopkeeper? A captive audience and a gigaton of unshared gossip. What was the verse? "My cup runneth over."

"What's that? You quote the Bible, friend?"

"Hmngh."

"Fine book that. A little overdone at times, but consistency in anthologies is hard to come by." The old fellow adjusted his green shawl and satchel; the ancient leather moved easy and supple as velvet. Over the other shoulder hung the gargoyle tail. If the weight bothered him, Belial couldn't tell.

Belial stopped on the next stair, turned, and took his companion by the upper arm. The spines dug painfully into his palm and fingers, but he didn't flinch. Pain was the one virtue he was familiar with. "When and where have you had the leisure time or the opportunity to read the Bible? Because the last time I checked, there weren't a lot of literary types floating around down here."

Porcupine pulled himself free and worked his shoulder in a circle. "Easy, big guy. You hurt my arm."

"And I asked you a question, too."

"Alright. I had a copy for several years. I'm a trader. An importer of . . . things."

"Where is it now?"

"The library, I suppose. That's who I sold it to. Why does it matter?"

"You've spent a lot of time on Earth. You know too much to have been sitting in this pit for the last thousand years."

"So what? You a Warden now?"

Belial got right up in his face and locked eyes. "Are you?"

He laughed. "No, I've been many things, but never that."

"Then how—"

"No. The interrogation is over. We've stairs to climb. Come or stay." And with that, the old fellow trudged away.

Belial ground his teeth in frustration and, for the barest moment, considered putting an ice spear through the smug little bastard. Instead, he clenched his fists until his claws ached, then stomped off after his damnably annoying companion.

It wasn't much longer until they reached the second gate. Where the first had been black stone and metal, this one was a crisscrossing of silver threads that hummed and trembled with echoes of a sound past hearing. It was as insubstantial as a particularly elaborate spiderweb. The symbol appeared, woven so tightly with the rest of the gossamer that it seemed to form all at once. An aha moment like when man first traced lines between the stars. The symbol seemed to loop and spiral toward the floor, always circling back on itself but never quite getting anywhere. Belial didn't know the word, and he was loath to ask the old fellow so soon after their quarrel. He needn't have worried.

"There's not a clear translation for it. The closest word I know is 'misery.'"

"The Gate of Misery, is it?" Belial shuffled his feet and resisted the urge to unfurl his wings and turn their many eyes to examine this obstacle more closely. It wouldn't have been an issue if Old Porcupine had turned back at the first gate like he'd said he would.

How to open this one? Would it be as simple as just walking through it? He could never be so lucky. "You want to take this one, old timer? I can hold your stuff."

"If I could, I would, but you are the pilgrim and I'm just your witness." He smiled serenely.

Belial wanted to say something snarky, but the old fellow was without guile, so he turned instead and faced the gate. Misery. Wasn't that just another word for life? "Do your worst," he whispered, and stepped into the web.

He'd squeezed his eyes shut, expecting pain. It never came. He blinked first one and then the other, and found himself in a crude wooden home, notched logs chinked with a mixture of mud and grass. He sat comfortably on a log bench draped with furs. A fire crackled in a rudimentary hearth, casting a pleasant warmth across his outstretched feet. His very *human* feet. He wiggled his toes experimentally. Yep, definitely his.

Belial's stomach rumbled in response to the smell of food. That's when he noticed the clay cook pot nested in embers near the fire. It was fish stew, his favorite. He didn't know how he knew. He just did.

Movement drew his eye to the bench beside him and his breath hitched in his throat. There was a woman nursing her toddler, and from the looks of it, she had another baby well on the way. Her head was bowed. Shadows and blue-black hair obscured her face, but where the ruddy light fell, her skin was a deep olive. As if sensing his gaze, she turned to him. She smiled, her nose crinkled, and her mismatched eyes shone in the firelight.

It was Tais. A few years older than the last time he'd seen her, but still her. Still as beautiful as he remembered. She offered him the little boy with the sleepy eyes, and with a familiar gesture his arms took the boy of their own accord. "My boy," he whispered. Tais kissed him on the cheek and went outside to relieve herself, he assumed.

He examined his son, Xanthus; he wasn't sure how he knew the name, perhaps the same way he knew deep in his bones this child was his. The boy had a thick head of hair as inky as his mother's. He had her nose too, but his eyes were the pure blue of glaciers and when he brought the child up to eye level, Xanthus whacked him across the nose. Hard. And he giggled. What a fierce, perfect child. Belial beamed to himself even as tears filled his eyes. It was the hit on the nose, that's all.

When Tais came back, he was down on the floor with Xanthus, watching him alternate between an unsteady toddle and a well-practiced crawl. "What are you doing down there?" she asked with amusement in her voice.

"Playing."

"Let's eat before it is too dark."

Belial nodded and retrieved the wooden spoons and clay bowls they used to take their meals. Tais filled the bowls from the larger pot and passed him one that still boiled lazily and gave off a steady stream of steam. When it cooled enough to sip, he groaned in satisfaction. "Delicious as always," he murmured.

Tais's eyes lit with pride. "It is nothing, my love," she said as she blew on a spoonful of stew to cool it and then tipped it into little Xanthus's mouth.

In the late evening, they took a walk beside the sea. The sun fled the horizon; a gloaming of purplish light remained. It was enough to see the water break on the sand. They walked slowly because Tais tired easily this late in her pregnancy and because Xanthus walked between them, each of them holding a pudgy hand and keeping the little man on his feet and out of the water. The waves sounded in time with his heartbeat, or maybe it was his heart that marched to the rhythm of the sea. For the first time, the sea didn't worry him. He thought maybe it should, but he couldn't remember why.

Later, with the little fellow asleep in a makeshift crib, Belial found his . . . wife? Yes, he supposed she was, wasn't she? He found Tais amid their pallet of furs and slid in behind her, pressing himself against the warm curve of her back and hips, kissing gently at the back of her neck, and draping a hand loosely across her swollen belly. She pressed herself back against his chest and they fell asleep that way.

The next morning, he rose before the sun and dressed in the dark. He gathered his slender pole—the one with the horsehair line and bone hook—a net of the same making, and a woven basket that hung on his hip from a leather thong. He tied the door closed behind him and relished the kiss of the cool morning air. The tunas were on the move this time of year and the water would be thick with them for a few more days yet.

Back in the trees, a good distance from the water's edge, he found his boat. It was small compared to some others, but he liked it. There was room for three men to kneel comfortably and row. He pulled the vessel down through the sand to the water's edge. Danaus and his son Fabrice would join him soon. He unwrapped a piece of smoked fish from his satchel and broke his fast.

Just as the sun made orange glimmers in the farthest east, a voice boomed out a greeting over the noise of the surf. "Isidoros! Always so early!" His laughter rolled out in low basso. "Maybe it is because you do not have a whelp slowing you down." He banged a heavy hand against Fabrice's shoulder and almost sent the slight youth stumbling into the sand. For his part, Fabrice took the jibe with good humor.

"Maybe you are just lazy?" Belial offered back with a large grin. They traded grips and began loading the boat.

"How is Tais? The baby must come soon, yes?"

"She is good, but she is tired and ready for it to be over."

Danaus smiled. "Maybe she gives you another son."

Belial shrugged. "Maybe."

Fabrice climbed into the middle of the boat and began to arrange his pole and line. Belial and Danaus guided the boat into the water and leapt in with practiced ease. As they paddled out to deeper water, the sun broke over the horizon in earnest and turned the sea azure. Gulls floated above them, moving in endless patrols along the coastline.

Fabrice baited his hook while the two older men paddled, so he was the first to drop a line when they reached a suitable spot. Belial smiled at the boy. He was almost grown and if he filled out a bit, he would look just like his father. Fabrice saw Belial looking at him and said, "How many you think we will catch today, Isidoros?"

Belial considered the question seriously. "I bet we each take home five fish today. The tunas are moving. It is a good time."

He rose, being careful not to upset the boat, and cast the line coiled in his hand as far as it would reach. When Belial knelt again, Danaus rose and flung his line in the opposite direction. They sat in companionable silence for the better part of an hour, with Fabrice casting his line from one side of the boat to the other several times. Danaus watched him reproachfully, but said nothing. Belial smiled. "Fishing is patience, friend." He clasped an affectionate hand on the boy's shoulder, but he made sure it was clear he was speaking to him as one man speaks to another, not as to a child. After this, Fabrice settled in to wait. Danaus nodded his thanks to Belial and turned back to his own fishing.

As the sun climbed into its second hour, Danaus grunted and gave his line a firm tug. It snapped taut and began to jump and tremble as he hauled it in hand over hand. "Isidoros, bring the boat around." Belial dipped his small oar and turned his friend to a more favorable angle. A few moments later, a blue fish with black stripes across its back was borne from the water and into a woven basket with a tied lid. Danaus lowered the basket into the water and lashed it to the boat.

Belial shook his head. "Danaus, not only are you lazy, but lucky, too? I am jealous."

The big man laughed, and Fabrice smiled, too. As the day wore on toward sweltering noon, they caught several large tunas. Enough to call it a day, but Fabrice, who had been unusually fortunate, wasn't ready to call it quits yet. At his behest, they turned and rowed farther out where Danaus joked the fish were likely bigger than their boat.

They saw several dolphins and a couple of sharks, but the heat of the midday sun seemed to have spoiled the fishing because there were no bites. Once, a whale swam right under the boat, a dark mass as large as the clouds in the sky.

"How long," Fabrice asked, "do you think a family could eat on a fish that big?"

Belial considered the question. "A village could eat for a week, maybe two, but there's no way to land such a big fish."

"Storm's coming," Danaus commented, nodding to the east where the sky was turning the color of a bruise.

Belial nodded in assent and dipped his paddle, turning for the shoreline. It took them a long time, and the storm caught them before they reached the shore, driving up waves that tossed the small boat. They held their course and with weary labor finally made the beach, hauling boat and basket free of the waves.

Later, by the fire with Tais, he recounted the day's adventures for his little family. Telling them about the whale, a fish big enough to carry their hut on its back. Xanthus's eyes grew round as he tried to envision such a thing.

"Are you going again tomorrow?" Tais asked.

Belial watched the shadows dance across her profile as he considered, then said, "The tunas are still moving. I think I will if the storm has cleared." She nodded, and they lapsed into companionable silence, though something in the smallness of her, the slope of her shoulders, spoke of vulnerability and left him uneasy.

Sunrise came behind a veil of rain clouds and Belial skipped the fishing. Tais had cried out in her sleep several times during the night and this morning followed his every move with haunted eyes.

"Tell me what troubles your dreams." He laid a hand on her shoulder as she stood in the doorway and watched the storm blow in along the coast.

She shook her head but said nothing. He thought to take her by the shoulders and spin her to face him, maybe give her a little shake, make her look at him with those mismatched eyes. He didn't though, and after a long moment, she spoke.

"I dreamed I was a wife to a king, that I lived in a great palace. There were many wives. I was not the first, and some of them were my friends, sisters even. I had children. Different children that I loved as fiercely as Xanthus."

"Not so bad as dreams go." He squeezed her shoulder. "Dreams don't mean anything."

Her eyes flashed. "Mine do." She turned back to the doorway, speaking so softly he had to lean forward to hear. "I dreamed you betrayed me, and the sea rose and carried me away. I dreamed I fell asleep in a palace and woke in a fisherman's hut."

"What are you saying?" His voice grew husky, tears filling his eyes. "You are not happy?"

She lifted her arms in an expansive gesture meant to encompass everything and turned to face him. "This is the dream. Don't you see? I want to wake up now."

Through the tears, her mismatched eyes reflected the firelight in a kaleidoscope of color. When he wiped the tears away, his hands had claws again and Tais was gone, replaced by the old fellow; his quills lay back as he peered down with concern. Belial pushed him aside roughly and rose. "Come on," he said, "we've stairs to climb."

37

VOICES OF REASON

"You can't do that! It's crazy." Mrs. Mays stood up, both hands flat on the table in front of her as if she intended to vault over it and bludgeon him senseless. She was capable of it, he knew.

He'd expected this reaction when he'd decided to share his plan. "It's her or them," Kurt said flatly. "They're never going to quit. I get explosives through the tunnel and under the manor. We get her clear and—"

"And I'd be fine with that if it were just them, but it ain't." She thumped the table with both hands hard enough to make the saltshaker jump. "It's our friends, too. It's Erina and her girls, it's Tristan, Brianne, it's all the people that still call the place home. Your people, most of them. And that doesn't even account for any regulars brought in to cater or perform. What makes her life worth so much that you'd sacrifice all of theirs?"

She's my son. But, he couldn't tell her that. Not without exposing his failure, his deal with Azrael.

He doubted Brianne still counted him among her friends. It sure hadn't seemed like it when she was strangling him with his own shirt. "I don't like the idea any more than you do, Amelia." He softened his voice. "I just don't have a better one, do you?"

"How about anything that doesn't cost innocent lives?" she boomed, slapping the table again for emphasis. "If you can't come up with something, then maybe you ought to consider doing nothing. You had no right to lock her up like that in the first place. She's a grown woman, not a child. If she wants to go to the conclave, what gives you or me the right to stop her?"

"She'll die if she goes. You know that."

Mrs. Mays crossed her arms and leaned forward on her elbows. "She might, but she knows that. It's her choice." She reached out then and took his bony hand in her plump one. "Kurt, we're both of us past raising kids, and judging by the fact we've both outlived our sons, I reckon we weren't too good at it, anyway."

"Which is why—"

"You're doing it different this time? Because if that's what you were about to say, you're not. Doing it different would be if you stop trying to control everything and everybody." She sighed, sitting back, blinking. "You think if you'd locked Tyler up, he wouldn't have found a way?"

"I don't know. Maybe he wouldn't have."

"Well, *she* will."

She probably would, too. Why couldn't Brooklyn be made to see reason? If he couldn't keep her safe this way, then he couldn't keep her safe at all. If he took her only opportunity away, would she ever talk to him again? He remembered the look on her face when she'd realized he'd trapped her, and knew the answer to that. "Damn it!" He pushed himself up from the table.

"Where are you going?"

He scratched at the back of his head. "Damn it," he said again, more softly. "I'm going back to get her."

Riley crossed the threshold into Kurt's former office hesitantly. The two men who'd escorted him remained in the hallway. The door closed with an ominous thump behind him. Two men were seated across from Nathan Goodrum staring at nothing, one in a policeman's uniform. His old friend, Santimo. Riley's heart dropped. They weren't talking and there were empty cups on the desk in front of them.

As he stepped further into the room, he became aware of a figure to his left near the fireplace. It was Father Logan. As if being noticed cued him somehow, he spoke. "I understand you've had a breakthrough on our little project?"

Riley wondered how much Father Logan knew and how he knew it. "I'm making steady progress," he offered with a shrug.

"Show me. I know you have it in your pocket." He turned from the fireplace wearing a curious expression.

Fumbling the golden knuckles from his back pocket, Riley slipped them over his fingers. Instantly he felt a connection with the four lesser demons he'd been experimenting with, as if tiny filaments ran through his hand and out into the world, binding them the way threads bind fabric. He concentrated and exerted his will, and they sprang into reality in front of him.

Dravin Logan clapped his hands, delighted. Then he flicked his eyes to the back corner, and Eric Stewarth stepped out of the shadows. "Let Eric try."

Riley shrugged, dismissed the quartet, and handed the tool over. Eric slipped it on his hand and furrowed his brow. Long moments passed in silence. Father Logan's focus on Eric never wavered until the same look of concentration and effort was written on his face. Still, nothing happened. It gave Riley chills to see Eric dancing like a puppet on a string. He didn't like the guy, maybe even hated him, but this . . . What if it had been him? What if it still might be? He'd do whatever it took to avoid that fate.

Riley cleared his throat. "I suppose . . ." He trailed off when Father Logan raised a hand to forestall him, his face gone pale and sweaty.

Crossing his arms, Riley rubbed at the chill bumps.

Not going to work, his companion thought.

One of the four demons flickered faintly into existence and vanished fast enough for Riley to doubt his own eyes. Simultaneous groans of frustration erupted from Eric and Father Logan.

"Why doesn't it work?" Father Logan demanded.

Riley chose his words carefully. "Whatever you did to him that night seems to have broken his ability to impose his will. With practice you could probably help him do it."

Dravin Logan ignored the answer and snatched the golden knuckles from Eric and slipped them onto his own hand. He gave a grunt like a man lifting a heavy load and then the four demons spun into being from the shadows. A feral smile split his lips. "It requires a certain force of will."

It wasn't a question, so Riley didn't answer it. He just watched the older man think and hated himself for handing this power to his captor. It wasn't his fault. He was only doing what it took to survive and keep his free will intact.

To his right, Goodrum watched them both, and Santimo and the other man sat as still and disinterested as marble statues. Though Riley was sure they'd unholster their weapons and gun him down if he moved against Father Logan. They'd clearly had something dark to drink before his arrival. He felt bad for the three of them and Eric, too. How close he had come to the same pitiful fate. He shuddered.

"You've solved it. Not the whole thing, but it's possible now, isn't it? Remaking the ring?" Father Logan asked.

Riley nodded carefully. "There are still unknowns, but this is a big step forward."

"More time, huh? That's what we need?"

The question felt like a trap. Riley judged the distance between himself and Father Logan. *This may be the only chance we get. Kill him quick and get away*, his companion hissed. But he didn't. There was no getting away. In the office, it was five against one. He had no weapons. Outside the door there were guards. Even if he could make it to the window, could he survive that fall? No. He needed a clean getaway. He wasn't willing to die trying.

"I'm a researcher, like you," Dravin said, clearly mistaking Riley's hesitation for uncertainty. "Though my work is field work, not lab work, I believe our interests may run the same path." He walked to the window, glanced out, then hiked one hip up to sit on the ledge.

"How so?" Riley asked after several heartbeats of silence hung between them.

"I control Nathan. Through him I control Officer Santimo and Investigator Richmond. Connections within connections, yes? Like nesting dolls."

"Still not sure I follow," Riley murmured, though almost as soon as he said it, his companion had unraveled the implications for him.

Connections within connections. You see? You've made a direct connection with each of these four demons. It's inefficient.

Seeing his dawning comprehension, Father Logan smiled. "You want to take control of an army? You don't seek control of individual soldiers. You go after the general . . ."

Father Logan droned on, but Riley tuned it out, his mind spinning with thoughts. The ring, the original ring, must have taken its hold at the top, or very near it. That's why its power was so broad. Whose will would be strong enough to bind the baddest of the bad? He couldn't fathom it. Neither could his companion. The most powerful being he'd ever encountered was Prosidris, Father of the Wardens, a grade-two demon. He could command oceans. Who or what could command him? What sigil was inscribed on Solomon's black stone? And with whose blood was it written?

"—to figure out which that is. I had my reasons for disliking your brother-in-law, but I'd like us to start fresh, work together on this, as equal partners. To show my good faith, the locks are being changed on your door right now. Roam the grounds to your heart's content. All I ask is that for now, you don't leave the property."

"Partners . . . ," Riley said, trying to regain the thread of conversation.

"Equal partners," Father Logan said; with a smile so sincere, Riley couldn't disbelieve him.

Riley nodded. "Yeah, okay. That sounds good."

What is this nonsense? Stockholm syndrome?

Shut up, Riley thought back.

"Wonderful! Another token of good faith," Father Logan said as he tossed something at Riley that glittered in the firelight.

Reflexively, Riley snatched it out of the air. It was a crystal vial with a cork stopper in the neck. Inside was a liquid as dark as tar.

"I call that Devotion. Don't drink any . . . but see if it can be improved, so something like this"—he hefted the golden knuckles for emphasis—"can be made to work more easily by proxy."

Riley nodded numbly and pocketed the vial. His thoughts spiraled in complex patterns like orbiting soul stones as he and his companion wove the possibilities and implications into probabilities and theories to be tested.

38

DICTIONARIES AND BIBLES

David saw the world unraveling. He watched through many eyes as food and product shortages turned people into hoarders and then into animals. Men were stabbed at gas pumps, and women beaten and robbed in grocery store parking lots. The national guard and police forces were stretched to a breaking point by the riots and overwhelmed entirely in the big cities. An imbalance in supply and demand caused all of this chaos. Fuel shortages crippled the distribution network. In the Midwest, milk, beef, and pork rotted by the ton waiting for trucks that never came, and in the cities people starved. When milk could be had, it ran as high as twenty dollars a gallon in some places.

All of this because of an insect the size of his thumbnail with a taste for corn, and a transmissible fish fungus.

Urban families were fleeing the cities in search of food and safety. They flooded rural communities, much to the locals' chagrin. Resources were quickly exhausted, and those that survived moved on to the next small town. It was the zombie apocalypse minus the zombies.

This was the problem with humanity. All interest was personal interest, no regard for the good of the whole. A more cooperative people would have easily navigated these hardships, making coordinated adjustments and sacrifices to keep the machinery of commerce in motion.

To this end, David had commissioned the construction of several satellite hives near major cities, such as Chicago, New York, and Atlanta. They received the refugees with open arms and a complimentary beverage. Unfortunately, the supply of their special cocktail was running low. If not for his own problems with supply and distribution, he might have held the world in his palm already. It was something he needed to discuss with Azrael if she ever bothered to drop in.

Somewhere out there in all that collection of catastrophes was Brooklyn. Assuming she was alive, of course. Which he always did because the alternative was unbearable to think about.

David pulled his guitar off the stand in the corner and sat down on the couch. He didn't play immediately, though, just held it, running his fingers over the delicate curve of the body and neck. Music could stop the noise in his head, cut away the chatter and the flickering images for a bit, but only for a bit.

He played. The first struck chord stilled the voices, all but one. One too often lost in the cacophony, his own. That voice whispered what it had for weeks. *War. War is coming and you aren't ready.*

Later in the evening, when the shadows stretched for sleep, David slipped out a side door and navigated by memory and the cool blue, crisscrossed beams of energy that marked the utility lines underground and high above on their poles. He followed a stone path that wound out to a large clearing. The grass would be brown now instead of the rich green it had been on his last visit here.

David shifted the bouquet into the crook of his left arm and counted his steps carefully to arrive at the correct grave. First running his fingers over the engraving to be certain, he then placed the flowers in the stone vase and said the same thing he always said on these infrequent visits: "I'm sorry, Nicole."

Like always, a little knot of terror weighed in his stomach like cement. What if she answered?

He'd had it built for her, but there were other gravestones now, too. An organization as large as this one had its fair share of deaths. Especially now. One perk of running a church, he supposed, nobody raised an eyebrow if you had a few dead bodies out back.

On the return trek, he paused to watch the pulsing energies of his church. The connections between the people were as intricate and delicate as a spider's web, and the people themselves were as brilliant and multicolored as the stars. Amid the cool colors of contentment, the blues, greens, and shades of purple, there were three points of sullen redness and all around those spots, the connections were slowly changing color to match. It was Eli, Nicole's boyfriend, and her parents, knowing things they shouldn't know. He'd quelled them before. Lulled them into unknowing the source of their hatred, but it never lasted. Left unchecked, the discord would spread like an infection. David knew of only one way to remove them from the network. He thought of the graveyard and shook his head. It wouldn't come to that. He was no murderer, but . . . But what? *But what about Nicole?* he thought, and for once there was no answer. It didn't do to dwell on regret. She was one person and he had a whole world full of people to worry about. What was the loss of one life measured against the needs of so many?

The next morning, he summoned his right-hand man. Avery was a stoutly built guy in his late thirties. He was ex-military and had worked overseas as a private bodyguard for the better part of a decade. He remained one of the most autonomous of David's organization. Dravin Logan apparently had a much lighter touch than David. He'd been unable to duplicate the feat. He could reap the benefits of Dravin's work, though.

"Avery, what can you tell me about the elixir? Where does it come from? Is there more?"

The man didn't answer right away. His eyes clouded over, David felt a ripple spreading through the network of the Prophets, and a few moments later, Avery shook his head in negation.

Not to be put off, David tried another question. "Can you remember a place Father Logan would visit in private, not permitting others to accompany him?"

After a lengthy pause. "The bathroom, his private quarters, his office."

"Okay, and did you or anyone else ever notice that he came out of those places with elixir?"

Almost without delay this time. "His office."

"Thank you, Avery. Come with me. I need your eyes."

They crossed the hallway. He wasn't hopeful. A hiding spot in the office seemed too easy, too obvious. David had Avery search the desk first, though he didn't expect to find anything, as he'd been using the desk off and on for more than a year. Avery was very thorough. He checked each drawer methodically, checked them for false bottoms, too. He crawled under and felt around beneath the desk. Nothing.

David turned Avery's head this way and that, scanning the room. "Check the coat rack, the guest couch, and the closet." He settled into blindness and let Avery do his work. The sounds of the search were oddly comforting. Around him the energies of the house and the people in it pulsed a strange staccato rhythm.

A few minutes passed and then, "Nothing, sir."

"Was afraid of that." He looked through the other man's eyes, ignoring the odd sensation of looking back at himself. "When I was a kid, my grandpa had a safe. He kept it by his bed like a nightstand. Even had a tablecloth long enough to hide what it was. He used to let me spin the dial. I'd press my ear to the door and try to hear the tumblers."

"That's very clever," Avery rumbled.

"Not clever enough. When I was older, in high school maybe, someone broke in while my grandparents weren't home. They found it and carried it out. Probably they busted it open somehow. The police never figured out who did it."

"That's too bad."

"Yeah, granddad was upset. He had a lot of old documents and pictures in that safe. But mostly he was mad they broke his lamp. They didn't need to do that."

"Seems trivial, considering all his valuables were taken."

"I asked him once how much money he'd lost in that robbery. You know what he told me?"

"I don't, sir."

"He said, 'A man would be a fool to keep more than five hundred dollars in a safe he paid five hundred for.'"

Avery barked a laugh. "That's not an answer."

"That's what I said! Then he just smiles and points at the bookshelf and tells me to bring his dictionary and his Bible."

"Hollowed out, weren't they?"

"They were." David smiled and watched himself smile. "He said that anybody sorry enough and ignorant enough to be a thief wouldn't think to reach for either of those books."

Avery cracked his neck. David was watching, but he wasn't moving the man's eyes when they came to rest on the bookshelf behind him.

39

GATES AND DOMINOS

Brooklyn made a fine-toothed saw of her will and set its teeth to the steel bars between her and freedom. Sweat ran steadily down her face and torso as the effort taxed her already fatigued body and mind. The growing pile of silver shavings on the floor encouraged her, and the fire in her belly steeled her resolve. The bars couldn't be broken outright; she didn't have the strength, but she could wear them away. For three hours, she'd done just that and had a groove in one bar big enough for her thumbnail to fit into. Brooklyn ran the math. It would take nine hours to cut one bar clean through. There were four bars, and each would need to be cut twice—once at the top and once at the bottom—to make a hole big enough to wiggle through. That was seventy-two hours of hard labor and didn't account for sleeping or eating. Brooklyn had less time than that before Kurt returned. He'd said when she walked out of here in three days the scales would be balanced, that she'd have nothing to fear from anyone. That was bullshit, and she knew it. Oh sure, he'd be back in three days if he said so, but even if the supernatural players left her alone, every law enforcement agency in the country still wanted to get a hold of her.

Letting the thread of her concentration slip, Brooklyn sat heavily, pawing through the provisions Kurt had left. She settled on a pack of peanut butter crackers and tried not to notice how her hands shook and rattled the wrapper. Intermingled feelings of betrayal, anger, and despair chased one another through her stomach and chest like playful kittens. She understood on some level that Kurt thought he was helping her, saving her life even, but she was damn tired of being treated like a child. And despite what he thought, she wasn't *his* child to save.

Brooklyn finished the crackers and studied the door while she waited for her hands to steady. This was working, but it wasn't working fast enough to do her any good. What would her dad have done? He'd have had the right tool for the job, she supposed, an angle grinder or something like that. "Work smarter, not harder." That's the advice he would give. The sort of maddening, nonspecific suggestion that made her feel dim-witted and then petulant. What else would he have said? "There's an easier way to do most things than the way we do them." Was there an easier way?

She dug in the bag for the flashlight, switched it on, and played the beam over the doorway, pushing back shadows the overhead incandescent couldn't touch. The grooved cut in the bar flashed silver. Something on the left side of the door caught her attention. Brooklyn thought of the last three grueling hours and blushed. How could she have been so stupid? There, clear in the flashlight beam, the dead bolt that locked the cell door into the wall. It was smaller than the bars. If she'd spent her wasted time on it, she might be halfway through by now.

Fumbling in the bag again, she pulled out more food. Cans of beanie weenies, canned pasta would be good for energy, too. Not seventy-two hours, but six hours, maybe less, and she'd be free. Just one cut to make.

The next two gates came in quick succession. The first was marked with a jagged glyph that the old fellow read aloud in a rumbling sigh: "Retribution." And clear enough to read through the translucent red bars of the third gate was a fourth of a melancholy purple material that seemed to drink in the light from the high windows and give nothing back. Porcupine took a long look at that one, squinting, before pronouncing it the Gate of Sorrow.

Belial put a clawed hand to the sigil and felt it pulsing with a strange warmth that ran along his arm. His heart quickened. The gate opened outward abruptly, pushing him back several steps.

A man with a familiar face strode through the gate. Belial knew him but couldn't say from where. He was tall and broad through the shoulders, and moved with the casual fluid grace of a young man. His hair was dark and long and he had eyes to match. His complexion spoke of long days under a Mediterranean sun. He wore a robe of crude fabric, and then Belial remembered his face.

"Friend of yours?" Porcupine asked mildly.

"Isidoros," Belial breathed.

"I was once," he murmured, "but look closer."

The answer was in the man's eyes. A brown so dark it presumed blackness, but around the irises a glimmer—just a glimmer—of glacial blue.

"You're me!"

"The stronger, braver you. The part that sees the bigger picture and is willing to make necessary sacrifices."

"Like Tais?"

"The bitch," he agreed.

Rage and loathing boiled in Belial, fuel ready for the spark. "So brave you're afraid to defy your father, so strong you tossed a young girl into the ocean?"

"Don't know why you romanticize these human sluts so much. Her bones are old enough to have turned to dust. No matter what decisions you made back then, that won't change." He smiled; it was beautiful and cruel. "Besides, I heard you have a new pet now. What's her name? Broo—"

Belial cut him off with a slap and rake of claws that would have made a grizzly bear proud. The righteous satisfaction was short-lived, however. Isidoros turned back to face him, face unblemished, still smirking. Then pain blossomed across the left side of Belial's own face like a spreading fire. When he cupped his cheek, his fingers came away wet.

"That doesn't appear to be working," the old fellow offered conversationally.

"No shit!" Belial roared at his companion. "Do you ever say anything that isn't obvious?"

Porcupine considered. "Obvious to whom? Everything I say seems obvious to me, but then again, I'm cleverer than most."

Isidoros cleared his throat. "Brooklyn, right? Except this time around, you are so pathetic that it's the human using you? Am I right?"

Belial lashed out with a savage kick and instantly regretted it as he doubled over.

"Of course, even when what I've said is obvious, the person I'm saying it to rarely seems to listen. It's very frustrating." Belial would have cursed the old fellow and his prattling if he could have gotten a decent breath. "My advice, well the first piece anyway, would be to keep our focus on what we are doing here."

Belial groaned and straightened his spine. His doppelgänger regarded him with something like amusement. *Focus on what we are doing here.* The words resonated in his thoughts. He drew back a pace from his adversary and regarded him thoughtfully, letting the indignation and anger evaporate. Would he have been so reckless and easily provoked if he weren't feeling miserable from the last gate? Maybe not.

"Not the quickest thinker, are you?" Isidoros mocked.

Belial approached him. Obviously, force would not work. He darted to one side to go around. The adversary mirrored him flawlessly. Just as quickly, Belial changed directions. He may as well have been trying to outrun his own reflection. Tentatively, Belial raised a clawed hand and pressed it against the man's chest. Belial pushed and felt the force against him grow in equal measures until he stumbled back. It was a disorienting experience.

"Hey, Quills!" he hollered over his shoulder. "Come here."

If the old fellow took offense to this new nickname, he didn't show it. He shuffled forward and raised a bushy eyebrow.

Belial spoke without looking away from the adversary. "We are here to get through that gate and this guy is in our way."

"An apt assessment."

"I can't hurt, get past, or move him."

The old guy grunted his acknowledgement and nodded.

"So, can you take him out?"

"I don't think it is a wise plan."

"Why not?"

"What happens if . . ." He paused to pluck a quill from his shoulder. The end glistened in the dim light.

"If wha—ouch!" He cried out as the old fellow stabbed him in the forearm. Muttering a curse, Belial ripped the needle out of his flesh and threw it at the old bastard.

Unperturbed as always, Porcupine pointed at the adversary. "Shhh . . . look." He gestured insistently.

At first, Belial didn't see anything. Just the man, his dark eyes, and their glacial halos, but then the bloodstain began to darken the adversary's sleeve and a trickle of crimson ran out and down his wrist before dripping onto the stone stairs. Belial looked down at his own arm, where blood ran freely to drip from his claws.

"You see. There's no killing one of you without killing the other."

Belial pressed his other hand over the wound in his arm. "And there wasn't a less painful way to test that out?"

Porcupine shrugged. "Now we know it works both ways."

"How does that help us?" Belial asked quietly.

"Now we know what not to do." The old fellow turned and unslung his pack, dropping it on the wider side of the stairs, near the outer wall. He sank down beside it, rummaged around muttering to himself, and produced a sheaf of parchment and a glass vial of ink. Porcupine plucked another quill, unstoppered the bottle, and began to write.

Several minutes passed; Belial cleared his throat twice and then a third time before the old fellow looked up at him. "What the hell are you doing?"

"I'm making notes. No one has a record of these gates and the challenges they present. Accounts don't even agree on how many there are, or the order of them. It could be valuable information if we make it out alive." He turned the pages around so Belial could see. "What do you think of my sketch?"

Belial peered. It was a good rendition of him slapping his doppelgänger. A caustic remark rose to his lips, but he swallowed it. The old fellow was looking at him expectantly, almost like a small child seeking a parent's praise. The thing he was about to say, he realized, was a lot like something this phantom of Isidoros might have said, sharp words meant to cut.

Instead, he said, "That's uh . . . that's actually a really good drawing, Quills."

"You two are making me sick!" the adversary called out from his place before the gate. "Why don't you just kiss each other's asses already and get it over with?"

Another thought occurred to Belial. "Hey, shouldn't we have climbed high enough that we'd have seen doors opening out onto the balconies by now?"

The old shopkeeper shrugged.

Belial hunkered down on a step higher than his companion and leaned back against the wall. He was careful to keep his green cloak pulled around his shoulders. The old fellow was busy with his pages again and the adversary looked on like a petulant child but was, for once, silent. Belial didn't sleep, not a necessity for his kind, but he did relax and let his mind toy with the problem at hand. It was, he'd decided, a puzzle, and puzzles have solutions. What was the point of the gate if it was impassable, after all?

"Suppose I went to sleep, very deep. Do you think he'd sleep too? Maybe you could drag me past him and through the gate?"

"Hmm . . . his mood seems to follow yours closely, but I'm not sure that would work. I'm thinking we won't pass unless he lets us."

"Well, that's never going to happen. He's an unreasonable asshole."

"No, it's worse than that," Porcupine said, "he's you."

Azrael Uzrahai found herself pressed into service. Her force of reaper assistants couldn't keep up. Not with the wars engulfing Africa and the Middle East, not with the contagion turning the ocean's fish into biohazards, and especially not with the corn crop failure. War, Pestilence, Famine, and she supposed she was Death. There was an old-school biblical grandeur to it she found intoxicating. Maybe she could round up a pale horse someplace.

She missed the freedom she'd enjoyed in the beginning, but she'd have it back once the dying slowed down. There would be people again that worshiped her, and there'd be few enough of them that the tether that bound her to her nature would never again be yanked taut. She could do just one thing and be wholly present for it. Maybe read a book on the beach, or watch the sunset from Everest.

As far as she knew, she'd been the last untainted with human blood. Azrael wished she'd had held on to that badge of honor, but there was nothing for it. She had sunk down from her high place to get the sustenance she needed to survive, and didn't regret it exactly, but there was a tug, weak as a kite string, but constant. Urging her to some other place where she belonged now. That would not be a problem much longer, she hoped.

Her people were as ready as they were going to be. David had them prepared as much as it was possible to prepare for something like this. Azrael had one more domino to nudge, and then she could sit back and watch things unfold. It was time for Kurt Levin to do his part.

She hefted a book bound in human skin and stepped over the body of the woman who had owned it. The woman was once pretty, with dark hair and big eyes to match. Not now, with her neck disjointed and purpling, and her hair and cheek matted with blood. It was a shame the negotiations about the book hadn't gone better.

40

Unlikely Reunion

"You want me to do what!?" Kurt spluttered. He had been halfway back to the farm after discovering Brooklyn's escape when Azrael descended into his path like a flock of jeering crows.

He remembered how his stomach had dropped when he'd found the steel door ajar and Brooklyn gone. How he'd turned circles trying to make sense of it, and screamed her name until the echoes in the tunnel were deafening. He'd chased his own voice to every chamber and dead end looking for her, and finally with dread pooling in his belly, he'd headed back to the farm, hoping she'd turn up there.

"Summon them." Azrael pushed the leather book against his chest hard enough to make him stumble back a step. "All of them."

Dread turned to horror. "I'm not strong enough. It took me years to capture the first hundred."

"Then die trying and we will see if the child has it in her to finish what you failed."

"That wasn't the deal. She's off-limits to you."

Her face softened into an expression of amusement, or maybe derision. It was hard to say in the moonlight. "If you want to hold me to our terms, then don't die, because once you do, all bets are off."

"At least let me use the ring. That's the only way I could summon and bind so many, and I know you have it."

"The ring is beyond even my reach now." She looked wistful. "I don't need you to capture them, only to call them across. The Pull isn't what it once was, and your strength is backed by mine." She tapped her temple. "Or had you forgotten?"

A buzzing chorus of chitinous voices echoed through his memory and made him shudder. "I haven't forgotten."

She flickered, but less than he remembered. "Good. Get some sleep so you're sharp, then get it done."

Before he could reply, she was gone in a gust of wind. He threw the book on the ground and swore. He needed to find Brooklyn, but he couldn't afford to defy Azrael. If he'd had hair long enough, he would have torn it out in frustration. Instead, he sat cross-legged in the dry leaves and tried to work out a way to keep Brooklyn safe and do what Azrael wanted at the same time.

How could he have let this happen? He'd lost Brooklyn again and now he wasn't even going to have time to look for her. Maybe he could enlist Mrs. Mays to search along the nearby roads.

Maybe when he got back to the farm, she'd be there. Furious but safe. He didn't put much stock in the thought. Where would she go? Back on the road? Maybe, but she wouldn't stand a chance of not getting caught. Every law man and his three closest friends were looking for her. If they found her, it would be his fault for having driven her to it. Mrs. Mays had the right of it: he wasn't much good at raising children. Then again, she wasn't one, and that, he supposed, was the thing he'd been missing all along.

When first light came, he was making his way across the barren cornfields; a new day to face and he hadn't slept at all. Early as it was, Amelia was up and about her chores. He slipped inside and stowed the grimoire in the guest room with his other belongings. Kurt would ask Mrs. Mays to start searching the roads as soon as she returned to the house for breakfast.

As he poured a cup of coffee in the kitchen, his mind ticked through a list of supplies he'd need for the summoning and likely locations. He definitely wanted to be in a rural place. The damage something like this would cause in a populated area would be unthinkable. Then again, he had deduced that was exactly what Azrael wanted.

Brooklyn idly ran a finger over the scar on her chest that spiraled down toward her heart like a tangle of thorns. She'd hiked away from the tunnel and away from the path back to the farm until she found a place to hunker between two trees on the opposing ridge. She had a good view of the mouth of the tunnel, but was far enough down not to be silhouetted against the sky. At least it would have been a good view if the surrounding night wasn't pitch black.

She stopped there because her legs were trembling violently, and she needed to eat. The exertions of her escape were weighing heavy, and she cursed herself for all the wasted effort. The backpack of supplies was substantially lighter than it had been twelve hours ago, but she did find a pack of crackers and some beanie weenies. Once her belly was full, she pulled her arms inside her shirt and leaned her head against the tree and closed her eyes just for a minute.

A loud thump in the leaves and a yelled curse startled her awake. Her eyes snapped to the only source of light, a figure sitting near the hidden tunnel entrance. It was Kurt. She recognized the shape of his face and the slope of his shoulders by the illumination of his flashlight. He must have already been inside and discovered her escape. How deep asleep must she have been not to hear his approach in the dry leaves? The night creatures held their breaths after his outburst and Brooklyn was careful not to move lest she rustle the leaves and draw his attention.

He did nothing but sit for a long time. The longer she watched him, the more forlorn he appeared. An irrational part of her wanted to call out to him and offer some comfort or condolence. He hadn't meant her ill after all. She understood that, but she also had some things she needed to do, and he'd already demonstrated that he was more likely to hinder than to help. When he stood up, she opened her mouth to call after him, but didn't. Brooklyn watched until his light passed beyond her sight.

She was covered in dust and grit from the excavation, and she wanted a shower and a warm bed. Instead, she made herself get up and walk back to the tunnel. Kurt had probably searched the place to see if she might be hiding somewhere else in the tunnels, so she didn't think he'd be back this way anytime soon. It didn't take her long to find the way back to the stones they'd excavated almost two days ago. The debris sloped up to the ceiling, large boulders on the bottom and finer stones the higher you went. She climbed as high as she dared, the pebbles shifting and cascading beneath her feet.

It was a large problem, one she would have tried to blast through a year ago and wound up collapsing from overexertion. Riley had told her once to focus on the small, precise side of the craft rather than the big flashy displays. He'd even said something about moving just the atom at the center of an object. She didn't think she could do that and wasn't sure he could either.

This was going to be about having the right tool for the job, or being the right tool, rather. Brooklyn took a steadying breath and focused her will into a blade, then into a nail, and finally into something as small and pointy as a needle. She sank that needle into the dust-fine detritus near the ceiling and pushed it forward, wanting some idea if the other side could be reached.

Displaced dirt showered down steadily for several long minutes. An ache was starting behind her eyes and she struggled to hang on to what she had. The further she went, the greater the resistance seemed to become. "Right tool for the job," she mumbled to herself. Her mind went to the auger she'd seen her father use for postholes. She imagined an incline plane spiraling around her needle of will and set it to turning. The dust cascaded down, forcing her to pull her T-shirt over her mouth and nose. She felt a trickle and knew her nose was bleeding again, a sure warning she was dangerously overexerting.

Brooklyn gave that needle a shove, and the pressure gave way. Her ears popped, and she felt the barest stirring of air.

She wondered about ballooning her tool on the other side and yanking it back through. She wiped her bloody nose. No. The effort would probably kill her. Instead, she imagined the continuous flow of water, the way it could carry dirt and silt away. Brooklyn let the needle melt and flow through the hole. The small debris began washing down.

Maintaining the flow was a small effort compared with the heavy lifting she had been doing the past few days, but as the minutes stretched on, it wore on her resolve as steadily as it eroded the collapsed stone and dirt. When the opening was as big around as her arm and in no danger of closing, she let it go with a gasp. She fumbled in the dark for her sack and the food inside. Then she closed her eyes, just for a little while.

Brooklyn woke without knowing how long she'd slept. She didn't have a phone or a watch. Panic seized her. What if she'd already missed the conclave? Could she have slept a whole day away? Her bladder, she reasoned, would let her know if that much time had passed. Regardless, she felt a renewed sense of urgency. She clambered up the slope and reached into the hole, scooping out handfuls of crushed stone as fine as sand and a smattering of larger pebbles and clots of clay.

After a few breathless moments, she'd widened the mouth of the hole to accommodate her shoulders and allow her to reach farther in. She shone the flashlight through the opening to where it narrowed at the far end and guessed it was about three feet from one side to the other. Brooklyn had a steady throb behind her eyes that blossomed into sharp pain as she reached out with her mind and began pushing the debris out to widen the far side of the tunnel. Instinctively, she reached for Belial to bolster her failing strength. She felt a faint coolness, far away and a little less tired, but the agony in her brain didn't stop.

Minutes or maybe hours later, she pushed her backpack of supplies through the other side and tumbled bonelessly after.

Brooklyn felt giddy and lightheaded as she shouldered the bag and followed the faint glowing stones set in the tunnel wall. She worried about encountering another cave-in and knew she wouldn't have the strength to bypass it. She need not have concerned herself. The tunnel curved, sloped up, and opened on a chamber illuminated by a weak, gray light, bright in contrast to the tunnel. It was a large room strewn with broken rockwork, shards of granite, and a fine layer of gray dust. The floor on the far side had been swept clean recently, the rubble moved into orderly piles on either side of a path that led from a grand set of stone stairs to a wooden door.

There was a figure in the shadows beside the door, watching her. When she froze, the figure smiled and stepped into the light and said, "You look like a ghost."

After all this time, something in her chest unclenched. "Riley," she breathed.

41

Putting Puzzles Together

Riley ushered Brooklyn into his lab, casting furtive glances at the stairwell. She was leaner than he remembered, almost gaunt. Her eyes, bloodshot and fever-bright, and her once chestnut hair bleached. Every inch of her, from hair to toes, was covered in pale dust.

"What day is it?" she demanded. "What time?"

He told her it was Wednesday, midday, and she sagged with relief.

"Do I still have clothes here?" she asked, gesturing toward the bedroom.

He nodded. "Where have you been? How did you get here? Why are you back? It isn't safe." He bit his tongue. Too many questions.

Brooklyn dropped her backpack, and it made a hollow thunk on the stone floor. "Shower first. Then we can talk." She trudged off to the bathroom and left him staring after her in disbelief.

She was gone a long time, so he went about securing his lab. The Tome in the fireplace he hoisted from the dais with an effort of will and hid it in plain sight amid the ash, soot, and half-burned logs.

Why do you suppose she's here? his companion wondered.

To hide maybe?

Can't think of a worse place to do that than here.

Riley cleared his old workbench, swiftly plucking beakers, burners, and various mundane and arcane materials up and placing them on the shelves around the room. He had a lab upstairs, but he suspected it was being surveilled, so there were some things he hoped to do here instead. To his knowledge, Dravin Logan was not aware of this lab, and it didn't look like much had been done to clean up the wreckage from the rocket blast.

Riley wasn't sure how Brooklyn had come to be here. The tunnels were impassable; he'd checked only a couple of days ago, thinking his newfound freedom might afford him an untraceable escape.

Well, I guess we'll just have to ask her if she ever comes out of the bathroom.

He nodded a silent acknowledgement. Riley had the vial Father Logan had given him, and he was eager to examine the contents more closely. He was setting up his microscope when Brooklyn emerged from the bathroom in a cloud of steam. She was human again and had her color back, and her damp hair was blonde instead of granite gray. Dressed in jeans and a Panama City Beach T-shirt, she still looked exhausted.

Brooklyn smiled, came to him, kissed him softly on the lips, and pulled him into a fierce hug. She smelled good and tasted of peppermint toothpaste. "I need you to make more ICMs for me," she said as she lay herself facedown on the workbench he'd just cleaned off and lifted her shirt, exposing her back.

"I thought we were calling them soul stones?"

"Just trying to speak your language, baby." She smiled tiredly. "Take some spinal fluid; I need them as soon as possible."

He rested his hand on her bare back. Her skin was hot from the shower and he had to resist the urge to trail his hand down over the inviting swell of her hips. Did she know David was alive? What would that mean for their budding relationship? Half-formed memories flashed through his mind. He licked his lips and attempted to push the thoughts aside. "They take weeks to make."

She sat up and turned to face him. His hands rested on her knees now. "I don't have weeks, not even days. I only have hours." She shrugged. "Guess I'll have to figure something else out."

"So, you didn't come here to lay low with me, I guess?" He tried to keep the disappointment out of his voice.

"Not my style."

"Whenever I made soul stones for any of us, I made extras in case the originals were lost or broken. I have three of yours." Riley walked over to the shelf and poked around until he found a small wooden box. He opened it and the orbs floated out and over his shoulder to their master. One a swirl of crimson and black, another striated between shades of peach and orange, and the third brindled brown and gray. They settled into uncertain orbits and then a flash of green leapt from her pocket to join the complex pattern.

"I see you still have one."

She nodded, then asked, "You've been here this whole time? 'Laying low'?"

He wasn't sure if it was an accusation or a question. She didn't meet his eyes. He felt a flash of irritation but tamped it down and tried to put on a casual humor he didn't feel. "Been a professional prisoner, mostly. Initially with Eric Stewarth here at the mansion, later at one of his family's estates over in Nashville, and now back here with Dravin Logan."

"Oh."

"Yeah, they just started letting me out of a locked room about a week ago."

"Why did they do that?"

He shrugged. "I've been trying to reason that out myself. I'm watched pretty closely, and I'm not supposed to leave the property."

"You must have some idea?"

"I'm an asset?" He frowned. "I guess Logan thinks he'll recruit me. With Kurt dead, I don't really have any loyalties."

Brooklyn smiled at him. He couldn't help it; he smiled back. It was so good to see her.

She reached out and put her hand on his. "Kurt is a manipulative egotistical idiot," she said, smiling, "but he's alive."

Kurt was alive. All this time? He felt relief and a bit of resentment. Better part of a year and Kurt never came for him, tried to contact him, nothing?

Brooklyn must have read his expression, because she squeezed his hand until he looked at her. "He was a prisoner until recently"—she gestured over her shoulder—"back in those tunnels. Father Logan starved him almost to death and let him believe you were dead."

"That psychotic son of a bitch!" Riley growled. "I should have killed him when I had the chance."

She shrugged as if to say that it wasn't worth dwelling on.

Do you think Logan dosed Kurt? his companion whispered.

"How did Kurt seem when you saw him? Was he zoned out or flat or just anything unusual about the way he was acting?"

She looked thoughtful for a minute. "Nope, same old Kurt. Thinks he knows best and everyone should go along with what he says."

Riley frowned thoughtfully. "Oh. That's good actually."

"What about Nathan Goodrum? I hear he's the Protector. He's here?"

"He's pretty much always here."

"And Eric Stewarth, the boy that led the attack last year, has he arrived for the conclave?"

"Also, pretty much always here."

Why is she asking these questions? the companion wondered. He need not have wondered for long.

"Good, I'm going to kill those two, but we need Father Logan alive."

Riley sighed. "Things are not that simple anymore. They are just puppets, now. Dravin has them on a psychic leash."

Brooklyn looked pale. Combined with the dark circles under her eyes, she almost seemed a ghost. "He'll know if I kill them?"

"And they'll know if you try to capture or kill him. And anyone else he's dosed."

She looked confused. "Dosed?"

Riley fumbled for the vial of opaque liquid and showed it to her. He told her what it did and filled her in on everything leading up to that night at her parents' barn. When he got to the part about the night at the Everses' barn with David, he watched her face, trying to read her emotions. Trying to understand if this knowledge changed things between them.

"So, David's alive? He's really okay?" She smiled with relief.

"I mean, he was."

A flush of unmistakable rage twisted her features. "Did Father Logan take David's mind, too?"

"I'm not sure. I know he took Eric's, and he gave me a 'stay of execution.'" He made quote marks in the air to emphasize the words. "I know they got the funnel in David's mouth, but then he vanished. Nothing left but a charred feather."

"A feather?"

"Azrael's feather. I have it in my upstairs lab, actually."

"The death angel Kurt made his bargain with?"

"Same," Riley agreed.

"Well, what's David got to do with her?"

"That, my dear, is the million-dollar question."

She hopped down from the table and paced the room. Brow furrowed in thought. Finally, she looked up at him.

"Did you know he thinks it's me? Kurt, I mean. That I'm his resurrected little boy?"

The look of shock on his face must have given her all the answer she needed because Brooklyn nodded before he could speak and resumed her pacing. "He tricked me and locked me up in those tunnels to keep me from coming to the conclave. Said he'd be back in three days, and I wouldn't have anything to fear after that. He said the scales would be balanced or some bullshit like that."

"This isn't a fight he can win. Not even with our help. All the Protectors will be there. All the major families. There will be the Heir's armed guards, Goodrum's Demonriders, Dravin's acolytes, and no telling how many others, and none of them on our side."

Unmitigated disaster, his companion agreed.

"Can you get communications out?" Brooklyn asked suddenly.

"Probably so." He nodded at the old-fashioned phone on the far wall.

She walked over and grabbed the handset off the cradle and pressed it to her ear. Then Brooklyn smiled. "It's got a dial tone."

"Who do you want to call?"

She grinned again. He thought it looked damned good on her. "I want you to call Eric's mama."

"That's me? You're sure?" Belial asked for the fifth time, contemplating his damnable double and his spiky companion by equal measures.

"Oh yes, I'm sure. The resemblance is uncanny."

Was Quills suppressing a grin? Belial thought he might be. He rolled his eyes at the old fellow and turned his attention back to his doppelgänger.

As he approached, he said, "You know you're everything I hate, right?"

His double puffed up and said, "Strength, power, purpose. You, on the other hand, are pitiful, weak, mewling, barely better than human."

"I would have said petty, cruel, and blindly obedient. And yet you are me and I am you, and we are in each other's way."

The twin tilted his head, considering for a moment. Apparently unable to think of an insulting retort about the observation.

Belial took it as a good sign and went on. "You are everything I can't accept about myself, and I'm everything that rejected self cannot reconcile."

"Are you reciting a love poem or getting to the point?"

Belial lunged forward and his double rushed to meet him. Belial wrapped his arms around him in a bear hug. "The point is," Belial grunted, "I accept you. I accept myself for what I was and what I am. I embrace it." He gave another squeeze, and the doppelgänger melted into him. It was a strange, warm, vaguely gross sensation, and then it was over. He was whole, and the third gate was open to them.

Belial rushed through the red gate quickly, half expecting his more irritating half to materialize in the way. Fortunately, the fourth gate was in sight. It was a majestic purple that seemed to tug at the light and bend it in strange ways.

"You said this is the Gate of Sorrow?"

"That's what the glyph reads, old friend."

"You're the old one," Belial grumbled.

"And the friendly one," Quills offered amiably.

Belial approached slowly. After the first gate, he'd thought this was going to be as easy as pie, but the last two gates had taken a toll, especially the second one. He wasn't sure how a Gate of Sorrow could make him feel any sorrier than he had after the Gate of Misery. And he shuddered at the thought of finding out. Belial checked the clasp for his cape and pulled the green leather farther around his shoulders.

To his credit, Quills didn't rush him. Finally, with a sigh, Belial reached out a clawed hand and touched the opaque purple latch.

The gate swung open, and nothing happened. Belial looked back at Porcupine and the old fellow shrugged. Belial braced himself, closed his eyes, and stepped through the gate. Still nothing.

He turned back to Quills and shrugged, then jerked his chin to indicate Quills should follow him up the winding stairs.

42

Trust Fall

Kurt drew his circle in pig blood. It spanned the central chamber of the underground tunnels, fully eighty feet across. He'd pounded a spike into the center of the granite floor and tied a rope to make a crude compass. He shortened the rope and made a circle within a circle, connecting the inner circle to the outer with lines of blood at the four cardinal directions. Then he did the same in the intercardinal directions. On and on, dividing the circle until there were sixty-four sections around the perimeter.

He stood up to take a break while his handiwork dried. His back and knees ached, his eyes weak from straining to see by lantern and flashlight. He would have preferred to do this on an uninhabited island or Antarctica or some such remote place far from humanity, but he had the luxury of neither time nor travel. This was the safest place available to him. The tunnels wouldn't hold what he summoned indefinitely, but he hoped they would keep them contained for a long time. Since there was only one way out, he planned to complete the summoning, run like hell, and blow up the tunnel entrance on his way out. And good riddance to this damned underground prison.

Walking back to the cells where he'd spent so many months, he examined the latches and locks that had held him. Then he examined the door to the antechamber that hadn't held Brooklyn. He still couldn't figure how she'd done it. She'd had some sort of cutting tool. She'd started on the bars and then attacked the lock bolt directly. A hacksaw blade was the only thing that made sense, but where would she have gotten one? He kicked an empty Vienna sausage can and sent it skittering away into the shadows. Damn, he wished he hadn't locked her up. Now she was out there somewhere, probably doing something stupid, and he should be with her to keep her safe. This was all his fault. All of it. He scratched the back of his head. There was nothing for it, and he had work to do. He wouldn't be any good to her if Azrael cut him loose and let the madness creep back in. As soon as this was done he'd get back to looking for her.

He returned to tracing the symbols from Azrael's book, one by one into the trapezoidal sections he'd created between the inner and outer circles. The blood stank and sweat ran into his eyes. The complex shapes of the sigils gnawed at his mind like the beginnings of insanity. Something in the angles and swirls took a ninety-degree turn right out of reality, and his brain struggled to process it.

After eight were finished, he rested until he felt like he could look at the remaining sigils again without going cross-eyed. It was going to be a long day.

"Did that seem a little too easy to you?" Quills asked. "I mean, every gate has seemed harder than the one before."

Belial kept trudging as he considered the question. "Maybe I've experienced enough sorrow in my life to get a free pass on this one."

The old fellow guffawed. "You don't really believe that, do you?"

"It could be the case." Belial bristled.

"Don't be prickly, young pilgrim. But what makes you think you've had more sorrow than any of the rest of the desperate fools who've tried climbing the tower of despair?"

Was Porcupine really telling *him* not to be prickly? Belial couldn't decide if it was intentional irony or not. Had Quills just made a joke? "Let's see, I've spent most of my life in service to a megalomaniac who also happens to be my father. I sacrificed the love of my life to the furtherance of his goals, and I don't even know what they are. I've killed hundreds of humans and destroyed a young girl's life and family in the process. I've possessed people and generally left them dead or ruined. I made a promise to a child, well, a dragon child, and it cost her life." Belial slowed, then stopped and turned around, sitting down on the obsidian stairs. "Every decision I've ever made has been a mistake. I poison everything I touch."

Quills took a seat beside him. "And you think you're making another mistake now?"

"Maybe." Belial leaned back against the curving wall and drew his legs up and rested his crossed arms on his knees. "I have a friend who needs me, and she might die without my help, but if I don't do this, she will almost certainly die, even with my help."

"This has to do with the father you talked about?"

"To some degree."

"It's a woman, isn't it? Another human girl?"

Belial nodded and closed his eyes.

The old fellow grunted his acknowledgement. "They die so fast... like goldfish."

"They die faster around me," Belial murmured.

Porcupine smiled. "Everybody has lost somebody, even me."

The old fellow sounded pensive. Belial knew if he asked who he'd lost, he'd get a true answer and probably learn something about his strange companion. He didn't ask, and the silence stretched, as it often did, until Quills broke it.

"You know what the problem is down here?"

Belial shook his head.

"There's no purpose. The Raff, the Wardens, the winged. Nobody has purpose anymore. Humans get purpose, but we got cut off from ours a long time ago. All of us are mindlessly trying to cross over because, even though most of us don't know it anymore, there's something on the other side that was taken from us. Something we're all trying to get back to."

Belial nodded.

"It was my mate I lost, in case you wondered. Or she lost me. It's a little muddy."

"This was a bad idea. I'm wasting my time here. You are wasting yours." Belial slumped. "It doesn't matter what you do, how hard you try, nothing gets better. You can't undo what you've already done, or make up for what you didn't do. Nothing ever changes."

"You're feeling sorry for yourself, and you ought not."

Belial's irritation with Quills flared, but it was a faraway feeling. "Why the hell shouldn't I?" he asked.

"All those poor bastards out there have no purpose and here you are struggling to choose between at least two of them."

"I guess . . . ," Belial muttered. He wished the old fellow would shut up and let him rest. He was tired. They'd been climbing for what felt like months.

"So, which will it be?" the old bastard persisted.

Belial forced his thoughts to turn away from the growing list of failures and shortcomings taking shape in his mind. He could bail on this tower of despair, get back to Brooklyn, and help her. She needed him. There was no guarantee Prosidris was here, and even if he was, Belial didn't think he was strong enough to even slow the old shark-face down.

On the other hand, if he didn't even try, then it wouldn't be much different from the way he'd handed over Tais.

The whole thing was so futile. If he could just wait a while here and rest until he felt better . . .

There was a loud crack, and pain flashed across Belial's face. His eyes snapped open. There was Quills drawing back to slap him again. "Quit wallowing!" he bellowed as he struck again.

Belial leapt to his feet, knocking his insane companion aside. "What the hell, old man?"

"Pick a path and follow it, damn you." Porcupine gestured up the stairs and back down the stairs. "Choose to go on or go back. Where's your spine?"

Belial glanced in both directions. His head was spinning, and his cheeks were on fire. He wanted to go back, reconnect with Brooklyn, and make sure she was okay. But that was the easy choice, and he understood now that he had to make the hard choice. That he had been making hard choices for a reason. As soon as he decided to go on, the thoughts that hung over him like a dark pall were swept away. He felt something he hadn't felt in a long time. Optimistic.

They pressed on, Quills apologizing for what he'd done and Belial waving his apologies away, thanking him for bringing him out of his stupor. He'd set off on this mission alone, but now, for the first time, he realized that if he'd come alone, he'd have already failed.

"Why don't these gates trouble you?" Belial asked. "Doesn't each person have to overcome the obstacles for themselves?"

Quills shrugged. "I can't say. Maybe the tower knows who's here on a pilgrimage and who's just a spectator?"

"So, the tower is alive now? Is that what you are saying?"

"I believe it is sentient after a fashion."

Belial scoffed. "It's a damn stone tower."

He didn't hear the reply as he climbed the last few steps to the place where they stopped. They hadn't reached the top, just the end. The stairs just weren't there anymore. Peering up, Belial could see the rest of the tower floating some thirty or forty feet above them. It was as if someone had removed a couple of stories from the middle without damaging the integrity of the structure.

He stood on the last step and looked over the edge. Belial could see the ground, what seemed an impossible distance away. He suddenly felt dizzy and took an unsteady step back from the edge and went down several stairs until the tower walls rose around him again.

Quills plodded past him and looked. Then he called back down, "There's a sigil up there floating in the empty space."

"What's it say?" Belial asked thickly.

"Gate of Ascension."

"Christ, how many more gates can there be?"

Belial stood and looked at the distance between the two stairways, resisting the urge to spread his wings and turn their many eyes to the task. He could fly it easily, but Quills couldn't fly and Belial couldn't carry him.

As he contemplated the dilemma, he felt Brooklyn reaching out for him. Belial clamped down on his power before she could draw it away. He couldn't afford to be weakened now, and, thinking back on it, hadn't sensed her the entire time he was climbing. Maybe because he was technically outside again?

Belial joined the old fellow on the top stair, looking up at the silvery sigil floating in the air, then looked down at the stair beneath his clawed feet and saw an inscription carved into the stone. He poked Old Porcupine. "Hey, translate this."

Quills furrowed his brow and ran his eyes over the flowing characters several times. Finally he said, "To fly is to fall."

Belial frowned. "A hint? None of the other gates had hints."

The old fellow shrugged. "This one does. It must be important." He smiled. "Doesn't matter though. Flying was never an option for us, was it?"

"Hmm," Belial said thoughtfully. "Maybe the stairs are still there. We just can't see them. Kind of like a trust fall."

"What's a trust fall?"

"Oh, it's this thing, a game that Brooklyn and her sister used to play as kids where one person closes their eyes and falls backwards and trusts the other person to catch them."

"Brooklyn. Is that the girl's name? The one you are worried about?"

Belial nodded, but he was distracted. He stood on the last stair he could see, picked up a foot, and stepped where the next stair ought to be. His foot passed through empty air, and he teetered on the edge until Quills snatched him back by the green leather cape. Strangling him in the process.

"I guess we can rule that theory out." Quills took a few steps back and leaned against the inner wall.

Belial took up a place on the opposite wall. "Yeah, definitely not a trust fall situation."

43

SECURITY MEETING

"Why is he here?" Brianne asked, cocking a thumb at Father Logan.

If you only knew..., Dravin thought. With a theatrically long suffering sigh, he stood and said to the others gathered around the conference room table, "I can step out if you—"

"No," Eric said sternly. "He's here because I asked him to be." He waved for Dravin to sit back down.

With a shrug, he did. Maybe he was a masochist? Why did he put himself in these situations when he could have controlled the meeting from the comfort of his recliner?

Goodrum crossed his arms and grunted his disapproval at Father Logan.

Dravin smiled at him serenely.

Brianne looked stunned, as if Eric had slapped her. Her response was curt but respectful. "As you see fit, sir."

Michael Benson pushed his glasses up his nose and shifted his eyes back and forth between Eric and Brianne.

Dravin found the whole thing amusing. He wondered what fun debates they might have if he gave everyone a drink of his special cocktail. But no. One compromised Protector was an inconvenience; four of them would be an unthinkable burden to manage and useless as investigators and exorcists. They had important jobs after all.

Goodrum continued to glower at him so convincingly that Dravin had a moment of doubt and checked their connection. He found nothing amiss, and when he willed it, Goodrum looked away gladly enough.

Eric cleared his throat. "Father Logan is here because I would value his input on certain spiritual matters." He turned his attention to the last person at the table, the only new face. "Let's start by exchanging introductions with our newest team member, Victoria Cortez."

They went around the room, introducing themselves to her. Of course, she already knew Brianne, who had hired her. Michael stumbled over his words and, for a heartbeat, seemed to forget his own name. She was of an age with him and quite pretty. Apparently, he'd noticed. When she smiled at him, he blushed. Dravin remembered what it had been like to be so young. It really didn't seem like it was so long ago.

When his turn rolled around. Dravin shared his name and background and flashed his warmest smile.

Eric leaned over and whispered something to Goodrum, and they both snickered. It was intentional. Dravin wanted to be viewed as unimportant and benign. Better to pull strings from the shadows than to be a puppet dancing in the spotlight.

"You must be Nathan Goodrum," Victoria said, her smile disarming. She had a melodious voice, though lower than Dravin had thought it would be. An accent, too. Dravin could hear it in her vowels and liquid consonants. The overall effect was pleasing to the ear. Victoria looked Goodrum over. "The first Demonrider to be named a Protector, right?"

"One and the same." He made a show of proffering a seated bow.

"How does that work, exactly?" she asked, raising her eyebrows.

Goodrum sat a little straighter, and Dravin had not told him to do it. The new girl had just struck a nerve. Dravin decided a hands-off approach would be best, so he left his old pal Nathan to his own devices.

"Well," Nathan grumbled, "I had to let my familiar go. Fly straight for the job."

She nodded and said, "Where I come from, the Demonriders are the bad guys. The reason we need Protectors in the first place."

"There's no law against riding a demon," Goodrum growled, sounding genuinely offended.

"No," she agreed, "but there is a law against summoning them."

Goodrum shrugged. "Archaic law that needs to be rewritten. Don't the Heirs take demons into service? Didn't Solomon himself summon them at will?"

She stared him down, her gaze smoldering. "I just want to know if, down the road, we have to take some of your old pals out, whose back are you going to have?"

The question hung in the air, unanswered, until Eric waved it away impatiently. "Protector Cortez, we are very honored to have you join our team. Protector Goodrum has proven his commitment to me and to my family again and again, which is much more than I can say of his predecessor, Protector Levin. Given the geography of your districts, I doubt your paths will cross often, but if they do, I assure you Protector Goodrum is a good man to have at your back."

Brianne smiled across the table at Nathan. "And you'd do well to stay on her good side. Or you might find you've gotten into a fight you cannot win."

A round of chuckles and then Eric raised his hand, calling for silence. "Let's talk security. We've less than a day to make our final preparations."

Goodrum opened a notebook and said, "All contractors, caterers, entertainers, and their staff will arrive by the front drive, and enter through the east doorway. It was hard to find outside help this year, what with the world basically disintegrating out there. Because of the food shortages, the menu will be a bit more basic than we're used to." When no one commented, he went on. "We will employ the usual mundane security measures, metal detectors, visual inspections, and pat downs. Checking for possession, involuntary or otherwise, isn't as precise. We will have two Protectors at the door to lay hands on anyone who seems suspicious.

"For obvious reasons, we will have guards in the kitchens and all kitchen knives will be inventoried prior to the serving of each course."

The others nodded in acknowledgement of the point. Everyone remembered Brooklyn Evers's attempt on the Heir's life at the last full conclave gathering.

"For the closed session of the meeting itself, the Heir's guard will act as security in addition to the four of us"—he nodded at Brianne, Michael, and Victoria—"and I think that covers everything."

"What about everyone's favorite way to kill kings?" Victoria asked.

"Beheading?" Goodrum asked.

She smiled thinly. "Poison."

Eric sat a little straighter, suddenly more interested in the conversation. Dravin wondered why that was. He could have probed the boy's mind, but he didn't want the others to start drawing conclusions about their young leader.

Brianne cleared her throat. "We will already be searching everyone at the door. We will have guards in the kitchen so we can have them keep a close eye on the food preparation. We could have Protector Goodrum's trusted kitchen staff directly oversee the preparations, and we could avoid identifying which plates are going to whom prior to leaving the kitchen."

"That would work," Nathan said slowly. "There's also the matter of drinks. It's easier to hide poison in wine than in food."

"We could either have a bottle kept on the table in plain view, or else only fill the Heir's cup from fresh, unopened bottles," Dravin interjected. Everyone seemed to agree.

The conversation droned on, but Dravin lost the thread of it. He couldn't have cared less. Eric would be the one with a target on his back. If he took a steak knife to the heart or a lethal dose of warfarin, it would be an inconvenience, but after tomorrow night, he would have served his primary purpose and would no longer be a crucial piece on the board.

"No luck?" Riley asked.

Brooklyn opened one eye and glared at him. "I'll let you know if something happens." She closed her eyes again and tried to relax and focus on emptying her mind. Meditating had been the idea of Riley and whatever spirit shared his skull. She had been willing to try it because she figured it couldn't hurt, and they probably understood more about her tether with Belial than she did.

The connection had re-established sometime after her helicopter ride. It was no longer a kiteless string, but it wasn't the strong bond she remembered that had let them communicate and had given her access to some of his abilities. Now it was muffled, obstructed somehow. Maybe he was too far away, or maybe he was intentionally closing himself off. She didn't know. Brooklyn could sense him, a cold presence, a flicker of shadow on her mental horizon. The words she thought at him bounced around in her own head and didn't seem to go anywhere. When she tried to draw on his power, she felt a slight chill trickling up her spine and then it just stopped. If she waited long enough, she could do the same thing again.

She stilled her mind and visualized this connection as a great blue rope stretched taut between them. Instead of drawing energy through, she pushed it along the connection toward him. Brooklyn sensed a moment of hesitation, like the slightest vibration in a spider's web, and then the energy met resistance and she couldn't push past the barrier.

Sighing in frustration, she stood up. "I can't get through. What did you find out?"

Riley stroked his beard, pulling it down from his chin into a point. "I spoke with Del Stewarth. I told her what I knew and what I suspected. She didn't want to believe it, but she has noticed the changes, however small, in his demeanor since Dravin forced him to drink this." He hefted the vial Father Logan had given him to study. "He calls it Devotion."

"What is she going to do?"

"I don't think even she knows the answer to that. I stressed the risk I was taking in calling her, the need for discretion given that Dravin Logan likely knows anything that Eric knows."

"Did you tell her about me?"

"No, but when she arrives later this afternoon I'm going to meet with her, if I can do it discreetly. She doesn't trust me because of my close ties to Kurt. The banquet is tonight, and the conclave starts tomorrow morning. I need to feel her out in person to see if we can count on her to be a part of any plans we make for tomorrow."

"I see."

Riley patted her shoulder. "Calling her was a good idea. A genius idea, actually. We just need a little time to sort out how she can help us, and if she's willing to."

Brooklyn nodded and sat on the edge of the bed. He came, sat beside her, and asked, "Are you nervous?"

She shrugged. "Some."

"You sure you want to chance this?"

"No, the opposite, actually. I don't want to do this, but I have to."

"You don't though, you could just hide out until after the conclave, and then you and I, well, we could slip out through the tunnels and go someplace."

Brooklyn smiled. It was a pretty thought, but he didn't get it. She wasn't sure how to explain it so he would. "I had a normal life. I had a family and plans for the future. Then that all got taken away. Then I had a new life in this new world full of crazy magic and strangeness, and now that's been taken away, too."

"Yeah but—"

She held up a hand. "Let me finish."

He nodded, so she went on. "I'm never going to have a normal life again. I'm not. I'll always be a wanted serial killer. Even if that goes away, my family is already gone. I don't have anything or anyone to go back to except Devin, and I can't live in his world. If I can keep him free of this world, I feel like that's the kindest thing I could do for him. So, if I'm going to have a life, I'm going to have to carve it out in your world because there's no going back for me, not now. And anyone in this world who might be a threat to Devin has to die. It's just as simple as that."

Riley was quiet for a long time. When he spoke, his voice was a little thick. "That makes perfect sense. If I can, I'll help you do it." He threw an arm around her shoulders and squeezed.

She smiled. "You already are."

44

PATIENCE

Belial crawled to the edge of the precipice and peered down. The tower stretched away below him, straight and unerring, black stone as smooth as finished marble, no visible balconies. Quills crawled up beside him. The inscription was on the stair between them.

To fly is to fall.

He rolled onto his back and looked up. With his head hanging out beyond the circumference of the outer wall, the tower above seemed like a guillotine, poised to strike his head from his shoulders. He waited for several long seconds of nothing happening, then felt a tug. It was Brooklyn again. This was the fifth time. She was persistent today. He pushed the feeling away and eased back from the edge.

"Hey, Quills, any thoughts on the inscription here? I don't see any way someone could pass this gate without flying."

The old fellow gave a shake, not unlike a dog. It sent waves through his quills as they flexed up and settled back into place. Belial thought it might be a gesture of irritation. This wasn't the first time they'd had this discussion, or even the fifth.

"I still think there must be a way. The tower is not only for the winged, but it doesn't matter because we don't have that option."

Belial considered the implications—as he had every time previously that his odd companion had used this line of reasoning to dissuade him—of coming clean. Looking the old shopkeeper up and down, he couldn't say why, but he trusted the little bugger. "Alright, Quills, I haven't been honest with you."

The old fellow smiled. "And now you've decided you will be?"

"Tell me why I shouldn't fly." Belial dropped the green cloak from his shoulders and spread his wings. They felt stiff and sluggish from disuse.

Quills laughed. "I was wondering how much longer you'd keep up the charade."

Belial folded his four wings gingerly. "You knew?"

"Yep."

"The whole time?"

"Uh-huh."

"Why didn't you say anything?"

"I know who you are. I figured you had your reasons and you'd tell me when you decided you should."

Belial turned to the precipice and looked up. "I think we can cut the capes into strips and knot them together. I can fly up and use the rope to pull you up after."

"Hold up. You asked me why you shouldn't fly, so let me tell you. Someone, probably the creator of this tower, felt it was important to carve a warning in this last step. The Wardens and the other winged have been flying around this tower since forever. None of them have ever reached the top. I think you are meant to find another way."

"There is no other way." Just then, Brooklyn tried to connect again, but it was different. She didn't try to draw from him; instead she pushed energy toward him. He had a sense of her for an instant. She wasn't in danger, at least not immediately. The surprise of it overwhelmed him, but he recovered a heartbeat later and closed off the connection.

Quills was watching him shrewdly. "What happened just now?"

Belial grimaced. "Brooklyn again."

"Your feet came off the floor for a second."

"No, they didn't."

"I wouldn't lie to you. I saw it, truly."

"Even if they did, floating a micrometer up from the floor isn't going to get me up there." He jabbed a finger toward the tower above them.

Quills sat back down on the top step, his legs swinging over the abyss. He patted the stone beside him and raised one spiky eyebrow at Belial. "Come," he said, "let's talk."

Reluctantly, Belial sat next to him. He itched to spread his wings and make a go at the gate, but something in the old fellow's warning gave him pause. So instead, he worried with fastening the green leather mantle back around his shoulders. When he was done, he looked up to see Quills staring at him intently.

"Yeah," Belial grumbled, "what do you want to talk about?"

Quills put a hand on Belial's knee, an intimate gesture that brought to Belial's mind a couple of old women swapping gossip. "I want to talk about the gates so far."

"What is there to talk about? You were there with me. You know as much as I know."

Quills nodded, conceding the point. "As much as you know, and probably more besides."

"So, what is there to talk about?"

"What they all have in common."

"They have nothing in common," Belial rumbled petulantly. "Each was completely different. The first was a test of determination, the second was a test of pain and regret, the third was confronting demons, irony intended, and the last one was another test of willpower and determination." He sighed theatrically. "And this damn gate is a test of frustration and patience."

Quills nodded. "That's one way to see it."

"You have another?"

"Maybe. It seems to me that every gate has required you to accept something. The first gate had you accept that you were going to see this through, and it gave way before your determination to do so."

"Maybe, but that doesn't really follow through to the rest of them."

"Doesn't it? The Gate of Misery required you to accept the choices you didn't make, the lives you could have lived, all your regrets."

"And the third made me accept myself to move on," Belial began slowly, "all the things about myself I wished weren't a part of me."

"Yes," the old fellow crooned. "Yes! And the gate that followed? What about that one?"

"It . . ." Belial stumbled. He couldn't quite say what the last gate had been about. "I'm not sure." He felt like a particularly dim-witted pupil under Quills's gaze.

"It's a tough one to parse. Do you think it might have been about allowing yourself forgiveness or absolution?"

"Maybe?" Belial wasn't sure. This was an odd way to look at the trials. "Say it was. If that's the case, then maybe this gate is about getting you to accept that I can fly and pull you up with a rope."

Old Porcupine laughed, and after a moment, for once, Belial did too. It felt good.

"No, young friend. I think you've forgotten that these things run both ways. You want to help your companion, Brooklyn, you might need to accept a little help, too."

"Well, how could she help?"

"I suppose, until you stop blocking your connection, we won't know."

Belial closed his eyes and tried to open the tether between himself and Brooklyn, but his mind went as far as the outer ring of the tower and no further. After a few moments of thwarted effort, he let out a growl of frustration and a few expletives. "I can't reach out to her," he admitted after a moment. "This damn tower won't let me."

"Hmm." Quills nodded. "Then I guess your first assessment of this gate was correct, after all. Frustration and patience."

"Well, what do we do now?"

Quills patted him on the knee again, a show of affection a grandpa might have showed a grandson, and said, "Now, my friend, we wait."

David fought to stay calm. He'd found the stash of Father Logan's dark drink, and the places where several bottles had been removed recently enough the dust hadn't settled. His first thought had been to check Eli's memories. The connection with Eli and those he'd influenced was degrading. It was something he'd need to deal with soon, but not now. That had been a dead end. Oh sure, he was full of grief for his girlfriend and homicidal anger toward David, but it was quickly apparent he had no knowledge of the secret stash and had not been a part of taking it.

Azrael may have had some insight to offer, but she'd been absent for many weeks. David ran his thumb and forefinger over the soft raven's feather he wore on a thong around his neck. He could call; she would come, he knew, but was it the right thing? He let the feather hang loose.

Having taken what he needed from the office, David locked the door and sat on the edge of his bed. "You think it was him?" he asked Avery for the hundredth time.

"I don't know," the big man answered from near the door.

David saw himself slumped on the edge of the bed through the other man's eyes and sat up a little straighter. "No one else knew it was there, or what it does, how to use it. It had to be him, didn't it?"

Avery shrugged. David couldn't see the gesture so much as sense the intent of it through their connection. "Stands to reason."

"He's going to rebuild the Prophets," David mused. "Or get allies enough to come at me head-on."

There was a grunt of negation. "Head-on isn't his way."

"Send out feelers. Find out if he's still staying at the Protector's manor." David cursed himself inwardly that the idea hadn't occurred to him sooner, days ago.

45

A New Alliance

Kurt shuddered with exhaustion as he made a minor correction to the last of the sixty-four demon sigils. Looking at the whole conglomeration made him dizzy and nauseous. If setting up the summoning had been this taxing, he couldn't imagine how he'd muster the strength to pull this off.

A part of him was ready to try now, to have this be over and done, but he knew better. He grunted as he stood. The old knees weren't what they had once been. He slung a small sack across his shoulders and made the hike back to the entrance.

Stepping into the fresh air was a relief. He'd almost died in this hole, and he was quite looking forward to blowing the whole damned thing up. For now, he sat on a bed of fallen leaves and dumped the sack full of snacks out in his lap.

Nuts and peanut butter crackers for protein, potato chips, several types of chocolate bars, and a can of beanie weenies. Kurt munched and enjoyed the feeling of the open air moving against his face and through his hair.

He saved three chocolate bars. Two to eat before the summoning, and the third in case he needed it after. Kurt wiped his hands on his jeans and stood up. He set about arranging the explosives in parallel rows, extending about thirty feet into the tunnel. It was probably unnecessary, but he wanted to be sure there was a thick barrier between himself and any of the demons that might try to follow him out.

Kurt unspooled the wires and made the connections with the detonator. He'd be about sixty yards downgrade when the blast happened. Hopefully, that was far enough. He kicked leaves over the wires on the way back to the cave mouth, though he couldn't have said why. Nobody would pass this way to see them, anyway.

"So, you are the woman who tried to cut my husband's throat?" Del Stewarth demanded.

"She was possessed—" Riley began, but the widow waved a gloved hand for him to be silent.

They were in an unused guest room, near the stairs to the basement. The room was small, without enough chairs for them all to sit, but it was somewhere Brooklyn could reach unnoticed and far enough out of the way nobody would look for Del there.

"I am," Brooklyn said with a shrug.

"Tell me why Kurt Levin put his life on the line to see you live after your treason."

Brooklyn started to say she didn't know, but that probably wasn't an answer that would help her move toward her goals. So, instead, she said, "He thinks I'm his reincarnated son."

Mrs. Stewarth let out a hiccup of laughter. "Oh. You're serious? What an old fool he is. Reincarnated son. It's bologna."

"No, ma'am. I don't believe it is."

Del looked from Brooklyn to Riley and back again several times, finally settling on Riley. "You believe this nonsense?"

Riley shrugged.

"So what, you have two souls?"

Brooklyn shrugged uncertainly. "That's how he made it seem, yes."

Del nodded. "You cut him pretty good, but not deep enough."

"I'm sorry. I really didn't mean to—"

A NEW ALLIANCE

Del raised a hand, stopping her. "Can't say I don't understand the impulse."

Brooklyn paused, unsure how to respond.

Del laughed, sensing Brooklyn's confusion. "Alexander killed my father, you know."

"No, I did not know," Brooklyn assured her.

"I suppose you wouldn't, would you? I forget you didn't grow up as one of us. It's been a source of gossip in the community since Alexander took me as his wife."

Brooklyn thought to sit on the bed where Del was perched, decided against it, and sank to the floor against the wall instead. Riley remained standing near the door, as if he did not know whether to stay or flee. He looked like a child, shifting uncomfortably from foot to foot.

"You don't . . . hate me?"

Del laughed again, a breathy sound that might've been a nervous tic. "How could I hate you? I don't even know you."

Brooklyn felt like nodding in agreement was the safest response.

"When Alexander died, well, I thought, now things can be better. Now Eric can lead and be a better, kinder, wiser man than his father. But he has that same self-righteous arrogance that was in his father, and now he's gotten himself into a mess I might not be able to get him out of."

"I don't know what we can do for your son, but I know Father Logan has to be stopped. Maybe when he dies, Eric will be set free."

"Why should I trust either of you? An assassin and a traitor's brother-in-law?"

Riley cleared his throat. "Well, because what we are telling you isn't what you want to hear. I haven't studied the Devotion very much, but my understanding is that it breaks down, changes, or alters a person's free will and subjugates them to another person.

I'm not sure that killing the leader undoes the damage. There might not be a happy ending for Eric in this."

"But you don't know that. Right? You don't know that it can't be undone," Brooklyn insisted.

"No," Riley conceded. "I know nothing for sure."

Del Stewarth ran fingers through her long, black hair. Brooklyn realized Del was quite a bit younger than her husband had been. She looked up at the older woman. "Will you help us? Will you help me?"

Del shook her head. "I don't know. I don't know what's the right thing anymore."

Brooklyn sighed. "I don't know if killing Father Logan will free your son, but I do know that doing nothing is choosing for the situation to remain the same. In essence, doing nothing is choosing for Father Logan to rule instead of your family."

Del shook her head slowly. "I'll help you, but I have a condition."

"What's the condition?" Riley and Brooklyn asked in unison.

Steel gilded Del's eyes and twisted her delicate features into a determined mask. "No harm comes to Eric."

"Of course—" Brooklyn began.

Del spoke over her. "No harm comes to Eric and we take Father Logan alive. If anyone knows how to set my son free, it's him."

Kurt Levin knelt in the leaves, relishing the fresh, cool mountain air and the last rays of sunset warming his face. Then he did something he hadn't done in many years. He prayed. He prayed for Brooklyn, for Mrs. Mays, and for Riley. And for Father Logan to cut his toe on rusty metal and die a slow, painful death from gangrene. Lastly, he prayed for himself, for safety or at least a chance of survival and maybe even a little forgiveness for what he was about to do.

He gave the ground a mental shove to take some of the strain of getting up off his aching knees. Kurt checked the detonator and wiring for the third time. When there was nothing more to do and no more excuses he could make for further delay, he trudged reluctantly back into the mountain.

"Kurt Levin's mansion? Are you sure?" David demanded of Avery. Speaking wasn't really necessary. David could read Avery's mind, but old habits die hard.

"I'm fairly sure, sir. We used to have prophets placed in the medical wing and among the cafeteria and cleaning staff, but those were killed in the conflict with the Heir last year."

"Logan had eyes in the Protector's mansion?" David's mind was reeling. The man had highly placed puppets in dozens of governments, law enforcement agencies, and military organizations, so David wasn't sure why this revelation was such a shock. "If our people inside were killed last year, how do we know Logan is still there now?"

"More . . . standard ways of obtaining information."

"He's been seen again?"

"Mhm. With Protector Goodrum and Heir Stewarth."

"Odd company. He despised Goodrum, or at least that's what he told me when he visited me while I was being held captive. Believe he likened their relationship on the night of my capture to that of a hunter and his dog. Based on that night at the barn . . . well, I could see the tether connecting Goodrum to him."

Avery nodded and settled into one of the leather chairs opposite David's position. "Will you go to the conclave tonight?"

David hesitated. "He's compromised the Heir and the Protector and who could guess how many others now that he's replenished his supply of Devotion. For Logan, it would be a simple matter to make charges, hold Judgment, and execute me all before suppertime and without uttering a word or even being present in the room."

Avery cleared his throat. "Yes. But will you go?"

"Can you keep me safe?"

"I will die trying, but no. This can't be done safely."

"Logan has to be stopped now before his influence grows out of control." David's voice shook with some emotion he couldn't name. "Yes," he answered thickly. "I'm going. Prepare a guard, thirty men."

46

Check

Dravin Logan put a hand down on the table to steady himself. The room was suddenly a ship deck tilting on rough waves. Was that really the Blind Prophet that just walked in with a full posse of guards? And not just any guards, but *his* guards. And there, bringing up the rear, Avery. His oldest follower and confidant, stolen from him. Did Avery still feel any loyalty or connection to him? Probably not. Damn David Sterling. He ruined everything!

So great was his distress that all those who he'd dosed with Devotion started toward him, sensing his alarm but seeing no clear cause for it.

This was unfortunate, but he couldn't let it rattle him. David's eyes found his, staring through him as if they could see, which he knew they could not. He'd made certain of that. With an effort, Dravin looked away and urged his followers to hold their places.

David made his way to one of the unoccupied and unreserved tables and took a seat. Avery sat beside him, and the others stood along the back wall behind him, flanked by the less prestigious members of all the other groups who didn't warrant a voting seat at the conclave. There were Demonriders, Witches, guards of the Heir, Adepts of the Protectors, and many others. All here for observation or security.

There were still empty seats, most notably those reserved for the Heir's family, but it was time for the meeting to start, so Eric took his place at the lectern and called them all to order.

Dravin took his own seat at one of the least prestigious tables furthest from the Heir. Eric was greeting the member groups one by one, working his way around the room from right to left. Dravin let him do it. He didn't need guidance for this part, but he listened through the boy's ears.

Tristan Barrett was exchanging pleasantries, lilting on about the state of affairs in Scotland where he held a role commensurate with Brianne Moore, the leader of the American Protectors. Mrs. Mays was in attendance; Dravin was happy he didn't need to speak to her directly. Her comments were curt but respectful and Eric's attention quickly shifted to Erina Craft. She was tall and fierce, her jet hair streaked with lines of silver. She put Dravin in a mind of Elvira. Beside her sat her daughter, Bryssa Craft, and from the looks of her, she was well into a pregnancy. She wore the same soft dress as her mother in shades of emerald and purple, but hers was cut for maternity.

Eric was on the cusp of commenting on the pregnancy when Dravin stopped him. Didn't the boy have any manners? There was an awkward silence that stretched until Dravin prompted Eric to say, "As always, such a pleasure to see the ladies Craft." Erina nodded and reclaimed her seat.

The next table was empty and should have seated Eric's mother. He skipped over that one and came to the table of Protectors next. Eric made a show of thanking them for their service to the community. They stood one by one as he addressed them: Goodrum, Brianne, Michael, and finally the newest member, Victoria Cortez.

Eric turned to greet David Sterling next. David was halfway to his feet when Dravin guided the Heir's eyes past him to the next table.

For half a second, the Blind Prophet looked confused; then his mouth pressed into a thin line and he settled back into his seat. *That's right, little boy*, Dravin thought smugly. *We're greeting members, not interlopers.*

When the introductions concluded, Eric Stewarth fastened his dark eyes on David Sterling. Slowly, the other gazes in the room turned his way as well. "The conclave is for sitting members. Why are you here?"

David did not flinch or indicate he'd heard the man at all.

"I'm talking to you, Mr. Sterling."

David rose to his feet with a rueful smile. "Apologies, Heir Stewarth." He made a show of waving his splayed fingers before his face. "I did not realize you were addressing me. I'm a touch on the blind side."

"That's alright," Eric mumbled. "Why are you here?"

"Oh. As you said, the conclave is for sitting members of this council."

"Yes. So why are *you* here?"

David looked genuinely perplexed. "For the conclave."

"You are not a member."

"I am. Are the Prophets not long-standing members? Doesn't my place as their leader give me a voice on any matters that come up for a vote in the conclave?"

Eric ran his fingers over his long, black hair, smoothing it in a gesture of Dravin's irritation. "Father Logan is the leader of the Prophets."

"He was," David offered with a bland smile. "But no longer."

The other council members were watching the exchange with rapt attention. Mrs. Mays was half out of her seat.

"In fact," David went on, "if anyone is no longer a member of this conclave, it would be Father Logan."

Dravin rose to his feet. "Liar and heretic!"

"Sit down," Eric's voice boomed at him.

Dravin dropped heavily into his chair. Had he told Eric to say that?

"What proof do you have to support your claims?" Eric demanded.

"Thirty witnesses, some, like Mr. Avery, well-known to the other conclave members as long-standing prophets."

A low murmur ran through the room and Dravin cringed. This was not going as planned.

Address me. He sent the demand silently along his connection to Eric.

Slowly, as if waking from a dream, the Heir turned to Dravin and smiled. "What do you have to say, Father Logan, about these claims?"

Dravin cleared his throat and rose again to his feet. "I don't deny it. Mr. Sterling has usurped me, taken my followers, changed our faith, and cast me out. I don't agree with his theology, but I can't deny his claim to a seat on this council on the basis of having replaced me." His heart chugged like a locomotive. "I would posit that Mr. Sterling's faith is not the faith of the Prophets that have traditionally advised the Heir of Solomon, however. I am still of that old faith and so the question becomes, is it the prophet with the most followers that holds this seat, or the prophet of the true faith?"

Another murmur circled the room.

"It is a complex issue, but one I'm sure the chosen Heir of Solomon's wisdom can unravel. I will accept whatever Judgment comes, but respectfully I suggest the Protectors might interview Mr. Sterling and determine what dark god he serves and perhaps ask him about the feather he wears on a leather cord beneath his shirt."

Eric cleared his throat. "This does seem a matter that merits some in-depth deliberation that would be beyond the scope of the proceeding here tonight. So, in order to move on with other business, I grant you both a shared provisional seat on the council for the conclave tonight. This means you'll need to sit at the same table and the Prophets will have no vote on any matter unless the two of you are in agreement."

Dravin rose dutifully and made his way over to David's table. He stood expectantly for a moment, until Avery stood and took a place along the back wall with the others, then dropped heavily into the vacated chair, leaned close to the Blind Prophet's ear, and whispered, "Have you ever played chess, Mr. Sterling?"

"Yeah."

"*Check.*"

Brooklyn had imagined her entry into the conclave many times over the past few weeks, had, in truth, fantasized about it. Sometimes she thought of entering by force, blasting the doors from the hinges, sending a hail of lethal shrapnel to tear apart her tormentors. Other times she imagined stepping quietly from the shadows just as the council's conversation turned to her. In her imagination, she made them see she was a person who should be left alone. In some of her fantasies, they even apologized and begged her forgiveness.

She had even thought about the preparations. The strapping on of weapons, maybe a smudge of war paint across each cheekbone. In none of her imaginings was she in the formal gown she wore now, with Del Stewarth applying her makeup. The older woman insisted that they would walk right through the front door of the council room and take seats at the center table.

Not being so sure, Brooklyn had taped the three new soul stones and the remaining old one inside the dress under her arms. She trusted Del, but she wasn't going in unarmed.

The time came and went. A servant knocked and stuck her head into the room twice to let them know the conclave was being called to order without them. Mrs. Stewarth waved a dismissive hand. "Nothing interesting ever happens at the beginning of a meeting. We'll be fashionably late. Now stand up and let's have a look at you, darling."

Standing, Brooklyn examined herself in the full-length mirror. She hardly recognized herself. The makeup Del had used created a dusky complexion that gave her eyes a brilliant contrast. The dress was elegant, emerald, and probably more expensive than anything she'd ever owned. Black heels rounded out the ensemble. Though a bit small, she'd managed to cram her feet into them. Brooklyn's normally straight hair was curled and hung like so much light fluff to frame her face. She hadn't looked this good at prom. "Wow."

"You attend enough of these, you learn to throw something together," Del said with a modest shrug and a pained smile. "Now, let's go get my boy back."

Brooklyn turned to check the dress from different angles. It wasn't the battle garb she'd imagined, but if Del's plan worked, this wasn't going to be a typical battle, and if it didn't . . . Well, the backup plan ran a lot closer to her violent fantasies, anyway.

47

CHECKMATE

Kurt reentered the chamber and set up disposable LED lights around the perimeter to illuminate the disgusting, blood-scribed sigils that filled the floor and made the closed, hot space reek of death and rot.

This was suicide. Unless Azrael's support went beyond quieting the voices of insanity in his mind, he would die of a brain hemorrhage before successfully drawing this multitude of demons through the Pull. And, if he did somehow manage it, being torn to shreds seemed an inevitability.

He could just walk away. Go find Brooklyn and make amends. If he was going to commit suicide doing something stupid, it would have been a damn sight better to have done it keeping her safe during her ill-advised mission than to be back in this stinking prison.

But you were willing to lock her away down here, weren't you? Kurt sighed. This was his own voice. If only Azrael could have silenced it, too.

Enough of that. He'd drawn this sixty-four-part sigil oriented toward the tunnel that led out. Kurt took up position on an outcropping of rock just inside the chamber that gave an elevated view of the floor while also keeping him close to the exit.

He thought fleetingly of the ring, Solomon's ring, and how easy this might have been with that ancient power at his disposal. It didn't matter. There was only one way forward now. Only one way at a chance to stay alive and a chance at sanity.

Kurt drew in a deep breath and let it escape slowly through his lips. He treated the sigil like a clock, starting at twelve and working his way around the dial, etching the shapes into his mind's eye.

Over several long minutes, he constructed the sixty-four-part sigil, feeling the essence and shape of the entities it represented. The connections popped into being a few at a time, like popcorn, and a steady pressure built behind his eyes.

It would be easier to pull them across a few at a time, but that would leave him in the dangerous situation of keeping control of the ones he'd brought across and still wrestling the new ones through the barrier as well. It would have to be an all-or-nothing heavy lift. So, he made himself wait, gritting teeth against the spike of pain. Over fifty now. Almost there.

If Azrael was going to pitch in, he hoped she'd get on with it soon.

Fifty-three. The pain spread around the sides of his head.
Fifty-seven. Christ. That was close enough, wasn't it?
Sixty-one. Blood dripped and tickled his nose and lips.
Sixty-four.

"AZRAEL!" Kurt's voice echoed around the cavern like thunder as he gave a tremendous yank like a fisherman drawing a net. The bloody sigil on the floor began to smoke and stink of burning meat. Just when he thought his mind would break and send him collapsing into sweet darkness, the feather beneath his shirt grew hot, burning like a brand against his skin, and a strange, new pressure grew inside his skull. Then all hell broke loose.

"Pompous ass," David whispered back to Dravin Logan. "Wish you'd have stopped in to say hello when you visited."

David couldn't have said what expression crossed Father Logan's face. He could only see the back of his head beside the back of his own. That was a disadvantage of having all his eyes lined up along the back wall.

Eric was moving through the agenda now. David had a copy on the table in front of him, but little good it would do him unless he had Avery come read over his shoulder. David's mind was suddenly drawn back to middle school. He remembered how they used to disassemble ink pens and use the barrels to launch spitballs at one another. The urge to have Avery pelt Father Logan in the back of the head with a spitball was strong enough that Avery was busy searching his pocket for a pen when David came back from the petty little fantasy. This wasn't middle school.

"Protectors, what of the search for our wanted woman?" Heir Stewarth rumbled.

Brianne rose to her feet. "We are running down a few leads still, but nothing very promising. As you all know from the news, Miss Evers evaded the regular authorities several weeks past and vanished in a helicopter."

David perked up, paying close attention to the mention of Brooklyn.

"That's disappointing," Eric murmured.

"We expect she's found someplace to lie low. Only a matter of time before she shows herself again. We are just trying to be ready to respond quickly when that happens."

"Thank you."

David leaned over to Dravin. "What's the point of this charade? Why didn't you just have him throw me out?"

"I do not know what you are talking about."

"Don't give me that shit. I was there that night, or have you forgotten?"

"I wish you'd pull the same vanishing act now. Walk away, squinty."

David yawned and stretched his arms wide, taking Dravin across the face and almost tipping him backward off his chair.

"Is there a problem over here?" Eric demanded.

"Apologies, Heir Stewarth," David purred, trying to contain his laughter. "Sometimes I lose track of where people are."

Eric stared at him hard. He could see it through Avery's eyes, but David just pretended he was unaware, smiling serenely.

After a moment, Eric shook his head irritably and moved on, but he had barely begun when he was interrupted again. A hollow boom thundered as someone let the main door in the rear of the council room slam shut.

A collective gasp went up. David craned Avery's neck to see who the newcomer was, and when he did, almost fell out of his chair. *Brooklyn!*

Dressed to kill and as gorgeous as he remembered, she walked arm in arm with an older, elegant-looking woman. *Del Stewarth, Eric's mother.* Avery supplied him with the knowledge. The two women walked straight to the center table, reserved for the Heir's family. Brooklyn pulled out a chair for Mrs. Stewarth, then seated herself without a word.

Eric Stewarth broke the silence after several uncomfortable moments. "Mother. What's this?"

"Please excuse our tardiness, Lord Heir. Time got away from me."

"No. I mean, is this who I think it is?"

"At the last meeting, you said to bring Miss Evers before this council, before the police get her. Well, here she is."

"Yes, I see that," Eric spluttered. Confusion twisted his features as Father Logan scrambled to put the pieces of this puzzle together for him.

"You also said she'd be offered a place with our family. As the matriarch, I've extended your generous offer and Miss Evers has accepted. She's an Adept of our house now." Del Stewarth smiled proudly.

"What I said was that we should bring her before this council for Judgment and for *my* offer. You've overstepped, Mother."

Erina Craft's mouth was hanging open and most others had averted their eyes. Probably ashamed to be present for this family drama.

David was watching the exchange with a dozen eyes, but Avery's gaze had not wavered from Brooklyn.

"The offer is withdrawn. Miss Evers will be held for Judgment tomorrow morning."

"Then the Prophets will offer asylum!" David leapt to his feet, banging his knee on the table.

Eric turned slowly, eying David like a particularly gruesome insect. "You and Father Logan agree, I take it?"

Shit. Brooklyn was looking at him with a shocked expression. Apparently, she'd just noticed him. David turned to Dravin and whispered, "What do you want?"

He smiled grimly. "Judgment first. Offers after."

"Dravin. Come on, man. You can stop this."

"I don't know what you mean."

"Guards. Take Miss Evers into custody."

Two men stepped away from the back wall. David readied his men to intercept them, but before he could, Brooklyn stood up and her high, clear voice rang out.

"On what charges am I to be judged?"

Eric made a show of rifling through a stack of papers, then said, "Forty-seven counts of murder, summoning demons, exposing our community to the regular authorities, and conspiring to commit treason with the late Protector Levin."

"I came here on my own tonight, and I'll stand Judgment if that's what you want. But I will not be imprisoned. Not now, not ever again."

"You don't seem to understand. You don't have a choice here. You're not in control."

"How would it look to these fine people gathered around if you killed your mother's guest in the middle of a conclave meeting? I was dragged into this mess kicking and screaming and your 'community' has cost me everyone I ever loved. You'd do well to remember that I have a lot less to lose than you do."

David noticed that Brooklyn was speaking to Eric, but she was staring straight at Father Logan. She knew then. Interesting.

"Now you make threats?" Eric's voice was low and deadly calm.

"He tried to murder me." She pointed one finger at Nathan Goodrum and pulled her dress down a little to show the wicked barbed wire scar above her heart. "When will he face Judgment?"

"If you'd like to file a complaint—"

"I'd like to file several," Brooklyn interrupted. "You were there the night it all happened in the cornfield at Mrs. Mays's farm, weren't you, *Father* Logan?"

David noticed Dravin shifting uncomfortably beside him.

"You took my boyfriend and blinded him, didn't you?" Brooklyn was pointing right at Father Logan.

David nodded. "I can corroborate all of that."

"I can too. At least the bit at my farm," Mrs. Mays bellowed out.

"Mrs. Moore, are you getting all of this down for future investigation?" Eric asked.

Brianne looked up sharply. "I am."

"Good. Any further allegations, Miss Evers, or are you done?"

"I am only stating facts. I've been possessed, falsely imprisoned, kidnapped, drugged, and named a fugitive all for things I didn't do or at least didn't do willingly. I never asked for any of it. My mom and dad are dead because of it. I don't care what you do with either of these scumbags. All I want is to be left alone. Is that too much to ask?"

Eric's stony face softened. David could see it through Avery's eyes. "I know what it is to lose a parent, and though you once tried to take my father from me, I recognize the role the demon played in that. I'll make this concession. Be my mother's guest tonight, and tomorrow we will hash this all out in a special session and find a solution everyone can agree on."

Brooklyn nodded and breathed a word of assent before taking her seat.

"Wonderful," Eric murmured, raising a glass of wine to the room. "To diplomatic solutions!" The words echoed back from around the room as those gathered lifted their own glasses and drank the dark wine.

David gasped. Like filaments of dewy spiderweb catching the sun, half a dozen or more lines of pulsing light sprang to life and traced their paths across the room to Dravin Logan. He'd just dosed more than half the room with Devotion.

"And . . . ," Father Logan whispered. "Checkmate."

48

Reunited

Brooklyn retook her seat, heart pounding and palms sweating.

Del placed a hand on her knee and leaned close. "You did well. I believe you have the support of every table from here to the left side of the room. The only people who would cast a vote against you tomorrow are the ones you've accused of misconduct. Now, it is time to hold up your end of this bargain."

"Here and now?"

"I didn't drink the wine, and I noticed you didn't either, but a lot of people did. We have to assume they could be compromised. You need to move the plans up, and it needs to look accidental. Do it as soon as everyone's attention is elsewhere."

"Okay. As soon as I have an opportunity." Brooklyn swallowed. She felt off balance. David was here. He was really here. And Riley, too. Kurt was out there somewhere. All the people she'd set out to find were found. Everybody except Erin, that was.

The meeting was droning on around her with much talk of logistics and of stockpiling fuel and resources to ensure the smooth operation of their little shadow government.

"This is a time when stability is imperative to our survival. This is not a time for infighting and petty disagreements. Both Hell and Earth stand upon a precipice. As you all know, the traitor, Kurt Levin, stole the very Ring of Solomon, the scales with which we balance and separate worlds. But my family is old, and Solomon was wise before the ring. I will reforge that power."

A low murmur went around the room.

Eric slapped the podium and Brooklyn felt the hair on her arms stand up. She looked around and saw similar discomfort evident on other faces. Four gruesome-looking demons snapped into being on the raised dais with Eric Stewarth. "A demonstration to assure you all that the old power will be reclaimed and perhaps even expanded upon."

Several people gasped. All eyes were on Eric Stewarth. There would be no better chance than this. Barely daring to cut her eyes upward to find the chandelier above Father Logan, she yanked it free of the vaulted ceiling and nudged it left to fall directly on Dravin. At the same moment, she tipped David's chair backward, sending him sprawling to safety. There was a crash and a tinkling. Now she looked. They all looked with wide-eyed confusion at the unconscious man lying amid broken crystal with a puddle of blood forming under his head and at the dust drifting in slow, lazy spirals down from the gaping hole in the ceiling.

More than half the room looked dumbstruck. It was Riley who moved first to check on Dravin, followed by Del. "He's alright I think," Riley called out, hoisting Father Logan's mostly limp form to a sitting position, head lolling. "We need to get him to medical. You. Help me get him up." Riley pointed at Avery, who stepped forward obligingly and helped hoist his former liege to his feet. Dravin's head hung limp. He was out cold.

Eric might have stopped them and called the medics up with a stretcher, but he looked like a man roused suddenly from a dream, yet unsure what was real or imagined. It was a look shared by many in the room. The Protectors, save Goodrum who appeared similarly addled, were looking suspiciously at David as he fumbled his way off the floor and righted his overturned chair.

A dull roar of conversation broke out at once and a moment later, Eric was banging his flat hand on the podium for order and probably wishing he had a gavel. The four demons that had flanked him earlier had vanished. Amid the chaos, Riley, Avery, and Del vanished through the double doors with an unconscious Dravin Logan in tow.

Brooklyn came to her feet as David crossed the space between them—with a sureness his blindness shouldn't have allowed—and wrapped her in a hug so tight she thought she heard her ribs creaking.

49

Convergence

Kurt Levin felt the world break. The smell of death and pig blood burned away by the heat of another world encroaching into this one filled the large chamber and washed over him in an arid wave. When the light of the summoning faded, Kurt found himself night-blind, with only the vague shapes of hideous monstrosities burned into his retinas. He turned and ran. The path ahead was familiar, though running it blind had never been part of the plan.

He was halfway to an exit when his eyes began to feed him information again. That was a good thing. Now at least he might not do himself in by running face first into a stalactite. His head throbbed like he had already done just that.

Kurt risked a quick glance over his shoulder and then doubled down on his running. They were coming. Several of them. Moving with the effortless grace of predators. One seeming to whip across the space like a side-winding snake on meth, another resembling something like a scorpion crossed with a cheetah, and there may have been a wolf. Raff, then. All lesser demons, bestial and probably not very smart, but insanely fierce and maybe fiercely insane.

Something took him across the left calf like a fiery whip and Kurt stumbled, almost going down. His shoulder slammed into the tunnel wall. He hop-skipped and found his rhythm again, though the burning in his leg was spreading with the slow inevitability of flowing lava.

The entrance to the cave lay just ahead, propped open, waiting. Kurt burst through it and tumbled down the hillside, branches and briars tearing at his arms and face. He reached for the detonator just as something closed around his ankle like a bear trap and began dragging him backward.

Kurt turned, kicking with his free foot. It was the wolf creature, and it appeared unfazed by the assault. Kurt had dealt with demons before and much more powerful ones than this mindless thing, but always with a talisman, and usually while they were being hosted. All he'd needed to do was break their hold on their host or this world, and poof, the Pull did the rest. Except if the Pull still functioned, this would not have been possible, and this wasn't just one. There were half a dozen on his trail last he'd seen.

He turned back to the detonator, wishing he were on the other side of it, down in the safety of the hollow, but he wasn't and there was nothing for it. With an effort of will, Kurt reached ahead of himself, ignoring a spike of pain behind his eyes, flipped the safety switch, and pressed the red button.

A tsunami of hot air rolled over him, dirt and rocks pelting like scalding rain, and then there was a blow that drove the air from his lungs.

Kurt came awake in the stillness after the explosion, ears ringing and nose bleeding. His left leg throbbed with venom and his right ankle looked like a chew toy. The demons that followed him out appeared to have been thrown away by the blast. He guessed being manifested in this world meant they got to follow some of the same laws of physics he was currently suffering the aftereffects of. Good. The motherfuckers weren't invulnerable.

Lying in the leaves feeling his heart pound, but unable to hear his own breathing, Kurt thought about what he'd just done. Sixty-four at once. It was an impossible feat and he'd just done it and, for the moment at least, survived. The thought brought a weak smile. He'd locked them away deep in the earth where they could do no harm. Hopefully.

It was a good ten minutes before he struggled into a sitting position to take stock of things. Both legs hurt, but he was pretty sure with some teeth gritting he could walk out of here. The poison worried him more than the wounds. It might be fatal. There was no way to treat it or even know what it was. Nothing he could do about that, so he turned his thoughts to his right leg. The leather of his boot had protected the joint, but those dagger teeth had pierced through in several places. It was bleeding, but there was no sense taking the boot off now. He had some hiking to do.

Brooklyn followed David back to his table and sat with him, twining her fingers with his below the table in the same easy way they always had.

Riley and Del would have Father Logan squirreled away in the basement lab someplace by now and on something to keep him from waking up. That wasn't her problem. Riley and Del could interrogate the bastard. Her problem was glowering at her from a couple of tables over. Nathan Goodrum. She remembered cutting his tendons with broken glass, smiled, and wondered if he walked with a limp now. She hoped so—running a finger over the black scar on her chest—he had left her a souvenir of their first encounter; only fitting if she had returned the favor.

Eric Stewarth was winding down the meeting. Cut free of Dravin's control, he seemed to have settled on an irritated scowl, perhaps intended to mask how off balance he must have felt. He was speaking about the banquet that would be held later in the evening and inviting both herself and David to be his guests at the main table when a sudden frown twisted his features.

A murmur of unease ran through the room. Brooklyn looked down and saw the hair on her arms was standing at attention. It was like when Eric had demonstrated his summoning earlier, but times ten. Her skin itched and crawled. Everyone felt it.

Brianne Moore took to her feet and let her full voice carry through the room. "The Pull has failed."

It was a statement of fact and nobody present disputed it. Judging from the looks of incredulity around her, she suspected nobody really had a concept for what that might mean, anyway.

"I can't believe this is happening," Eric Stewarth mumbled, the microphone carrying his dismay to all ears. "Can't be real."

Brooklyn thought someone might answer back, words of reassurance or of derision, but none did. It was a shock to her when it was her voice that broke the disbelieving silence. "We need to keep people safe, regular people. We have to fix this."

"Shut up." Goodrum's voice cracked like a whip. "You have no idea what's coming. Protect others? You won't even be able to protect yourself." He stood and swiped an arm across the table, toppling drinks and papers onto the floor. He pulled a penknife, sliced his fingertips, and began drawing a sigil in blood on the tabletop, using four fingers at once.

"What do you think—" Eric began.

"You don't get it either. It's over. Your rule. These politics. Over. None will walk safely through this world again save my kind." As he spoke, he finished the sigil and smoke rose from the table.

Brianne moved to stop him, but it was too late. The demon appeared and vanished inside of Nathan Goodrum.

"I wouldn't do that if I were you, Brianne." It was Goodrum's voice, and it wasn't. It had taken on the strange, controlled cadence of a Demonrider. The others, the ones along the back wall, stepped forward, taking their places at Goodrum's back.

Eric opened his mouth to say something and was interrupted again. This time by an enormous boom that rolled over the house like a thousand thunders and rattled the windows all around the room.

"What!?" Belial growled irritably. The old fellow stood over him, hand drawn back for another slap. Belial had been asleep, or at least what passed for sleep among spirits. It never ceased to amaze him how irritating his companion managed to be. "Hit me again and I'll toss you off this damned tower."

The old fellow blinked at him.

If the threat troubled him, he didn't show it. "Something's happening."

Belial pushed himself up and looked out across the world. At first, he didn't see what the fuss was all about, but then something caught his eye. Green. "Is that—it's grass?"

"Mhmm."

There wasn't grass in Hell. "What's happening?"

The quills on Old Porcupine's face stood up and lay flat again in a gesture Belial interpreted to be agitation. "Don't ask questions you know the answer to."

"I know the Pull has failed. I mean, why is grass appearing in certain spots?"

The old fellow considered the question. "The worlds are bleeding together, forming points of connection."

Belial looked up to where the spiraling stairway resumed above him, beyond reach. "We're running out of time."

"Patience is our only path forward."

Belial opened his mouth to say something snarky, but just then a jolt of icy power rushed out of him and Brooklyn was there again, on the other end of their connection, and she was in trouble.

50

Left to Melt

The Heir's guards interposed themselves around Eric and demanded Nathan Goodrum's surrender. Instead, Goodrum advanced on them. As gunfire erupted, Brooklyn dragged David under the table. Some Demonriders fell, but most were strong enough to shield themselves.

Splinters flew as bullets ricocheted into the great wooden tables. A stray shot took one of David's guards in the chest and Brooklyn saw David wince as if struck. Odd, but no time to think about it just now.

She peeked her head up. The Demonriders were wrestling for control of the guns. They had greater numbers and an unnatural strength the Heir's guards couldn't match. Brooklyn shoved David down and kicked off her shoes, and before she knew what she was doing, her legs had carried her halfway across the room toward the melee.

Eric Stewarth was trapped behind a press of bodies; the men trying to protect him were also blocking his escape. Brooklyn saw his eyes flash and felt the air charge with static, and the four monstrous demons from the demonstration earlier popped into being and began tearing into the attackers with mindless savagery. Though they appeared spectral, the gashes they opened gushed real enough blood.

A flicker of movement caused Brooklyn to flinch and raise a wedge of shield as the wooden lectern careened at her head. It followed the wedge clear of her and she brought a curve of energy up behind it, the way Kurt had taught her, forcing it to bank and turn back toward its origin. Her eyes found Nathan Goodrum's smirking face just as the massive projectile headed back his way. He shunted it aside, and it crashed into two demons and the unfortunate Demonrider caught between them. All three were driven into the far wall and crushed. Brooklyn saw the broken body of the man, but the demons just fizzled and blinked out of existence.

Nathan made a mocking gesture of thanks and grabbed one of the two remaining creatures, crushing its head like a rotten melon. It, too, flickered out of existence. With the tide turning back in his favor, Nathan strode toward her, without a hitch in his step—damn *it*—and drew a familiar black blade as he came. "Tonight's a night for tying up loose ends, it seems."

Eric's guards were dying all around him as Nathan Goodrum broke away and turned his attention to Brooklyn Evers. The black shadow that had lain heavy across his thoughts these past few weeks had lifted, and the scene unfolding came to him with terrible clarity.

Demonriders with guns. Eleven of them on the dais with him. Dozens more in the room beyond. Every possible escape blocked. He had two guards and one demon left. One of the guards held his rifle one-handed while the other arm hung limp and bloody at his side.

The demon moved among his enemies like a wraith. Claws and teeth flashing. Eric reached for the other three and tried to will them back into being, but couldn't draw them together again.

Three of his enemies pinned the demon and tore it apart.

Eric brought up his best shield and shaped it around himself. He could have shielded his guards, too, but it would have prevented them from shooting. Bullets skittered along the edges, each bringing a jolt of sharp pain to his head. His men stood their ground, firing aimed shots with careful discipline. Three Demonriders fell before the onslaught. A bullet caught the injured guard and something wet splattered across Eric's face.

The final guard charged forward, spraying bullets wildly. More Demonriders fell, but he never reached them. The return fire tore him to shreds, and more enemies piled onto the dais to replace the fallen.

Christ! If he'd had his father's ring, his birthright, he could have ripped the demons from every last one of them and turned their own power against them. This was Kurt's fault for stealing the damn thing and losing it.

One of the men stepped forward. Eric had seen him with Nathan Goodrum before, but didn't know him.

"Name's Cyrus," the man offered. "This is quite a pickle you're in, but you don't have to die today."

"What do you mean?"

"I'll accept your surrender. You'll publicly submit to our rule and encourage all the others to do the same."

"I'm the last Heir of King Solomon. I'll never bow to a Demonrider."

"We are all descended from Solomon."

"I'm a direct descendant. My blood is pure."

"Is it worth dying for?" Cyrus stepped through the shield with both hands up in a placating gesture.

Eric backed up a step and bumped the wall. He reached for the four demons again, but couldn't muster the concentration to make them materialize. In frustration, he clenched his fist around the golden knuckles until his fingers ached. "Stay back."

Cyrus took another step.

Eric swung with everything he had. The golden knuckles slammed into Cyrus's jaw with a meaty thud. The Demonrider went down on one knee, stunned. He should have been out cold. Eric drew back and punched again, but this time his opponent was ready.

Cyrus's hand closed around Eric's wrist like a vise. The bones creaked and pain exploded all the way to his shoulder.

The Demonrider pulled him down so that they knelt in front of one another. There was cold rage in his eyes. With his free hand he plucked the knuckles free of Eric's nerveless fingers and slid them onto his own hand. "I know what Dravin Logan did to you. I know he's done it to Nathan, too. You know, I made up the rhyme Cindy used that night, but I think we need to add a couple more lines."

Eric looked up into his tormentor's dark eyes. His vision swam with the pain. How could a human hand have such a grip? "What?"

Cyrus smiled. "The rhyme. Heir without a ring, little boy playing king, he's a puppet on a string, let's make him dance and make him sing."

The pressure on his wrist increased and Eric thought he could feel the bones grinding against one another. He gritted his teeth. He would not scream. "I . . . am the Heir . . . of King Solomon," he began haltingly, each phrase a labor that took all his breath. He remembered the feeling of wearing Solomon's ring. Remembered the thrill of holding even the mighty Prosidris thrall. And something his father had told him once, that the ring takes something from those who use it and leaves something behind. He called to the demon inside Cyrus, reached for it with his mind. For a fleeting moment he had its name and it was in his grip. Then it wasn't.

Cyrus stumbled back as if slapped, an unmistakable glint of fear in his eyes. Eric cradled his damaged arm against this belly.

"Let's see this pure blood you are so proud of," Cyrus growled, lifting the golden knuckles high. A heartbeat later the four demons sprang to life and Eric braced himself as the closest leapt on him and snapped its jaws closed on his throat. This couldn't be happening. He was the blood of Solomon. He couldn't lose to a Demonrider. There was a moment of pain, much worse than his arm, and then all the pain went away.

The black scar on her chest tingled at the memory of the fiery poison from that dark blade. Brooklyn took a small step back from Goodrum. Then another. But there was nothing behind her but David. David, who was blind and couldn't fight something like this. David, who was blind because he'd tried to once before.

"Just run away, little girl. Leave the Blind Prophet to me. I'll take care of him," Goodrum murmured.

Brooklyn stood her ground and reached for Belial, and—blessedly—he was there. The familiar cold power rolled up her spine like adrenaline. She channeled it into her right hand and a shard of ice formed, working itself into a large, daggerlike shape. It was a glacial blue that hurt to look at and wisps of steam trailed the blade. It tugged a dim memory from her nightmares in the house of blood. She remembered the bodies, mutilated, stacked like firewood and thawing. She shook her head to clear the cobwebs. No time for regrets just now.

Goodrum's steps faltered, only for half a second, and though he came on, he came more cautiously.

She made herself smile at him, hoping he could feel the frost in it. "There doesn't have to be a fight today."

"See, that's where you are wrong." He closed the distance between them and lashed out with a series of low slashes aimed at her belly.

Brooklyn stepped back and to one side, parrying the first attack with her forearm against his. Without stopping, he spun and whipped the knife from the opposite direction. She pivoted, the way Mrs. Mays had taught her, and blocked that one, too. She reversed her grip on the ice dagger and, when she blocked his arm a third time, it was with the edge of her blade.

Blood sprayed, but if Goodrum felt pain, she couldn't tell. He moved with the same easy grace Mrs. Mays had demonstrated during their lessons. He slashed for her face and she dropped, spinning into a sweep that took his legs out and dumped him on his back.

Brooklyn leapt astride him and brought the ice dagger down fast. Goodrum got his bloody forearm up against her wrist and stopped the blade a scant inch from his breastbone. She leaned forward, getting her weight on top of the blade. His arm trembled, and the blade dipped near enough to graze his shirt.

She saw the demon glint in his eyes. Or maybe it was just panic. Either way, he forced her back with unnatural strength, hoisting her entire weight on one arm. The blade rose until the tip was seven inches away from Goodrum. The icy handle sent aches deep into Brooklyn's bones, but she wouldn't let go. Couldn't.

"Death is better than living as a puppet," Brooklyn growled, in a voice she hardly recognized.

"Fuck you!" Goodrum grunted.

She drew on Belial. More of the cold power flowed into her body, awakening senses, filling her with energy. Then the blade began to lengthen, growing toward Goodrum's chest.

His eyes widened as the long dagger became a short sword and its tip found his skin again.

A flash of movement drew Brooklyn's eye. The other Demon-riders charging to Goodrum's aid, and David's guards rushing to block them, along with Erina Craft, the Scottish man, and Mrs. Mays. They were buying her time. Time to finish this.

Another flash of movement at the corner of her eye. The black knife, its tip trembling at her temple, and beyond it, David, straining to hold back Goodrum's arm and slowly failing, his feet sliding across the wooden floor.

Brooklyn rolled away from the blade and kept rolling as Goodrum overpowered David and scrambled after her, stabbing wildly into the floor where she'd been a split second before. She crab-walked under the great table where David and Father Logan had squabbled earlier, crunching shards of broken chandelier into finer fragments.

As Nathan flipped the table, Brooklyn came to her feet. She stopped it with an effort of will just before it toppled and crushed her. Goodrum pushed. Brooklyn pushed back.

The pressure built behind her eyes. The table slid forward one step, then two. Goodrum cursed at her from the other side. She reached into the cold well of energy, and the pain in her head grew distant. Goodrum gave ground until he was trapped against the wall between the table's solid sides. If it were facing the other way, she'd have crushed him already, but the legs wouldn't allow it.

He was trapped, though.

"Are you going to lose control now like the last time I bested you?"

"Shut up, you bitch!" Goodrum snarled with a shove. The table moved a couple of inches back her way.

"That's how it started last time. Rage. Impotent rage. After I cut your legs out from under you. Then the demon got the better of you."

"That won't happen again," Nathan snarled, and hoisted himself up on top of his wooden prison.

"So, you admit it happened?" an unfamiliar robotic voice called out behind and to one side of Brooklyn.

The color drained from Goodrum's face.

Brooklyn followed his eyes, half turning to see the speaker. She didn't know him, but had seen him somewhere before. He was taller than Nathan and about a decade younger. His skin was dark and his eyes were darker still. He held a rifle taken from one of the Heir's fallen guards.

"You know what that means. Turn it loose."

Nathan Goodrum's eyes hardened. "You don't lead here, Cyrus."

"We live by our code, or we die by it."

"Put the gun down."

"Let the demon go."

Goodrum's eyes flicked to a spot behind Brooklyn, and the broken shards of crystal from the chandelier lanced across the room into Cyrus's back.

Brooklyn leapt aside as Cyrus screamed and the staccato boom of gunfire filled the room. More of Eric's guards streamed into the room, weapons barking. Cyrus cast a disgusted look at Nathan, turned, gave a shrill whistle, and dashed for the far door, returning fire all the while.

Brooklyn slid one side of the table away from the wall. There was blood spatter on the wood paneling. She found Nathan crouched inside, holding pressure on his shoulder where one of Cyrus's stray shots must have clipped him.

"I told you there didn't have to be a fight today," she said with a casualness that belied her thundering heartbeat.

"Fucking bitch," he grunted. "You'd never beat me in a fair fight."

She squatted so they were eye to eye and rested the tip of the ice knife against the floor. "Name-calling is rude, and what would you know about a fair fight? I don't believe we've had one of those yet, have we? It's always been you and a demon against just me. Hell, the first time you had half an army with you, too."

"You choose to be weak! You could have been the first grade-three Demonrider. There's never been one. You could have been special."

"See, that's the thing I didn't realize for a while. Unlike you, I don't need a demon to be special or powerful." The green soul stone floated up between them. "Take it from me. I dare you."

His mental grip slid across it as ephemerally as a cobweb, and for once that superior grin wavered. "What kind of trick—"

"The kind that lets me put holes in you," she whispered. The orb drifted toward his face and she saw real panic glinting in his eyes as he tried and failed to stop it. "What life is left to you now that your secrets are out? The Demonriders won't have you, and when Father Logan wakes up you'll be one of his zombies again."

"Shut up!" Goodrum screamed as he produced the black blade from some hidden place and leapt for her, dodging around the hovering soul stone.

Brooklyn was ready. She shifted her weight back onto her heels and the new soul stones zipped free and hammered into the Demonrider's arm, driving it into the floor. At the same time she lifted the icy tip of her dagger up to meet him, and his own momentum drove it between his ribs.

She knew he was dead when the demon rose out of him. Standing tall enough to bump its head on the chandelier and covered in lichenous growths that hung like Spanish moss in the Deep South, it took a step toward her and paused. They made eye contact, and some understanding passed between them. The creature turned and fled the room.

Kicking the poisoned blade aside, Brooklyn knelt to check Goodrum's pulse. He was truly dead. Something like sadness put a hitch in her breath. This was her moment of triumph. It should have felt good. In reality, it didn't fix anything. She pulled her icy blade free, raised it high, and drove it into his lifeless heart with both hands as if she could kill the feeling along with the man. When it was done, she touched the ugly scar he'd given her and left the knife to melt.

51

NEED AN ARMY

Azrael severed the souls of Nathan Goodrum and Eric Stewarth personally. Her indentured demons handled the rest of the fallen. For a moment, it seemed the souls would linger rather than go wherever they went; she considered eating one, but slowly, like mist burning away under a summer sun, they vanished.

She found her prophet—he never seemed to stay where she put him—and followed his sightless gaze across the room to Brooklyn Evers. Cursed girl had never stopped being a pain in the ass since the moment she was born. Even so, Azrael harbored a small affection for Brooklyn. Doubtless a byproduct of sheltering and protecting her for more than two decades while the ever-incompetent Kurt Levin collected demons enough to purchase her.

He'd done his part, though. The Pull was no more. The worlds were reconnecting and, for the first time in nearly millennia, thanks to a little famine and pestilence, the humans were dying faster than they were being born. The next part of the game would be a matter of controlling the destruction. As resources continued to dwindle, war would become inevitable. So long as she and David kept a firm hand on the reins, everything would be fine.

Azrael approached her prophet, felt the moment his attention shifted from Brooklyn, and smiled. "You found her, I see."

"And now that I have, you're here to drag me back to the church, I suppose?" David grumbled.

"Not at all. Bring her home if you like."

"Just like that? No big speech about endangering your plans and ruining everything? Nothing about my responsibilities or how you can't interfere with her?"

"I haven't interfered. I'm still not." She gestured around the room. "You brought guards this time. The danger has passed, and you never listen anyway. There's nothing left to do but drop the bombs."

"The bombs?"

Is he serious? Does he really not see the plan, even now? "Why do you think we've worked so hard to place our prophets in positions of power? We must be careful that too many are not killed at once. A nuclear autumn may be weathered, but not a nuclear winter. The only question is where to begin."

Comprehension dawned slowly, but he got there.

"You expect me to cause a nuclear war? To bomb cities?"

"Cause one? Of course not." She cocooned them in her wings, holding back the flow of time so they could remain unnoticed. "That's going to happen regardless of what either of us does. The dominos are already falling. Resources are dwindling, demons are spilling over into this world, war is inevitable. What I'm saying is, you can minimize the impact. Without your guidance, humanity will extinguish itself like a candle, but with your leadership, humanity will survive and thrive in the aftermath. An apocalypse doesn't have to be a finality."

She saw conflict written on his face.

"I could stop it entirely."

"No. Not even I could. Not now. The best we can hope for is to redirect and minimize the destruction. The world is at a tipping point, and you are its savior. You can control which way it tips."

David appeared ready to argue the point, but the pressure of holding back time was mounting, so she cut him off before he began.

"Goodrum is dead. The line of the Heirs of Solomon has ended. Only Father Logan remains. You must deal with him."

"Deal with him?"

Yes, stupid boy. "You must kill him."

"I'm not a killer."

"You are a leader. And this new world is going to need one." Azrael reached down into the collar of David's shirt and tugged the leather necklace with the feather free so that it hung on the outside. "Wear that proudly. Never hide it."

"I don't see how killing—"

"He's a monster. You'd be one of his bootlickers right now if it weren't for me. Kill him or have your girlfriend do it for you. She's got experience."

David opened his mouth to retort, but Azrael was already gone. *Must be nice to always have the last word.* He searched the room with other men's eyes until he found Brooklyn again. She looked lost.

"Brooke!" he called out, making his way to her. "Are you okay?"

She nodded. "Goodrum's dead. We need to find Mrs. Mays and Riley and get the hell out of here."

"Who's Riley?"

"He's a friend. Look, there's Mrs. Mays."

David turned to look, then chided himself for trying. When would he ever get used to seeing only the cool lines of energy and not people? Probably never. David turned Avery's eyes in the appropriate direction and saw Mrs. Mays picking her way over the debris to join them. He scanned the rest of the room and plucked a list of survivors from Avery's impeccable memory. Erina and Bryssa Craft. A number of Demonriders who'd beaten a hasty retreat with the Protectors and Heir's guards on their tail. Abram Randall, patriarch of one of the lesser Tennessee families who seldom attended council meetings. Boy he picked a doozie to show up for. Mrs. Mays, of course. A dozen and a half of David's own surviving retinue, and around twenty other attendees who'd fled the room when the conflict broke out. Del Stewarth, Father Logan, and Brooklyn's *friend* Riley rounded out the list.

David tried to remember who had been sitting at which tables when Dravin Logan dosed the room. Only some people had been affected. Whether that was just luck of the draw or by design, he didn't know. He directed his own eyes to the Craft women, who were engaged in some sort of whispered debate. The pregnant one, Bryssa, radiated a warm energy; the other woman kept a coil of some power David had never seen like a compressed spring, full of potential energy, and then he saw the thread, barely there, a darkened filament that left her body and disappeared into the floor. She'd drank the wine; thanks to the unborn baby, her daughter had not.

Would killing Father Logan free her, free all of them? He didn't know. They might go through life with this filament trailing behind them, attaching to anyone or anything with more willpower. David had taken all of Dravin's followers once. Maybe he could do it again. That wasn't really a solution. It didn't undo the damage, only changed who benefited. Images of Emily stabbing Nicole washed through his mind and carried away any desire he had to follow that line of thought.

"Why are you young-uns standing around like you don't know what to do next?" Mrs. Mays demanded.

"What next?" Brooklyn sighed wearily.

"There's a small war going on downstairs, or ain't you noticed?"

David cocked his head and listened. There were distant sounds of fighting. "Who?"

"The Protectors and the Heir's guard are after the Demonriders, I expect. Trying to end them before they scatter, or before they take over. They killed Eric Stewarth. The Heir is dead."

That news stopped everyone cold for a long moment.

"We should help the Protectors," Brooklyn said. "We have to."

"We need to get to gettin' while we can. We can't beat the Demonriders. Too many of 'em. Too strong."

"There must be something we can do. We can't just leave the good guys to die," Brooklyn argued.

"I'm telling you. It'd be like pissing on a house fire. Take an army to beat them now."

David shuddered. Something, either excitement or dread, was pooling in his gut. When he spoke, his voice sounded strange to his own ears. "As it happens, I brought one."

52

SPRING THE TRAP

"You brought one?" Brooklyn repeated. Why was he saying something so outlandish when the situation called for seriousness?

"An army. I brought one."

"You've got a dozen guards. That's not an army," Mrs. Mays said, crossing and uncrossing her arms.

The two Craft women joined their little circle. The pregnant one had her hands clasped around her belly.

"I didn't come to this meeting with any intention of being imprisoned again," David said softly. "I can have my men, two hundred and eighty-four of them, here in about seven minutes."

Brooklyn felt a prickle on the nape of her neck and looked around to see the men who came here with David drawing together in a circle around them. One man, who appeared to be the leader, nodded at David as if acknowledging an unspoken command.

"We'll push the conflict outside, onto the front lawn, and then I'll end it," David said.

A cold weight settled in her belly. *Is David controlling people like Father Logan?* "*You'll* end it?" Brooklyn ran a hand through her hair in agitation. "How will you end it, David? You can't see. You need to wait here where it is safe."

"No," David murmured. "Avery, I need a weapon."

The man he addressed pulled a bulky black pistol from the holster of one of the fallen guards and tossed it at David.

David raised a hand, casually snatched it from the air, and then racked the slide, a move that would have been cooler if a round weren't already chambered. The bullet clattered to the floor.

Brooklyn knelt and retrieved the round and tossed it at David, intending to plink him with it. He caught it easily and loaded it back into the magazine.

He smiled. "I'll get by."

How in the hell... She let the thought go. It didn't matter. She'd seen much weirder things in the past year. Instead of asking more questions, she ran her eyes around their motley crew. "Is everybody in?"

"I'm in. I won't raise my baby in a world run by Demonriders," Bryssa Craft whispered.

The girl's mother looked at her strangely, but then nodded. "Me too."

Mrs. Mays looked dazed but said, "I'm with you."

David smiled at her. "Of course, I'm in. This is my plan."

After he spoke, all his retinue murmured their commitments in unison. Something about it made the hair on the back of Brooklyn's neck tingle again. She pushed it aside, a concern for later.

The armed men went first, followed by Mrs. Mays, Brooklyn and David, and then the mother and daughter duo in the rear. As they snaked through the hallways, following the sound of the conflict and trying to be both swift and stealthy, Brooklyn recognized a door. It was her door. She leaned close to David and whispered, "Call a halt."

He didn't say anything, but the men ahead came to an abrupt stop. *That is definitely suspicious.*

Brooklyn tried the door. It was open. She slipped inside and latched it behind her. Crossing the room to the closet, she pulled the door open. Blessedly, there were her clothes, just the way she'd left them. Ditching the ruined dress and formal shoes for the familiar comfort of her own clothes and a pair of tennis shoes was amazing. She slipped the soul stones into her pocket. Lastly, she pulled her hair back. Now ready to fight, she rejoined the posse.

"We've stopped in the middle of a battle for you to change wardrobes?" Mrs. Mays growled.

Heat rose in Brooklyn's cheeks. "I'll be more help if I can move freely." She looked around. Bryssa Craft was nodding in agreement and a ghost of a smile played across Erina's lips.

"Let's move," David called out.

The sounds grew louder as they descended the stairs to the main floor. That would make it easier to push the fighting outside. Twin hallways diverged from the main entrance and curved away to the right and left and reconnected near the rear of the mansion. A great ruckus of sound and intermittent gunfire came from the one to the right.

David's man Avery peeked around the corner, but it was David who spoke. "The guards and Protectors have them trapped in the middle of the hallway. Both sides are shooting and shielding. There's two, maybe three times the number of Demonriders. Even attacking from two sides, they won't be able to hold them long. We need to make sure this side falls first, so the others can drive them this way and out the front door."

"How do you—" Brooklyn began.

"No time."

"So we circle around and reinforce the other side?"

"No time."

Three of David's armed men stepped around the corner and opened fire on the Protectors and Demonriders alike.

"No!" Brooklyn pushed David aside and reached out, shoving the gun barrels down and away.

Return fire lanced out of the hallway and one man went down in a bloody mess. The other two made it back to cover. David howled and scrambled back to his feet. "Why did you—"

"No time." She cut him off and dashed around the corner, drawing on Belial's glacial power again and raising a wedge of a shield.

The scene before her was breathtaking. Plaster dust spun in turbulent motes like tiny universes being born, flickering in the muzzle flashes. The projectiles churned the whole conflagration into ever-new and more complex patterns. She didn't have long to admire it before bullets screeched along the edges of her shield. Each impact was like a solid thump between the eyes.

Brooklyn found what appeared to be the woman in charge on this front of the fight and approached her through a hail of detritus, bullets, and panicked cursing. Several of the Heir's guards turned to fire at the new threat. She raised her hands in mock surrender. One of the guards tapped the woman on the shoulder and shouted something that was lost in the din.

The woman cast a quick glance back at Brooklyn and jerked her head in a "come here" gesture.

Brooklyn approached cautiously and touched the woman on the shoulder. She was older, maybe sixty, thin as a skeleton, and blood sheeted one side of her face from a scalp wound.

"Here to help, or shoot us in the backs?" the woman asked curtly.

"You need to fall back," Brooklyn shouted. "Let them out the front. We've laid a trap."

Something tore into the ceiling above them and splinters rained down.

"How do I know I can trust you, Brooklyn?" The woman cast a handful of broken wood into the air and shoved it down the hallway at the Demonriders.

"Kurt Levin trusted me. You're a Protector, like him, right?"

"Yes, Brianne Moore, and Mr. Levin's judgment was not always the best," she shouted over the ruckus.

Brooklyn remembered a rusty cell door clanking shut. "At least on that, we agree."

"Fine! But this better not be a trick, or I'll hunt you down, little girl." Brianne raised both hands, and the already chewed-up ceiling collapsed between their position and that of the Demonriders. Gypsum dust filled the air and covered their hasty retreat. Brianne came last, shielding the rear.

Free of the hallway's confines, Brianne and her cohorts sought cover with the rest of the survivors. Tense moments passed and then the Demonriders boiled out of the hallway in a cacophony of yelling and pounding footsteps, the rearmost shielding and lobbing projectiles at the pursuers.

The man from earlier, Cyrus, came last of all, dancing past Brooklyn with a smile and a roguish wink. "Ditched the dress?"

She opened her mouth to reply, but he was already through the door, rushing headlong into the trap she'd helped set.

53

Questions and Answers

"So, what's the endgame here?" Del Stewarth gestured at Dravin Logan laid out on a table connected to an IV and a heart monitor.

Riley bit back a retort. He was tired and jittery all at once. The Pull had failed less than half an hour ago and he felt it acutely, like an itch he couldn't scratch. Endgame? The end may have come already, and it definitely wasn't a game. Instead, with a long-suffering sigh, he asked, "What are you asking me exactly?"

"How do we undo what this monster has done to my baby?"

"I don't know. I need time."

"Does he know?" She slapped a hand down on Dravin's chest, hard enough Riley winced.

"If anyone does, it's him."

"Can his men get to us here?"

Riley cast a sidelong glance at the reinforced steel door and the granite barrier blocking the entrance to the chamber beyond. "Not without some dynamite and a cutting torch, or somebody who knows the secret way."

"Wake him. Let's make him talk."

"Torture him, you mean?"

"Torture, truth serum, forced possession, whatever it takes."

Forced possession? Is that even a possibility here? Riley inquired of his companion.

With the Pull in shambles, probably.

I hope it doesn't come to that.

Del raised her brows and tilted her head expectantly. "Alright, I'll bring him around."

Dravin drifted up from nothingness and longed to return to it. His eyelids seemed to be weighted with stones and his arms were heavy and clumsy. Nearby, a monitor beeped. His head ached, but he couldn't remember what had happened. Car crash?

"Little caffeine might help," a familiar voice murmured in his ear, and a pair of hands raised him into a sitting position and pressed a cold can with a straw into his hand.

Dravin brought it to his lips and tasted a sweet, fizzy cola. Opening his eyes and blinking against the dim lights, he identified his nurse and apparent captor. "Riley Martin." He groaned. "To what do I owe the pleasure?"

"You are going to release my boy or we are going to start cutting bits off you." A woman's voice, distinctive accent, coming from behind him.

Dravin smiled. "Del."

"You think we won't?"

"I think you might, but I know it won't do you any good." Dravin took another sip of Coke. "As far as I know, there's no undoing Devotion."

"Anything that is done can be undone," Riley growled.

"Maybe so," Dravin agreed amiably. "I just don't know how." He reached out to his web. He could sense the connections, but his brain was too fuzzy to bring them into focus. Another few minutes, that was all he needed.

"Maybe the first thing we should try is killing you," Del suggested. "That might set my Eric free."

"Your son was a petty tyrant on the rise until I gave him guidance and perspective. You saw the executions out on the lawn. What he did to those Adepts."

"He did the only things he could to hold us all together. It was you, and Kurt, and those damnable Demonriders that put him in that position. He didn't choose it."

"You left out one."

Del scowled. "Excuse me?"

"Left out yourself."

"Myself?" Del hissed.

"Sure, if you hadn't poisoned your husband, none of this would have ever happened. Really, you are the one who set all this chaos into motion."

Dravin saw the rage on her face. She squashed it. She'd probably had to do that a lot with Alexander Stewarth for a husband. Dravin had seen the kind of man he'd been at home in Eric's memories.

"Wait a minute," Riley cut in.

"Let him talk," Del murmured. "For the first time, it seems a prophet got it right."

"I didn't think you would deny it," Dravin said. "I'm sure you had your reasons."

"He was a cruel, arrogant man."

"My point exactly. Eric was becoming a crueler version of his father when I intervened. In a way, I saved him from becoming the sum of the worst parts of you and his father."

Del made a choking sound. Riley watched the exchange with an alien fascination.

Dravin reached for the scattered strands of his web and pulled it back together. "Oh, damn."

"What?" Riley demanded.

Dravin shook his head wearily. "I guess the whole thing is a moot point. Eric's dead."

Kurt stumbled through what had once been a cornfield, climbed the farmhouse's front porch steps, and settled himself wearily into a chair. Nausea came in waves. The back of his calf sported six parallel welts that were slowly swelling together. Kurt pulled the boot off that foot for fear it would swell to a point he couldn't remove it.

He pulled the other boot free and found several deep punctures around his ankle, oozing blood. Beyond that, his battered body was alerting him to half a dozen lesser bumps, bruises, scrapes, and burns. Where the hell was Amelia?

Kurt hobbled inside and rummaged through the cupboards until he turned up a bottle of aspirin. He'd have liked to wash it down with some liquor, but Mrs. Mays didn't have any. At least, not that he could find.

Back on the porch in a rocking chair, Kurt sat still and waited to see if his churning stomach would accept the aspirin or send them back up. "My God, what have I done?" he asked aloud.

"I assume you are talking to me?" Azrael asked. "I am your god now, right?"

Kurt grunted a reluctant assent to that assessment, looking around until he found her lounging against the porch railing.

"Let me see," Azrael said, kneeling to examine the back of his leg. She ran a warm hand over the welts, and Kurt stifled a groan. As she drew her hand away, a pulling sensation sent a frenetic itching through his entire leg. She sat back on her haunches and wadded up strands of something that looked like fishing line. "Barely worse than a bee sting. I thought Protectors were made of sterner stuff."

"Too damn tired to argue with you. I've just ruined the world."

"Not ruined. Remade. Even now, connections are forming like nerve synapses in the human brain. You are the corpus callosum."

"Doesn't feel like that from where I'm sitting. Not to change the subject, but I have another question. What did you do with Solomon's ring?"

"Knowing would be of little use to you. It is beyond human reach now."

"Then what's the harm in telling? Curious minds want to know."

She laughed then. He'd only seen her smile a handful of times over the years. It lit her face.

"Curiosity got you booted."

"Eden?"

"That's right."

"You're talking about the actual Garden of Eden? From the Bible?"

Azrael just smiled.

"You know, it might be a lot easier to remake this world if you fetched it back and put it on the right finger."

"Hmm. Who would you suggest? David Sterling?"

"Oh, no. I think we need to keep church and state separate. I was thinking maybe, me?"

Azrael laughed. It was an unsettling sound. "Your mind is broken, held together by me alone. It is too much power for any human to hold. That's why I've placed it where no human may ever go."

"What about Brooklyn? Do you know where she is?"

No answer came. Instead, the wind whispered against his sweaty face and he was alone again.

54

SOME SAY FIRE, SOME SAY ICE

From the flash of pain in David's eyes, Brooklyn could see when one of his men died. The sound of gunfire and men screaming had them all crowded into cover on either side of the open doorway. The creeping suspicions she'd felt earlier settled in the pit of her stomach with the weight of certainty. Whatever Father Logan was, David was the same thing now.

After a few more tense moments, the gunfire became sporadic, like the last few kernels of popcorn popping. Then the air filled with an expectant silence.

David cleared his throat. "Thirty-four dead. Five escaped into the woods."

"Escaped? You have to be kidding!" Brianne said, color rising in her cheeks. "We had them. Had them all hemmed up. Surrounded. Then we went with your plan and now the whole thing is fucked."

"You would have died," David murmured.

"Yeah, if you'd had your way, with your men shooting us in the back."

"That was a misjudgment. I'm—"

"No, it was a crime. One I intend to see you answer for." She stepped toward David.

Brooklyn moved between them. "We don't have time for this."

"Get out of my way, little girl," Brianne growled.

"She's right." It was the skinny, dark-haired Protector.

"There will be time later," the third Protector, a Hispanic woman, said softly, but Brooklyn couldn't recall her name either.

Brianne's shoulders sagged wearily. "Fine." She jabbed a finger into Brooklyn's chest. "I'll deal with both of you later." The elder Protector jerked her head at her two subordinates and strode out onto the battlefield to survey the damage.

"I could kill her now with only a thought," David whispered low enough that only she heard.

Brooklyn sighed and leaned back against his chest for a moment. "No. There's been too much blood."

Wrapping his arms around her, he said, "We should check on Riley, Del, and our good friend Father Logan."

"Yeah, let's regroup in the basement," Erina Craft called out.

"We should get out of this place while we can. I don't want to risk my baby," Bryssa said.

"It will be safe," Erina insisted, turning to trot away without a glance to see who followed.

They all followed.

As the steps wound down to the basement below, Brooklyn drew on Belial, just enough to frost her fingernails and open the connection between them. It was the first time she'd done so lately, when her life wasn't in danger.

Belial?

I need your help.

Show me.

The memories sped through her consciousness in a blur that nearly sent her stumbling down the stairway. She understood the tower and why it was imperative Belial stop his father, and saw the journey he'd been on. Even the shameful parts of passing through the gates, and finally the moment she'd pushed the energy his way instead of taking it. The way it had lifted him a few scant inches closer to the goal.

I'll find a few moments alone and help you.

When?

Soon. She dropped the connection without awaiting a reply.

"Are you alright?" David asked.

"Just woozy for a minute. I'm fine now."

They arrived at the bottom of the stairs and Erina led them directly to the section of granite wall that wasn't really a wall at all, but a secret entrance.

Erina pointed a finger at Brooklyn. "You know how to open this?"

"I—yes." Brooklyn ran her fingers over the familiar stonework until she found the hidden catch, and several tons of stone slid aside with barely a whisper.

"And the door? You can open it?" Erina gestured to a locked metal door.

Brooklyn shook her head. "Don't have the key for that one."

"Come inside and close the outer door," Erina commanded.

They all entered the inner chamber, which was shaped like an egg with the doors set opposite one another in the middle of the long walls. Brooklyn pulled the door shut.

"No! Don't!" David shouted, lunging across the space between them. But it was too late. The door snapped into place with a click.

Father Logan rolled his head back and forth, trying to work out the kinks in his neck and shoulders. "It seems we find ourselves at an impasse."

"How's that?" Riley asked.

"I want to leave and you don't want me to."

"You're not going anywhere," Del Stewarth growled. Whatever grief she felt over the loss of her son, he couldn't see it on her face or hear it in her voice. Maybe she didn't believe it yet, or perhaps she was in shock.

"That's the trouble. We've gotten ourselves into a bit of a hostage situation."

"What are you talking about?" Del snapped.

"Open the window in the metal door over there and have a look outside."

Dravin watched with grim amusement as Riley opened the window and gasped in shock. The orange flames colored his face.

While Riley and Del were distracted, he pulled the IV needle free of his arm. "If you cannot make out their faces through the flame, that is Bryssa Craft and her unborn babe, Amelia Mays, David Sterling with several of his guards, and of course the ever-troublesome Brooklyn Evers.

Riley rounded on him with murder in his eyes.

"You both just stay right there where I can see you or all those good people go up in smoke."

"What do you want?" Riley's eyes darted back and forth as he spoke. It was a bit unsettling.

"I'm going to walk out of here. I'm taking David Sterling with me. Once we are safely departed, my associate will quench the flames and everybody goes home."

"No way!"

"Why do you care? You don't want me, she does." Dravin gestured contemptuously at Del Stewarth. "You don't want Sterling either. You only have eyes for the girl. Seems like I might be doing you a favor."

"I suspect if I kill you, the flames will go right away."

"Except I'm holding Erina in check. My concentration slips even for a second, and they flare out of control. Everybody dies. And don't be too long about releasing me. It's quickly becoming an oven out there."

The flames sprang up like molten walls. Brooklyn found herself corralled into a corner with Bryssa Craft. She couldn't see the others except in flickers. The temperature in the small cavern soared and sweat ran in rivulets.

"Mom, what are you doing!?" Bryssa shrilled.

There was no answer. Brooklyn watched her cellmate plunge both hands into the wall of flame and begin to push it apart, seemingly without being burned. The fire seemed to push back and Brooklyn had to steady Bryssa to keep her from falling.

"I can't beat her. She's stronger than me. A lot stronger."

"Maybe I can do it," Brooklyn murmured.

"Don't try. You aren't attuned. You'll just get burned."

Brooklyn sheathed her arms to the elbows in ice and plunged her hands into the flames as Bryssa had done, but unlike the other girl, she could gain no purchase on the wall. It was as ethereal as someone else's soul stone.

The steel door clanged open and Father Logan strolled out, walking a corridor of flame from one door to the next. Brooklyn saw a section of the opposing fire wall flicker out of existence, and David stumbled free of his cell. Dravin Logan took him by the arm and tugged him toward the granite door.

"You are not taking him," Brooklyn shouted, and set her will against the mechanism that unlatched the stone door.

Riley stood in the other doorway, watching.

"Riley, stop him."

"I can't. He'll burn you alive."

"It's okay, Brookie. I've survived this snake twice. I can do it again," David said as he reached out a hand, pinching delicately at something only he could see in the air. Sudden pressure built between her eyes and all at once Brooklyn's mental grip failed, and the door slid open. David, Father Logan, and Erina Craft stepped through and it shut again.

For long moments, the flaming walls continued to burn even after Riley had emptied a fire extinguisher; then all at once they waned and died away.

Brooklyn bolted through the door and pounded up the stairs, with the others calling after her. They were gone. She needed Belial up in the sky tracking them, but he wasn't here. She tried to summon him the way she had once before in a farmhouse kitchen in what seemed another life. It didn't work. The connection opened, nothing more.

55

GATE OF ASCENSION

Brooklyn needed Belial. That scared her. She'd never thought she needed him for anything. She'd been doing him a favor by keeping him topside and out of Prosidris's reach. Now, as she pushed open the heavy wooden door of what had once been Kurt Levin's office, she shuddered. Goodrum, whose corpse was still cooling in the meeting room, had predicted as much, hadn't he?

She settled into the plush leather chair and opened the connection with Belial, pushing energy through to him. A lot of energy and quickly. Brooklyn had a sense of what was happening on the other end. A sense of rising or being borne up on something. But mostly she just felt the expenditure of effort.

As Belial rose, Quills leapt and snagged the green leather cape, scrambling for purchase as they were both lifted through the missing section of tower to where the stairs resumed. Twice it seemed their ascent was slowing, but somehow Brooklyn found the reserves to keep at it.

When the first step came even with his face, Belial grabbed it with both hands and heaved them both onto the black stone. The hellscape below was a patchwork of chaos, and for a heartbeat

Belial teetered out over the emptiness like a drunk, but as ever, Quills was there to prod him in the right direction.

"Onward and upward!" the old fellow declared cheerfully. Then he bellowed, "You are the wind beneath my wings." Belial kicked him.

As they climbed, the spiral stair took them out of sight of the world below, and the connection with Brooklyn strained and broke. She was in trouble. He had to hurry. They took the stairs two at a time now, jogging.

"How many more gates do you think?"

"One more."

"Why do you think one?"

Quills shrugged. "I just do."

Belial was pondering that when the next gate appeared before them.

The symbol on this one was a patchwork of parallel wavy lines over an egg-shaped lump that seemed to rise out of the ground and sink back into it in undulating waves. Belial couldn't read it, but looking at it stirred a deep sense of shame in him, so he turned his gaze on Quills instead.

"Can you tell what it says?"

"Hmm. This is a different language than the others. Ancient." The old fellow stepped forward and ran a spiky hand over the glowing sigil. "Unpleasant to touch."

Belial reached out his own hand and felt something familiar. Dragon script. He plucked a quill from Quills and lanced the pad of his finger, letting it turn his blue claw red. When one fat drop gathered at the tip, he touched it to the gate's seal.

As they watched, blood ran in a rivulet along his flesh and flowed into the fiery symbol. New lines appeared and intersected the others at harsh angles. Black blood twined around the golden luminescence like a vine might a tree. The meaning came to Belial then. He said it aloud. "The Gate of Indignity."

At his words, the gate creaked and vanished. His blood, burned into a fine ash, drifted into a line on the step below. A line Belial was no longer sure he wanted to cross.

David didn't struggle as they herded him through the underground garage. Father Logan in the lead, David behind him with a man on either side, one or both of whom must have been police officers based on the fact they'd had handcuffs at the ready. Last of all, Erina Craft guarding the rear.

He'd caught a faraway glimpse of his little escort through the eyes of one of his guards. He could have summoned help, but that would have likely only gotten his helpers incinerated. There was the feather dangling from a necklace around his throat also, but David wasn't sure Azrael would help him. If he was facing death, she might swoop in, but otherwise she'd given him a task to complete and she would expect him to handle it.

Their footsteps echoed in the cavernous garage. David leaned on his captor, deprived now of any eyes that might aid his navigation. They came to a stop and David heard the snick of a latch opening. He readied himself to be forced into the trunk of a car, but it wasn't that. They lifted him *up* into something. He settled on a seat and the door slammed closed. The sound of other doors opening met his ears and whatever he sat in rocked gently as his new friends hoisted themselves in as well.

None of them spoke. They probably didn't need to. He focused and found the shadow lines connecting them each to the other and all of them to Dravin Logan. It at least gave him some awareness of where everyone was situated relative to everyone else.

David saw the faint pulse of blue as electricity flowed and an engine spun and sputtered to life. The engine rose to a roar that didn't correlate with the slow acceleration, but as they moved forward, he realized, *It's a plane!* Then the world dropped out from beneath them and David wished desperately he could look out the window.

With Belial safely on his way, Brooklyn looked around the once plush office. She still thought of it as Kurt's office, but it wasn't, really. It was Goodrum's, and so she felt no guilt as she rifled through his belongings.

Brooklyn found the bourbon that had been Kurt's, and two glasses. She sat them both on the desk, poured three fingers in each, and tossed them back one and then the other, managing not to splutter as she had done the last time. A chaser would have been nice, but the hell with it; it had been a rough day.

The liquor started a small fire in the pit of her belly and loosed a knot of anxiety she'd been carrying for weeks, maybe years.

Very little was the same as it had been a year ago when last she'd trespassed here. As if Nathan Goodrum had endeavored to erase all memory of Kurt's many years here. She opened the desk drawers one at a time and found the familiar stationery on which she'd written a letter to her mother but never sent. *Missed opportunity, that*, she thought wryly, and immediately felt ashamed.

The center desk drawer, like all the others, held all the things she remembered, plus one. Brooklyn reached inside and plucked a cheap, plastic cell phone from the drawer. It was the kind you could buy at Walmart and prepay for minutes. A burner phone. Nothing special about it, except that she recognized it. It was hers. *How did this get here?*

Brooklyn rummaged through the desk drawer, looking for a charger, but of course, it was in her car, wherever it was now.

She slipped the useless brick into her pocket with the thought of finding a charger later.

As she stood to go, the door swung open. It was Riley, face pinched and ashen.

"We have to get everyone out," he said without preamble. "There are demons in the basement. In the tunnels. A lot of demons."

Brooklyn sighed. *Of course there are.*

56

NEAR DISASTERS

Drop the bombs, a seductive voice whispered inside David's brain. *Far enough away to knock this little toy into a tailspin. I'll catch you.*

The idea had not occurred to him. He had incredible resources at his disposal. He could have a team of military jets here in less than ten minutes with orders to intercept and escort this plane to the nearest airport.

Drop the bombs, his flickering mistress whispered again. *Here.* A map of the world filled his mind's eye with red *X*s marked on several continents. As the idea of it captured his attention, David sensed the appropriate people around the world making ready to carry out his wishes.

No, he thought loudly. *NO!*

The map vanished and with a tinkling of laughter, Azrael did too.

David's heart pounded and an icy trickle of sweat ran down his spine. What had he almost done? He remembered Nicole the vegetarian, then shuddered. A misunderstanding, a bit of mixed signaling, and a girl died. What would happen if he made another mistake? A bigger one?

"How many did you dose with your poison?" David asked.

A long moment passed in silence before Father Logan's butter-smooth voice filled the cabin, half shouting to be heard over the engines. "More than half of Solomon's descendants are mine now. Soon, you will be too."

David had told Azrael he wasn't a murderer, but now with rage boiling behind his breastbone and the realization he had the power to do something about it, it seemed he might need to reassess.

"What are you—" That was all Belial heard of Old Porcupine's inquiry because as he set one clawed foot over the line of ash, he was abruptly alone on the stairway.

No. Not alone. There was another presence. A familiar presence just out of sight around the tower's gently curving inner wall.

Belial took a careful step back, then another, thinking he might leap back into the chasm between the tower's two parts and glide away from this fool's errand. But no. The stairway ended at a black stone wall. There would be no going back.

"Yes, try to run away. It's what I would expect. Ever the coward, aren't you, son?" Prosidris's voice filled the stairwell and echoed strangely.

Belial was afraid. Had been afraid since the moment he left Brooklyn with Mrs. Mays and let himself be carried back to this place.

"You didn't save the last girl. What makes you think you can save this one?" Prosidris taunted. "I'll drink wine from her skull before this is over, and you'll gladly refill my cup."

"No." Belial's voice came out puny and small. It carried no power here, but he squared his shoulders and forced one foot in front of the other anyway. This was what he came to do, after all.

Clawed feet clicked against the stone stairs as he climbed to meet his father.

Belial found Prosidris standing a dozen steps on from where the line of ash marked the floor. Tall as always, with a head that seemed to be a globe of water that flashed different faces. Finally, he settled on one and gave Belial that familiar, toothy smile.

"You aren't real." Belial climbed the stairs and made to push past the apparition. "You're only in my mind."

A heavy hand came to rest on his shoulder. "Son . . . How real do you want me to be?" Without waiting for an answer, Prosidris cupped a slimy hand to the side of Belial's face and rammed his head into the stone wall.

Belial stumbled away, dazed.

"You cannot win. To think you could overcome me is as foolish as a single raindrop hoping to quench a volcano. I've already won. I own you."

Belial shook his head, more to shake loose the cobwebs than to negate the things his father said.

"I won't let you kill her."

"You cannot stop me. In fact, all I need to do is keep you occupied here for a few more minutes and it will be a moot point."

"What do you mean?" Belial demanded, straightening his spine.

"Those rifts forming out there. The largest one opened right inside the Protector's manor and the Raff are flooding through. Incidentally, your little pet is sitting on a crate full of dynamite and doesn't even know it."

Belial reached for Brooklyn through their connection, but the way was blocked. He turned to look his father in the eye. "What do you want?"

"To watch you squirm and suffer for your betrayal and then to administer the sweet mercy of the final death. You know I gave you that name you carry for a reason. It means 'worthless.'"

Oh. That was nice. "Doesn't it bother you that the Pull has fallen? You worked so hard, with your friend the king, to see the Earth stripped of her spirits, imps, and demons, and committed all of our element to safeguarding it. Only to have it implode before your eyes."

"It is change, Belial, another change beyond my power or influence. I will adapt and prosper. Those who don't will perish along with you, the dragons, and most of humanity."

Though Belial's mind was spinning, he spoke with slow precision. "So, you've accepted this is beyond your power, but have you considered it might not be beyond *our* power?"

Prosidris made a sound like the surf breaking against a cliff. After a moment, Belial realized it was laughter. "Your power derives from mine. What could you possibly offer that I don't have already?"

It was the very question he'd expected. *The Tomes.* The answer that might save the worlds, earn his father's favor, and buy Brooklyn's life, danced on the tip of his forked tongue. Belial swallowed it. "You're right. I'm worthless. I have nothing to offer."

A cruel smile split his father's chosen features, and then everything around him blew away like smoke.

"These gates are just getting easier and easier! That was the quickest yet." Quills beamed.

"Yeah. Easier and easier," Belial repeated, rubbing his aching head.

57

Mass Exodus

Hurrying to keep up as Riley darted down the carpeted hallway, Brooklyn caught him at the elevator and gestured wordlessly to the red handle set in the wall that read *FIRE ALARM*.

Riley pulled it and the halls filled with a three-pulse buzz and flashing strobe lights. "Smart. I didn't even think of that."

Brooklyn stabbed an impatient finger into the elevator button. "Where are the others?"

"Buying us time to evacuate everyone."

Despite the alarm, Brooklyn noted the halls were empty as the elevator doors slid closed. When they opened on the main floor, there was pandemonium. Kitchen staff, janitorial, medical, and others whose clothing didn't advertise their roles scrambled and fought toward the door. Gypsum dust and gun smoke hung heavy in the air and gave the illusion that the building really was on fire.

Riley tugged her against the flow of bodies, toward the stairwell that descended to the basement. The crowd evaporated at the stairwell entrance, but a blast of heat and actual smoke broke across her face like a slap.

Taking the steps two at a time, they rushed past Riley's lab without slowing and climbed over a mound of rubble that still hadn't been cleared away after the explosion last year. On the other side was the tunnel she'd emerged from two days past.

Except now it emitted an eerie bluish light and there were shapes moving in the darkness beyond.

Before the tunnel entrance waited the remainder of their ragtag gang. Bryssa foremost, with both arms raised and sweat shining on the back of her bare neck even in the low light. Across the edge of the opening, a curtain of flame flowed and shimmered and beyond it, warped by heat, was a hoard of unearthly visages. Some were beautiful, some were misshapen, all were fierce. If she'd had time to dredge through her memory, Brooklyn might have remembered some of them from the house of blood.

Behind Bryssa, Mrs. Mays loomed with a pair of short sickles in her hands, the curved blades etched in strange flowing symbols. She looked unafraid, but the same couldn't be said of most of the others who stood behind Mrs. Mays, looking pale and wrung out.

Riley dashed into his lab and returned a moment later with a large book, a piece of playground chalk, and several duffle bags. He dropped the bags at Brooklyn's feet and edged up to the inferno Bryssa was maintaining. With the book open in one hand, he drew a half moon from one side of the tunnel opening to the other and scrawled a series of long, looping symbols along its edges. He occasionally glanced at the book, open on the floor beside him, but mostly he appeared to work from memory.

When it was finished, Riley pricked a finger on the tip of one of Mrs. Mays's blades and dripped blood on the chalk scribbles.

The hair on Brooklyn's neck stood up as the symbols illuminated softly, like neon lights.

Riley snapped the book shut and snatched up the duffle bags.

The wall of flame spit, hissed, and went out. Bryssa swayed on her feet. Mrs. Mays steadied her and guided her away.

On the other side of the half moon, the bestial demons paced and growled.

"How long will that hold them?" Brooklyn called out to Riley.

"Until the blood dries and its power is depleted." He shrugged. "Maybe twenty minutes. Long enough to get out of here."

Brooklyn stooped and grabbed two of the duffle bags. They felt like they were full of rocks. "Let's get going then."

They emerged from another tunnel into Kurt's garage. Maybe parking deck was a more accurate way to describe the scope of it.

Riley fumbled in a steel cabinet mounted on the wall and began tossing car keys to each of them. Brooklyn snatched the set he threw her and laughed. Chevy keys with a Dunder Mifflin keychain, they were her keys to her sister's Cavalier. The Demonriders must have brought the car and phone back here to Goodrum after they captured her. *That was considerate of them*, she thought wryly. Scanning the cars, she spotted it several rows away. Brooklyn hurried over and popped the trunk, dropping the absurdly heavy duffle bags inside with a thump.

Shortly, they were all lined up in a convoy, Riley out front in an oversized Jeep. He stuck his arm out the window and made some sort of hand signal that Brooklyn interpreted to mean "Let's go."

They did, the vast doors folding away to birth their motley parade into the world. Brooklyn spun the wheel absentmindedly as they rumbled through mountain curves and descended onto Main Street in the little town that was unfortunate enough to be closest to the Protector's manor. Burned-out storefronts and half-complete reconstruction were testaments to what poor neighbors the scions of Solomon made.

Beyond town, the roads meandered until they wound almost back the way they'd come to Mrs. Mays's farm. The graveled driveway was not large enough to accommodate so many cars. Several parked in the yard and what had once been cornfields. On the porch, Kurt waited, looking as nervous as Brooklyn felt.

As she reached the top step, Kurt stood up, stumbled, and righted himself. He limped over to her. "Can we talk?"

Brooklyn wanted to refuse. To push past him into the familiar comfort of Mrs. Mays's home, but she didn't do that. He looked old and weary. Pale dust streaked his dark face. Pain drew his features taut, and based on the way she felt right now, she might have been better off locked in that cell after all. She shrugged. "Fine. Talk."

He nodded his head and drew her aside from the others. "First, I'm sorry about tricking you. I thought I'd done the right thing . . . at least until I got back here and Amelia set me straight."

"Mrs. Mays knew you locked me up?"

"When I told her what I'd done, she sent me back to turn you loose. When I got there, you'd already broken out. I looked for you." Kurt shrugged.

Riley ambled up to join them. "Mansion is overrun with demons. I brought what we could carry. Hopefully bought enough time for all the people to get out."

Kurt's face grew ashen. "How? The tunnel was collapsed on the basement side."

"How do you know they came from the tunnels?" Riley and Brooklyn asked in unison.

Brooklyn would have thought he couldn't look any wearier, but a great weight settled on his shoulders just the same. Suddenly, she didn't want to know the answer. She was so sick of Kurt and his secrets, and Riley, too, for that matter.

Brooklyn turned her back on them and went back to the car, retrieving both Prosidris's shark-toothed dagger and the Demonrider's shuriken from the trunk. A quick search of the console turned up a phone charger. She plugged the phone in and the screen lit up. When it loaded, she saw there was no service here on the farm. So, she left it to charge.

Taking a deep breath, Brooklyn went back. Riley was babbling something about containing the breach when she interrupted. "Dravin Logan took David. We have to get him back."

"Azrael won't let David die. He's going to be okay," Kurt murmured.

"Azrael? The thing you made your deal with?"

"There's a lot you need to know. We need to do away with our secrets before they get us all killed."

That sounded to Brooklyn like a damned fine idea.

58

TOWER TOP

The walls of the stairwell fell away suddenly as Belial and Quills emerged onto the top of the tower. The floor, or roof rather, was of the same obsidian stone as the rest of the tower and seemed to drink up the harsh light from above. Around the periphery were plinths, nearly three men high, with capstones set between them to form crude archways. Directly overhead, the soul sun seemed close enough to touch, but burned with a brightness at which Belial could only stand to cast quick glances.

The view below was stunning. Belial turned in a slow circle. All of Hell and whatever lay beyond it spread out around him. The plains, cruel and parching, glimmered like rubies and rust. In the places where the worlds bled together, there were patches of color. Emerald grass, the azure glint of running water, the silver spark of steel and glass. Beyond it all, at the edge of seeing, was a mountain peak, shrouded in fog and mist. Belial wondered fleetingly if that might be the mountain that wasn't really a mountain.

"Hell of a spread, ain't it?" Quills sighed appreciatively. "Pun intended."

For once, they were in complete agreement. Belial turned in another slow circle, taking it all in. He approached the tower's edge and peered over. The distance was impossible. His wings twitched reflexively, and he backed away. Turning back to Old Porcupine, he said, "Well, now what?"

"What did you expect to find?" the old fellow asked serenely.

"My fa—Prosidris, I mean."

"I suspect he's never been here. Few have. The last gate would have held him back even if he passed the others."

"You know him?" Belial asked.

The old fellow shrugged. "He's kind of famous."

"Yeah, but I think you know him."

Quills smiled serenely. "There appears to be something inscribed in the middle of the roof over here."

Belial reached for Brooklyn and found her. Whatever it was about the tower that had blocked their connection didn't seem to have any effect up here. "She's okay," he murmured to Quills as he took stock of the situation. "With friends."

The old fellow didn't answer. He was busy examining the carved symbol beneath his feet. Belial walked over to take a look.

"That's . . ." He trailed off, looking more closely. "That's a version of Solomon's seal, isn't it?"

"Mhmm. Minus all the embellishments."

Belial ran the tip of a claw along the deeply cut grooves of the design. "Is it another gate?"

Quills grunted. "Don't think so."

With a pop, the air pressure changed and the faraway sounds of the Raff were suddenly absent. The spaces between the enormous plinths filled with color and light, each slowly resolving itself into a single image.

In the first, Tais embraced a familiar brown-skinned man alongside the ocean. Belial tensed, waiting for the water to erupt, but it never did. It was a moment frozen in time. The next gateway had Belial poised between worlds, gazing toward the supernova that was Brooklyn Evers. Scene number three was a void of blackness. The fourth image was the dragon girl, standing in the shadows outside the Tome room, the barest hint of firelight reflecting from her scales. The last gate was Belial himself, but not quite himself. Softer. He peered closer. Human, actually.

Belial turned in a slow circle, surrounded by these strange images. Some he recognized from his life and two he did not. Both outliers were unnerving. The image of himself made mortal and the inky nothingness of the void.

A woman's voice came to him then, ringing with authority, and vibrating through his feet as if the Colossus itself spoke. "Choose wisely."

Kurt was talking, but Brooklyn wasn't listening. She was watching the gateways atop the black tower fill with color and resolve themselves into still-frame images. And she heard the voice issue that two-word ultimatum.

Frost reamed her fingernails as she maintained the connection. She already had a dull ache behind her eyes that the effort made sharper.

"Choose what?" Belial shouted into the abyss.

The vast voice did not answer.

"Quills! Choose what? What does it mean?"

His friend shrugged.

Belial turned to the image of himself and Tais on a beach long ago. As he extended his hand toward the still frame, he noticed with an odd detachment that it was shaking. His arm vanished into the image with a tingle. When he drew it back, his claws were coated with wet sand.

It's real.

"Looks like it's real," Belial's strange-looking companion called out.

Belial shot the old fellow a look of exasperation and flicked the sand away.

"More gates. More chances to relive my mistakes?"

"Or maybe a chance to fix one of them."

Belial made another circuit, considering the prospect, and stopped in front of the black gate. He was just reaching to touch the inky surface when Porcupine's gnarled hand fastened firmly around his wrist. "I wouldn't test that one."

For one mad moment, Belial considered jumping in and dragging Quills along for the ride, but then the impulse passed and the old fellow let him go.

The next gate to the left was the moment before he had met Brooklyn and ruined her life, and to the right, mere seconds before he had met the dragon girl and ruined hers.

There's a theme here, he thought wryly. "Suppose I could go back to that day with Tais beside the sea and refuse my father's demand."

Quills furrowed his brow thoughtfully. "If it was something in your power to do, why didn't you do it to begin with?"

Belial blinked. That was true. He hadn't been a match for Prosidris then, so there was no reason to think he could fight for and win a different outcome now, even if he had the moment to live over. This was just another of the tower's puzzles to be reasoned through. And hadn't the earlier gate seemed to show Tais had lived a good life? The life she was supposed to live? Defying Prosidris meant the final death, which was why he hadn't done it way back when.

Passing a hand through the next gate, Belial felt the warm dry air of the corridor outside the Tome room. What was his opportunity here? To turn tail and run, keep the little dragon from being cast out? That seemed like a kindness, but for the two eggs now warm and buried alongside the sea. It was a chance to undo the one promise he'd actually kept. *Would she want her life back at this cost?*

The last gate was himself made flesh. He plunged an arm in up to the elbow and drew it out again. The skin on his arm was olive complected and ended at a clawless hand with five fascinating fingers. He gave them a wave. Slowly, the skin bubbled and turned blue again.

Quills watched him with wise, luminous eyes.

"Is this the one I'm supposed to pick?"

The old fellow shrugged. "It is not the worst idea. Go, forget everything that came before, be human for a while, die, and move on to whatever comes next."

"Whatever comes next?" Belial turned slowly back to the black gate, the one that beckoned with its silent call to oblivion. He looked away, shaking his head to clear it.

There was only one gate left to consider. Brooklyn's gate.

59

An Unusual Summoning

Brooklyn watched with desperate fascination as Belial approached her gate. The pinpricks of light were a map of the world and its life. Hers was twice again brighter than most, and blurring away from her, a shadow caught in still frame, sweeping across the west, like a great raven, and in its wake Brooklyn was a lamp unshaded.

She knew what this moment was. Knew because Belial knew. Every gate so far seemed a trap. Why would this one be different? Brooklyn tried to think it through, but she couldn't. He could step through that gate and make a different decision, one that wouldn't drag her into this strange world and ruin everyone she'd ever loved.

Someone was saying her name over and over again, far away, a woman's voice, but Brooklyn could not focus on it. She could urge him forward into the gate and out of her life forever. She was just about to do it when someone slapped her.

Her eyes shot open and came to rest on the silver pendant dangling at the end of her nose. Mrs. Mays gave her a shake. "Wake up!"

Frost had climbed her arms almost to the shoulders. Brooklyn blinked. The pendant spun, catching the evening sunlight as Mrs. Mays straightened up. "What's that?" Brooklyn raised a frosty finger to point.

Mrs. Mays caught the pendant between her fingers. "This? A gift from husband number two. Solomon's sigil."

Brooklyn focused her eyes with a great effort. A six-pointed star inside a circle with diamonds set in the spaces between the points. Her brain was tired, so it took a few long moments for the significance to click. *Six points. The sigil has six points.*

She dove back into her connection with Belial, found him stepping through the gate, and gave a terrific yank, summoning him back to Earth.

He didn't come. Something held him from the other side. Something as heavy as the Colossus on which he stood.

Ignoring a spike of pain between her eyes, Brooklyn redoubled her efforts. Something gave way with a sound like tearing paper and the pressure was gone. She sat up and searched for Belial.

She found him, standing not in Mrs. Mays's living room as expected, but just before her glimmering gate, a look of shock etched on his features. She was atop the Colossus, its stone warm beneath her fingers.

"That's a new one," a gruff voice said. "And a twin soul."

Brooklyn turned to find a short, spiky creature approaching her. She scrambled to her feet and took a step back.

He paused, raised both hands, and took a step back himself, but his eyes burned into her with a hungry curiosity.

The plains beyond glimmered like a desert where all the grains of sand were tiny rubies, and the sun, so close above she might have thrown a rock and hit it, cast an ethereal glow over everything save the black stones beneath her feet, which drank the proffered light greedily.

"How are you here?" Belial demanded.

Brooklyn shrugged. "Why ask? If either of us knew, the other would know, too."

"I was going to undo it all. Fix your life."

"Maybe you still will, but I'm not sure it works the way you think it does." She strode to the center of the tower, Quills scurrying out of her way, and knelt to examine the sigil carved into the stone roof. "Missing a point. Solomon's sigil has six."

"There must be another choice. Another gate." Belial finished her thought.

But there wasn't.

The three of them looked around.

Brooklyn sighed. "What did you come here to do? Why did you start climbing this tower?"

"To stop my—to stop Prosidris."

She snorted. "Well, thank you, Mario, but our princess is in another castle."

"I don't know what that means."

"Means who you came for isn't here," Quills growled.

"And he's not on the other side of these gates, either," Brooklyn added.

Belial gestured irritably at the shimmering seascape. "He's in that one, or he will be shortly."

Walking behind the gates, Brooklyn paced the perimeter. Viewed from the rear, there was nothing to see. She toed the edge, looking down the unfathomable length of the tower to the ground below. In a less arid environment, clouds would doubtlessly have obscured the view, but not here.

She stepped carefully back from the edge and turned to face the two demons who were arguing about the purpose of the gates and the merits of each choice. Brooklyn waited while they bickered, but when it showed no sign of letting up, she cleared her throat loudly and they both turned inhuman eyes her way.

Brooklyn smiled at them. "What do all the gates have in common?"

The two of them were perplexed, exchanging questioning glances with one another like two school boys caught goofing off during a lesson.

"What?" Quills demanded at length.

"They take him"—she jabbed a finger at Belial—"someplace else, or some-when else, or turn him into something else. Every gate gives him a chance to try to do alone, something he's already failed to do alone."

"Well, what other choice is there?" Belial growled irritably.

"You didn't get up here alone. Remember? The sixth way, perhaps the way to Prosidris, lies right over there." She pointed again. This time to the stairs beyond the two, which led back down into the Colossus.

Quills nodded and Belial shook his head.

"Look how vast it is out there. I have no idea where he may be."

"You thought he'd be here, on a lower level, or in the library. So, wouldn't the library be the next place to check?"

Brooklyn cast a quick glance up at the searing soul sun. Sweat trickled between her shoulder blades. How long would it be before her skin burned?

"If he's still here. With the Pull broken, he may well be back on Earth by now."

"That would be . . . not good."

Belial turned toward the library. "I could fly there and see."

"Another path you'd have to walk alone," Quills commented mildly.

Belial threw his hands up in exasperation.

Brooklyn felt her face split into a smile.

"What?" Belial demanded.

"I tried to summon you, but it was like your feet were bolted down to this damn tower and I got dragged through instead."

"And?"

"And what are the chances you can actually kill your father alone?" She pointed at the gate with Tais for emphasis.

"Not good."

"But when it was you and me together, we defied him and saved Devin. Remember?"

Belial shrugged in acquiescence. "Riley was helping us as well."

"Can a demon be summoned back to Hell?"

Quills's eyes lit up. "You'd summon Prosidris here?"

Belial flexed his wings. "Even if we summon him here, then what?"

"You gave me the strength and the weapon I needed to kill Nathan Goodrum." She touched the tangled scar on her breastbone and remembered the shock in his eyes when the blade slid in. He was weak and pitiful. She saw that now and almost felt sorry for him. Almost but not quite. "I believed the lies he told me last year. That there was nothing special about me. Nothing except you. But that's not true. I have something he'll never have."

"Two souls?" Quills asked.

"Friends."

Turning to Belial, she said, "You gave me what I needed to defeat him. Now I'm going to do the same for you." She fumbled in her back pocket and produced a black-bladed dagger. Prosidris's shark-tooth dagger, retrieved from the trunk of her car. It drank the light as greedily as the tower itself. She turned it around and offered it to Belial, hilt first.

He stepped forward and took it reverently. "I won't let you down. I promise."

Brooklyn nodded. "I trust you. We are in this together now. We kill your father, we check on Devin, we take care of those dragon eggs, and we find my sister. Everything together as a team, but we've got to hurry before things get worse." She gestured out at the plains where Earth and Hell were bleeding into one another.

60

BRAVE NEW WORLD

Kurt sat in the rocking chair on Mrs. Mays's front porch and tried not to nod off. He stretched his ankle, feeling the swollen tissue compress uncomfortably. It was the witching hour, maybe a bit later than that, and he scanned the fields and tree line with a careful eye.

The demons had showed up the first night, mostly in ones and twos. He and Bryssa took it in shifts to teach them the farm was off-limits. If only they'd been so plentiful when he'd had a quota to meet.

Pregnant women needed their sleep, so he'd taken the nights. Driving the stragglers away wasn't hard, but with no Pull to drag them back to Hell, it wasn't particularly efficient either. They needed to come up with a way to imprison them or kill them. That would be an excellent project for Riley, but he was busy with his studies, trying frantically to make sense of Brooklyn's disappearance, which he believed was almost certainly the doing of the rogue Warden, Belial.

Kurt got to his feet gingerly and made his way down the wide farmhouse steps. It was a new moon night, stars so bright and far away they made everything here seem insignificant. Maybe it was. Looking up at them, Kurt could almost forget the world was crumbling. Forget the sporadic news reports of disease and starvation that were causing wars to break out. That had always been the way of it. Better to die trying to take someone else's food than to starve watching them eat it.

He could have used a stiff drink about then, but the farm was dry. He would have almost hiked back home for it. Well, not home anymore. Tomorrow evening—technically today—they'd vote on a new leader. Someone they could all support to make the decisions. *Christ! Was Eric really dead?* The world was going to hell in a hurry, and he'd helped push it along.

"You give yourself too much credit."

Kurt jumped at the familiar female voice and turned, and there she was. Pale skin and black wings. How far into his thoughts had she burrowed? Far enough, it seemed. "What do you want?"

"Makes you feel small, doesn't it? To look at something so much larger and older than yourself?" She gestured up. "Makes me feel the same way. The youngest stars you can see are billions of years older than me."

"You're destroying the world," Kurt growled irritably.

"Just making some adjustments so the world doesn't destroy me."

He huffed a laugh. "You've literally unleashed hell on Earth. You call that an adjustment?"

"You did that for me, actually. And it isn't the last wall we are going to tear down together. The first of many, in fact. This"—she made a circular gesture—"separation was never how the world was meant to be. *We* are just setting things back on the natural course."

"I can't be a part of this anymore. I can't."

"You want me out of your mind?"

Kurt sensed a subtle change and then the voices started scrambling like insects inside his skull. He could hear Tyler's voice and Mary's, but marred by an insectile buzzing, a bad connection that made them robotic and inhuman. The words were indistinct, but becoming clearer. He desperately did not want to understand what they were saying. "No, damn you."

The voices stopped. "Excellent. As it happens, I have work for you. My prophet needs a Protector and an advisor. One he doesn't control. Someone wise."

"You want me to protect David?"

"Nail on the head, and as much from himself as anyone."

"Bring him here. I can keep him safe here."

"Head west on the interstate. I'll be in touch with more specific directions. Be ready for a fight. You know who has him."

Kurt did indeed know, and was about to say as much when he realized she'd already gone. *Typical.*

A sizeable shadow detached itself from the side of the farmhouse and approached Kurt. "Seems like that demon has hooks in you," Mrs. Mays said without rancor.

"Less a demon, more an angel, or a god, or something."

"Ain't no angel. That much is clear."

"This is my fault, Amelia. All of it. I'm worse than any of them." Kurt frowned into the darkness at her silhouette.

"Somebody's got to lead, Kurt. Solomon must have an Heir."

"Not me. I can't be what we need right now."

"Well, we need to choose somebody before your lady friend or those Demonriders that got away do our choosing for us."

"I want Riley to have my vote, and you should cast Brooklyn's. She'd want you to speak for her above any of the rest of us, I think."

"Brooklyn doesn't have a—"

"Oh, I think she's earned it. And I hope making her an affiliate is one of the first orders of business."

"So, you're really leaving? Tonight?"

"I have to. At least until I can find a way to win myself free. Besides, I've an obligation to help David if I can. I'm the one that brought him into this mess in the first place."

Amelia looked like she wanted to say more, but she only looked away to the east where the inky darkness was shading toward gray, the first clue of the coming day.

Kurt wheeled Brooklyn's little Chevy down Main Street, where the morning bustle was just beginning. The hardware store, with a shiny new roof, was opening, and people already came and went from the post office. Evidence of the fire that ravaged the shops last year remained only in the presence of new construction, delayed by the chaos now gripping the world. How long would it be before the urban refuges found their way to communities as rural as this one? How long before the demons spilling into this world found their way here to wreak havoc? Not much longer, he suspected. Either way, the peaceful scene before him was a thing of the past. Was it his fault? Probably so.

He thought fleetingly of stopping by the police station to warn Santimo, but then dismissed the thought. He had no advice for the big man. The world was broken and it would take someone smarter than Kurt to fix it again. Maybe Riley.

Kurt took a southerly route, purposefully avoiding driving near his old home as he meandered backroads toward the interstate. There was a strange peace that came with letting go. Kurt wasn't a Protector anymore, and the line he'd sworn to protect was gone from this world. He'd seen his son's soul shepherded back among the living, and it hadn't brought the boy back to him like he'd hoped. Somewhere deep down he'd always known it wouldn't. He had a task ahead of him and, for the first time in a very long time, he thought he might just be up to it.

Not long after he merged onto the interstate, Kurt heard a shrill beep accompanied by a buzz. He looked down and found a cheap phone connected to the car's charger. A voicemail icon flashed on the display.

Curious, he picked it up and touched the icon. Just then, a horn blared. Kurt looked up and, realizing he'd left his lane, jerked the car back to the right. A silver Subaru blasted up beside him and the man in the driver's seat with long black hair flipped him off. Kurt gave a little wave of acquiescence and slowed down a bit to let the man go on.

Kurt risked a glance back down and put the phone on speaker and hit the play button. A man's voice with a Midwestern accent greeted him, jittery with excitement.

"Miss Elroy, this is Alvin Whittaker, Innovative Investigations Inc. You missed our meeting. I hope everything is okay. I need you to call me, okay? Soon as you get this message." A long pause followed. "Uh . . . look, I know who you are. Saw you on the news. I know it's not your friend you are looking for, it's your sister. I don't believe you killed all those people like they say you did." Another pause, this one so long that Kurt thought the message had ended when Mr. Whittaker went on. "You're gonna want to call me back," he said, his voice getting high with excitement. "I've got a lead and, well, I think I've found your sister."

Word From The Author

Thank you so much for reading *Soul Stones*. If you enjoyed it, please leave a review. Reviews help other readers discover books they'll love and give us authors some idea how we are doing.

For announcements, deleted scenes, and bonus material, join my newsletter.
To get started tap HERE on your device
or scan the QR Code below from your paperback copy.

https://tonygallowaywrites.com/newsletter-landing/

Acknowledgements

I'd like to thank the following people who helped make this book as good as it could be.

Timothy Repasky, the man who pores over every sentence, scrutinizes every comma, and threatens me with a dictionary when I misuse a word. His attention to detail and continuity keeps everything in this complicated story consistent. Without him this whole thing would be a jumbled, incoherent mess.

Lisa K Rich, the mystery reader who always unlocked my chapters almost as soon as I posted them on a certain serial story platform. She went on to tell me she only reads my work and the work of John Conroe on that site. It's an honor to be mentioned in the same breath with Mr. Conroe, but a greater honor still to have a reader who cares enough to seek out what I've created.

Andrew Hicks, author of *The Fern and the Rose*, who, after finishing my first novel, gave me honest feedback and encouragement in equal measures. Because of his forthright review, this book is a much better read than it otherwise might have been. I'm proud to call him my friend.

Sarah Henne, of the Facebook group "Fantasy ARC and Beta Readers." She volunteers her time reading random strangers' books and providing thorough feedback and detailed suggestions for improvement. Her beta read ran closer to a full developmental edit. *Soul Stones* is a much better book because of her insight.

Cara Galloway, my wife, who finally put an end to my procrastination and helped me power through an overwhelming number of beta reader edits and rewrites to get this thing out the door for proofreading. Together we muddle through all the business aspects of publishing such as cover design, blurbs, and ad copy. Her patience, love, and support gives me the confidence to put what I've written out into the world.

About the Author

Tony Galloway, author of *Solomon's Ring* and *Soul Stones*, was a voracious reader from a young age. In the long ago times, before e-readers and two-day shipping were a thing, he could often be found checking the mailbox for books he'd purchased weeks prior with postal money orders. Now with two, mostly useless, college degrees to back him up, he's balancing a day job with writing novels of his own. He lives in the North Georgia Mountains with his lovely wife and admires her as she does a much better job than him of raising four teenagers. In addition to novels, Tony has published various automotive DIY articles, one book review, and a couple of online serial stories. If you'd like to learn more and maybe even get some free bonus content, head on over to https://tonygallowaywrites.com and subscribe to his newsletter.